COMING
UNDONE

Staci Stallings

Spirit Light Publishing

14-20,294

Coming Undone
Copyright © 2010 by Staci Stallings
All Rights Reserved

Cover Design: Allan Kristopher Palor
Contact info: allan.palor@yahoo.com
Interior Formatting: Ellen C. Maze, The Author's Mentor,
      www.theauthorsmentor.com
Author Website: http://www.stacistallings.com

ISBN-13: 978-0615654317 (Custom Universal)
ISBN-10: 0615654312
Also available in eBook publication

Spirit Light Publishing

PRINTED IN THE UNITED STATES OF AMERICA

~*~

*To those who dedicate their lives
to helping those who are making the transition through death
into the eternity beyond
as well as helping the families through the difficult time
of a loved one's death.
Your courage, faith, kindness, and compassion
are appreciated more than you know!*

~*~

One

Don't give me that, bro. Come on. We want details. Lots of details."

At the stainless steel refrigerator in the kitchen, Ben Warren grabbed the handle as he smiled. "Oh, no. I don't kiss and tell." He reached in, snagged three cold ones, and headed back for the large round table currently taking up a good portion of his living room. Setting the other two beers on the table, he sat down and twisted the cap off his before taking a long drink.

Friday night and the living was good.

"Since when?" one of the guys on the other side of the table said.

"Yeah, come on, Ben," Kelly Zandavol, Ben's best friend since high school said as he nailed Ben with an I-don't-believe-that-for-a-minute look. "You can't leave us hanging like that. What's she like?"

"No. Uh-huh." Ben shook his head even as he took another drink. "You ain't getting any more."

"Dude," Logan Murphy said, surveying his cards although there was only sparse attention to the actual game, "you know that you're our in with the ladies. Now you're gonna freeze us out just when it's getting good? What's up with that?" He rearranged the cards in his hand though presumably that didn't help. God Himself couldn't help Logan with cards or with the ladies as he called them. "If I can't live through you, I'm doomed."

"Not to mention the shape Kelly'll be in," Todd Rundell added. "You know what that marriage thing can do to a guy."

"Hey. Hey." Kelly lifted his chin. "Speak for yourself there. Me and my lady are doing just fine."

"Uh-huh." Todd put down his beer, picked up his cards, and shuffled them back and forth in his hand. "That's why you're over here at nearly midnight on a Friday night."

"That's better than you turkeys," Kelly retorted. "At least I've got a woman to go home to."

Logan laid three cards on the table. "Three." He waited for Kelly to deal him three new ones. "The man does have a point. Yes. Yes, he does."

Ben took one more drink of the beer before setting it down and getting down to the business of raking more of his friends' money to his side of the table. "Well, I'll take beer and cards over having some chick looking over my shoulder all the time an-y-day. Two." He waited and accepted the two cards Kelly gave him. He fought not to let the disappointment in the hand show, but it didn't work very well. "Dang, Kelly. I think you need to go back home to that lady of yours. This dealing thing is not your forte."

"Ha. Ha. Funny-man. You in or out?" Kelly nodded to the table, indicating the betting had begun.

A long breath that Ben exhaled very slowly. Finally he pushed his cards together. "I'm out. No sense playing trash like that." He stood to go back into the kitchen, figuring if no one was leaving, they might as well get some sustenance. Pushing the unbuttoned and rolled sleeves of his blue pin-striped work shirt up to his elbows, he reached into the cabinet and pulled out a bag of chips and another of pretzels. With two rips he had them open. He didn't bother with the dish. The guys didn't care about that kind of stuff anyway.

"Ah, dude! Aces? You're kidding me!" Logan exclaimed as Ben headed back.

"Hey, you play, you pay," Kelly said, raking all the money in the middle to his side of the table. "So, are you at least gonna tell us her name?"

Ben put the bags in the center of the table. He pulled a chip out and sat down, crunching loudly. Truly, truly, he wished they would stop the questioning. If they didn't, he might have to resort to making things up.

Unfortunately, Kelly had known him too long. He stopped gathering the cards and looked right at Ben who was crunching and drinking but not really looking up. "You don't know it, do you?"

"Know what?" Ben asked as if he had no clue what Kelly was

talking about. Then he shrugged and grabbed another chip. "Of course I do. It was…" For one second too long, his brain went on vacation. "Cheris. Her name was Cheris." He bit into the chip and smiled widely. "See. I told you I knew it."

"Uh-huh." Kelly's look told Ben he wasn't at all sure if he believed that or not.

Truthfully, Ben wasn't completely sure whether to believe himself or not. That whole night after the company party was a little fuzzy. In fact, there were very few nights when he ended up in his bed or someone else's that weren't more than a little fuzzy. Of course, the guys didn't need to know that part, and they were on a need to know basis, if that.

The phone in the kitchen rang precluding anymore discussion of the subject.

"Speak of the devil," Logan said as Ben's gaze jumped at the sound.

Puzzled by who might be calling at midnight, other than Cheris—if that was her name—he got to his feet. Then again, he didn't think she had his phone number although she might. Those details weren't exactly clear either. The thoughts swirled in his brain as he headed for the still ringing phone.

"Hi, honey," Logan said sweetly. "Oh, sure, you can come on over. I'll just chase the guys out…"

Ben wanted to deck him, but he was already to the phone. The guys all cracked up at the kissy noises Logan was making. For grown men who were all 30-something, they certainly could be childish sometimes. "Hello."

"Uh. Mr… Mr. Warren?"

In the background he could hear the too familiar sounds of a medical facility. Worry dropped on him as he spun and ducked next to the cabinet. "Yes, this is Ben Warren."

"Uh, Mr. Warren, I'm sorry to bother you so late, but this is St. Anthony's Hospital. Your father has just been admitted. You are listed as his next of kin…"

The rest of the words evaporated in a swirl of alarm and concern. "What? Is he okay?" He put his finger in his ear to block everything else out. "What happened?"

"I'm not really authorized to discuss it, but the doctors think it would be a good idea for you to get here as quickly as possible."

Ben ran his hand through and over his thick, dark hair. "Uh.

Yeah. Yeah. Okay. I'll be there as soon as possible."

Somehow he ended the phone call, but it too was lost in the spinning of the world around him. He closed his eyes and fought to breathe, hoping to make it stop. However, when he opened his eyes, it was still tilting and shifting around him. Decisions. He had to make some decisions. First, he needed to get to the hospital to see what was going on. Pushing away from the cabinet, he stumbled through the myriad of possibilities as he headed through the living room.

Three surprised and very concerned faces gazed up at him.

"Something wrong?" Kelly asked.

"Uh. Yeah. I guess. I don't know. It's my dad." None of the words seemed to even correlate with reality. "I don't know. Something happened."

At the little closet, he pulled out the first jacket his hand found, and he yanked it on. "You guys just lock up when you're done."

"You want me to go with you?" Kelly asked, standing. His dark face was ash-washed with concern.

"No." Ben tried to shake the looks on his friends' faces from his consciousness. "No. Of course not. I'm... I'm sure it's nothing." *Do they call you from the hospital at midnight if it's nothing?* He couldn't answer that question, and he didn't even want to try. "I'll just..." The words were jamming together in his brain in no distinct pattern. "Um... Just let yourselves out when you're finished. And be sure to lock up."

Remembering he would have to drive, he patted his pockets and then looked around. "Keys? Where are my keys?"

"By the front door where they always are?" Kelly asked, clearly tipping toward legitimate concern for his friend.

"Oh, yeah. Right." Ben nodded, having no idea why.

"Are you sure you don't want me to go?"

"Yeah. Yeah. I'm sure. I'll let you know." Taking the keys from the little hook, Ben wrenched the doorknob and for one second, considered reconsidering his friend's offer. He didn't want to face whatever this was alone. Then he took his ego by the collar and gave it a good shake. He was Ben Warren, and Ben Warren didn't back down from any challenge. With that thought, he yanked the door open and headed to the hospital.

The final credits rolled up and off the screen as Kathryn Walker swiped at the tears streaming down her cheeks. The only good thing was that she was alone, no one here to witness this pitiful display of sap and desperation. She could hear Misty or Casey or her mother. Ugh. Her mother. That was enough to dry all the tears with one single sniff.

Her mother would count this as verifiable proof that being unmarried was the single worst disposition a woman could have on this earth. Especially a woman of 32 and three-quarter years. As Kathryn stood, she sniffed again and walked over to the DVD player to replace that disc in its proper case. It was strange how somewhere north of 28, she had started counting the months to and from her birthday like a ten-year-old.

"I'm still six months from being 30." "I'm only 30 and two months..." It was pathetic really—as if there would be something magical about the four months before she was 30 and six months, or 31 and six months, or 35, or whatever. At one time she had vehemently sworn to herself that by such-and-such an age, she would've found Mr. Right. But when such-and-such became six months ago and then a year ago, and then five years ago, she had given up that game and morphed into the newest incarnation of singlehood—the defiant, "I kind of like it this way. No, really, I do. It's easier..."

She wasn't sure if anyone believed her. She didn't even believe her. Especially on nights like tonight. The movie that was supposed to cheer her up had hardly done that. Instead, it had brought her face-to-face in vibrant color with the fact that everyone else found that perfectly perfect person for them through these neat, cute little coincidences that just, for whatever reason, never seemed to happen for her or to her. She couldn't quite tell which it was. She wondered for the millionth time if they knew some secret that she didn't. However, she was pretty sure it was all just one big, stinking luck of the draw thing. And she was about as unlucky in that department as anyone had ever been.

As she flipped off the light and gingerly made her way through her dark apartment toward her bedroom, she went through the inventory of herself once more. Weight—not bad, could be better, but not bad. Looks—above average but definitely not model territory. Financial standing—quite good actually. Good job—

check. Moral with values—check. Although honestly, she wasn't sure if that one counted for her or against her.

Certainly she could have bedded many in the past if she had been into that existence, which she most definitely was not. No. Even snagging a guy wasn't worth giving up her self-worth. Besides, she knew quite a few who had done just that only to find divorce papers on the other side of the marriage certificate.

With a sigh, she climbed between the pressed cotton sheets. Nope, the hard truth was all the good guys were long gone. The only ones left had track records that read like rap sheets not to mention baggage from their several failed marriages and a couple of kids thrown in for good measure. Still, as she did every night, she closed her eyes, snuggled into the covers and thought about him. She had no real picture of him although she had seen him in her dreams on a couple of occasions—never his face, just vague pieces.

She snuggled deeper thinking about those pieces. Like his hands. She'd always liked his hands, with nice long fingers and a presence she couldn't quite put into words. And his dark hair. That one always made her heart snag. She would know that hair when she saw it. Of that, she was sure. She had seen it so many times in her dreams. Slowly sleep began to take over her senses, and as she drifted off, she let out a long sigh. "God, please be with him wherever he is. Keep him safe and guide him. And please let him know that I already love him. Amen."

The disorienting transition from the darkened parking lot and street lights into the blinding white light of St. Anthony's emergency room cut right through Ben's skull with the precision of a sharp scalpel. He blinked it back, hoping he wouldn't trip over something he couldn't see because he never even slowed down all the way to the counter. The nurse on the other side looked both bored and half-asleep.

"Excuse me, I need to know…" he started.

"Please get in line," she said with no feeling to her voice at all.

"What?" He glanced around in confusion. "There is no line."

"All patients must get in line behind that sign." She pointed to the ceiling without so much as looking at it.

Ben looked around and up at the sign. *For privacy, please remain behind this line until you are called forward.* The same was written again in Spanish and then in some language he neither spoke nor could decode.

"Please step behind the line and wait to be called."

Man, he wanted to argue. More than he'd ever wanted to do anything in his life, he wanted to argue, but he sensed from Ms. No-Nonsense that doing so would only prolong this nightmare. Tilting his head at that understanding, he nodded. "Okay." He pushed back from the counter and took the four steps to the front of the non-existent line. After a moment, he put his hands out to his side to indicate that he had fully complied with the request.

The nurse took her own sweet time as she finished up whatever she was doing. Then, looking like she was bored to tears, she looked up. "Next."

Finally. Ben rushed forward.

"Name?" she asked.

"Um, it's for my father."

"Name?"

Frustration growled through him. "Mine or his?"

She checked him with a condescending scowl. "Are you the patient or is he?"

"He is. They said they brought him in…" Composure slipped away from him as he looked at his watch. "Like an hour ago or something like that."

"Okay. His name?" She put her fingers on the keyboard.

"Ron… uh, Ronald Warren."

"Ronald F. Warren?"

"Yes."

She nodded but didn't continue. As panic set into his heart, he arched forward, straining to see what was on that screen. With a deepening scowl, she looked at him and turned the screen from his line of vision as he backed off.

"Sorry."

You should be went through her eyes. "Mr. Warren has been taken to the 8th Floor, Neurology."

"Neurology?" Ben repeated the word, trying to understand the horrors it hid in its depths.

"Yes." The nurse glanced behind him. "Next."

It was a fight to keep his balance on an even keel as he turned from the desk and hurried to the elevators at the far end of the room. This part he knew. This part he had memorized. The riding the elevator part—up to see doctors, down to see administrators—working to incorporate his company's newest line of life-saving drugs into the hospital's current regimen of patient care.

At the elevator, he hit the button and stepped back, putting his hand on the beltline of his jeans. He arched first his gaze and then his neck to watch the numbers above the elevator slowly slide downward. Part of him wanted them to speed up. Part of him wanted them to stop altogether. If they just stopped, then he wouldn't have to deal with whatever came next. He tried to think about what that might be—what neurology meant, what he should do if this was truly serious.

He let out a quick I'm-being-stupid breath and fought to tamp down the clutch of fear around his chest. His father was fine. Of course, he was fine. He was, after all, only 66. That was hardly old. With the back of his hand, Ben scratched the side of his face as indiscriminant nerves attacked him.

The elevator dinged, yanking his attention upward. He stepped back as those on the elevator disembarked, and then raking in a breath, he got on and hit the round number 8 button. So many things. So many memories and thoughts of the past and future crisscrossed in his brain as the little box slid upward. Should he call his mother? She would probably want to know. Especially if it was serious.

What about Jason? Surely his mother knew where his brother was. She should make that call. Ben certainly didn't want to—even if he knew the number, which he didn't. Truth be known, he didn't want to do any of this. If he could somehow just skip over the next hours or days or whatever this turned out to be, he would with no questions. He didn't do serious or responsibility very well. How had the universe not gotten that memo? Or maybe it had, and this would in fact turn out to be nothing. False alarm. Nothing to worry about.

The bell dinged, and he forced all the other thoughts and worries down into himself. First, he would find out how bad it was. Then he would figure out how best to proceed.

It wasn't like there was a barking dog or even traffic noises this high up, so there was really no excuse for not being able to sleep.

However, Kathryn had endured more than one night like this, and she knew there was no forcing sleep. In frustration, she flipped the covers off her legs and swung herself to the edge of the bed.

"Ugh." Why did life have to be so impossible? She stood carefully and got her balance before turning her steps for the kitchen.

Over the sink, she turned on the little light and squinted into it. Two blinks and her eyes began to accept the invasion of the light. On auto-pilot and with a yawn, she went first to one cabinet, then to the other, gathering what she needed for chamomile tea. It was her first line of defense on nights such as these. If this didn't work, she'd be back for hot chocolate in an hour. Then melatonin if all else failed.

She filled the little cup with hot water from the tap. It would give the tea that funny after-taste she hated, but it was quicker than going the kettle route, and since she'd read that stupid email about not heating water in the microwave, she'd been too much of a coward to try that again. Instead, she took her mostly lukewarm water to the counter and put in the teabag.

In no time the clear water had turned to a dull brownish-yellow. With one half teaspoon of sugar, she lifted it to her lips. "Ugh." Terrible as she figured it would be. Not caring, she lifted it again, switch off the light, and headed back for her bedroom.

"Mr. Warren, your father has suffered a massive stroke." The doctor, in the white coat, gave Ben the news softly but with noted firmness.

The little consultation room seemed to close in on Ben as he shifted in the chair. He swallowed that feeling down. "Okay."

"As next of kin, where we go from here is pretty much up to you and the good Lord," the doctor continued obviously assuming Ben had some connection to the Creator that he really didn't.

Ben narrowed his focus, trying to find the answers the doctor seemed to think he had. "I… Okay. Um. What are our options?"

"Well, we've stabilized him as much as we can. At this point, we could try surgery although with his heart history and his present condition, I can't guarantee anything."

Ben absorbed the news with another swallow, a nod, and a small shift backward. "Heart. Yeah… Okay. So…"

"We have an MRI scheduled for the morning to determine the

exact extent of the damage. Once we get those results, we will probably know more about how to proceed."

"Okay. Good." It was incomprehensible that he should know what to say. "Um, can I see him?"

"He's in ICU right now. They're getting him settled. You can have a seat in the waiting area. ICU visits don't really start until 8 a.m., but for you, I'll make an exception. Your father and I played many rounds of golf together. I know he would want you to have this time if…" The words stopped. "Well, he would want you to have this time."

Although Ben tried to wrap his mind around all of this and think it through, the truth was he was lost, like being in a forest with no trail and only brambles and briars for as far as the eye could see. How or why he had gotten dropped here, he had no idea. Where he was supposed to go from here was even vaguer. "Um, do you… do you think I should call my mother and… well, should I let everyone know?"

The pause was almost imperceptible, and then the doctor nodded. "I think that would be wise."

Two

The night in the hospital waiting room, propped up next to the wall, was the longest of Ben's life. He didn't really sleep, only nodded off once or twice. He'd tried to call his mother. She wasn't home, but the help would leave a message. His mind had gone around and around the question of calling Jason, but he'd finally decided against it mostly because he didn't know his number or even the exact name of the town where he lived.

They'd only let him back to see his father once sometime around three in the morning. The best thing Ben could say about the visit was it was mercifully brief owing to the hospital rules about ICU visits. Those five minutes had been spent with his hands in his pockets, back practically pressed to the wall by the door. He didn't want to go closer. He didn't want to see.

Beeps from the monitors were the only indication that the man lying in the bed wasn't already gone. Gone. It was such a strange word—especially in association with his father. There was a time, before the divorce when his father had been gone a lot. Actually, his father was there, just not in a traditional sense. As head of the regional neurology department for the hospitals in the area, his father was a very busy man. He was charged with saving lives, and the fact that other things paled in comparison was just reality.

And then the divorce came, and everything changed...

Ben let the breath go from his lungs as he thought about his mother and his parents' marriage. The time when she had been present was so far gone that he hardly remembered them being together. At least that's what he told himself. It was easier that way. Easier to forget his mother leaving him to watch Jason in the car while she went into that house on Macasy Street. Yes, he wished he could forget that. And he wished he could forget the fights and the tears and the ripping of his heart as he watched her car turn the corner out of sight that last day after being in court.

At the time he hadn't had all the pieces, and in truth he still didn't. But in adulthood, he'd filled in many of them so that the story at least made some sense now. His father's absence was the excuse she used to find comfort in the arms of another man—Macasy Street. That had always been his name to Ben. Honestly, he'd only seen glimpses of the man, but they still brought up an irrational anger so dark that it threatened to swallow him whole.

Even now when he let the hard-clamped mask over his heart slip, he felt that fury clutch his throat, choking the life from him. No. It was better not to remember. The problem was, with so much time, remembering was harder to keep at bay than usual. He shifted in his seat next to the wall. The room was again coming to life, slowly, a few bodies at a time, they drifted in. He looked over at the clock and mentally had to search for how long from 7:34 it would be until 8 o'clock. Taking a breath, he closed his eyes to push it all away. He didn't want to be here.

The bleep of his phone brought him forward, and he yanked it from his pocket. With one touch he had it to his ear. "Warren."

"Hey, bro. I'm sorry. Did I wake you?"

Ben laughed at the thought and scratched his head. "Hey, Kell. How's it going?"

"I'm fine. How's it going with you?"

It was strange how hard it had become just to breathe. He looked around, tilted his neck to stretch it first one way and then the other. "I've been better."

"How's your dad?"

His head fell forward on the weight of the situation. He couldn't find the words. They just were not there. "I… Um… It's not good, Kell. It's not."

Kelly didn't say a thing for a moment as he absorbed the news. "I'm sorry to hear that. What happened?"

"Well, I'm not real clear on the details, but at like 11 last night his maid found him in the kitchen. He had a stroke."

"A TIA. Right?"

"No. This one was massive. Almost like an aneurysm from what I can figure based on what they're not telling me. He's in

ICU." Defiantly, though he couldn't clearly determine who the enemy was, Ben sat back and put his head on the wall. "I just… I wasn't ready for this, you know? I mean, I just talked to him the other day, and he sounded fine. We were going to go golfing next weekend…"

"Do you want me to come down there?"

Ben deflated. "No. There's not really anything you can do."

The pause stretched between them.

"Are you going to call your mom?"

"I tried. Last night. She's out. I don't even know what that means. Out. With Mom, that could mean in the Caribbean, in Hawaii, or on the moon."

"The moon?"

"You know what I mean."

Ding. The speaker cracked on. "It's 8 a.m. Visiting for ICU."

Looking up at the speaker, Ben wanted to punch it to get it to shut up. "Listen, Kell. I've got to go. Visiting hours." What he really wanted to do was act like he'd never heard the announcement. What difference would it make? His father couldn't hear him anyway. Besides, he was not equal to this task. No possible way.

"Call me. Okay? Whatever. You don't have to do this alone."

"Yeah." But he didn't believe a word of it. He was alone. More alone than he had ever been.

"Don't start." Kathryn stirred her oolong tea as her steamed rice sat heaped on her plate Saturday afternoon.

"I'm just sayin'," her sister, Casey said. Casey, who was younger by three years, had moved two-hours out to the suburbs so these little get-togethers had gotten few and far between. Now she sat like a pixy on the edge of her chair flicking things back and forth on her plate.

Anger plowed over Kathryn. "No. No just sayin'. I don't want to hear it. Okay?"

"Kate, if I didn't love you, I wouldn't suggest it, but I see how miserable you are."

"Oh, and you're not? I don't see you doing cartwheels, Mrs. Married for eight years with two kids."

"Well, but it's different for me. Brett makes me crazy. You

know that. He always has." Casey laid her hand across the table until it rested on Kathryn's wrist. "But I love him, and he loves me. I just want that for you, Kate. Is that so wrong?"

"No." Kathryn picked up her fork and rearranged the white grains as she yanked a long piece of blonde hair over her ear. "It's just… It's not the same for me. You fell in love in college. College wasn't exactly a picnic in that department for me."

"So, you were a late bloomer. So what?"

"Cas, I'm 32. Thirty. Two."

"Almost thirty-three, but who's counting? Come on, Kate. You're smart, and you're so kind and helpful and…"

"Doomed to be single forever."

"No. Not true. You just have to get out there. You spend entirely too much time at work and in that apartment of yours."

"I like my apartment."

"And I'm sure it likes you back. Come on, Kate. Face it. If the only places you ever go are work and home, how are you ever going to meet someone?"

"I go other places." Kathryn hated the defensiveness in her voice.

"Like where?"

"Church." Okay. It was lame. But it really wasn't. She'd been in the singles group until she got too old. Of course, she could join the re-single group, but that had no appeal.

"Are there any prospects at church?"

Her heart skipped just a little at the thought. She smiled before she could stop it. "Well, there is this one guy. He came in a couple weeks ago. He sat a couple benches ahead of me."

"A ring?"

"Not that I could tell."

"Alone?"

"Yes." It was like pushing the words off a cliff. She didn't want to think them, to go down that road because she'd been disappointed after getting her hopes up so many times, she had this feeling memorized.

"No ring. Coming to church alone. Good. Good." Casey considered those for a moment as she ate her noodles slowly. "Age?"

"I don't know. A little younger? A little older. That's kind of hard to tell anymore." Kathryn let her fork go and sipped her tea.

"So, in the right age-range roughly, new to church. I think you should introduce yourself."

Horror painted her face red hot as she shook her ponytail back and forth. "I'm not introducing myself. Are you crazy?" She ducked at the thought that anyone in the restaurant had overheard the conversation. "He'll think I'm insane."

"So you'd rather some other insane chick gets him first?"

"Casey!"

Her sister frowned. "What? You do your level best to melt into the woodwork, Kate, and then you wonder why no one notices you."

"I can't…. I couldn't…. I'm not like you." She went back to her rice though she had lost her appetite completely.

"And you have thanked God for that on regular occasions."

"That's not true," Kathryn said although she knew it was a lie.

"Yes it is, but thanks for trying." Casey spun her fork in her noodles three times. "Look. All I'm saying is it wouldn't hurt to go out once in awhile. You know, get yourself out there."

A thought traced through Kathryn's head, and she bit her tongue to keep it from coming out. *No. Don't say it. Don't tell her. You know what she'll say. Don't say it. Don't say it!* "Well, Misty said…" Kathryn ducked, hating herself for saying it the instant it was out.

"Yes? Continue." Casey circled her fork in the air, her gaze suddenly excited and full of anticipation.

Kathryn shrugged, smiled, and then laughed as she ducked over her rice. "Well, she's got this cousin or something."

This time Casey laid her fork all the way down. "And…?"

"I don't know. She said he's back in town, and he's single…"

"Hello! What are you waiting for—an engraved invitation?"

"I don't know." Kathryn scrunched her nose in embarrassed apprehension. "A blind date? Isn't that kind of… I don't know… desperate?"

"Well, I guess that would depend on what you wear and if you sit on his lap and ask him to marry you before you get in the car."

Annoyance flooded over Kathryn. "You're terrible. I would never do something like that."

The laughing taunt left Casey's face. "Look, all I'm saying, big sister, is that Mr. Right is obviously not going to just fall into your lap. You've got to stop waiting around and be a little more proactive in the search. Who knows, Mr. Cousin Guy might be him, or maybe he knows him, or maybe when you're at the restaurant, him will come around the corner, and you'll just know. It's not like it's an exact science, you know."

Kathryn picked up her tea and sipped it carefully although it was by now only tepid. "Yeah, tell me about it."

Sleep sounded heavenly. After being at the hospital for 18 hours straight, Ben boarded the elevator that made him sway as it started downward. He ran his hand over the back of his head wishing any of this made sense. He still hadn't gotten in touch with his mother, and his father's condition, though stabilized, did not look any better. In fact, the MRI was inconclusive because of some swelling on the brain.

The doctor told him that was normal, but nothing was normal now. Nothing. On the ground floor, he followed the others out, thinking how long of a walk the parking lot seemed. He had run marathons that were shorter.

"Ben?"

Instinctively he turned at the sound of his name as Travis Steele, one of the younger doctors in oncology, stepped up to him. He put out his hand, and Ben shook it.

"I was sorry to hear about your dad," Travis said. "He's one of the good guys. How's he doing?"

Ben stepped back into his cocoon of personal space. "Not great. They're waiting for the swelling to go down so they can figure out what to do." Was it just him or did the whole world seem like some strange, psychedelic dream all of a sudden? Who was this saying these things? It couldn't be him. He didn't even understand them himself and yet somehow he sounded like he understood it all perfectly.

"Oh. Sorry to hear about that." Travis looked to the side. "Listen, I was just about to go get some coffee if you'd like to join me."

Not really. But he heard himself say, "Okay. Sure."

In fact once they sat down, Ben found it was nice to have someone to talk with that understood at least a minimum of his situation. That was comforting.

"I wish I knew," Ben said as they discussed what happened if things went south with his dad's condition. "It's just me here. My mom lives in Oakland, and my little brother… Well, I'm not even real sure where he lives. I don't know if they'd come for the funeral or not." Once again the sheer weirdness of the whole situation descended on him. He thought about Dr. Steele, a young man— probably younger than even himself, and for the first time, Ben thought about the other side of saving lives. "How do you do it?"

"Do what?" Travis took a small drink of the coffee.

"How do you come here every day when you know some of your patients aren't going to make it? Doesn't that make you crazy?"

"It can. At first it was much worse, and even now, sometimes it's rough, but you learn to do what you can, care as much as you can, and then let go. Sometimes what you do works. Sometimes it doesn't. The final call's not up to me. God makes that one. But sometimes it's easier than others to agree He made the right one."

God. There was a topic Ben did not want to discuss. He wondered then if every doctor who practiced at St. Anthony's had to swear by some oath of faith or something. He'd never really thought about it before. However, before he could ask, Dr. Steele looked at his watch.

"Well, I'd better get back. I'm on call tonight."

"Oh, well." Ben scrambled to his feet, his spirit lagging a good six inches behind every move he made. "Thanks."

Dr. Steele extended his hand. "I hope you get a miracle. I'll be praying for one."

"Th-thanks."

Macaroni for one. Kathryn pushed it around her plate and then around again as she sat at her counter, a single glass of water the only other thing on it. Bored, she turned and grabbed the day old newspaper from the coffee table, propped it up and leaned forward on the stool. It wasn't interesting. Politics and foreign affairs— neither of which were more than distractions for her. She read the first few paragraphs of three stories before giving up and pitching it back onto the coffee table. She would never see what others found so fascinating.

After taking her plate to the sink, washing it off, and putting it in the dishwasher, she trekked into the living room. Curling onto the couch, she grabbed the remote, aimed it at the television and started flipping through the channels. One led to the next and then to the next. How could there be that many channels and nothing to watch? Putting her head back onto the cushions, she continued through the channels, hoping she had missed something. She hadn't.

Finally she clicked the thing off and let the darkness envelope her. Her spirit plummeted into it and through it. Maybe Casey was right. Maybe she should tell Misty she'd go out with what's his name. She bounced her toe up and down trying to decide. It couldn't be any worse than sitting alone in her apartment for hours on end. Could it?

Try as she might, she couldn't find one thing that wasn't completely depressing about her current existence. The plain truth was, she was tired of being alone. "God, why are You making me wait?" she asked the ceiling. "I don't understand this. I really don't. Look. If he's not coming, would You please just tell me so I can quit thinking about it?"

Silence.

Utter, total, complete, maddening silence.

Even the soft ringing of her ears was louder than God's answer.

"Great." She sprang to her feet. "That's just great, God. Thanks for that. Really. I'll be sure to put an extra five in the collection plate tomorrow." Stomping to her room although she had to be careful what with her sock feet on the hardwood floors, Kathryn let the anger and frustration boil over. She didn't need a man. She'd survived this long without one. Besides a man meant she'd have to deal with kids. The others at work were always complaining about how expensive day care was, not to mention braces and dance lessons.

As she brushed her teeth, she reasoned at least she didn't have to waste money on things like that. No. She had a whole apartment all to herself. If she left her underwear on the floor, nobody was there to complain. If she let the dishes stack up, that was okay too. No one cared.

And yet, as she went into her bedroom and sat down on the bed, sadness took over. She laid her clasped hands in her lap and closed her eyes. "God, really I don't understand this. I don't." Slowly she slid from the bed to the floor. Kneeling there, she laid her head on her hands. "God, please. If being married is not what

You want for me, then please, please take this desire away. I can't take living like this all the time, feeling like something should be happening when it isn't. Please. Somehow, just give me peace. I don't know how much longer I can do this."

But she knew she really had no choice in the matter. If God didn't send her soulmate, there was really not much she could do other than to continue to wait and pray. Her heart filled with thoughts of the "him" she didn't even know, and the familiar words came once again. "God, please be with him tonight, keep him safe, and guide him in the ways You want him to go. Dear Lord, please put Your hand on his life, guide him, protect him, and give him peace. Amen."

The brakes under Ben squealed the car to a halt as the white car flashed by him through the intersection. "Hello! What does red light mean to you? Jerk!"

Collecting his scattering nerves, Ben smashed his foot on the pedal and took off through his light which was still green. "Stupid, idiot drivers. Get a clue or get off the road!"

He knew in some deep place in himself that he was out of control and on the edge of completely losing it, but he didn't want to think about that. The street lights flashed over the top of the Mustang, drifting across the shiny paint like ghosts from another existence. Putting his elbow up on the armrest, he let his head down onto his hand as he stopped at the next red light. At this rate it was going to be midnight or better before he got home.

Home. That would seem odd in a way it never had before. That's where he was, where he had been before his world had turned upside down. Pushing that and everything else back down, he drove through the crowded Saturday night streets, hardly realizing that had this been a normal Saturday night, he would surely have been cruising these same streets looking for some action. Right now all he wanted to find was a pillow and a bed.

It was another 30 minutes before he pulled up to his apartment. Another five before he closed the apartment door behind him and leaned up against it. Home.

He didn't bother to turn the lights on. What was the point? Instead he pitched his keys to the little hallway table and wrenched his jacket off. Tired had never felt like this. Even hangovers were better. At least with them, he had a vague memory of fun and partying to remind him of why he felt so bad. This just felt bad through and through.

Going into the kitchen, he considered a beer but decided against it. Instead he got some water from the tap, which he hated but downed the whole thing without tasting any of it. He felt at the moment like he might never again slake his thirst or be fully rested. He was so tired. So incredibly tired. Two steps back to the door and he saw the blinking message light on his answering machine sitting on his counter. Like a robot, he punched the button and leaned his head against the door post to keep himself from sliding to the ground.

Beep. "Ben. Dude. I've been trying to get a hold of you." Kelly.

Ben wondered what time that one had been left, but somehow he had missed that part of the message.

"Don't worry. I'll try your cell."

Beep. "Ben. Hi. This is Charissa… from the party."

His eyes rolled upward before letting them fall all the way closed. *Not now.*

"Listen, I got your number from Cameron. I hope you don't mind. I really had a good time the other night. I'd like to see you again. Call me. K?"

She left her number in a sultry tone just before the machine went beep. And then it went dark. Without bothering to even think of responding to either, Ben picked himself up off the wall and headed for the shower. He wanted to get off this nightmare of a ride. He wondered if someone could let him off. It would be nice.

The hot water from the shower sent humidity into the air, and although Ben wanted to get in under it, he found himself at his sink, knowing he should be doing something but not at all sure what that something was. Then he looked into the mirror. His eyes were sunken and sad. He didn't remember ever seeing them like that before. How could he ever get through this? This wasn't the life he wanted. He didn't do responsibility well. Never had. Careless and reckless were much more his style.

Too tired to dwell on that, he headed for the shower and was already under the current before he remembered he was going to shave. Oh, well. Granted, two full days of stubble were becoming far more than a mere five-o'clock shadow by this point. If he kept this up, even he wouldn't recognize himself. The shower was accomplished only by marshalling all of the energy he had left. Still, each movement was made in ultra-slow, by sheer-force-only motion. It seemed slow was the only gear accessible to him anymore.

When he cut the water, he grabbed the nearest towel, put it around him, and went back out to the bedroom. Sure, he normally did things like brush and dry his hair, brush his teeth, dress for bed. But little things like that were lost in the thick haze of exhaustion. He wasn't even sure he was in the bed before he was asleep.

Sunday mornings always dawned with glorious sunrises followed by soft white and pale yellow light streaming in her bedroom window. Kathryn loved Sundays. She awoke bathed in that heavenly light as she did every Sunday. Sundays were always special because she got to sleep in a bit later and so the sun had a little more chance to break over the horizon and make it into her room. Breathing life in, she smiled. Maybe today was the day. Maybe today she would meet the guy two rows up at church. Before she was even out of bed, she started plotting. If he was there before she was, maybe she could just innocently sit next to him.

That wouldn't be too forward, would it? It might be, she finally decided. Maybe she could sit behind him. Then when they did the sign of peace, he would turn and shake her hand. A fantasy played out featuring the two of them, their eyes meeting, their hearts beating as one. She let those thoughts run their course because they were so much better than reality ever was.

Dragging in an excited breath, she arched her shoulders over the possibilities. Maybe today was the day.

Three

"We can do the surgery," Dr. Vitter said. He was the same doctor as the first night only this time Ben had been able to tease the right name out of his still-exhausted brain. Dr. Vitter. Richard as his father had always referred to him. They played golf. They went to the same fundraisers for the hospitals in town. Yes. And now here was Dr. Richard Vitter opining on the best course of action to take with the man, his friend, lying just down the hallway, hooked to three dozen wires and six dozen tubes.

Ben wanted to ask him if he even recognized his father amidst it all. Ben certainly didn't. Far from the tall, suave man he had always known as his father, this man, the one lying in the bed, looked bony and weak and frail. Even the perpetual tan from trips to Florida had evaporated, replaced by a sick white hue that scared Ben to death.

Dr. Vitter continued laying out the options, but Ben could not keep his mind on them. This should be someone else, someone who knew what they were doing. What were they thinking naming him next of kin to anyone? He didn't know how to be next of kin. He didn't know what to do. He was having a hard enough time not completely freaking out. And yet, here they were—not asking his opinion but for his decision.

"And what if we don't... do the surgery?" he heard himself ask, presumably to fill the silence he had realized had descended on the room.

"Well, we could keep him alive indefinitely on the life support, but I do not believe he will ever wake again without some form of intervention."

"And if he does... wake again?" Ugh. Just getting the words out was horrible. "What then?"

Dr. Vitter's gaze slipped to the pen in his hand. "I expect there will be quite a bit of paralysis, drastic loss of speech and coordination, although I cannot give you any idea of percentages. There's just no way to know with something like this."

"Will he ever...?" Ben cleared his throat and shifted in the chair. "I mean can he ever... be like he was... before?"

The pause answered the question for the good doctor. "We're doctors, Ben. We're not God. We do what we can based on what the family thinks is best, and then we deal with that. Do I think your father will ever be who he was on Thursday night? No. Can he come back from this in some form? Possibly." He took a long breath. "I've ordered one more scan for this evening. I'm hoping we've missed something, but right now, we're looking at almost certain paralysis, speech impairment if it comes back at all, severe mental issues if we could even prolong his life, and if he were to wake up after we do. This is not a perfect solution, but in this situation, unfortunately, there just isn't a perfect solution.

"I suggest that you give yourself some time to think about what your father would want in this situation, what he would tell you to do, pray about it, talk it over with some of your loved ones. We'll talk again tomorrow and see where we are."

Ben nodded. Why, he didn't know. He stood because the doctor did, and he shook the doctor's hand because he knew he was supposed to. "Thank you, Doctor."

"You're welcome." But there was real sadness in the doctor's eyes.

Like he was a zombie, Ben walked out of the office and down the hall. He hated this place. Strange how he had walked these halls most of his life but he had never seen them like this. Never.

On either side of him, patient doors stood in various states of open and closed. Beeps and quiet conversations emanated from beyond them. He wondered what they were talking about. Were they having the same conversation he was having in his head? The one in which the options swirled with no real place to land? Were they considering who to call and what to say?

Each breath brought with it the very real possibility of tears, and he hated that. He'd never been weak like this. He was always the positive one, the one who didn't let little stuff get him down. Granted this wasn't so little, but the principle was the same. In the waiting area, he pulled out his cell phone and dialed the only number he knew.

Leaning forward, he put his elbows on his knees and pressed the bridge of his nose into his fingertips. "Hey, Kell. What's up?"

"I was starting to get worried, man. Where've you been?"

"Trying to survive this nightmare."

"So things aren't any better?"

"Uh. No. And if my discussion with Dr. Vitter is any indication, I don't think we're going to find better either." Because he knew Kelly would listen and because he so needed to give voice to the disparate thoughts in his head, Ben started at the top and outlined every detail he could remember. When he came to the end of the details, all he wanted to do was scream at the absurdity that it was him sitting here, saying these things.

"So what're you going to do?" Kelly asked, and the fear and concern were evident in his voice.

"I don't know. I really don't, man. I hate the thought of him laying there like a vegetable forever. He wouldn't want that. But how do you make a decision like that? How do you say, 'I think it's better if he dies'? God, that even sounds horrible."

"Yes. Yes, it does, but sometimes…"

"I know. I know." He didn't want to hear it. He didn't want to hear the platitudes about when it was your time to go and doing what's right and letting go. What he wanted was for someone to wave a magic wand and get him out of this situation. "Listen, Kell. Thanks for listening. I'm going nuts here. It's nice to have someone to talk to."

"Well, you're welcome. I'd like to think if the tables were turned, you'd be there for me."

Ben would like to think that too, but he couldn't be at all sure of that because the times he hadn't been spun through his tired soul. "I'll let you know how things go."

"Okay. And remember, we're here for you whatever you need."

"Thanks, man."

Kathryn pulled at the side of her skirt, smoothing and fixing it. She should be listening, of course, but her attention kept straying from the pulpit to that nice-looking set of shoulders just two rows ahead of her. She should have sat up there. Ugh. Why hadn't she? Then she would be in the same row as him.

Her face heated at the thought of the glimpse she'd caught of him striding down the aisle as he came in. He had such a nice walk. Firm. Confident. Yes, he did look a little younger than she'd at first thought he was, but then those things were so deceiving, how could she know for sure?

The sermon ended, and she stood with everyone else. It wasn't proper, but her gaze went right to his back. He had on a soft yellow shirt, buttoned down, nice—like something someone would wear to a casual office. She wondered what he did for a living and tried to guess. Maybe he was in sales or management. Management. Yeah. That could be it.

The thought of what kind of car he drove or what kind of apartment he had drifted through her mind. Nice. Yes, they would all be nice. They had to be. Nice-looking guy, nice place, nice ride. Yes, they would be nice. She tipped her head as her thoughts strayed even further to what it might be like to go on a date with him. Where would he take her?

She could see him getting out at some nice restaurant to come around to help her out of the car. Of course he was a gentleman. Why wouldn't he be? After all, he was nice. Movement next to her snagged her attention, and she jumped. "Oh."

The Our Father. Time to hold hands. She smiled at the older man who was offering her his hand even as the rest of the congregation had gone on with the prayer. Quickly she obliged and jumped into the prayer mid-stream. When she returned her gaze to the front, she let the words continue without even hearing them. He was tall. She wondered how tall he was up close because the floor of the church was sloped so that she couldn't really tell. Maybe six foot, maybe even a little taller.

Yes, that would be perfect next to her. The prayer ended and the rest of everything drifted by her in a haze of what ifs and maybes. By the end, she was certain that they were destined to be together forever. Now to get his attention. The final hymn ended, and it was then that she realized he was on the outside of the bench, but she was in the middle so that he turned and headed for the doors with no way for her to get to him through the crush of the others. Man, she was bad at this.

She smiled in his direction, hoping he would look at her. Instead, he shook someone's hand on the other side and strode right on by her pew. This was not how the story was supposed to end. Hello! she wanted to yell. Soulmate over here!

But he just kept walking. Even when she was out of the bench, the crowd pouring out with her impeded her progress. She caught a single, solitary glimpse of him as he exited the doors. "Oh, excuse me," she said to the little old lady she almost tripped over. Her hands shot out to steady the woman, but her gaze was already at those back doors.

He was gone. He couldn't be gone. That wasn't fair. Ugh. Ten more steps through the molasses of people, and she knew he was gone for good, in the parking lot, in his nice car, with his sunglasses on... At first she was upset by that, but then she rationalized that at least she knew he did come to church on a semi-regular basis and he always sat in the same pew. Alone. All she had to do was change where she sat, and they were as good as a couple.

"Ben," Dr. Vitter said, shaking his hand.

"Dr. Vitter." There wasn't a thing Ben liked about this. Dr. Vitter looked far too concerned, far too serious.

They sat simultaneously, and Ben fought not to squirm right out of his chair.

"We got the MRI's back this morning, and unfortunately, there has been more bleeding overnight."

"Um-hm." More bleeding. That did not sound good. "But you can fix that, right? I mean, you can... with the surgery."

Dr. Vitter's gaze slipped to the desk. "Even with surgery, your father's chances of ever coming out of this are very, very slim."

"But..." Air, words, hope—they all escaped. "But there is... I mean, there is still a chance. Something. Some drug or something."

Although he never actually shook his head, Dr. Vitter's whole demeanor said, *No, there isn't.* "I'm sorry, Ben. Really, I am. If there was any way I thought we'd have a chance, I would give it to you. But he's too far gone. There's too much damage, and to keep him 'alive' like this..." He put quotes around that word, raking right over Ben's heart with the gesture. "Your father wouldn't want this."

"I…" He cleared his throat because suddenly he wanted to cry more than he ever had before. He blinked the tears back. "Okay." Reaching up, he scratched at his shoulder which suddenly felt like it was crawling with something. "Um. Then what…" The lump grew in his throat so that he had to clear it again. "What do we do now?"

We. Such a strange word. There was no we. Only I and me. He'd loved those words for so long. Suddenly they felt very, very lonely.

"Well, I think it's time to consider the possibility of hospice."

"Hospice. Hm." Why could he not get more than a word out without choking up? "What's that?"

"Hospice," Dr. Vitter explained as the world did that tilt away from Ben thing again. Why could he not concentrate when the doctor was spelling out the options? Why did it seem that the doctor's mouth was moving but no sound was coming out? "It really is not as ghoulish as it sounds. It gives the patient a place to die in peace without heroic methods being used to prolong a life that is fading."

"Hm. I'm sorry. And where is this… this hospice place?" Ben could think of no place bad enough for this to be. The deep recesses of hell came to mind.

"On the northwest side of the building. It's a smaller building although it is connected to the hospital."

Ben nodded, not at all sure that those words even made sense. "And he would be moved there?"

"Yes. Once you sign the papers, we would do the transfer."

"Uh-huh." There was no catching any thought in his head. He stood and stepped over to the window, not wanting to be in this room anymore, having this discussion. He looked out at the traffic longingly. "And what if I don't sign the papers?"

"Well." Only now did Dr. Vitter hesitate. "We would continue to keep your father on the life support systems as long as they worked, but you have to understand, he will almost assuredly not come out of this comatose state."

"Yeah, but if I do this, if I sign those papers, then that'll be it. He will definitely die?"

There was a slight moment of hesitation. "Yes." The doctor's tone was grave. "He will."

Ben wanted to run more at that moment than he ever had before. Looking out into the parking lot far below, he put his hand on the back of his neck, feeling knots he didn't remember ever being there. They were giving him a terrible headache. "I don't know. I don't think I can do that... sign those papers I mean... I mean, how... how can I do something like that? How can I make that kind of decision? I don't think I could ever do that."

"No, seriously, Kate," Misty said on Monday afternoon as they stood at the nurse's station in St. Anthony's Hospice. "I get it. There was a good-looking guy at church, and he's probably wonderful and perfect for you. But you didn't even talk to him. You don't even know if he's single. I mean, that's great, and maybe it will work out, but in case he... I don't know... shows up with a girlfriend next weekend or something, why don't you just go out with Nathan and give him a chance too? He really is a nice guy, and I've actually talked with him."

Kathryn rolled her eyes. "Why does this have to be so complicated? Why can't I just find a guy, fall in love, have a couple babies, and live happily ever after like everybody else does?"

"Uh, because nobody does that?"

"Yes they do. Look at you and Casey. You're both married with kids and the whole thing."

"Yes, but it's not a bed of roses for us either. I can't tell you how frustrated I get when I'm thinking new bedroom furniture and Zac comes home with a new power mower. Ugh. I'd like to shoot him, and sometimes I think I would if I didn't love him so much."

"But that's what I mean. That's what I want. I want to be so frustrated with him that I want to shoot him but know I never would. I want that, and I'm so tired of waiting and thinking maybe it's never going to happen for me."

"So, then why are you afraid to go out with a guy that might make it happen?"

Kathryn's shoulders slumped forward. "I don't know. I guess I'm just afraid of being disappointed again."

"Uh-huh. So you're going to refuse to even try even though you keep telling me you want that more than anything."

The phone next to Misty beeped, and she picked it up.

Kathryn knew to politely find something else to listen to. She was good at doing that. Her own thoughts seemed as good a place as any to disappear. Misty was probably right. What was she doing pining away for some guy two rows up that she had never met when another perfectly nice guy might be waiting for her if she just said yes?

"Yeah, she's right here." Misty put her hand over the phone. "Dr. Vitter for you."

Snapping back into work mode, Kathryn stood. "I'll take it in my office." She strode down the hall, knowing what was waiting on the other side of the phone call. Another patient. Without really thinking and because it was always her first line of defense, she whispered in her heart, "Lord, please be with this person and their family as they begin their transition to You."

In her office she sat down, wiped her eyes as if Dr. Vitter could see her pathetic state, picked up the phone, and pushed the blinking button. "This is Kathryn."

"Kathryn, oh, good." He sounded genuinely relieved, and she knew this was more than a routine call. "Listen, I've got some rather bad news, and I'm afraid I'm going to need some help with this one."

"Okay. What's up?" Her prayers kicked into a higher gear.

"Well, I'm sure you remember Dr. Warren with the oversight office."

"Yes."

"Well, he was admitted on Friday night, and I'm afraid I just got the MRI's back. It does not look good."

"Oh. I'm sorry to hear that." On her desk, she wrote, *Dr. Warren. MRI.* "Is this a stroke or a car accident or what?" Not that it really mattered, but it was always nice to have the information going into any meeting with the family.

"A massive stroke. The family's really struggling with the hospice decision. I think it's a matter of not understanding the program. I was wondering if you could come talk with them just to maybe put their mind at ease, you know?"

"Yes. All right. Are they there right now?"

"I can let them know you're on your way."

"I'll be there in ten."

"Thanks, Kathryn."

She almost said her good-byes.

29

"And Kathryn?"

"Yes?"

"Go easy, okay? This is really a tough one."

Nodding, she steadied her heart. They were all tough. "I will." She hung up, stood, and left the rest of her work behind. As many of these meetings as she had had over the course of her career, they never got any easier, and she never wanted them to. It was too important that she not become hardened to the difficulty of the transition of death. No matter how many times she went through it, she had to remember that the family had not had nearly so much practice. Most had had none at all.

She boarded the elevator and let her gaze slide up to the numbers above. "Dear Lord, please be with the Warrens. Give them Your love. Help me to help them through this difficult time. Give me the right words, God. Please, do this through me…"

Never had Ben ever wanted to feel like this again—like his world was shattering and there wasn't a thing he could do about it. He remembered this pain with crystal-clear clarity. In fact, it was still so fresh, he wondered if he had ever truly forgotten it. Tears came to his eyes, but he beat them back. He couldn't start crying now. If he did, he might never stop.

Hunched over his knees in the waiting room, he pushed his mind to topics that he might be able to deal with. Things like how things were at work and if Simon had called the Naxel Company yet to explain the situation. Explain the situation. Ha. That was a joke. Ben wanted to scream, "How did this happen?" And inside he was screaming that and so much more. How he was managing to keep it all on the inside, he had no clue because it felt like it might burst from him at any moment.

"Ben?" Dr. Vitter suddenly appeared right in front of him, and Ben snapped to attention, yanking himself out of the chair. He shook the doctor's hand without really understanding where reality had gone. "Ben, this is Kathryn Walker. She's the social worker in our hospice program."

"Mr. Warren." Ms. Walker stepped forward and shook his hand although the world was tilting into that not making any sense realm again.

"Ms. Uh Walker." He nodded, tried to smile, knew it didn't

get that far, and hoped he wouldn't completely break down right there in front of everybody.

"Um, we could go into my office," Dr. Vitter said, and Ben nodded again, wanting no part of making that walk.

"Okay."

Ragged. That was a good word to describe Dr. Warren's "family." It wasn't a family. Just one guy, and Kathryn wished she had thought to ask a few more questions. As they walked down the hall, Dr. Vitter in front, her in the middle, and the guy behind her, she sank into prayer because that was all she could think to do. God had better show up for this one because she was definitely out of her league. He looked just barely this side of death himself.

In the office, Dr. Vitter motioned toward the little couch on the far wall, and Kathryn accepted his invitation. When she was seated, she watched Mr. Warren sit on the other side, gaze down, looking like he might fall off the earth if someone didn't hold onto him. She smiled softly, hoping her compassion was evident and not condescending. It was then that she realized Dr. Vitter was not planning to stay.

"Take as long as you need," he said, and with that, he turned and hustled out, closing the door behind him.

Oh, help, God! her heart screamed into the abyss where she was now staring. She looked over at the guy who looked positively ripped to pieces. Where to start and how? Words failed her. "I'm sorry. I didn't catch your first name."

When he looked up, his blue-green eyes were filled with a pleading for her to do something, anything someone hadn't already thought of. "Uh, Ben. Ben Warren."

She nodded, wishing she could do or say something to take away the immense pain in his distraught eyes. "Mr. Warren…"

"Please, call me Ben," he said with the saddest of smiles.

"Ben," she said softly, "I'm sorry about what's happened." The words stopped because compassion choked the rest from her chest. She had learned not to force herself to keep talking in such situations. Time was a stabilizer that rushing simply couldn't match. "Dr. Vitter said you're considering hospice care for your father."

Ben's dark eyebrows arched in slight sarcasm. "I guess." He

exhaled and put his elbows on his knees and his hands to his mouth. "I don't really know what I'm doing to be honest with you. All of this… stuff is totally new to me. I don't know what's best. I don't even know what's worst at this point."

She watched him, her emotional radar searching for any and all signals that would guide her words. "I take it you will be the one to make the decision."

"Yeah." He laughed a hollow laugh. "Lucky me, huh?"

Kathryn didn't push it. He was working this out in his head and his heart, and she had to let him in his way, in his time.

When he looked at her, there were a myriad of questions in his eyes. "Um, can I ask you some things? I mean, they didn't really tell me much about your… program."

"Certainly. Ask whatever you want."

Ben swallowed hard and let his gaze fall to the floor at his feet. It was brown. That registered. He was glad something did. Words were becoming harder and harder to come by and harder to say without breaking down completely. "Um, well, I take it from what Dr. Vitter said that once Dad is transferred… there, that's pretty much it. Right? I mean he won't get any care after that."

"If you mean do we put him in a dark room and wait for the end, no that's not what we do." Her voice was soft and very kind. "We feel we're a place that can provide the needed transition time for your father and for the family. Hospitals are wonderful for those who are going to survive, but they are not great places to die."

Die. Man, he hated that word, but he nodded anyway even though his gaze was still firmly on the floor.

"The staff and machines and keeping the family at bay are just not conducive to giving everyone the time they need to say good-bye," Ms. Walker continued. "We don't make you say good-bye on a schedule. The schedule is whatever you set. You come when you want, stay as long as you like, leave when you're ready. It's totally up to you."

Something akin to hope brushed his heart, and he picked up his gaze. "No five minute visits every two hours starting at eight and ending at eight?"

She smiled clearly getting the reference. "No, you do what

works for you. We have round-the-clock staff who specialize in end-of-life issues. We can help you through not just your father's transition, but we can point you to services that can smooth life out as you go forward as well."

His shoulders relaxed as he let out a slow, choppy breath. As he looked at her, the need to tell someone how overwhelmed he was overtook him. He looked down quickly trying to squelch it. However, even after several long seconds, he couldn't. "I'm… Uh, I've never dealt with anything like this before. I feel like I'm in the dark with no idea which way to even go."

"You're not alone. Most people feel like that," she said like the touch of an angel's wings. "Believe me, no one feels equal to this one. What you have to understand is that you're not being judged. You get through it in the best way you can. You just have to learn to be really gentle with yourself. That helps."

He laughed that hollow laugh again.

She joined him. "Well, it's pretty much a learned skill. We're all so programmed to think we have to know what to do and what to say that when we don't, we feel like utter failures. I know. I've been there." Her eyes were soft as was her smile. "But this is not some kind of competition. It's not a pass or fail test. It's doing your best and giving yourself the space to do it the way that makes the most sense for you."

"So you think I should sign the papers."

"That's not my decision. I haven't seen the medical reports. What I want you to know is that our facility is not some draconian echo chamber. We really do care, and we want to help when you're ready."

A moment more and Ben nodded. At least he'd stopped looking only at the floor. That was something. And he was calm—at least on the outside. She had seen families screaming and yelling at one another in these situations. This was definitely better although she could tell he was struggling mightily to get through this minute to the next.

He stood from the little sofa and offered her his hand. "Ms. Walker, thank you very much."

She shook his hand. "You're welcome. And for the record, it's Kathryn."

"Kathryn." There was almost a smile there. "That was my grandmother's name."

"Really?" She tilted her head in surprise. "Most people call me Kate, but I really prefer Kathryn. I don't know why. It sounds more old-style Hollywood or something." With a saucy smile, she tossed her blonde locks over her shoulder as if she was anywhere near as glamorous as those ladies. "Hey, a girl can dream, can't she?"

This laugh made it all the way up to his eyes. They were nice eyes, kind of a hazy bluish-green. "That she can. That she can."

After a moment the laughter fell away from her. "But really, if you need anything, here's my card." She slipped it from her pocket and handed it to him. "Just call anytime. Of course, I'm not the only one on staff, so if I'm not there, Clyde or Yvonne will be able to help also."

He took the card and looked at it for a long, long moment. When he looked up again, there was genuine gratefulness in his eyes. "Thank you."

Her only wish was that she could do more. "You're welcome."

After she left, Ben went down to the cafeteria, got some coffee, and found a little corner to disappear into. It was only three in the afternoon, but it felt like midnight-thirty. He took a sip of the coffee and set the cup on the table. Reaching in his pocket, he pulled out her card. Kathryn Walker, St. Anthony's Hospice, Social Worker.

Who signed up for a job like that? He would run for the hills. Slowly he turned the card over and over in his fingers. What to do? She didn't make it sound as horrible as he had envisioned, and yet a good salesman could sell anything. True, she didn't seem like a pushy salesperson. But it was her job to make her facility seem as user-friendly as possible. He thought it through again and took another drink.

It wouldn't hurt to check the place out. At least then he could give Dr. Vitter a logical reason why he wasn't going to take that option. Downing the last of the coffee, he grabbed his cell phone out of his pocket. With a hard blink, he forced himself to dial the number correctly. As it rang, he realized she probably wasn't even back yet.

"St. Anthony's Hospice, this is Kathryn."

His heart snagged on the softness of her voice. He spun the phone's speaker down to his mouth. "Uh, yeah. Kathryn? This is Ben Warren. I just talked to you?"

"Oh, yes. Ben. Did you need something else?"

"Um, well, yeah. Kind of. Um, I was wondering if maybe I could come over and see the… facility." There were certain words he just couldn't utter.

"Oh, well, sure. Of course. Do you want to come now?"

Now? Now was a little soon. His spirit recoiled at the thought. He'd long before given up the nursing home route on his sales trek through the city. There were just some things he did not want to subject himself to. "Uh, well, I don't want to bother you. I've already taken up so much of your time…"

"Oh, it's not a problem. Tell you what, I'll meet you by the elevators on the neurology floor. Will that work?"

"Uh. Yeah. Sure."

"I'll be there in five."

"Okay."

And she was gone. Only then did reality occur to him. What was he thinking? He wasn't anywhere near the elevators on the neurology floor. He jumped up, nearly knocking the chair to the ground. Two doctors from the table near him glanced his direction. He quickly resettled the chair, ditched the cup, and headed out.

Kathryn strode from the elevators over to the partition leading to the waiting area. Glancing in, she frowned with concern. How could she have missed such a simple thing as where they would meet? Or maybe he had reconsidered the meeting? Or worse, he was worse off than she thought and connecting A to B was becoming an issue.

The elevator dinged, pulling her attention that direction. Air re-introduced itself to her lungs when he stepped off, running his hand over his hair, his gaze down. When he looked up, his smile was sheepish.

"Sorry. I was down in the cafeteria getting some coffee."

"That's okay," she said, feeling really silly for all the doomsday scenarios she'd been running in her head.

They stood like that, five feet apart, not saying anything for a long moment.

Finally, glancing up at the elevators, she let out a breath slowly. "You ready?"

His gaze yanked up with hers. "Oh, uh. Yeah. Sure."

Together they stepped to the elevator, and he pushed the button. Standing there next to him, she could feel the trepidation in his stance and his demeanor. He would hardly look at her, not that he was really focusing on much of anything. That bothered her. The truth was, in the last hour, she had come to see him as her patient as much as his father. Caring. It was always her downfall.

The elevator dinged, and he let her board first. There were already three people on, so she didn't want to broach any heavy-duty subject, but she didn't want to make him more uncomfortable than he obviously already was either.

"I guess all of this is wreaking havoc with your work schedule," she said, hoping that was a safe topic.

His laugh was soft. "You can say that again. But I'm on commission, so... it's mostly my wallet that's taking the hit."

"Commission. So you're in sales then?"

The elevator stopped on floor 3 to collect more people.

"Yeah," he said as they all swayed forward to compensate for the renewed movement.

Kathryn lifted her chin in acknowledgement both of the response and the understanding that he wanted no more to do with that topic. She waited until the elevator dinged on the first floor and they had disembarked and turned for their destination before she tried again.

"I'm assuming," she said, stepping lightly around the question, "that there aren't other family members involved in this decision." Her gaze went over to him as they walked. "Not that that's really any of my business, but I kind of like knowing going in what pitfalls there are. You know, people showing up that we're not aware of, that kind of thing."

"Oh, yeah." He walked four more steps before he said any more, and she wished she wouldn't have asked. "Well, besides Dad's work colleagues, which I couldn't really give you much of a run-down on who might come, it's pretty much me. I've been trying to get ahold of my mom, but that's been a little more difficult than I thought it would be."

"So they weren't together then… your parents?"

"No." He seemed to laugh softly at that, and the response puzzled her. "No, they haven't been together for a long, long time."

She lifted her chin in acknowledgement. "But you have called her?"

"I've tried."

At the large glass doors, he pushed through and held it for her. "Where is this place anyway?"

"Just down this hallway. We're almost there."

He continued to walk although she could feel him careening backward. She could only imagine what he believed would be at the end of this hallway.

Never before had Ben wanted to turn and run so badly. Death. He didn't do death. He didn't even do sickness. Even when he was sick, he hated being there for it. And now he was going to a place that people went to die. It was overwhelming, intimidating, sickening. In fact, if this walk lasted much longer, he might actually be sick on his shoes.

Focusing on his breathing, he forced the air in and out and then in again. At least he was breathing. Moving and breathing. Those were two tallies in the good column. Now if he could just skip this next part.

The sunshine from outside streamed in through the large windows edging the outer wall next to him. Covered in mustard yellow and brown, the floor did its best to look cheery. But it didn't succeed. And the beige walls, though not the bright white of the hospital still were not exactly welcoming.

At the end of the hallway, they came to a glass door marked *St. Anthony's Hospice*. On the walls next to the door were plaques proclaiming the date of completion for the unit and those responsible for its existence. Not wanting to, Ben opened the door and held it for her. His father had taught him to be a gentleman if nothing else.

With one more exhale to calm his scattering nerves, Ben followed her inside. The décor and atmosphere upon entering were decidedly more homey than the hospital they had just left. The lights were softer, the carpeting more plush, the sounds less machinery and more personable.

On the table in the center of the entryway stood a large vase of burgundy flowers that was two feet taller even than he. He glanced up at the arrangement, noticing the touch of elegance and wondering who thought it was a good idea to spend so much money on a place where people came to die.

"Misty," Kathryn said, walking right up to the rounded counter in the center of the large room, "this is Ben Warren. He's come to check out the facility. Ben, Misty Clark, one of our nurses."

He fought to smile as he shook the hand of the young woman with the dark bob. "Misty."

She smiled sweetly. "Welcome, Mr. Warren."

"Thank you."

Kathryn turned to the large lobby area, and he followed like a lost puppy. "This is one of our lobbies. We have another down the opposite hallway that's the same."

He stuck his hand in his back pocket, trying to appear casual. "You have two units?"

"We have two areas, but the staff roams the two freely. Our nurses work both sides."

"So why do you have two areas? Wouldn't it be simpler to just have one?"

"The two areas allow us to keep the atmosphere quieter for our families. This way, we can split the incoming patients between the two areas, which gives our families more room and more privacy. That way, they aren't stacked on top of one another." She was so calm about all of it, like they were discussing hotel reservations instead of death preparations. Something about that unnerved him even more.

"We really try to give our families what they need, and we've found one of the most important things is to maintain a sense that they are not cattle being herded through to make room for someone else."

Ben sighed at that thought. *Hurry up and die. We need the bed for someone else.* Strange how ghastly thoughts like that now attacked him on a rather frequent basis. Was he always this morbid, or did the situation just warrant it? He wound his hands up under his armpits, trying to look like he was interested and not repulsed by what she was saying.

"It can be such a stressful time for families, but we've found it can also be a very healing time if we set up the situation to allow for that healing. Rushing the process doesn't work."

"Rushing." He'd never thought about not rushing. Some part of him thought that was the point. Suddenly he was very tired—as much from the situation as from thinking of the rush of life he'd been living. He dropped his hands to the back of the chair in front of him and put his foot up on the little brace at the bottom.

"We don't rush here," she said gently. Her soft brown eyes held a degree of sympathy and compassion he wasn't sure he had ever seen before. "We support. We assist where we can. But we never rush anyone."

Ben nodded, appreciating what she was telling him personally as well as professionally. He glanced up as an older lady supported by two younger ladies exited the room straight in front of them. Ducking, he waited until they had meandered off down the hall. "So, how many patients do you have here at one time?"

"The number varies, but we have rooms for twenty. Ten rooms here. Ten on the other side."

"And they're… private rooms?"

"Yes. Actually they are really rather nice with chairs and a couch, fold-out for those wanting to stay the night."

"People do that? Stay the night I mean?"

Kathryn seemed to sink to an even more peaceful level if that was possible. "Every family, every person handles this situation in their own way. Some want to be very hands on. They have a family member here round the clock. Others simply want to know their loved one is taken care of in their final hours, but they do not feel comfortable doing anything more than visiting."

He put his hands back under his arms. "And how long do people usually… stay while they're here before they… you know, pass on?" Was it him or was this conversation immensely surreal to the rest of the world as well?

She smiled in a way that made him wonder what she knew that he didn't. "That's hard to answer. Some stay only a very short time. Others are not as ready to go. Sometimes they wait for a loved one to come. Sometimes they wait for everyone to leave. Sometimes they pass with no real discernible reason why. Each situation is very unique—as I imagine is each soul."

Interested perplexity drifted through him. "So you really

believe that—that they have a soul and all of that?"

"Oh, very much so. I've seen too many things to believe otherwise." Then she caught herself and jerked her gaze to his. "Not that anyone else has to believe that or anything. It's just what I believe."

He narrowed his gaze, trying to see the catch.

"Um, we also have a small chapel if you're interested in seeing that." She jerked her gaze down the hallway.

"Uh, no." That uncoiled him. "I think I've pretty much seen enough for today."

"I'm sorry," she said, exhaling in understanding. "I shouldn't have said that earlier..."

"No." He stopped her with one word and after a second, held his hand out to her. "Thank you for the tour and the talk."

"Anytime," she said, shaking his hand but clearly not believing she hadn't completely messed up. "You have my number."

Reaching in his pocket, he pulled out the little cream-colored card. "That I do."

Four

In minutes he was gone. He. Ben Warren. Such a nice guy. Lost and unsure of how to proceed but nice and wanting to do the right thing. Kathryn had lost track of the time during their discussion and by the time she walked him to the door and said her good-byes, she was shocked to find it was only twenty minutes from shift change.

Quickly she went back to her office and righted the paperwork on her desk. Then she quietly went out to check on each of her seven families. They were a perfect blend of people from all ages and races. Having saved Mrs. Baker for last, Kathryn pushed through the little beige-green door.

"Knock. Knock." She ducked inside and found Rachel and Sadie sitting with the woman she had seen them come out of the room with earlier.

"Kathryn," Rachel said, getting up and coming to her. The young woman with the dark brown tresses pulled her into a hug. "Thank you so much for coming. This is our aunt from Illinois, Aunt Abigail."

Kathryn sat on the couch next to the chair where the woman sat. "Aunt Abigail, it's nice to meet you."

"You too, dear." The old woman held out her wrinkled and veined hand.

"How was your trip?"

"Lumpy and bumpy just like me." She smiled, and Kathryn was sure had the situation been different, she would have laughed as well. "You know, this is the first time I've been here in 12 years. Emma always came to visit me. I've got a bad hip, so I don't get around like I used to."

"I'm sure Emma is glad you could make it," Kathryn said with a soft smile as she glanced at the woman lying in bed, unmoving. "She sure has brightened our corner of the world with her lovely family."

"The girls have just been dears," Abigail said. "They've kept me abridged of all the developments ever since Em got sick. They kept telling me to just stay put that it wasn't worth it to come, but I'm glad now I did. I think Em needed to see me once more."

Kathryn fought the tears welling into her eyes. These kinds of heartfelt searches for confirmation always did that to her. "Yes, I know that Emma loved her family so much. I'm sure she was extra glad to see you."

"Kathryn," Rachel, who was at least half a decade younger than she, said. "Would you pray with us, with Grandma?"

"Of course." She stood and helped Sadie, who was on the other side of the chair, help Aunt Abigail to her feet. The woman was incredibly frail, and with her sister pushing 93, she probably wasn't too far behind. Together they made their way over to the bed. When they were in position, Rachel looked at Kathryn who took a breath and closed her eyes. She reached down, took Emma's hand, and held it up to Abigail who smiled as she put her hand on her sister's.

"Dear Lord, we thank You so much for the gift of this family," Kathryn prayed quietly but firmly. "We thank You for Emma's life and for the love she has given to her sister and to her granddaughters who love her so very much. Lord, we ask You to welcome her home, welcome her back into Your love at Your best time."

Next to her, Abigail sniffed, and Kathryn let go of her arm to put her arm all the way around her back. She leaned in as Abigail leaned closer to her. "And Lord, we ask You to be with us. You know how much we love Emma and how very hard it is for us to see her go. Please touch our hearts with Your love and Your peace as we let go. Comfort us and love us in our time of need. These things we ask in Your name. Amen."

"Amen," Abigail whispered next to her.

When Kathryn looked down, Abigail reached up and touched the side of her cheek. "Thank you."

Kathryn could hardly hold all of the emotions in. She tilted her head and smiled. "Thank you for allowing me to be with you all." Her gaze went back to the fragile hand still held in her own. "We all love you, Emma. You will be in our hearts forever."

Fighting back the tears, she laid the hand on the bed, ran her hand once over the wiry locks of gray hair, and said one more silent prayer for a safe and peaceful transition for this beautiful soul. It took more than a moment to gather herself before she turned back for the three women.

"Will you be here tomorrow?" Sadie asked from the other side of the bed.

Kathryn smiled. "Eight o'clock as always."

"I don't know, Kell. This is like the impossible decision from hell. How am I supposed to sign those papers?" Ben sat in the neurology waiting area watching the clock. Ten more minutes and he would get a five minute visit with a man he had relied on and trusted his whole life. Unfortunately that man's life now hung in the balance, and his finger was on the nuke button. Where in the world did that make any sense at all? He kept asking himself that even as he hunched over his knees.

"So is the place like... awful?"

"Hospice?" Ben asked, straightening and going all the way back to the wall. "Actually it's very nice. Kind of like a retirement community only much quieter." He raked his hand over his eyes. "How did I get into this? I'm not the one to go to for stuff like this. You? Yeah, you can handle this stuff. Me? I'm a screw-up who hasn't made a rational decision in a decade."

Kelly laughed, but it was soft. "You give yourself far too much credit there, my man."

"Huh." Ben's laugh was soft too. He fooled no one. "I don't know. Part of me thinks they are right. I should just sign the papers and get it over with. I mean we're not getting anywhere like this. But the other part..."

"Have you heard from your mom?"

"Not yet." He couldn't hide the frustration. "I don't even know if she would come if I could get a hold of her."

A moment and Kelly sighed. "Man, I wish I could give you some advice, tell you what to do, but I just don't know. This is a tough one."

"Tell me about it." Ben sat, trying to think of a way to prolong the conversation. He was not looking forward to another night alone. But then again, that's what he was... alone.

"Listen, Ben, I need to be..."

"I know. Thanks, Kell, for being there."

"Hey, where else would I be?"

Ben smiled at that and signed off with his friend. Once the connection was dissolved, he put his head back on the wall. The waiting was pure torture, and yet, what exactly was he waiting for? What was going to happen in this realm that would do anything but make him wait even more? Short of another stroke or something else failing in his father, he could be here until doomsday.

If he believed in God, he might even have gotten angry at that moment. But what sense did it make to argue with an entity you didn't even believe in? None. He looked at the clock and pushed to his feet when he realized visiting hours would be starting in only a couple minutes. It was odd how accustomed he'd become to making that walk down that too-well-lit corridor to those double doors with the windows at the end of it.

He made it to them just before they opened and went through on the push of some family in front of him. There was no need to ask for the room or directions, he knew them by heart, and when he pushed into the second door, the nurse tending the body on the bed with the tubes and wires strung to it looked up.

"Mr. Warren," she said, addressing the man in the bed, "you have a visitor."

"How's he doing?" Ben asked, absurdly hoping that she would tell him fantastic and he would be going home tomorrow.

"He's stable."

"Stable." Ben raised his chin and lowered it slowly. There were just certain words that made his heart fall into his shoes.

"I'll be out here if you need me." And with that, she went to and out the door.

The world tilted away from him as his senses swirled. He let out a hard exhale. Why was this happening? Why? "Um, Dad." Man, it felt weird to talk to someone who couldn't even hear him. "We... we need to talk." He took a hesitant step forward, seeing the face amidst the wires, but not wanting to. "Uh, I went down today to the..." Bile rose in his throat, and he swallowed it down.

"To the hospice unit. I… I don't know if you've ever been there before, but it's not so bad. Um. They… want me to sign some papers that would take you off life support. I don't really know how I feel about that, or how you would feel about that."

Anger bubbled up in his gut. "You know, this really isn't fair. You always said I could come talk to you about anything, and now I could really use your advice. I don't… I don't know what to do here. I really don't. So if you could like, I don't know, give me a sign or something, something so I know what you want me to do…"

A different nurse pushed into the door, and Ben took a full step backward. It was almost time to go anyway.

"I'm sorry," the nurse said, "we had a monitor malfunction out there. I just needed to check on his oxygen levels."

Ben shook his head as if the intrusion was no big deal, but his sniff gave him away.

"Yep," she said, checking several cords. "Everything's working just fine." She turned to go and smiled at Ben as she left.

He hated those smiles. They tore more holes in him than he could deal with. He wished they would quit doing that, looking at him like they didn't know what to say. Of course, he knew they didn't. How would they?

"Well, Dad, I guess I'm going to go too. I may just head on home. It's after six, and with traffic…" There was an end to that sentence, but he didn't bother finding it. "I guess I'll see you in the morning." And with that, he turned and fled.

Instead of getting easier, these visits were getting harder. What do you say when you're the only one talking?

Anger reasserted itself as he banged through the double doors and headed out and down to the parking lot. What was the point of living if it just ends in such a distressing mess? He couldn't tell, and he was tired of thinking about it.

In the parking lot, he climbed in the Mustang, glad for once for the shred of normal one-upsmanship between him and Kelly that had brought him to make this purchase. He looked good in the silver Mustang, in control, invincible. Right now he needed that feeling more than he ever had before.

Before leaving for the evening, Kathryn went into the chapel. It was one of her favorite places in the world. Quiet. Serene. Holy. It had a way of wrapping around her and making her believe once again that Someone greater than she was in charge. She needed that more often than not. This job, the one she had been led to, was not the job for someone who thought they knew it all— because on a rather frequent basis, she was reminded that she had no clue.

Like today. As she sat in the pew, just looking forward and up at the large crucifix hanging there, she remembered Rachel and her sister, their aunt and the great-grandmother who had raised them. At one time Kathryn had tried to talk with those families like she knew it all. Now if humble had a name, she was sure it was Kathryn. Over and over she had walked into rooms filled with grief, knowing she had no words to ease their sorrow, and slowly but surely she had learned that although she couldn't, God could.

Her thoughts turned to Mr. Warren, the man with the incredibly sad eyes. He was struggling so hard. He wanted to do the right thing. That much was obvious. But how do you do the right thing when that means giving up? Kathryn shook her head at his dilemma. "We're not programmed to be quitters, God. We're not. We're raised—the whole lot of us—to believe we can do anything we put our minds to or that we should be able to." She closed her eyes to the pain that surged in her soul. "But when we can't, where do we even go with that? Especially when we don't know You. God, please be with Mr. Warren and with his dad. They need You so much, Lord. Both of them. Please guide them through this difficult time. And Lord, if I am to be any part of this, please give me the words to be part of Your solution. Do it through me if that is Your will. This I ask in Your name. Amen."

"Good morning," Kathryn said as she strode into the unit the next morning. A good night's sleep had done wonders for her disposition.

"Kate." Misty didn't even let her get a step down the hallway.

Coffee in one hand, briefcase in the other, she stopped. She never liked that tone.

"Kate," Misty said, coming around the desk, and a list of the patients streamed through Kathryn's mind. When Misty was only an arm's length from her, she stopped and gazed at her friend for a very long moment. "Mrs. Baker passed away overnight."

The coffee shook, nearly spilling from her hand. "What?"

"Here, let me take that." Without brooking an argument, Misty took the coffee. "Come on, let's go to your office." She took hold of her friend's elbow and steered her down the hallway.

"What… what time?" It felt like a knife to the gut. Many, many patients went through. Some she hardly remembered, but there were some she knew she would never forget. Mrs. Baker—Emma was one of them.

"I don't really know. Janet checked on her at two, and she was sleeping. At four, she was gone."

"Have they… Have they notified the family?" Slowly the wheels of her role started to reassert themselves.

"Yes. They've already been here to get her things. In fact, I think housekeeping has already cleaned the room."

In the office, she sat down on the client side of the desk in one of the two chairs. Misty got her some tissue, and they sat like that for a moment. Kathryn could feel her heart cracking in half as she dabbed at her eyes.

"I didn't even get to say good-bye."

"No, but you helped them to. That's what matters."

There had been no change overnight in his father's condition. That was so frustrating because if he just went one way or the other Ben would know what to do. He checked on everything at the eight a.m. visitation time, and then realizing he had to make this decision or stay in limbo forever, he pulled out his phone and dialed her number. Closing his eyes, he made a deal with the universe that if she didn't answer, that would be his answer.

"Let the service get it," Misty said when the phone on Kathryn's desk rang.

Determined to do her job the best she could whether or not she felt like falling apart, Kathryn stood. "No. It's okay. I'm all right." She stepped over and picked up the phone. She hadn't even had time to make it forward to her cell, which was usually accomplished no later than 8:05. One glance told her 8:05 had long passed. "St. Anthony's Hospice, Kathryn Walker." The first words had sounded so professional and then she sniffed, totally blowing her act.

Misty ripped three more tissues out and handed them to her.

"Uh, Ms. Walker?" Ben knew in a heartbeat he shouldn't have called. "I'm sorry. This is Ben Warren, from yesterday, if this is a bad time…"

"No. No, Mr. Warren, this isn't a bad time. What can I help you with?"

He swallowed, feeling the decision in his heart but not being able to get it to his voice. "I was wondering if maybe I could come down and take a look at one of the rooms." It was as good an excuse as any to delay the decision.

"Oh, of course. Certainly." She sniffed twice in quick succession. "Are you…" The pause was a mere second, but he heard it just the same. "Upstairs?"

"Uh, yeah." He looked around the waiting room to make sure. "I can just come down if that's okay."

"Sure. Of course it's okay. I'll…" She sniffed again. "…see you in a few at the main doors."

"Okay." Ben hung up and dropped the phone to look at it. That was strange, and if he wasn't so very unsure of his own stability, he might even be inclined to question hers. But as it was, he was in no position to question anything about anyone. So he stood and headed on the long walk to the little building just off-set from the hospital.

"Are you sure you're okay?" Misty asked, her voice filled with overwhelming concern. "I can call Yvonne."

"No. Don't be silly. This is my job." Kathryn ran the tissue under her eyes once more as she looked into the mirror. The grief was etched there, but maybe she could fake alive and happy long enough to get through this. "I'll be fine." She turned from the mirror knowing she could do no more. "Seriously. I'm fine. You, however, better get back out there. I don't want you getting into trouble."

Misty frowned but knew as well as Kathryn there wasn't much

that could be done about the situation. "Okay." She stepped over and gave Kathryn a hug, which Kathryn wasn't sure helped at all seeing how it put another crack in the mask she was desperately trying to get back on. "But if you need me, you know where I am."

Quickly Kathryn nodded but ducked her head lest Misty see and know how badly her heart hurt. "I'm fine. Go on." She pulled her shoulders back and stretched her neck side to side. "I'd better get too. Mr. Warren will be at the doors in no time."

"Ooh, Mr. Warren. He's cu-ute." Misty stretched the word out to two syllables.

"Stop it." Kathryn whacked her on the shoulder. "He's a client who's going through a really rough time right now."

Shrugging, Misty opened the door. "Doesn't mean he can't be cute."

Kathryn widened her eyes in warning at her friend as they walked down the hall, where from the entrance, crossing to the empty nurse's desk stepped Mr. Warren. He was more than cute. He was downright handsome. She whipped those thoughts from her brain in horror. What was she thinking? It must be the emotions of the morning. She snapped professional back over her and walked right up to him as he turned on their approach. "Mr. Warren."

"Uh, Ben," he reminded her as he shook her hand.

Her alert system blared to life at that touch, and stunned by it, she forced herself to smile and remember the situation. He was going through enough. He certainly didn't need the hospice social worker mooning over him. "Ben," she said softly, hoping it wasn't too soft. What was wrong with her?

She tipped her head, fighting to get herself back under control. "You mentioned wanting to see a room?"

"Y-yes." He glanced over at Misty. "I did."

Holding out her hand to indicate the lobby, Kathryn smiled. "Please."

Side-by-side they walked the ten steps to the lobby, which looked more like a vastly over-sized living room and which owing to the early morning hour was empty but for them.

"Has there been any change in your father's condition?" Kathryn anchored her arms over her chest, hoping she wasn't hopelessly wrinkling her soft white shirt.

"No." His gaze swung over to hers, and seas of deep blue-green washed over her. "Things are still pretty much the same."

She nodded, forcing herself not to look away. He needed her to be professional, and one way or the other, she was not going to let him down. Going to the angled wall along the edge of the room, she opened the door where the Bakers had been the day before. As she figured, it was already ready for the next family. Walking into the room, she sucked in a breath of stale, sorrowful air and let it out in small ragged burst of air. The bed was so very empty and too sterile for her grieving heart. She hated this part. She truly did.

Tears slipped up into her chest, but she beat them back. "As you can see, the rooms are quite large."

"It's kind of dark." He followed her in and then stepped past her to the chair next to the side wall.

"Oh, it doesn't have to be, but most of our families like it that way." She went back to the door, determined not to notice anything about him. At the entrance she turned on the overhead light. "When patients come to us, they are usually beyond the point of consciousness. I think because they look asleep, families generally feel more comfortable keeping the lights low."

From the door, she watched as he walked across the room to the little end table with the lamp on it. Before she had turned on the overhead light, it had been the room's only illumination. He picked up the little Death and Dying brochure that was always put out for new families.

"We try to give our families as much guidance to know what to expect as we can," she said, her gaze never leaving his back. "We have counselors on staff 24/7 and a chaplain on call as well."

He lifted the brochure for her to see though he didn't turn. "Looks like you've thought of everything."

What to say to that? He sounded annoyed or mad. She couldn't quite tell.

"It's a lot like the time issue we talked about yesterday. Every family is different in their approach. For some this time is peaceful and calm and prayerful. For others, confusion and fear reign, and calming that confusion is a very real component of our role. Many people have never gone through the death of a close loved one. It can be an overwhelming experience."

With his back still turned, Ben raised his hand and then laughed that little laugh that tore her heart out. "I'm thinking a trial run would've been nice right about now."

"It wouldn't matter."

This time he turned just slightly. "Oh, yeah? What? You don't think it would get easier?"

Her heart knew the truth all too well. "It's never easy to say good-bye."

She said it so gently, so without judgment or condescension that he almost believed she meant it.

Ben considered everything, thinking it through one more time, and then knowing what he had to do, he turned to her. For all of two seconds he thought he could lay it out for her like an adult. Then that wall crumbled. He reached up and scratched his head. "I... I think it's time. I do." His gaze slipped up to hers and then fell.

"Okay." With a single nod, she waited for more.

He glanced up at her again, hoping she wouldn't think him stupid or unbelievably weak. "I don't... Um, this isn't..." Hating himself for sounding like an idiot, he crushed the tears back inside him and cleared his throat.

In two steps she closed the space between them. "Please, let's sit," she said, indicating the couch.

Truth was, he was thankful for that. His legs were starting to feel like jelly. Once he was down, he searched for the words to explain the unexplainable. "I'm normally not like this... with things. It's just... My dad was my hero. I looked up to him in a way I guess most kids look up to their fathers, or maybe they don't. I don't know." He let out a slow breath to calm the racing of the emotions. "My mom and dad split when I was 13. I chose to stay with my dad.

"He was really busy with work, but he always made time for me. He always wanted to know how I was doing and what was going on in my life. Even when he was super busy, he always found a way to include me in his life."

"He sounds like a great dad."

"He was." Ben nodded, a smile coming to his face as his hands came together at his knees. "I always wanted to be just like him, you know? Carry on the tradition. But doctoring was not my specialty. I think I liked partying a little too much." He laughed softly. "It was a lot better than Anatomy and Physiology, that's for sure. So I went into pharmaceuticals, and when I got out, Dad helped me swing a job with a drug company."

Falling into the memories, Ben hardly realized he was still talking out loud. "Everyone loved my dad. I couldn't go anywhere that they didn't know him, and I think that made me even prouder of him. And I wanted him to be proud of me, you know? I wanted him to be able to say, 'That's my son. Ben Warren.'

"I…" The story stopped for a moment as he remembered his father as he had been what seemed a blink ago, not as he now was. "I never wanted to let him down, you know?" He sniffed back the sudden tears and wiped his nose that was betraying his effort not to cry. "I guess that's what I feel like I'm doing now, with this, like I'm letting him down."

"Is your father living the life he would want to live now?"

Instantly a picture of his father in that bed flashed into his mind. "No."

She let that word hang there in his heart for a long moment. "There is nothing wrong with heroic lifesaving if your efforts actually bring that life back. That's what they did to begin with. But there comes a time when holding onto a life that needs to go on only prolongs the inevitable."

The tears were overwhelming him now, and he sniffed them back angrily.

"This option is not about tossing that life away. It's about honoring life and the end of life. Death is a natural part of the process. That's not a good thing or a bad thing. It just is. Your dad lived a strong, healthy, vibrant life. He helped a lot of people. He gave a lot of good to this world. You are not going to diminish that by accepting that the time of his death is near."

Sorrow crushed over his spirit, crumpling it. "But I don't want him to go."

The touch of her hand on his shoulder brought the tears springing out of his eyes.

"I know. And that's okay. One thing you have to learn is to be very gentle with you. Let yourself feel and grieve and hurt. It's part of the process."

Overwhelming panic gripped him as he looked up at her. He could not do this alone. That much he was perfectly sure of. "Will you go with me? To sign the papers?" For a long moment his gaze searched hers, and then his bounced around and fell to the floor. "I really don't think I can do this alone."

Her soft brown eyes under the fall of blonde waves soothed his overwrought emotions when he glanced back up. "If you want me to go with you, I will."

Five

Kathryn sat in one chair in Dr. Vitter's office, Ben in the other. Dr. Vitter sat like a stone statue on the other side of the expansive desk. She watched the pen just touch the paper, and then Ben jerked it back. Closing her eyes, she prayed for God's will to be done. If Ben was having this much trouble, maybe there was a reason. Maybe he wasn't supposed to sign those papers. She didn't know, but she knew Who did.

"And there's nothing," Ben said as if he was pleading for his own life. "Nothing else you can do."

Dr. Vitter's gaze never left the other side of the desk. "We've done everything, and nothing in any test we've done gives us the slightest hope that he could ever come back."

Ben nodded but did not move.

"Ben," Kathryn finally said, and he turned to her with that same pleading in his eyes, "if you're not sure, there's no need to rush. Maybe you know something we don't."

She felt Dr. Vitter's gaze snap to hers, and she felt the anger too. But she didn't flinch. He could think what he wanted. She knew only to be there for this family that needed her to do what was right for them—not push them into a decision they were not ready to make.

A moment and Ben looked up at Dr. Vitter. "Um, could you give us a few minutes?"

The doctor looked both shaken and confused, but quickly regained his composure. "Certainly." Standing, he went around the desk and to the door. "Take all the time you need." And then he left.

When he was gone, Kathryn fought to keep herself under control. She had no idea what Ben might be thinking, but she was pretty sure whatever it was, she wouldn't have the answer.

"What do you believe," he began slowly, "about Heaven? About God?"

Whatever she thought his question would be, this was not it. "Uh, well. I believe that God exists, and so does Heaven. I believe that when our bodies die, our souls go on into eternity."

"So you don't think this is it?"

"No, I don't." With everything in her, she wanted to ask where this was coming from, but she didn't want to push him. These were steps he had to take on his own.

He laughed in that way she was getting used to, that little disbelieving, short little sound. Then he raked in a long breath. "My dad believed that too. He wanted me to believe it, but all that stuff that heaven and hell stuff—it was just stuff they said at church to me." His gaze fell to the papers. "Now I almost wish I believed it."

She let the thought drift in the air between them. "Why?"

When he looked over at her, it was as if he thought she had to know the answer to that question. She knew for herself, but she didn't know for him.

"All my life, things have been easy for me. I played soccer in high school, made captain of the team my junior year. I was all-state my senior year. I went to college had a great time, graduated, got a job, got my own apartment. I never really thought I needed a God, you know? I never saw the point." He stopped and took a breath. "Now, I guess I see that if I could believe Dad was going somewhere, that this wasn't the end, that maybe someday I would get to see him again... Maybe I could sign those papers."

"Have you ever seen a cross?" she asked, truly wondering where those words came from.

He shrugged. "Yeah. I mean you see them all the time."

"Have you ever seen one with Jesus on it?"

This one made him shift in his chair. "I'm not crazy about that kind. It's kind of... ghoulish to worship some statue of a guy hanging there being tortured, don't you think?"

Her voice grew softer. "There's one down in the chapel in the hospice unit. I was there last night. I go there a lot, and I look up at that man on the cross and I see what He gave up for me, how much He loved me, and how much He believed in God's love not just for Him but for me too. He believed right to and through the point of death. And sometimes when I sit there and look at Him, all I can think is, 'Jesus, please help me with my unbelief. Please help me in those times that I can't see You in the situation. Help me believe like You did, like You do.'"

Ben's forehead creased in consternation. "I thought you said you believed in God."

"I do."

Confusion piled on confusion. "But you prayed about your unbelief. If you believe, why would you pray about unbelief?"

"Because sometimes it's hard to believe. And believing doesn't negate life. Believe me, there are many times in my life that I want to question God. I want to question His timing and His plan and His wisdom. I look at things that happen, and I just get so angry with Him because I don't understand, because what He's doing makes no sense." She glanced over at the papers. "Like these papers. I hate seeing families going through what you're going through. I hate that. I hate that they are so sad and confused and scared. I want to make it all better, but I don't know how. That's when I have to go to God and ask Him to help me to know what to say and how to say it, to know what they need, and if I don't know, then for Him to just do it through me because I can't. I don't know all of the answers. I wish I did."

"Do you think I should sign the papers?"

The question was spoken with such a trust that she could hardly think of an answer.

"That's not a question I can answer," she said slowly. "I don't know what's right for you and for your dad." The next words went through her heart three times before she said them. "But I know Who does. I believe if you will ask Him, He will give you the answer you need."

Ben scratched the side of his face as he sat back away from her. "God, right? You're talking about God."

She should back off. She knew she should. Yet... "I am."

He sat there for the longest moment of her life. "Okay. Then how do I ask Him?" Ben pointed at the ceiling with the pen. "What, do I take out a telegram or something?"

"No." The words took a barrelful of courage. "You pray."

"Pray?" How he could sound so incredibly sarcastic she didn't know. "You think I should pray about this?"

Her gaze went to the papers still lying on the desk. "If it was my decision, I know I would be doing some serious praying over it." Then she resettled her gaze on him. "But you have to do what you feel comfortable with."

He let his gaze fall to the pen now in his fingers at his chest. "And if I were to pray, what might I say? I mean I don't exactly know how to talk all that Thee and Thou stuff."

Kathryn smiled and laughed. "Well, I don't think you're alone there. But prayers don't have to be some stylized version of King James. You just speak from your heart and then listen for what God has to say."

"My heart? Wow, you certainly don't go for the easy answers, do you?"

She smiled again. "I try not to."

A moment during which she had no idea what might come next, but she sat through it, knowing the next move was his. Finally, Ben shook his head slightly, pulled up, and then leaned forward toward her. When his gaze came to hers, there were only fragments of his normal arrogant manner in them. Mostly they were filled with fear and uncertainty.

"I don't know what to say," he said softly. "Would you pray it for me?"

How did she get into these things? *God, help.* "Of course."

In front of him Kathryn leaned toward him, and Ben wondered at the veracity of his own mind. What was he thinking asking her to pray with him? What was that? He didn't pray, and he certainly didn't go around asking other people to pray for him or with him. Even as he bowed his head with hers, doubts and insanity swirled through his thoughts. Had he met her in a bar, praying would not have been his first thought at all.

Of course, considering what they were about to do this moment that was probably not what he should have been thinking about, but it went through his mind just the same. She was, after all, quite beautiful. Blonde hair that hung in waves down to just past her shoulders, beautiful brown eyes, a nice smile—yes, he would have taken her for a spin or two. And now, somehow, absurdly, here he was praying with her. What sense in what realm did that make?

"God, we come to you today," she said, and he shifted in his chair suddenly uncomfortable with all of it, "to ask for Your guidance. We know that all things are of Your making, that all times and seasons obey Your command, and that You have a plan in everything. Lord, we ask You to make Your understanding available to Ben. Show Him what to do, God, and give him the strength and the peace to do it."

Thinking the prayer was over, Ben shifted back but stopped when she continued. Her head was still down, her eyes closed; she never knew he was looking right at her.

"And Lord, I ask a special blessing on Ben. You know how much he is struggling in this decision and with his belief in You. I ask only that You reveal Yourself to him so that in the coming days he will always know that at this moment You were truly right here with him."

If the angels were not singing, it sure felt like they were.

"Thank You God for every great and perfect gift that You give us—even the ones that sometimes don't feel like it. All these things we lift up to You. Amen."

Stunned and feeling like he'd just been hit by a bolt of white, hot lightning, Ben blinked twice, searching for reality. Two feet from him, she opened her eyes and smiled in a way that pierced right through the center of his heart.

"Did that help?" she asked after a moment of silence between them, and the softness in her voice cradled him as he had never been held.

"Y-yeah. It did."

A moment of her eyes being only on him, and then she cut her gaze to the papers. "If you want me to let you have some time…"

"No." He knew he shook his head, but he didn't know how. "No." Peace flooded his soul. "I'm ready now." And as if it was the easiest decision he had ever made, he turned and signed the four sets of papers that suddenly didn't seem nearly so scary or overwhelming.

When they were signed, he let out a long sigh as a huge weight lifted off his shoulders. He thought through it all once more and then turned to her. "Thank you."

"You're welcome."

Things began moving very quickly for Ben at that point. In no time he was back in the neurology ICU wing, standing outside the double doors waiting. They had let him have one more private moment with his father before they removed all the wires and tubes. He hadn't been any better at this visit than the last. The whole ordeal was grating on his nerves so that he felt like he might jump out of his skin at any moment.

He wished she hadn't had to go back to work after the signing the papers thing, but honestly, he knew she couldn't be there to hold his hand every step. However, he smiled slightly as he remembered her sitting there in Dr. Vitter's office. For that moment it was certainly nice to have a friend.

"Ben," Dr. Vitter said, coming out of the doors, and Ben's attention jerked up as he straightened from his leaning post on the wall. "They're taking him down."

It took more than a second for him to understand what the doctor was saying. Then he remembered the vast labyrinth of back hallways and staff only elevators. Of course they wouldn't transfer a patient through the lobby. "Okay." His senses came back to him, and it was humbling how very far afield his sanity had gone in the last couple of days. "Thank you, Doctor."

Ben held his hand out to shake the older man's hand.

"I wish you all the best. Your father really was a wonderful man."

"Thank you."

And with that, Ben turned and headed for the last time to the eighth floor elevators.

"Kate," Misty said from the telecom.

Kathryn pushed the button. "Yeah?"

"They're on their way with Mr. Warren."

As he traveled down the elevator with the twelve other passengers, Ben wrapped one arm around his middle and let the other trail up to his neck. This was so awkward. He wondered if he wore a big sign on his forehead that said, "I just sold my dad down the river."

Others in the elevator bantered on as if nothing in the world was wrong or out-of-sorts. He wondered how often he had shared an elevator with someone who had just signed papers, or just gotten the call, or just lost someone. He tried to think, to remember, but he couldn't. Things looked so very different from this side of reality.

The ding of the elevator brought his attention back to the present moment. That was a good thing because there were times he felt like he might just zone out for good and never come back. Tired was part of it to be sure. But some of it was just existing in a realm he didn't really understand and had never prepared himself for. Not that anyone really prepared for such things, but surely others had been much more prepared than he was.

Walking through the lobby and down the long hallway with the windows that looked out onto traffic, he let his steps slow and then slow some more. His heart was slamming in his chest. He didn't want to do this. He didn't know how. Maybe by the time he got there his dad would already be gone. After all, they had said he might not be able to breathe on his own very long.

Disparate parts of him warred with each other—saying this or that would be better and then adamantly disputing that suggestion. At the door to the hospice, he stopped and heaved a sigh. What would life be like on the other side of the door? Yes, he had seen the lobby. He had even seen a room. He'd just never seen his father inside a room, and that scared him.

Trying to act like this was all perfectly within the realm of normal for him, he opened the door and strode up to the nurse's desk in the middle.

The nurse from the first day looked up, and he turned on the charm that had always served him so well in the past. "Yes, they just brought my father..."

"Ben."

He fought to corral himself before he turned to greet Kathryn. It was much easier to play act I'm-fine with someone he didn't really know. As she came to him, he lifted his hand to her. She smiled, but there was sadness and pity in it. That was such a trap. It asked him to remember that he was really here and why. "Kathryn."

She shook his hand and then turned them both toward the lobby. "He's in the corner room."

They stepped away from the desk, and he noticed the nurse purposely go back to her work as if disappearing into the woodwork.

"Would you like to see him now?" Kathryn asked, walking next to him but not reaching out to him or hurrying their steps.

"I…" He cleared his throat desperately trying to get more out. "Hm. Um, I…"

Calm, compassionate brown eyes turned to him. "It's okay. Everyone is nervous the first time. But it's really not so bad."

Only because she had the strength did he feel like he might not completely fall apart. "Okay."

At the far end of the lobby and off to the right, she opened the door. Ben closed his eyes, feeling like his heart might turn him around and run without his even telling it to.

"It's okay," she said softly, beckoning with her eyes as she stepped into the room.

One more swallow and Ben followed her inside. This room was the other's twin. The same furniture, the same set up. The only thing different about it was the figure lying prone and motionless in the bed. Ben's heart caught at the sight. The white hair, always so very dignified, was perfectly in place. His father would like that.

Grief overwhelmed him, and he balled his fist at his side, fighting the memories—the Sunday mornings when he would wake and take the paper to go into his father's room, laying with him as he explained the world and life. How did they get here so fast?

"Dad…" Tears flooded into Ben's eyes, and he covered his face with his hand, ducking to hide the anguish. Even when his father was in the hospital, he'd never gotten this close—close enough to really see him. Now he was only steps away, no tubes, no wires to mask how very close to the abyss his father had come. "God, why?"

Choking on the emotions, he fought to breathe. Like the brush of a soft angel's wing, her hand rubbed his shoulder and down his back. Knowing he would fall through the earth if he didn't have something to hold onto, he turned and grabbed for her. Desperately he clung to her as pangs of heartache wrenched over him.

Over Ben's quaking shoulder Kathryn looked at the man lying in the bed. The love of his son was palpable. It spoke of how very much the son must have been loved. She closed her eyes then and offered up a prayer for them both and a quiet plea for the strength and wisdom of God to be in her to get them through this.

Finally Ben pulled back, nodding and sniffing. From his pocket there was a small beep, and he dragged in a hard breath as he reached for it. With a beep, he had it on and to his ear. "This is Ben." He scratched his head and turned from her into the depth of the room before going over to the couch. "Hey, Kell. Yeah…"

Kathryn caught his gaze when he glanced up, his eyes red, his face blotchy under the scruff of his darkened jawline. Her presence was no longer needed. "I'll just be…" She pointed to the door and left to give him some privacy.

It would've been better for Ben's nerves if she had stayed. He didn't want to be left alone here. He thought about running after her, but he'd already shown himself for the pathetic weakling that he was. Crying on her shoulder? That had to be some kind of sick cliché somewhere. He sniffed the embarrassment down.

"Ben?"

"Yeah. I'm here. We just got him moved."

"How is he?" Misty asked as Kathryn came back out, trying to come up with enough paperwork to do that she would never have to think about how horrible that was.

"Not good." She glanced back at the door, feeling her own heart splintering into sharp shards. With a sigh, she shook her head. "Sometimes I really hate this job, you know that?"

Misty reached across the desk and patted her arm, which only brought up anger in the face of the helplessness. "They're lucky to have you."

"Sometimes I really wish I could do more."

"They don't need more. They just need someone to care."

Memories of Mrs. Baker and her granddaughters slipped across her heart, and overwhelming grief swamped her. "I think I'm going to go down to the chapel for a few minutes. If you need me…"

Misty nodded. She'd seen Kathryn like this on more than one occasion. She'd even asked a couple times about Kathryn's trips to the chapel. After awhile, the nurses all had come to take these visits in stride. They were just a part of Kathryn and how she chose to cope with the difficulties of her job.

She walked down the hallway that separated the two units and in the middle, she turned and went into the chapel. The lighting was soft and reflected off of the reddish-brown wood of the pews. There were only seven benches on each side of the small aisle. She took a seat in the back one by the stained glass window on the opposite side of the door in case anyone who needed to get closer came in.

Her heart was so very heavy with grief and helplessness. It panged forward, aching with the understanding of how useless she really was in the face of all of this. She wanted to make a difference. She wanted to ease the pain. But how could anyone do that? She, of all people, knew how little anyone else could really do.

She swiped at the tears now sliding down her face. "God," she said softly, "I know You have a plan. I know You do, and I really believe that, but I have to be honest, this really hurts. It really does. These are good people, God. Why do they have to suffer so much?"

Reaching over, she snagged up a couple of tissues and wiped her eyes. As she sat there, the words of hurt and anger still pouring from her heart, her gaze slipped up to the crucifix. She looked into the sorrowful, anguished face of her Savior. "You know, huh? You do. You know what we're going through. You watched Your Son suffer and die. I've got to tell You, God. It never gets any easier. I thought it would. It doesn't…"

The snap of the door behind her sent her gaze scurrying downward and her words into silent mode. If the families knew she came in here and talked to God out loud, they might think she'd truly lost it. They didn't need thinking she had sanity issues. They had enough to deal with.

She was sitting over in the corner. Ben glanced up at the huge, ugly rendition of Jesus on the cross at the front of the room. He hated those things. They creeped him out. After only one glance up, he turned his steps to where she sat, questioning every step. They'd said she was here, and she was. He thought, though, now that he was here he really shouldn't disturb her. Not like this. However, his heart kept dragging him forward as if it wasn't even listening to his head. Two steps from her, he took a deep breath to steady his nerves and to keep him from running outright.

At that moment, her gaze jerked up to him as she caught the movement of his approach. In a heartbeat she was on her feet, swiping at her eyes. "Oh. I'm... I'm sorry. Did you need something?"

The look of pure anguish on her face stopped him cold. It was unshrouded agony such that he had never seen. Somehow until that very moment he had seen her as invincible. The truth stunned him to the core. "Oh. Um." He had no idea what words came after that. All he knew was how much she had done for him and how badly it hurt his heart to see her so sad.

He stumbled through what he should do, what he could say, standing there mere feet from her as she sniffed and swiped at the tears tracing down her beautiful face. Not knowing what else to do, he put one arm out to her, to touch her or comfort her or something, but the gesture had no certainty that he should. For a single second she looked at him with pure panic, but he had already made the decision. With one more step, he collected her into his arms. She stiffened at his touch, and for a second he thought he had made a horrendous mistake. But then with no more warning, she melded into him as her grief once again spilled over its banks. She clung to him, and he held her there. Putting his head down next to hers, their tears mingled into one.

He cupped the back of her head with his hand as eternity slipped through itself. They stood together in the shaft of light streaming in from the stained glass window on the other side of the pew. He could do no more, so he just held her and hoped that was enough. She fit snuggly in the circle of his arms, and he closed his eyes, needing the hug as much as she did.

After many more minutes, she finally sniffed and pulled back, still swiping at her eyes, clearly reaching for normal and stable. "I'm sorry. Um. Did you... did you need something?" She took a full step backward, looking truly unsteady. Her breath came in ragged, uneven jerks.

Still in the trance of the hug, he reached over, touched her hair, and pushed it back over her shoulder. "Just..." It took another breath to settle the words. "I just wanted to say thanks for everything you've done."

"Oh." She swiped the tears from her cheeks and smiled,

obviously fighting to make him forget the past few minutes, but he would never forget. Never. "You're welcome."

The next moment passed between them as he stood there, looking at her, knowing and yet not at all able to say how. The truth was he should let her go. She had work to do, and yet somehow he couldn't.

He had no right to ask, but he glanced down at the pew just the same. "Can we talk?"

She glanced around nervously. "We could go to my office if you'd rather."

There was a time he would have jumped at that chance. Somehow this was not that time. "I'd rather stay if you don't mind."

"Oh." Quickly she nodded clearly trying to get the mask of professional snapped back over herself. "Okay." She backed up and made room for him in the pew.

He followed her down, feeling her gaze on him, and not at all sure of anything anymore. Life was sliding around him in surreal patterns he didn't recognize. Words jammed into his mind, making no sense whatsoever. He glanced over at her and laughed softly. What was he doing here anyway? How was he suddenly sitting in a church, wanting to ask questions he'd never even known were a part of him?

"It's okay," she said softly. "Whatever it is. It's better to just say it and get it out."

It was so strange how he knew he was not being judged by her though he would feel better if that statue thing wasn't staring down at him. "You…" He glanced up at the thing hanging on the wall. "Um, do you come here often?" It wasn't until it was out that he realized how incredibly stupid that sounded. He closed his eyes, knowing she was going to think he was an idiot.

"Actually, yeah." Her gaze went to her lap. "I do."

His gaze swept over to her when he realized she wasn't laughing at him.

She sniffed. "Some days it's the only thing that keeps me sane."

Strangely he felt for her in a way he wasn't sure he'd ever felt for anyone else. "Like today?"

One small nod, and she pursed her lips together in a tight smile. "Sometimes it gets really hard to keep your arms open."

That scraped across his understanding. "Your arms?"

There was only the smallest of smiles in her eyes when she looked up at him. Then her gaze fell back to her hands on her lap. Although he really wanted her to explain, he sat watching her as she blew out a hard breath and looked up at the cross. He refused to follow her gaze. It was better for him not to look. A moment, a sniff, and her gaze fell back to her hands.

"Sometimes I think that's why they nailed His hands to the cross."

"Why's that?" He really did not want to get into a theological discussion at the moment, but he couldn't help himself.

"Because that way He couldn't close His arms." She glanced over at Ben, and the anguish was back. "See, I think in this life we start out with our arms open. We love everyone, and we want to experience everything. Then things happen that convince us that keeping our arms open is not smart. People hurt us or they leave us, and we think that it would just be better if we would close our arms—either to protect ourselves or to hang onto them."

Never before had Ben been so enthralled with anyone. Sitting in the light, her hair shone like the gossamer on an angel's wings. He looked up at it, taking it and all the rest of her in. When she sniffed, he knew she was not play-acting. This was for real with her. That drew him even closer.

Her gaze jerked up to the cross, hanging there, and after a moment her eyes closed. Something close to anger went across her beautiful features followed by a desperate attempt to not break down again. "Sometimes it would be so easy to close up and close down and not want to care anymore."

"But…" He wanted to protest, but he had no words.

The softest smile he'd ever seen drifted over to him. "I know." She nodded and let her gaze fall back to her hands. "I know."

Behind him, the door snapped open, and he spun as an elderly couple came in, him helping her although they both looked like they needed assistance. Like a shot, Kathryn stood, wiped her eyes, and went around the other side of the bench. Ben was caught somewhere between the conversation they'd just had and watching her with the couple.

She went over and sat on her heels next to where they sat. The conversation was so quiet that even just across the silent chapel, he couldn't make out all the words. He had a lot of thinking to do. That was for sure. With one more glance up at the cross, he tried not to shake his head but he did just the same. That was one he would never understand.

Six

"Come on, Kate. You need a night out. Look at you." Misty gazed at her friend as Kathryn made final notes in the stack of charts that would be turned over to Clyde in twenty minutes. She should have done this in her office, but it was too quiet, or her brain and all its whisperings was too loud. She wasn't sure which.

"I don't think so."

"But Nathan is a nice guy."

"I'm sure he is, but right now… it's just not good for me." She finished the last note, picked up the charts, and turned. However, somehow she had missed the approach of one very attractive young doctor coming from the front doors. Barely hanging onto the stack, she yelped. "Oh!"

He smiled as they both came to a sudden, jerky stop, and she smiled back.

"I'm… I'm sorry," she said, pushing a strand of hair behind her ear. "Were you looking for someone?"

"Oh, uh, Dr. Nelson sent me to check on…"

"His wife's mother," she finished.

The doctor in the white coat tilted his head. "Very good."

"She's in Room 8. I believe Mrs. Nelson is with her. I can show you if you'd like."

His gaze traveled all the way down her, and she caught the meaning with no trouble. She also knew Misty caught the meaning.

"Oh, no. That won't be necessary. I was just supposed to check to make sure there have been no changes."

"No," Kathryn said, remembering what they were talking about. "No changes."

He nodded once and turned for the door. With a roll of her

eyes and a slow exhale, she turned to go the other way down the hallway.

"Um." He turned back, and she spun toward him. "I'm Dr. Martin, by the way. Dr. Joseph Martin."

"Kate… Kathryn Walker." Stepping over, she shook his hand.

"Well, Ms. Walker. It was nice to meet you."

"Yes it was." For a full second she didn't realize what she'd said. "I mean it was nice to meet you too."

He smiled a half smile that struck a flirtatious note in his eyes. "I hope to see you again soon."

"Me too."

And then he turned and pushed out of the door.

Barely corralling her excitement, Kathryn turned for the nurse's desk. "Wow," she breathed.

At the desk Misty was fanning herself. "Whoa baby."

"Ye-ah." And with that, Kathryn went to her office to finish up.

Ben knew he couldn't keep bothering her, but when he looked at his watch, he knew she would be leaving any time. He needed something to drink anyway. This sitting around waiting thing really made one much thirstier than he would have thought. Quietly he left the room and shut the door behind him. He went to the nurse's station where they were in the midst of shift change. Leaning on the desk, he cleared his throat to get the two nurses' attention.

"Oh, Mr. Warren," Misty said. "I didn't see you there."

"I was just wondering where I might get a Coke."

"Oh, just down this hall, make a right, then another right. There're vending machines in that hallway."

"Thank you." He pushed away from the desk, fully cognizant of the two gazes that went with him. Three days of hanging out in hospitals hadn't made him a male supermodel, but they hadn't completely destroyed his way with the ladies either.

Checking the current state of his attire, however, he knew he was a little more undone that normal. Shirt tail completely out, sleeves rolled to two very different lengths. Plus he hadn't seen a razor in more time than he could remember. Just as he was about to assess how bad he must look, Kathryn stepped out of a door off to the right and came up short when she almost bumped into him.

"Oh!" She started, jerking herself up short.

"Oh. Hey. Fancy meeting you here," he said, and he couldn't stop the smile.

Sometime since their meeting in the chapel she had come back to some semblance of control. Truth be known, in that knee-length peach business skirt and white button down blouse, she was anything but ordinary. "Did you need something?"

He laughed. "No. Well, yeah. I was just headed down for a Coke. I'm getting a little behind on my caffeine quotient."

"Ah." Turning only slightly, she locked her office door.

He watched, absurdly feeling like she was abandoning him. "So you're headed home then?"

"Yeah. Clyde will be here in about five minutes if you need something."

"Clyde." Ben raised his chin, thinking Clyde probably wouldn't be quite the same. "So." He leaned on the wall, folding his arms, trying to appear completely casual. "Will you be back tomorrow? Surely you don't just work all the time."

Door locked, last of excuses not to leave complete, she turned to him. "No. Not all the time. I will be back tomorrow about eight."

"Eight." He nodded. "Okay." Wow did it feel a long time to eight.

"You'll be in good hands." She laid her hand on his wrist, and for the first time he saw her fingers and nails. Both nice though not showy. More than that, he felt the gentleness of her touch. "Trust me. Everyone here wants to help with whatever you need."

"I'll remember that." In his pocket the phone beeped, and he straightened like a shot. He grabbed it up, looked at the number, but didn't recognize it. Holding up his finger, he turned. "Warren here."

"Ben? Ben is that you?"

"Mom?" He took two steps down the hallway in utter shock.

"Ben, what's wrong? I called home, and Teresa was in a panic. She said you'd called like four times."

"Yeah." Ben half-turned back to Kathryn, trying to figure out how to tell her a proper good-bye without saying it.

I'll just go, she mouthed, and he nodded though he didn't want to. He watched her walk off down the hall. The long sigh sunk him

70

right back into frightening understanding that he was in this alone.

"Ben?"

"Yeah." His gaze dropped to his shoes as he leaned his back against the wall.

"What is going on?"

"Hmm." Slowly he closed his eyes and then looked at the ceiling. "It's Dad…"

Kathryn hated to leave him like that, but then that was dumb. On the clock he was her responsibility. Off the clock, he was merely a client that might still be there when she got back the next morning and he might not. The thought of him being gone when she got back jabbed into her. She hadn't thought about it like that.

As she climbed into her car, she berated herself for being so unprofessional. That whole scene in the chapel. What was she thinking? He wasn't there to comfort her. The feel of his arms around her came once again to her consciousness even as she tried to say she didn't remember. It felt so good for that one minute to not have to be the strong one. But then she reminded herself that it could never happen again.

If he was even there in the morning…

"You can call him if you like." Nothing his mother did should have surprised him, but this did.

"Mom, Jason doesn't want to hear from me. He doesn't even know me."

"He's your brother."

"Huh. That's convenient now."

"Well, this is between you, your brother, and your father."

If it didn't hurt so badly, he would have laughed. It was going to be a little tough to include his father at this point. He jerked his fingers through his hair, pretty much knowing the curls and waves left in its wake were already out-of-control. What else to do? "Well, if you're not coming, could I at least have Jason's number?"

"You don't know it?"

He wanted to scream at her. Really he did. "Uh, no. I don't know it. If I did, I would've called him three days ago."

"Oh, well, I would've thought your father would have given it to you."

The comment struck him as odd. He wasn't aware that his father even knew where Jason was. It was becoming apparent there were a lot of things he wasn't aware of. "No, he didn't."

"Well, it's 55…"

Then he realized he had no way to write it down, and he no longer trusted his memory at all. "Hang on. Let me get something to write it down."

She sighed like this was some dramatic imposition on her time.

As he strode down the hall, he realized he should at least act like an adult. "So what are you up to anyway?"

"I'm in Cozumel for a month. Sand, sun, surf."

"Ah." At the desk, he motioned to the nurse who after a nice little game of charades gave him a pen and some paper. "Vacation?"

"Actually we're treating it as an early honeymoon. We may go to Hawaii after the actual ceremony in a couple weeks."

"Honey…" He let out a breath. "Moon. Okay." Not that he was surprised. He knew enough from his father's off-handed comments about the money situation that his mother had considered remarrying at least twice. Both times it had fallen through due to the possibility that she would lose her right to alimony if she did.

"Who knows, I might actually go through with it this time," she said.

"Great." He stretched one syllable to seven. "Okay. I'm ready." He really wasn't but, he was already sick of this call and everything else about his life.

"Casey told me about Misty's cousin," her mother said as Kathryn spun a strand of hair around and around and around her finger.

She curled further on the couch, the phone in her hand. "Mom, don't start."

"Who's starting? I'm just saying…"

"I know what you're just saying. You're always just saying."

"Well, must I be the one to point out you are almost 33?"

"I am not. I'm only 32 and eight months." She smirked at the phone, hating her defensiveness. Why did she always feel like second hand garbage in this department with her mother? She was a successful, professional woman with her own apartment and life. So why could her mom make her feel like she was the worst failure on the planet with only ten words?

"Like I said, you're almost 33, and what prospects do you have? You work all the time…"

"Mom…"

"You never go out."

"Mom…"

"You haven't had a boyfriend since that guy you brought to Hannah's wedding…"

Kathryn fought not to wither under the barrage. "Mom!"

"What?"

"Do we really have to do this every time?"

"I just don't want to see you alone. That's all. I want you to find someone."

Sighing to keep her anger in check, Kathryn's mind spun back and forth through her day.

"I want you to be happy," her mother continued. "Is that so wrong?"

"I am happy."

The snort was past sarcastic. "You are not happy."

Why did she so want to convince her mother what was truly not the truth? No, she wasn't happy—at least in this area. She wanted to be, but short of throwing herself into the meat market at the bar, she had no clue how to do that.

"I was going to tell you, there is this guy that came to the salon the other day…"

"Mom!"

"What? He was cute, and Janie said he's single too. I could ask…"

Kathryn pushed her fingers onto the bridge of her nose. "No. Mom. Don't. Please."

"What would it hurt to ask? It's not like I'm setting you up on a blind date with a beast. He was a very nice young man."

This was getting worse. "No. Mom. No blind dates with guys you don't even know. No."

"Well, then I think you should go out with Misty's friend or how about that guy Casey knows, that neighbor of her friend from the choir…"

"Ugh, Mom. I'm hanging up now."

"She said he's very nice looking…"

"Good-bye, Mom." Kathryn took the phone from her ear, waited a second, and put it back to see if her mother had stopped going down every rabbit hole she could find. She hadn't, so Kathryn hit the off button. Laying her head on her knee, she thought through it all. They all meant well. Surely they did, but every time the conversation turned to her lack of a love life, it made her feel like an utter failure.

"God, please, bring me someone… just to shut them up."

That was a bad reason, but at this point she was desperate to find any reason He might actually listen to.

"Uh, yes, is this… Uh, I'd like to speak with Jason Warren please." Ben leaned back on the couch in the lobby. He'd waited to make the call until darkness had overtaken the landscape outside. He told himself it was because Jason was on West Coast time and probably wouldn't be home before then. The truth was, this wasn't a call he wanted to make.

"This is Jason."

The slamming of Ben's heart hurt. He let out a breath, remembering to his core that voice that now sounded so very different. "Uh, Jason?"

"Yeah?"

"Um, Jason, I don't know if you remember me or not. This is Ben. Ben Warren."

Could the aftermath of a bomb explosion have been any more silent?

"Ben?"

"Yeah."

It was amazing how two syllables could twist things in such a confusing jumble.

"Um. Hm. This is a surprise," Jason said, being the first to come up with words to put to the situation.

"I know, I know, and I'm sorry. But listen, something's come up." Ben raked his fingers through his hair, hard. At least the pain told him he was still alive, though the numbness was honestly more comforting. "Listen, I called Mom. She gave me your number."

"Why? What happened? What's going on?" There was real panic in his brother's voice.

"It's Dad. He had a stroke a couple days ago."

"A couple days? Why didn't you call sooner? Is he all right?"

"Jase, slow down. Look, I've been trying to call Mom, but apparently she was out of the country. I didn't have your number."

"You didn't? Why not?"

"Why not?" That question threw him, and he squinted into it to try to come up with an answer. "Why didn't I have your number? How would I have had your number? I haven't talked to you in…" Did he have to come up with an exact number? If he did, he was in trouble.

"I know, but Dad had it."

The news pushed Ben back into the couch cushions. *Dad had it.* "Dad? Are you sure? He never… he never told me that."

"Yes, I'm sure. He's been calling me every so often for a couple years now—ever since I got married."

Seriously, Ben just wanted to stop the ride and get off. It was making him dizzy and sick. "Oh? So you're married then?" He wanted to feel casual about the whole thing. But he didn't. He couldn't.

"Yeah." There was a suspiciousness to Jason's tone. "Didn't Dad tell you about the wedding?"

This was getting worse. "Wed… Hm. No." Ben scratched the top of his eye. "He didn't mention that."

"He didn't tell you why he came out here?"

"Out here?" The walls started closing in on Ben. The feeling that this was all some kind of dream, that nothing was real began inching up on him. He cleared his throat and shifted on the couch to stop its onslaught.

"To Colorado. When he came out here for that conference thing?"

Conference? His father went to a lot of conferences all over the country. Ben searched his mind for the one in question, but he couldn't find it.

"Dad came out for the wedding that weekend. He didn't tell you?"

Sick. Really he was going to be sick on his shoes. "No. He didn't."

Jason paused for a very long moment. "Well, that's weird. He said you were busy."

Well, that was probably accurate. He was usually busy with something. Then again if he had known… "I'm sorry, Jason. Really. I am. I've been trying to call, I just had no idea how to get a hold of you."

"That's okay."

He could tell it wasn't, but Jason was at least trying.

"So, how is he?" Jason finally asked, and Ben's gaze went over to the solid wooden door. He hated that door and that room.

Sitting forward, he put his head on his hand. How do you tell the brother you haven't seen in 20 years that his father is dying? "I'm not going to lie. It's not good. I had to sign some papers…"

"What kind of papers?" Jason's voice arched up two notches into near-panic. "Talk to me, Ben. What's going on?"

Pain sliced right through Ben. Saying the words hurt worse than he could ever have imagined. "Dad's in… um… they moved him to hospice. The stroke was really bad, and they didn't think…"

"What hospital are you in?"

"Uh, St. Anthony's."

"New York, right?"

"Yeah. Right."

"Okay, listen, I'm going to book a flight. I'll be there by tomorrow morning."

"Okay." Ben could think of no reason to argue.

The whole night Ben lay awake, tossing and turning in his bed, tortured by what might be in the cards for the following day. Jason was coming. That was a good thing. At least he hoped it was a good thing, but he couldn't be exactly sure about that. He still remembered Kathryn's comment about families screaming at each other, and that did nothing to calm him. He hadn't had many people scream at him over the years. The prospect frightened him more than he wanted to admit. After all, how did he know what Jason might think of him for signing those papers? Or what would he think of him, period?

That thought drove him farther into the covers. Opening his eyes, he tried to stop the thoughts, but they were like a train wreck jamming one car on top of the other.

Memories from so long ago he had convinced himself they

were not real suddenly attacked him in the quiet of the apartment. Fighting to breathe, he rolled over and fought not to think those thoughts. But every time he closed his eyes, they were there. Very few of them spoke of anything good. How could his mind remember things he thought he had forgotten? Really. He wanted to forget them all. He just wanted to make them stop.

Putting the pillow over his face and ears, he squeezed his eyes closed, trying to make them stop. If he could just make them stop...

Seven

Checking herself in the mirror once more as the morning came to life, Kathryn spun to the side. Not bad overall. Her hair was an issue. Up. Down. Which was best? She finally put it into a ponytail, anchored it upward, and fanned it out. Not bad.

She told herself the nice outfit was in case the good doctor decided to make a repeat appearance. That was as good a lie as any.

"Good morning," Kathryn said, floating into the lobby just above the ground—at least that's how it felt. "Anything I need to know?"

Misty turned and arched her eyebrows. "Well, don't you look nice?"

Kathryn pushed that to the side as quickly as it came. She picked up the three folders on the counter.

"Um, we've got a new admit coming at ten, scheduled for Room 12," Misty said.

"Okay. And Mr. Guthrey?"

"Made it through another night. I swear I think his family's about to break. Twenty days is enough to stretch even my patience."

"In his time and God's." She looked through the top two folders, wanting to ask about Mr. Warren but knowing that would be way too obvious. She glanced only once at the door at the far end of the hallway, but she yanked her gaze back to the folders. "Okay. Call if you need me."

With that, she walked down to her office. On the other side of the door, she stopped, closed her eyes, and said a very soft prayer only in her heart. "God, I don't want to make this big deal over him with the situation as it is. Please, God, keep me from making an idiot of myself." That was a tall order. Even she knew that.

Ben opened the hospice door, having no idea what would be on the other side. He figured if something had changed, they would call him, but he had never thought to ask that question, so he wasn't really sure. Trying to keep as low a profile as possible, he skirted the nurse's area. With his hand next to his hairline, he hurried around the lobby furniture to the door on the end. One hard breath and he opened the door.

He wasn't sure how much longer his heart could take this roller coaster. Not that he wanted to find out what came next, but this was taxing his coping abilities. Sleep was non-existent, and he hadn't had the stomach to even look at breakfast. How much longer he could keep this up was anybody's guess. If he was guessing, he would've said not much longer.

In the bed, his father lay, still motionless; however, his breathing sounded much raspier than it had before. Ben couldn't face the reality in that bed, so he went over to the couch and sat down like someone had kicked his knees out from under him. Sitting didn't make him feel any better. He was beginning to think nothing would.

Knowing he needed to check in with work, he pulled out his phone and dialed the number. Jason would be coming any time now. He hated that thought. It made him both defensive and worried, so he tried not to think it. "Uh, yeah, Jack? This is Ben." Yanking his jacket off, he tossed it over to the side chair and buried himself in the details of work.

"Good morning," Kathryn greeted Mrs. Edith Guthrey.

The older lady looked up from her rosary with tired eyes. *Twenty days* passed through Kathryn's mind. She stepped to the bed.

"How are we doing today?"

"Still here," Mrs. Guthrey said. "I always said he was too stubborn for his own good."

Turning to the older lady, Kathryn noted the abandoned cups on the end tables. "Are you here by yourself?"

"The kids had to get back to work. Can't put food on the table when you're not working." Mrs. Guthrey nodded. "I understand that. Really I do."

Kathryn heard the note of trying to talk herself into not blaming them or being bitter. Carefully she sat down on the couch and leaned her elbows on her knees. "Would you like me to pray with you?"

"Oh, darling, I know you've got better things to do."

But Kathryn smiled. "Actually, I think God penciled you into my schedule just for right now."

With a sad, grateful smile, Mrs. Guthrey reached over and put her wrinkled hand on Kathryn's. "Thank you for all you've done for us, dear."

"You're very welcome."

Wait.
Wait.
Wait.

For something Ben really didn't even want to happen. He drummed his fingers on the couch armrest. This was like the cruelest bad joke ever. Losing patience with the couch, he stood and paced first one way and then the other. He wished he had gotten some sleep last night. Maybe that would've helped, but he doubted it. Turning, he looked across at the bed. Both hands came up to his face and his eyes and rubbed there. This wasn't happening. It really wasn't. It couldn't be.

This was all just a very bad dream that he was going to wake up from. That had to be it. It was the only thing that made any sense at all.

"Wake up, Ben. Wake up." He shook his head hard, twice. But when he took his hands away, nothing had changed. Nothing in this surreal, insane nightmare. He could feel his mind slipping-sliding from his control. Control. There was a funny, ironic, moronic word. He hated that word. He really did. It held such a recrimination of his existence that it dug even deeper into his growing despondent acceptance of his own inadequacy. Had he ever been able to handle anything? He couldn't clearly remember anymore.

His cell phone beeped, and he yanked it out glad, for the

distraction. He really didn't care who it was. "Warren."

"Benjamin, my man."

"Kelly." Ben collapsed back on the couch. He was so exhausted even normal felt strangely odd and demanding.

"I was just driving in and thinking about you. I've got a call not far from where you are, wondered if I might stop by."

Ben's gaze snapped over to his father's lifeless form, and he swallowed. "Oh, Kell, you don't have to."

"Hey, Ben. Come on now. You've been hanging out there for five days. Tamitha is about to skin me alive if I don't at least go check on you."

He was too exhausted to argue. "Okay."

When Mrs. Guthrey's niece came, Kathryn quietly said good-bye and tip-toed out. She had other patients to check on. Misty was obviously checking on someone because there was no one at the station. Kathryn went to the center station, not because she thought anything would be out of sorts, but it's what they did for each other—watching each other's back. They were a good team.

Sure enough at the desk, the phone was blipping. It didn't really ring, more made this odd little sound that you could only hear if you were right on top of it.

She punched the two buttons. "St. Anthony's Hospice, this is Kathryn."

"Yes, I'm needing some directions to your facility from the airport."

In quick succession Kathryn gave the directions just as a tall, nice-looking black man with broad shoulders and a hesitant smile accompanying hesitant eyes approached from the entrance.

"Thank you," the caller said.

"You're welcome." She hung up and turned her attention to the visitor. It was easy to tell he was a visitor. They always had a look of wide-eyed, utter fear. "Hi there. May I help you?"

"Uh, I hope so. I'm looking for Ben Warren."

The name jump-started her heart, but she fought not to let that show.

The man fidgeted with his eyes and the words. "Oh, uh, not Ben... I mean Ron... Ronald Warren."

His fumbling touched her heart. No one looked comfortable

their first time here.

"They're right down this way," she said, going around the desk. "I'm not sure if Ben… if Mr. Warren is here yet. I haven't seen him this morning." He followed her all the way to the door where she knocked softly. "Knock. Knock."

The sight of Ben coming up off the couch simultaneously delighted and worried her to the core. He looked much paler today, much more on edge. His five o'clock shadow was fuller and darker than it had ever been since she'd first met him.

"You've got a visitor," she said gently as she pushed into the room.

The man followed her into the room where he took one look at Ben and stepped past her.

"Hey, bud."

In the center of the room they met in a bear hug. Kathryn was glad. Ben needed someone. She stepped out to give them some time.

"Dude," Kelly said, looking at Ben who hated the scrutiny.

He ducked and scratched his ear with his fingernail. How bad did he look anyway? He was glad when Kelly took his gaze from him and put it over on the bed. At least he was for the first two seconds. However, he hated how weak his family looked at the moment. This wasn't how it was supposed to be. He'd never been the weak one. In fact, between his dad and him, they had bailed Kelly out of several tough situations. This felt very different than those times ever had.

Without a word, Kelly went right over to the bed, far closer than Ben had ever gotten himself to go. He envied his friend that. He just couldn't bring himself to get that close. It was much safer way over here.

After a couple minutes, Kelly turned back to him. His gaze perused his friend. "You look fried."

Ben laughed sarcastically. "Thanks."

"No, seriously. I had no idea." Kelly glanced down at the bed. "Why didn't you tell me?"

Not sure how to answer that, Ben shrugged.

"What can we do?"

It would've been nice to be able to make a list that would

make any difference whatsoever. "I don't know." Then a thought occurred to him. "I haven't been out to the house, to check on things. I mean I know Maria's out there, but…"

Kelly nodded. "Consider it done. I'll go this afternoon."

The worry on his friend's face went right through him like a knife and twisted there.

"Thanks for coming," Ben finally managed.

Kelly's look fell even further with concern.

Ben hated not knowing what to say and nobody saying anything. "They don't really know… how much longer…" It was so hard to sound normal and fine. "I called Jack this morning and took an extended leave…"

"Have you made any… arrangements?" The concern had turned to sympathy.

Closing his eyes, Ben couldn't even think of such a thing. "I don't know. Jason's supposed to be here sometime this morning. I haven't really made any decisions yet."

Kelly lowered his head so he could look at Ben who had his gaze on the floor. "If you need me to look into it…"

Ben nodded, not sure what he was supposed to say. His heart ached with indecision. Was that something you asked a friend to do? In a way it seemed less personal. In another, it sounded wonderful that he wouldn't have to do it. "I'll let you know."

Kathryn was at the desk talking with Misty about whatever she could find to keep her there when the door down at the end of the lobby opened. The black man stepped out, turned, and closed the door very softly. Then he stopped and rested his hand on the closed door, and his obvious pain sliced through her. Carefully but decisively she ended the conversation and started across the lobby just as he turned to head to the outside doors.

She smiled to let him know she wasn't on the warpath. "I'm sorry. I didn't catch your name before." She held out her hand.

"Oh, Kelly. Kelly Zandavol." He had bright white teeth and a sad smile.

"It's nice to meet you, Kelly. Are you a friend of the Warrens?"

"Yeah, me and Ben go way back." He glanced at the door, and she saw the distinct worry lines cross his face. "I sure wish there was more I could do. I've never seen Ben like this."

"Like this?" she asked, pressing but only gently.

"Ben's usually the together one, the guy who can handle anything. I just know how close him and his dad were. You can just see that this is killing him."

Interesting choice of words, but then the irony of word choices in this place were usually more frequent than less.

"I wish I could be here with him," Kelly said. "I mean Jason's coming, but it's not the same."

Jason. She wanted to ask, but he didn't really give her the chance.

"I'm going to try to make it back tonight." Kelly's serious gaze came to her, pleading as so many did. "Will you please look out for Ben for me? He really needs somebody."

Gently she nodded. "I'll do my best."

After Kelly left, Kathryn, hearing his words again about taking care of his friend, went over to the door and knocked softly. It was time to start making good on that promise. "Knock. Knock."

Like a shot, Ben vaulted up off the couch. At first, he felt like a jack-in-the-box and then more like an idiot when she stepped in. Why he felt like an idiot, he couldn't really tell, but he did just the same. Everything about him felt so off, and he had no clue how to fix that.

"Hi," she said in that soft voice that touched his heart like an angel's whisper. "How's everything?"

With a quick nod trying to hide the ache in his heart and his head, Ben fought to smile. "Good I guess."

She glanced over at the bed and then came all the way across the room where she stopped and indicated the couch with a small wave. "May I?"

"Uh, sure." Hesitantly, Ben nodded and then followed her down. His heart was screaming at him that whatever this conversation was, he didn't want to have it. Whatever it was she had come to say, he didn't want to hear it. She looked too serious, too solemn. He couldn't handle serious or solemn. Not now. Not with his nerves right on the surface. What he really wanted was to find a couple shots of straight vodka and forget all of this. The way she was looking at him, it was too likely that she was going to want to discuss what came next, and nothing in him wanted to do that.

"So how are you doing?" she finally asked, and guns and shields flew up over the battle walls of his heart.

Trying to laugh it off, he made a strange sound even he didn't recognize. "Oh, you know, I'm fine."

Her gaze never left him as he tried desperately to find something else to look at that would help him not to feel her gaze.

"You know, it's all right to not be fine," she said, her voice floating between them. "You don't have to put on a show for me. I know this is tough."

Ben looked over at her, taken off-guard for a moment. Quickly he looked down, afraid she could see in his eyes what he felt in his heart—his weakness, his confusion, his pain. "It is tough." He felt her nod. "I'm just trying to figure out what comes next, you know? What to do, but then I don't really want to think about that. I don't want to think about making plans or anything like that, but I know I should be."

"You will do it in your time. It's not a race or a test. You've got to do it your way, but just know, it's overwhelming for everybody."

"Yeah, well, but I'm not everybody." Anger yanked him up off the couch. It was so much easier to keep his feelings in check when it was just him. Why did she have to come in here, asking all these questions? "I'm Ben Warren. Things aren't supposed to get to me like this."

"What? Ben Warren can't be worried or scared?"

"No." Four feet from his right hand was his father's foot, covered with a thin blanket. Ben didn't look. He couldn't. It all hurt too badly. His hero couldn't be lying there, not like this. And now he found himself trapped. The wall on one side, her on the other. There was nowhere to run. He reached up and ran his hand over his face, pushing hard to keep all the emotions down as he turned almost completely to face the wall. But the emotions were bubbling to the surface undeterred, and he had no idea how much longer he could keep up the act.

After a long moment, he heard her moving, felt her moving, standing, closing the space between them. His whole spirit recoiled away from her. Why couldn't she see he didn't want to have this conversation? Why couldn't she just leave him alone? He could hardly breathe, and it was getting worse.

"Sometimes the world pushes us to places we can't handle," she said, the words flowing softly and tenderly. "When we get to that place, we realize that all of those things we thought make us so Teflon-tough don't amount to much of anything. It feels so impossible because we don't want anyone to think we're weak, we don't want anyone to see us weak. We think if somehow no one knows, if no one sees, somehow they won't know how bad it really is, how much we're really hurting, how scared we are, how close to the edge."

He was holding his emotions in two white-knuckled fists, one at his side, one at his mouth.

"But it's all lies because the truth is we're all hurting, and we all need someone to be there, to lean on. And more than that, we need to learn to be more gentle with ourselves. That's not something they tell you or teach you anywhere, but it's true."

His whole spirit tightened at the thought. Be gentle with himself? What kind of psychobabble was that? It was a dead sure bet that he would be a complete and utter failure if he'd ever been gentle with himself... whatever that even meant. He dropped his hand from his mouth to his hip. "Yeah, well, I don't know about that."

"I know you don't. I didn't either, but I think it's important to see that slam-dunking yourself doesn't do anyone including you any good...."

The door across the way snapped open, truncating her sentence. They both turned toward it as a man stepped in. Not more than 25, he looked thoroughly out of place with no white coat and no stack of official-looking papers.

Not understanding this stranger's appearance, Ben looked to Kathryn for why he might be there. However, she didn't move to greet the man at all. A confused second passed, and then Ben realized she wasn't going to say anything. She obviously didn't know him.

"Um, can we help you?" Ben asked, stumbling over the words as he glanced at her once again.

"Yeah, uh, I hope so." The man with the light brown hair and smart pale blue shirt glanced at the bed. "I'm..." His gaze came back to Ben's as recognition hit him one second before the name.

"Jason Warren. Mr. Warren's son?"

It was a question, as if he was asking if this was the right room or how to get to Bermuda. Like an explosion detonated right in front of him, Ben careened backward, caught only by his understanding that there was nowhere to go. His heart slammed inside his chest as he fought to get all the pieces to line up correctly. Was this really his brother? Was this really the child he had played with in that car and held at night as the screaming down the hallway escalated? Could he really look like an adult, all grown up like this?

Kathryn was looking at Ben presumably because she wanted some confirmation of the man's identity. Ben had none to offer beyond vague memories that had faded even further with time.

Reaching up, Ben scratched the side of his head. "Uh, hi, Jason. It's been awhile."

Jason's eyes narrowed. "Ben?"

Ben let his arms drop as he fell back on who he had been in anything approaching normal circumstances. "In the flesh."

Why he expected Jason to be happy about that, he had no idea. However, happy never really materialized.

"Oh, well," Jason said, "I guess, then..." He glanced at Kathryn. "This is the right room?"

Awkwardness descended around them like a fog.

Her glance at Ben was barely there.

"Yes," she finally said, jumping into the situation with both feet. "Yes, it is." She stepped across the room and held out her hand. "It's nice to meet you, Jason. I'm Kathryn."

"Kathryn," he said, shaking her hand as something very close to relief slipped across his features. He raked his fingers through his sand-colored, wavy hair, pushing it back out of his face though it wasn't long enough to really stay there. In truth, he looked like a salesman—one of those guys who do all the work but barely make it in the company. Second or third tier at most. He glanced again at the bed. "I guess this means he hasn't..."

Once again she took charge, leaving Ben knowing he should be saying something intelligent but having no idea what that might be. "No. He's still with us." She held out her hand to indicate that Jason could step over to the bed, and like the professional she was, she followed just behind him.

From across the room, Ben's stomach was churning to the

point he seriously thought he might be sick. It wasn't that he begrudged his brother being here so much as that he couldn't fathom why Jason could be the one to walk in and look like the good son with no more effort than that.

"He's not on anything?" Jason asked, looking around.

"No." Kathryn stood not three inches from Jason, and Ben was having a really hard time keeping his anger with them both in check. "Only pain medication if he needs it, but so far, he's just been like this, sleeping peacefully."

A moment, and Jason reached down and touched their father's hand. With his head tilted and a small smile on his face, Jason looked at the figure in the bed. Then he dragged in a breath and sniffed. "Any idea how long…?"

"That's pretty much up to him and God at this point."

Jason nodded, and although they weren't six feet away, Ben felt an enormous gulf between where he stood and where they were. Was he really so bad at this that he couldn't be like Jason? Kathryn must think he was completely heartless or that he just didn't care. That thought stabbed his heart. It wasn't that he didn't care. He simply didn't know how to care like that—like Jason and… her.

The phone in Ben's pocket beeped, and when he turned to answer it, he caught them both looking his direction. Wishing he could disappear or walk through the wall, he pulled out the little device and punched Talk. "Warren here."

"Mr. Warren?" The soft female voice was thick with a Hispanic accent, and he put his finger in his other ear as if that would help.

"Yes?"

"Mr. Warren, this is Maria at your father's house."

Worry piled on worry. "Yes?"

"Mr. Warren, the electric company just called, something about a bill not being paid. They are coming to shut the electricity off if it's not paid, but I don't know anything about the bills. I don't know where they're kept or how to pay them…"

"Maria. Maria. Hang on. Calm down."

The longer she talked, the faster she went, and with her accent, it was becoming more and more difficult to understand her.

"Dios Mio! If they cut the electricity, that will mean to my house too! I will not be able to cook or clean or see…"

"Maria!" Ben was now practically yelling even as he stuck his finger further into his other ear. "I'll come. Okay? I'll be there. I'll take care of it."

"Oh, thank you, Mr. Warren. Thank you. I did not know what else to do, who else to call."

"Yeah." The syllable was short, but it cut her off. "I'll be there in an hour."

When he hung up, Ben cursed his life three times and then a fourth for good measure before he had the presence of mind to remember he wasn't alone in the room. He turned to find two concerned faces staring at him. With a half-laugh, he held up the phone. "Something's going on at Dad's. I guess I'd better run out there and make sure everything's okay." Yanking his jacket up from the side chair, he pulled it on, glad for something to do that at least looked like progress. "It shouldn't take me more than a couple hours."

Jason glanced at Kathryn who stood, looking at Ben with that helpless but wanting to help gaze that he hated. He ducked mostly to get away from that look but also hoping to make a clean getaway.

"I could go with you," Jason said as if he might get shot for the suggestion.

Ben exhaled a short laugh as he stopped. "You just got here. It's no big deal, really. I'll be back in no time." His skin was crawling with the looks on their faces. They just looked too... concerned, too close. He wanted to get away from them, from here, from all of it. In fact, a wild thought traipsed through his mind—he might just get in that car and keep driving. Jason was so good at this, maybe he could just handle it all from here on out. Would anyone really miss him if he did just drive and keep on going?

"Really," Jason said. His seriousness punctured Ben's attempt at levity. He glanced at Kathryn only once. "I want to."

Where was the escape? What could he say to tell his brother he wanted no part of this little reunion? With a sigh, Ben realized that like it or not, Jason was here, and he wasn't going to just dismiss him, even if the chance of having him around freaked him out completely. "Okay. Sure. Why not?"

Jason looked at Kathryn. "Are you coming too?"

The question hit her so full-on that she blinked to figure out the correct answer. "What? Oh, no. You two go ahead. I'll stay."

"Okay." Jason gave her another two seconds to change her mind. "Then we'd better get so we can get back."

"Yeah. Okay."

Ben was really worrying her. He careened back and forth from out of control to scarily in control so fast that she could hardly keep up. Worse, in his eyes, he looked two steps from the edge, and she wasn't sure just how long she might have to pull him back. When his father was gone, there was no reason for him to be here, and that scared her too though she was less inclined to admit that.

"We'll be back," Ben said to her at the door.

Kathryn waved him off. "Take your time. We're fine here."

With that, they left. When they were gone, Kathryn turned to Mr. Warren in the bed. Carefully she rearranged the pillow under his head. "You have a really great son there, Mr. Warren. I hope you know that. He's scared, but so is nearly everybody. I just hope he can find peace in all of this." And then, standing at the bedside, she closed her eyes. "Dear Lord, please help Ben find peace. Amen."

Eight

The little silver Mustang jumped out into the late morning traffic, and Ben held on, hoping he wouldn't get thrown off completely. Truth was, he was doing that a lot lately—holding on and hoping he could do that long enough that he could find normal again. This was definitely not normal. In the seat next to him, far too close for comfort, sat his younger brother who looked so much like he remembered and yet nothing at all like he remembered.

It was wei

rd how that was, but that's how it felt. He strained not to glance over. That wasn't easy. Instead he readjusted his sunglasses and glanced into the rearview mirror. New York. No place like it especially when your nerves were so frayed you could feel them crawling across your skin.

He didn't know if it was nerves or the stress, but heat began pulsating from his core outward. Had he been alone, he would've taken off the jacket. But he wasn't alone, and that threw what he would usually do right out the window.

"You said an hour," Jason said after clearing his throat. "Is this Dad's main house or the apartment?"

"Main house." Ben checked the mirror again.

The conversation faded for a long moment.

"Huh," Jason said, "it'll be weird seeing it again."

This time Ben did glance at his brother and then retrained his gaze back to the road. "Do you remember it?"

"Some. I don't know that I remember it exactly, it's more visions and feelings. Is there a big island thing in the middle of the kitchen?"

"Yeah." Ben glanced over. "It's got all the pots and pans on the rack above it."

Jason nodded. "We used to eat peanut butter and jelly sandwiches there."

"Strawberry because…"

"I was allergic to grape." Jason laughed. "Still am." He put his hand up to his mouth as awe drifted through his eyes. "Wow. I can't believe that was really for real. It seems more like a dream."

Many, many things seemed more like a dream to Ben at the moment, not the least of which was the moment itself. He glanced over. "So Dad came to your wedding then?"

"Yeah." Awe fled replaced by solemnity. "I had no idea if he would or not, but when I got his number from Mom and called him, I don't think wild horses could have kept him away. And Holly just loves him. They hit it off right away."

"Holly? Your wife." Carefully Ben made a turn and headed out on the expressway.

"She wanted to come," Jason said. "Of course, she's never been to New York, so the thought kind of freaked her out, not to mention we're six months pregnant with all that entails."

Suddenly Ben felt very old. "Pregnant. Well…" He stumbled forward, looking for the words. "Congratulations." He nodded, trying to keep his brain working. "Your first?"

"Second."

"Second." Ben lifted his eyebrows in complete disbelief. "Wow. You guys don't waste any time."

"Well, Ryley was kind of a surprise. That's why the whole wedding thing took place like it did, not that I regret it for a second, but…"

It was hard to drive, listen, absorb, and think straight all at the same time. Ben looked behind him and changed lanes. He fought to think of something to say—brotherly advice, that kind of thing, but he was sorely out of anything even approaching wisdom.

"So, how about you and Kathryn?" Jason asked. "You guys got any little feet running around your place?"

The question came from so far out of the blue that Ben swerved into the next lane and garnered an angry honk from the driver behind him. "Kathryn? Me and…? Uh, no. You…? You think we're married?" How those were all the questions he got out, he didn't know because there were so many more flooding his soul.

"Well, yeah." Jason shifted uncomfortably in the seat. "Aren't you?"

Ben looked over at him, trying to see if he was serious. "Kathryn from the... thing, Kathryn?" He searched in his brain to figure out why Jason would think such a thing. "Uh, no. We're not... married." What was that for a word anyway? How had it even come up? "She works there. She's like the counselor-type person or something."

"Oh." Jason sounded totally taken aback. "I'm sorry. I just... You were..." He cleared his throat. "I just assumed."

"Yeah, well, it's best if you don't do that." Ben knew his tone was harsher than it needed to be, but he didn't care. He was about to go off the edge, and Jason was not helping.

"So. Hm. Are you married then? Is there a Mrs. Warren in the picture?"

And this was helping? "No." Ben's hands tightened on the steering wheel. "There is no Mrs. Warren. I'm very much single. I live by myself in a great apartment. I come and go as I please, and I have many lady friends, if you can call them that."

"Oh." Jason nodded. "The New York thing."

That ratcheted up Ben's annoyance another six degrees. "What does that mean? The New York thing?"

With a shrug, Jason laughed it off. "You know, free as a bird, no attachments wanted or needed."

"I don't know that that's such a New York thing," Ben said defensively. "I think that's pretty much an everywhere thing."

"Some, but not as much."

This conversation was giving him a headache. He crossed over to the off-ramp and took it, glad they were only twenty minutes from the house. He was ready for this drive to be over.

"So, what do you do... for a living?" Jason asked, and Ben wished he wouldn't feel the need to try so hard. Couldn't they just make this trip in silence, get through this horrible ordeal, and go back to their own separate lives? Was that really so much to ask?

"I'm a pharmaceutical rep."

"Ah, a drug pusher." Jason laughed at his own joke although Ben really didn't see the humor.

"For your information, I was number two in sales last quarter."

Jason was clearly fighting to control the laughter. "No. I'm sorry. That's just what we call them at the clinic. Drug pushers."

Ben snagged on the word "clinic," and it was as good a reason as any to change the subject. "So you work at a clinic then? Are you a doctor?"

"X-ray technician. I wanted to do the whole doctor thing, but with Holly... It was just smarter to go the quicker route at the time. And I like it well enough. It pays the bills. Plus, I see the junk the docs go through. I wouldn't want that life."

Memories Ben wanted no part of flashed through his mind. "Yeah."

Thankfully the let's get to know each other barrage concluded as the freeway and its rush melted into the posh neighborhood that Ben had called home for the better part of his life. The homes were spaced to give each owner maximum privacy that the gate at the entrance didn't already afford them. Ben punched in the code, the gates opened, and he drove in.

"Wow. I had forgotten the gates." Clearly in awe, Jason gazed around them at the two and three story houses looming like sentinels on either side of the street. "I always knew it was big, but wow..."

At the end of the cul-de-sac Ben pulled up next to the curb. He could've gone around back, but he didn't plan on staying that long.

"It wraps around the block," Jason said.

Ben knew his brother was in the midst of remembering, but he didn't care. The last thing he wanted to do was to go on a stroll down memory lane. What he wanted to do was handle this and get the heck out of here. They walked together up the sidewalk, and at the door Ben punched the bell. He had a key, but he didn't want to scare Maria—even though she was expecting them.

After several minutes, the door cracked open and then swung all the way to the gapingly dark interior.

"Oh, Mr. Warren, thank goodness you are here." Maria's thick accent and slight, cinnamon brown features told a good deal of her story. "I was so worried when I got that call..."

"I'll take care of it." Ben took off his sunglasses and slipped the earpiece into the v at the top of his shirt. "I'll just go up to the office and see if I can find something to figure out how this happened."

"Do you want me to come with you?" Jason asked.

"No." The word was sharp, harsh even. Then Ben

remembered himself and let out a breath. "Nah. I can handle it." And with that, he left them at the foot of the stairs.

All morning, Kathryn had been thinking about him. As she made her rounds to the other patients, as she talked with Misty, and even as she sat eating lunch, his name and his face kept sliding across her heart. "Dear Lord," she said over her pasta salad, "please be with Ben… and with Jason."

"Well, hello there."

She looked up from her salad and found two electric pools of blue staring down at her. "I… Oh…" Grabbing up her napkin, she wiped her mouth. "Hi."

"I'm sorry. I saw you sitting over here alone and wondered if you might like some company." It was Doctor… wow, she couldn't find his name in the swirl of Ben's circling her consciousness.

He deflated slightly. "I'm sorry that was presumptuous of me…"

"No!" She practically jumped out of the chair. "No. It… wasn't. Please. Have a seat."

And then, somehow he was sitting down in front of her. If her mother could see her now, she'd be picking out the drapes for their new house and the names for the children. Then again, that's pretty much what Kathryn was doing too.

Papers. Envelopes. Bills. Junk mail. They were everywhere in the office. Ben had been in this office many times, but it had never, ever looked like this. He rifled through one stack and then another. Some of the bills were from as much as six months before, and there were stacks of letters that hadn't even been opened yet.

In one such stack he found an electric bill from two months before that hadn't been opened. He ripped into it and perused the information therein. The total at the bottom took his breath away. He blinked twice to make sure he was seeing it correctly, and then he noticed the bright red PAST DUE notice stamped at the top. His gaze slid around the room at the rest of the mess. The bill hadn't been opened, so presumably it hadn't been paid.

Quickly he sat down in the chair he'd only been in one other time, when he got the whipping of his life for playing doctor at his dad's desk. No one sat at this desk. No one. Pushing that and every other thought away, he grabbed up the phone and dialed the number on the bill. It took three more numbers through the company's phone bank to have a person on the line.

"Yes, this is Ben Warren." He started through the explanation about his father's house and the bill. It took only two more minutes for the iceberg to come into view. Three months behind, cancellation notice sent a week ago, electricity to both the house and the cottage set to be cut off in one hour.

Letting out a ragged breath, Ben sat back in the chair and rubbed his eyelids. This couldn't be happening. "Yes, of course I want to pay the bill. Yes, in full."

"I will need a valid credit card, sir."

"Oh, uh, sure." His body going one way, his mind another, Ben dug his credit card out and transferred the information. Thoughts swirled. Did he have enough of a credit limit to cover the mess surrounding him? Did he have the patience to sort through it all in order to even determine the extent of the damage?

"Thank you, sir," the lady on the other end said.

"Sure. Thank you." And he signed off.

When he sat back, that feeling of wanting to escape at all costs invaded his consciousness. Had he been specially selected for this hell? What had he ever done to deserve this? His stomach began to knot-up worse than it ever had. It was like someone was gripping it in a fist and refusing to let go. Doggedly, he pulled himself forward, knowing how easily the self-pity would pull him down if he let it. Slowly he picked up a stack of envelopes and thumbed through them. Water, gas, phone, credit card statements.

Fear crept over him as he turned one of those over and slid his thumb under the flap. He tried to steel himself for what he would find when he unfolded the pages. A shudder shook him to the core when his eyes adjusted on the numbers. He leaned forward and put his hand to his mouth. It was worse than he could have imagined. What and how questions played tag in his brain. How had this happened? What should he do now? How was he going to have time to sort all of this out and deal with his father too?

The quiet knock on the hardwood door yanked his attention to it. By some surreal phenomenon that Ben couldn't really understand or grasp, his brother stood there. Older and taller, but his brother just the same. "Did you find it?"

There really wasn't anything else to do. Ben let out a hollow, half-laugh in the breath of air. "Yeah. I found it all right. Along with about six dozen others." He let out another rush of incredulous air. "Ga…" Sitting forward, Ben threw the envelopes to the desk and put his hand to his forehead, pushing to get life to go away.

Jason stepped into the room, his face laden with concern. "What's going on?"

For a moment Ben tried to get all the words to line up in his head, but there were just too many to know where to start. He put his elbows on his knees and his face in his hands, trying desperately not to cry. The fist in his stomach clenched tighter. "I have no idea. Did you hear that? I have no freaking idea. That's the answer you want, right? I'm supposed to have all the damn answers, and I have no freaking idea what I'm doing."

Coming all the way into the room, Jason glanced around. Ben felt him moving though Jason said nothing.

"This whole thing is one big, freaking mess," Ben continued, giving voice to the utter chaos swirling inside him. "I don't know what to do. I don't. I don't know how to handle any of this. I don't even know where to start."

At the leather couch, Jason sat down and pulled a stack of mail from the little table next to him. Ben couldn't look. It was too overwhelming. If he could just think of a good place to run, somewhere with sunshine and vodka—lots and lots of vodka. That would be great. Anywhere but here where all he could do was watch his life crumble before his eyes.

One at a time, Jason paged through the documents. "Have these been paid?"

"How the hell should I know?" In a blinded fury, Ben vaulted from the chair and took three steps to the side wall. He wanted to punch it. Something in him said that would feel good, but something else by only the slightest power kept him from it. "How should I know anything? He didn't tell me about any of this. He didn't even tell me about you."

Anger and bitterness spilled over the sides of his heart, and he had no way to stop it. "Where have I been? Where? This isn't new. Look at those statements. Six months or more. And where was I?

How long has this been going on? How long has he been like this, and I didn't even realize it until I got that call..."

A soft knock on the door yanked Ben's hand up to his face to stop the words. This was embarrassing enough with his brother right here. He sure didn't want the world to see him like this.

"Hey," Kelly's voice drifted into the room. "Maria said you guys were up here."

Squeezing his eyes closed with his back still to them, Ben arched his head forward and then back, fighting to get the emotions to stand back down. It wasn't working.

"I'm Jason." Standing from the couch, Jason shook hands with Ben's best friend while Ben prayed to wake up from this nightmare. He would sell everything he owned just to wake up.

"Kelly Zandoval. I'm Ben's friend."

"Nice to meet you."

"You too."

How could they act so incredibly normal? How could anyone act normal? The world was spinning out from under their feet. Couldn't they feel it?

"What's... what's going on?" Kelly asked softly.

Jason let out a long breath, and Ben felt them looking at him. He didn't care. He couldn't face them or the absolute chaos of his life.

"We just got here," Jason finally said. The sound of papers moving dug into Ben. Did they have to look? Did Kelly have to find out? "I don't know, but it looks like Dad's behind on some of his bills."

The papers fluttered again as Ben forced his blood pressure to descend slowly. He was regaining control. It was a good feeling. Numbness overtook him in a wash, and slowly he turned to rejoin humanity.

"It looks like things just got too much for him," Ben said, testing his voice with each word as the two gazes from across the room came up to him. Each of the two men held a fistful of papers. How many could there be? Ben didn't want to know, but he also wasn't going to let them see any more cracks in his armor. This was his problem, and he would deal with it.

"How many are there?" Kelly asked, looking from Ben to the papers in his hands.

"I don't know. I haven't had a chance to look yet." Ben

stepped back over to the desk. Sitting down in that chair was one of the hardest things he'd ever done. It felt like death itself. It was strange how dark it was in this room. He had never noticed that. There was no outside light at all, only a couple of dim reading lights. He pushed that thought away as he picked up four envelopes. "The electric bill was three months past due. The lady said they only let it on that long because Dad was such a long and loyal customer."

He selected one envelope and tore into it. "This is the water bill. Past due." Picking up another, he opened it. "Trash bill. Past due." He shook his head as he flipped the papers onto the desk, gripping numbness for all he was worth. "I'm guessing they are all past due. The question is where to start and how to pay for it all."

"We may have to tap into some of Dad's stocks," Jason said, "if there's not enough in the bank accounts to cover it."

Overwhelm started its slow creep onto Ben once again. Where was he supposed to start? He didn't even know where his dad banked. There could be any number of accounts at any number of institutions, and he'd never even considered asking that question until this moment.

"Well," Kelly said, holding up one envelope, "here's a bank statement. I guess we could start there."

"How was lunch?" Misty asked when Kathryn made it back ten minutes late. She and Dr. Martin had shared salads and laughs for a solid thirty minutes. In fact, she hadn't even realized that much time had passed.

"Wonderful," she sing-songed back.

"Oh, really?" Misty's eyebrows reached for the ceiling. "Are you going to share some details, or do I get to make them up in my head?"

Kathryn demurred, but the truth was, she was dying to tell someone. "Well, if you must know, Dr. Martin showed up."

"Ooo!" Misty squealed, leaning forward on the counter. "This is good. Tell me everything."

"He's great. Single. Just finished medical school, this is his first job." Kathryn ran through the list she had been painstakingly making in her mind. "He's from somewhere in Ohio I think. Always wanted to be a doctor."

"Sounds promising."

"I know. And here's the thing. He came and sat by me! I didn't even know he was there until he showed up."

"Ooo, very promising."

Kathryn managed to hold onto her excitement. "But don't tell anybody. It's nothing… yet."

The smile on Misty's face told her she heard and fully understood "yet."

Kelly was on his cell phone down the hall with the companies attached to the overdue bills, Jason was on his cell phone across the room with the bank, and Ben was sorting through statement after statement trying to get a handle on where money might be and how to go about transferring it so they could make some sense out of this.

"The bank needs some Power of Attorney documentation," Jason said, snagging Ben's attention. "They won't give out the info otherwise."

"Power of Attorney? Dad gave me those a couple months ago." Just getting memories pulled up was becoming ever more difficult. "I think I have them in my safe at home."

"Great." Jason transferred the information and hung up. "They said as soon as we can get in there, if it's all in line, we can probably have control of it by tomorrow."

Kelly stepped back in. "Hey, I've got the gas company on the line. They want credit card info or something to cover this one. It's scheduled to be shut off tomorrow."

Ben held his hand up for the little cell phone. He felt the glances between the other two but tried not to let them sink in. "This is Ben Warren. I can give you my credit card if that will work."

"Are the Warrens not back yet?" Kathryn set the stack of papers on the counter.

"Haven't seen them," Misty replied. "Is there a problem?"

"No." But she didn't sound very convincing. Quickly she checked her watch and spun through her memory of their leaving. It was after two. Hadn't they said an hour? "I hope not. I just expected them to be back by now."

"Oh. Well, I can call you when they come through."

Kathryn nodded. "Yeah, do that."

"K."

It was really a good thing Jason and Kelly were there. They had taken Kelly's Expedition back into the city to find the Powers of Attorney. It was a minor miracle that it was where Ben had thought he put it. For good measure he called the attorney listed and filled him in on what was going on. That set other wheels in motion, like finding the will and readying the estate. Ben didn't want to think about that, so he thanked the attorney and hung up.

"Yeah," Kelly said, "it was real sudden. I don't think Ben even knew anything was wrong."

Jason turned in the front seat slightly to look back at his brother. "Anything?"

"Yeah." The word stuck in Ben's throat. He didn't like the two of them discussing this. He didn't want anyone discussing it. "He's getting some other things ready. I guess we'll have to go in there as soon as…" The words stopped the second they wound around to his heart. "Soon anyway."

He hated the looks the two of them exchanged. When did he get to be Pity-Case #1?

"You know," Kelly said. "I'm like starving to death. Have you guys eaten anything?"

"Not since peanuts on the plane," Jason said. "I could go for a burger."

The thought of food made Ben want to throw up. He couldn't remember the last time he had eaten, and it was looking like a worse and worse idea every minute.

"We can pull in here," Kelly said. "It shouldn't take long. We totally missed the lunch rush."

"Sounds good."

Ben wanted to deck both of them.

Kathryn's concentration was thinning. She could hardly get five minutes of work done without her mind registering that Misty hadn't called in yet. Finally at ten-'til-three, she hit the little button on her phone.

"Yeeees?" Misty said in that sing-song voice she used when patronizing Kathryn.

"Hey, did you forget to page me when the Warrens got here?"

"I don't... Hang on." Misty left.

Kathryn flipped through the top three pages on her desk. All forms to fill out. She'd never like the paperwork part of this job, but it was something that had to be done to stay in compliance, so she really didn't have much of a choice. That still didn't mean she liked it. If she could just concentrate, maybe she could make a dent in this stack before it was time to go home.

Beep. Her intercom buzzed to life.

Silliness drifted over her as she punched the button. "Yeeees?"

"They haven't come back yet."

All teasing left. "They haven't? Are you sure?"

"I went and checked. Brenda said she hasn't seen them all day."

Kathryn wanted to argue, but that made no sense. It wasn't Misty's fault. "Okay, well, let me know when they show up."

"Will do."

Putting her head down, Kathryn struggled to think of what she could do, but the only thing she could think of was to pray. "God, please be with Ben and Jason wherever they are."

Ben sat next to the window, looking at his meager cheeseburger and trying to find any desire anywhere in him to eat a bite of it. Truth was it looked cold and brick-hard. When he took a bite, it tasted about as good. He chewed and chewed but couldn't get himself to swallow it.

"So I guess we'll head to the bank next," Kelly said to Jason who sat next to Ben.

"Guess so. I hope everything's in order. I hate being gone so long." Jason looked over at Ben as he chewed on his chicken sandwich. "They have your number, right? In case something changes?"

"Wh...? Oh, yeah." Ben was having a monster of a time following the conversation. He kept looking at his cheeseburger, sitting there in front of him. Rational said he should eat, but emotional just wouldn't let him. When had he gotten so weak, so pitiful? No wonder they were looking at him with those sad-puppy-dog eyes that he hated. He deserved it. With a ragged breath, he picked up the burger and took a small bite.

It was all he could do not to let the feeble contents of his stomach come roaring back up. This was a bad idea, a thoroughly, unimaginably bad idea. He pitched the burger back to the table and grabbed for his Coke. It wasn't much better.

His stomach was roiling around the hard fist that was growing by the second. Where was the escape hatch? It had to be here somewhere. If he didn't get a grip, he'd be gasping for air in no time.

"You not going to eat that?" Kelly asked as if he'd just noticed his friend hadn't woofed down three.

"The bread's hard," Ben said, choking the words out. What he wouldn't have given for a bed and a deadbolt.

"We could get you another one." Kelly was looking at him with those eyes again.

"Nah. I'm not really all that hungry." Ben tried to slide back in the booth with that air of confident self-assurance that he'd always had, but wow was that hard to pull off.

An awkward silence settled on the table for a moment.

"So, you think you the bank's going to know what to do with all that paperwork?" Jason asked.

Ben nodded, afraid to trust his voice. He might either throw up or scream, and he wasn't sure either wouldn't feel better than he felt at the moment.

"Okay then. Well, let's hit it." Jason crumpled his wrappers up and slid from the booth.

The long sigh was the only thing that got him moving again.

"Yes, sir," the bank representative said as he checked the computer on his desk, "let's see what we've got. Hmm..."

Ben forced himself to stay up straight in the chair. It wasn't easy, but he knew if he leaned back, he would go to sleep or worse.

"Yes. Okay..."

If the guy didn't start saying more than yes and okay, Ben was likely to scream, "WHAT?!" so the whole bank would hear. He held the frustration down with both hands, wondering if he looked as frazzled on the outside as he felt on the inside.

A few more tip-taps on the computer keys, and the man

swiped out a pad of paper. "It looks like we've been receiving direct deposits of your father's salary on schedule, but there have been no checks written out on this account in... let's see... April, January, November... about six months."

That at least squared somewhat with the bills.

"But there is money in the account?" Jason asked.

"Oh, yes." The man wrote the amount on the paper and pushed it across the desk. "And that's just the checking. Let's see, I believe... Yes, there's a savings and a money market as well."

At least there was air again. It tasted so sweet, Ben thought he might pass out.

"Looks like those are around..." He pushed the pad back over, and Ben and Jason each took a look.

"And how do we go about getting the money out to the creditors?" Jason asked.

Half of Ben wanted to smack him, half of him wanted to hug him. It was a second-by-second see-saw.

"Well, since the Power of Attorney looks to be in order, I believe we can set something up this afternoon to let you take control over the funds immediately. If you're ready to do that..."

One more incredibly daunting step. Jason looked over to Ben, probably knowing this wasn't his call. Ben felt the responsibility shift inexorably back onto his shoulders. "Yeah. I guess we'd better."

"Very well, then. I'll go get the paperwork drawn up."

When the man left, Kelly stepped into the room as Ben let his head go forward, caught only by his hands anchored by his elbows on his knees.

"What'd he say?" Kelly asked Jason. It was strange how they felt like two sides of Ben's brain talking and rationalizing as the rest of him fell apart.

"We can get the money, and it's plenty to be able to cover everything," Jason replied.

"Thank the Lord."

"You've got that right." Jason shifted in his chair. "You know, I've been thinking. Didn't Dad have an apartment too? I remember going there a couple of times."

Kelly nodded. "Yeah. It's about six blocks from the hospital district."

Jason hesitated and then shifted again. "Don't you think we

should check it out? I mean, maybe the bills for it came there instead of the house."

More problems. More issues. More junk to deal with. Ben really didn't think he could take any more. He felt the two of them looking at him. *Make a decision, Ben. It's time to stop acting like such a baby here. For the love of Michael, sit up and say something!*

"That's probably a good idea," Kelly said, glancing away from Ben, even as he stepped in for him. "Then we can head back."

Somehow his feet were moving. Somehow his hands worked the key and let them into the darkened apartment. Somehow he wasn't curled in a corner immobile and numb, but Ben didn't know how that was.

"Nice," Jason said as they entered, and indeed, it was nice. Deep mahogany floors shone in the softly lit room. It felt old and impressive.

"I'll just go check the office," Ben said, wondering who was saying that and why. It was odd how detached he felt. And to him, that was much better than feeling attached. He strode through the living area and down the hallway. Everything was as if no one had touched it in months or maybe years. Not even dust. He vaguely remembered his father getting a maid and he wondered if he still had one.

As he entered the little study, he decided that yes, the maid had been busy cleaning everything for someone who probably hadn't been there in quite awhile. Thankfully, there were no stacks, no papers. Nothing.

It felt like a museum, set up to look like how someone would have had it if they had lived there. Ben quickly went through the desk drawers and found nothing of any interest. His mind slipped upon the thought that he would have to come clean this all out at some point, but he couldn't face that, so he closed the drawer quietly and went back out.

"Yeah, he's really worrying me," Kelly was saying down the hall. "This is not like him at all. I don't think he's been sleeping either."

Ben purposely made a noise on the floor, and the conversation slammed to a stop. Fighting to look normal, he strode into the living room. "I don't think there's anything here.

Nothing looks out of place."

"Oh, good." And there was genuine relief on Jason's face.

Kelly nodded. "Should we head back then?" He looked at his watch. "It's almost five."

Five? Where had that many hours gone?

"Yeah, I guess so."

Nine

"Clyde's here," Misty said as she crossed the threshold to Kathryn's office at ten after five. "You about ready?"

Lost in prayers, Kathryn looked up from the form she was trying to fill out. She'd been working on it for fifteen minutes and had gotten the First and Last Name written in. "Oh, I'm not quite done yet."

"You're never done yet."

"Ha. Ha." Kathryn wrinkled her nose and then fought to get a smile onto her face. "You better go on without me. I'm just going to finish up here for awhile."

"Dr. Martin's not coming, is he?"

If she'd had something to throw, she would have. "Ha. Ha. I just really need to get this filled out so I can skip out and go to Mrs. Baker's funeral in the morning."

Misty lost the happy-go-lucky stance and slumped against the door. "Oh, yeah. That's tomorrow, huh?"

Bending her head back over the paperwork, Kathryn nodded. "Yeah, that's tomorrow."

"Well, okay, but don't stay too late, they might not let you escape."

"I'll try not to."

Misty backed up.

"Drive carefully," Kathryn called.

Misty ducked back into the room. "You too."

And with that, she left. For one moment Kathryn considered following her friend. What was she planning to do, stay all night? What if they didn't come back tonight? The concern over what was taking them so long washed through her again. "Dear Lord, please be with him—with them." Then she shook her head to clear it of the thoughts and went back to work.

"I really think our best plan of attack is for me and Jason to go back to the house tonight and sort through everything," Kelly said as they walked up to the hospice doors. The late afternoon sun was blazing as post-five-o'clock snarled traffic snaked by on the roadway beyond.

The closer they got to those doors, the shakier Ben's legs felt, and his insides wobbled like unset Jell-o. If only he didn't have to do this... He opened the outside door and let the two of them cross in front of him. One more second to stall the inevitable. The gold tones of the walls and carpet wrapped around his senses, probably because he was no longer really taking in details anymore. Everything had become one, big, giant blur.

He followed the other two into the hospice unit and through the lobby as his mind went the other way—down the hallway to the chapel. How he wanted to feel her arms around him again. Shaking his head at the sheer absurdity of that thought, he crammed his hands in his pockets. It wasn't like that between them, and it never would be. Moreover, she was not what he was looking for. She was stable and compassionate. The truth was she'd be smart to run the other direction.

Then he wondered why he was even thinking about her at all. It must be about being in this building and needing something to hold onto. His fists balled inside his pockets.

At least he could keep them from shaking too. It was immensely difficult to breathe all of a sudden. That door in the corner and all the horror it held behind it tilted off-square in his mind. He closed his eyes, fighting the waves of fear washing over him. How could he ever survive this? He wished he could go talk to her, but then he realized with his last breath of sanity that she was long since gone. It was, after all, almost six. He couldn't account for that many hours. He couldn't even account for the last five minutes.

"Has there been any change?" Jason asked the young brunette nurse as she stepped out of that door. Ben pulled up short behind his brother, ducked his head, and ran his hand over his jawline that felt like a porcupine. He tried to remember the last time he had shaved. It was a memory he couldn't pull up.

The nurse jumped, startled by their approach but quickly regained her composure. "Oh, uh. No. No change."

"Can we go in?" Jason asked, taking the lead that Ben had somehow relinquished.

"Sure. Sure."

As she passed, Ben kept his gaze on the carpet at his feet. He felt like a skunk, too wrapped up in himself to do what he should be doing. The other two went through the open door as if it took nothing, and Ben hated himself for how hard that simple act was for him. He closed his eyes, squeezing them to get his feet moving. He forced the air into his lungs. It hurt. He had let his father down in the worst way, and now he was going to again. It was like being on treadmill that kept coming around to the same moment over and over and not being able to get off. He let out a long breath, steeled his determination, and got his feet moving one more time.

"Ms. Walker?"

"Yes, Sonia?" Kathryn looked up from the book propped on her desk. It was one she had meant to read several months ago when she'd gone to the conference on End of Life Issues. She'd never had time until now, and now it seemed she had nothing but time.

"The Warrens just got back."

The chair crashed onto the spring beneath her. "Oh, thanks, Sonia. Thank you."

"You're welcome." The young nurse ducked back out.

Suddenly Kathryn felt all undone. Her blouse was hopelessly wrinkled from the day's activities, and her hair was coming down too. Good grief, she looked a mess. Quickly she readjusted herself as much as possible, slipped her shoes back on, and grabbed for her suit jacket. Once ready, she closed her eyes and breathed a final prayer for him—for them. It was always such a challenge to remember to include the others, and she was sure that was not good.

Not having time to dwell on it, she strode out and locked her door.

"Oh, Kathryn," Clyde said from across the hall, his door open as always, "you're still here?"

She put her hand on the doorjamb, vowing not to go in. Clyde had a way of making five minutes turn into two hours. "I'm just going to run down and check on the Warrens. They've been out all day, and then I'm taking off."

"Well, don't let me keep you. Hot date tonight?"

"Very funny. Be good."

"Always."

She laughed and turned to head down to that last door. It occurred to her then how nervous she was. That was silly. What was there to be nervous about? She had talked to hundreds of families in this situation. Still, the closer she got to that door, the more she had to force her feet to keep moving. Probably no one on the outside would ever know the struggle inside her or that this felt like anything but a professional call. That was good because inside, it felt like anything but.

Carefully she opened the door. "Knock. Knock."

Three gazes snapped to her from various points around the room. Jason was closest, standing next to the bed. Kelly and Ben sat across the way on the couch. Instantly Kelly was on his feet. Although Kathryn glanced at the others, her heart snagged on Ben, sitting there, looking like death itself.

"Please, sit," she said, tripping on the words and trying not to focus only on Ben. "It's just me." Her only hope was to get her focus on the others, so she walked up to the bed and put her hand on Jason's back. "How's he doing?"

If there had been anything in his stomach to throw up, Ben would have. The ache tore through him as he watched her comfort Jason with that same gentle touch she had used with him. He suddenly felt like an idiot. Here all along he had thought she was that nice to him because she liked him. What a joke. What a stupid fool he was for even letting his stupid mind think that.

Hot anger flashed into his soul, and he let it melt there because it felt good.

"Kelly." Kathryn came over, offered her hand to his friend and then hugged him when he stood. Jason followed her over. When Kelly let her go, she looked down at Ben. "Ben."

"Hey." But he hardly lifted his gaze. She probably thought he was an idiot too. Had he done anything to show her how he felt?

Well, he had followed her into the chapel that time… Ugh. He slammed his eyes closed. *Make it go away, God. Please. Make it go away.*

"Did you get everything taken care of?" she asked, presumably to the other two because he was completely uncommunicative. He wanted to lash out at her that it was none of her damned business what they got done or didn't get done. What did she care anyway? She didn't. She was just being polite, and that angered him even more—why he couldn't quite articulate, but it did.

"Yeah," Kelly said. "It turned out to be a bigger headache than we thought."

"Oh, yeah?"

"I don't think Dad's been in very good shape for a couple of months," Jason said. "He hasn't been paying bills or keeping up with much of anything…"

"Say it!" Ben came right off the couch, and all three gazes jumped to him in surprise and alarm. "You're all thinking it. I don't know why you don't just say it! I should have seen what was happening. I should have known. I should have done something."

"Ben, dude." Kelly put his hand out.

"Don't dude me. And stop talking about me as if I don't have ears. I'm sick of it. You hear me? Sick of it!" Air. He had to get air, and there was none in this stifling room. His feet were going before he knew he was leaving. But he didn't contradict them. Just let them walk. Walking felt good. Running would feel even better.

"Ben. Ben!" Kelly called, but he wasn't stopping no matter what.

He wrenched the door open, and when he was out, he just kept going.

"I knew it," Kelly muttered when Ben was gone.

Kathryn, one step from following him, stopped. "Knew what?"

Kelly shook his head, his dark eyes flashing. "I knew he wasn't handling this very well. I knew it when I saw him this morning, and them bills…" He let out a hard breath. "That boy is in bad shape. He hasn't eaten, and I swear he hasn't slept decent since he got the news."

Worry took over Kathryn. "He hasn't been eating?"

"He ate like two bites of his hamburger today. Said the bread was hard." Jason shook his head and glanced at the door. "Maybe I should go talk to him."

"No." Kathryn stopped them all with the sharpness of the word. "Let me go. Maybe he'll talk to me."

Kelly started to argue and then nodded. "Good luck."

She was going to need more than luck. "Say some prayers."

"You got it, girl."

When he got outside, Ben realized he didn't know where he was going. His car was back at his dad's house. How or why that was, he couldn't really remember. Frustrated by being stranded by his own stupidity, he sat down on the curb and raked his fingers through his hair, yanking at the tangles and pulling for good measure. He wanted to stop thinking, but the thoughts just wouldn't stop no matter what he did.

Tears choked into his throat, and he sniffed them back and ran his nose over his sleeve, not caring about propriety or etiquette or anything else even vaguely resembling civility. Heaving air in and out, he felt the center of his heart wrench and twist. He'd never hurt like this. The ache swept his breath and his thoughts away as overwhelming tears welled up inside him, overtaking sanity and everything else.

"Hey." Suddenly she was bending down right next to him—how or why, he didn't know.

Ben said nothing. Instead he sniffed again and slid his nose over his sleeve, fighting to get the tears to stop. Anger bled through him as he wiped at one eye with his wrist. He really didn't care how rude he seemed by turning his head from her. He didn't want to talk to her or anyone else.

Without asking, she sat down on the curb next to him. It was strange because she was dressed in the nicest clothes—heels and silk and the whole thing, and yet, she sat right down there on the concrete without so much as a hesitation.

Thinking it would be much better if he just didn't look at her, Ben put his elbows on his knees and angled his arms in front of him as he anchored his gaze directly in front of him—stoically mashing the tears back. Traffic crawled by on the street one line of parked cars away. How he wished he could join that life again. It had at least made some sense. Well, at least what he remembered of it did.

He had thought she would start talking, start telling him why he was being an idiot and why he was doing everything completely wrong, but she didn't say anything, just sat there next to him, looking out at the traffic too. At first he thought that was better, then it began crawling over his nerves as if she was forcing him to tell her everything by some silent-drip-by-drip torture. Why didn't she say something? He glanced over at her, and she looked at him and smiled softly. There was light in her eyes, and compassion.

The anger slipped away from him as he looked back out to the traffic and sighed. Words began to form in his mind. Not harsh words or angry words, just words.

"He thought we should go out to a restaurant for Christmas this last year," Ben said, letting the words come up and out though they would make no sense to her. "He said he didn't want me to have to drive all the way out to his place."

Kathryn turned her attention from the traffic to him but said nothing.

"I didn't think anything of it at the time. I just figured he was staying at the apartment, you know, and that it would be easier for him too." The twisting of his heart made getting the words out more difficult. "I never once thought that…" Tears reached up from his throat and grabbed him again. He sniffed them back, fighting to breathe through them. "Was I so damn busy with my own life that I never even bothered to see what was really going on with my own dad?" He exhaled. "I feel like such an idiot."

"You're not an idiot." Her tone was so soft and wholly without judgment. "We all get wrapped up. It's easy to miss the signs."

"But I should have been there. I should have known."

"Beating yourself up over it is not going to help."

He laughed, a hollow, hurt-filled laugh. "Yeah? Well, I'm not the only one. They're doing it too." With a jerk of his head, he indicated the hospice doors. "Not that I blame them or anything."

"Hey, they don't blame you. They know this is killing you, and they're worried… about you."

"I wish they wouldn't."

"Why not?"

"Because I don't want anyone to worry about me. I'm fine."

"Uh-huh. And that's why you haven't been eating."

His gaze jerked over to her, and then he knew. He dropped his head in embarrassment and hard anger. "I... can't. I feel like I'm going to throw up every time I even look at food."

She took a long breath in and nodded. "For what it's worth, that's pretty normal. I really think you're expecting yourself to be super-human here, and you're not."

Ben thought about that as it twisted down into his gut. "If I just knew how to fix this."

"It's not something that can be fixed." She waited for a reply, but he couldn't find one. "This is just one of those times that you have to live through and learn as you go. You're not going to do everything right because there is no right... or wrong. There is just being as gentle with yourself as you can..."

Ben growled in frustration. "Ugh. There's those words again."

She backed up an inch in surprise. "I take it you don't agree."

"No. I don't. Look. Being gentle with yourself is a one-way ticket to failure and a life of misery if you ask me."

"And holding yourself to impossible standards is not?" It was her turn to laugh although he wasn't sure he totally liked her laughing at him. "Look at you. Look where beating Ben up has gotten you. You're out here, sitting on a curb because you feel like a failure. You think you let your dad down, your brother down, your friend down..."

"If this is supposed to be a pep talk..."

"No. It's not. It's about trying to get you to see that this is not working. You are being harder on yourself than anyone else would ever be, and that includes your dad."

His gaze swung over to hers. "What do you know about anything? You didn't even know my dad."

"Not personally, but I knew of him. I work in a hospital. People talk. Your dad was one of the most trusted, well-liked doctors around. You don't get to be known and respected like he was by being a hard-ass."

Ben raised his eyebrows both at her tone and her language. "Do you talk to all of your clients like this?"

The smirk came although she tried to hide it. "Only the ones that need it." Her gaze fell to her hands on her knees and then picked back up to his. "This whole façade thing you've got going on here might look like it works in the world, but it's not real. I think what scares you is knowing it's not."

"Oh, yeah?" He leaned back onto his hand as if they were just at a Sunday picnic. "What makes you think I'm scared?"

She looked right at him. "That."

Confusion drained through him, and he shifted slightly. "What?"

"That I'm so cool nothing can touch me attitude you get sometimes."

He folded his arms as anger slithered into him. "Maybe it can't."

"Oh, yeah? Then why are we sitting out here on the concrete?" She looked around at the day for emphasis. "I mean it's a nice day and everything, but…"

That put a small crack in his well-oiled and executed life strategy. He reached up and scratched the top of his head before refolding his arms.

"I've seen you," she continued, and the softness in her eyes and voice called to a place in him he hadn't felt in many years. "The real you. The one who doesn't know everything and wants to do the right thing but doesn't always know what that is."

He uncoiled. "But…"

Quickly she sat up in anticipation of his protest. "And that's okay. That's okay. It is." She slumped slightly when she realized he wasn't going to fight further. "It's just that I've seen what being real can be like, and I've seen the other road too. I don't think putting on a mask to impress the world is what God had in mind for our lives."

Ben scrunched his lips at that reference but tried not to show his annoyance. "Well, don't go getting all spiritual on me. I just want to get through this in one piece."

"And you will." She nodded. "You will. You will get through this. There will be another side. That's why right now it's so important not to set yourself up to hate yourself forever when you get to that other side. I don't care who you are, losing someone you love is tough. This situation is tough. Don't make it tougher by trying to be Superman."

The late day sun warmed the earth, and the breeze carried the warmth right over them. Tired came, and hungry followed. He let his arms go, put his head down, and rubbed the back of his neck. It, like everything else in him, hurt. Maybe she was right, and

115

maybe she wasn't. His mind was so crammed full of thoughts, he couldn't really tell.

"Is the cafeteria still open?" he finally asked, looking back at the building.

"24/7."

As tired took over, his stomach unknotted, and he nodded. "I think I'll go get me something to eat."

The hesitation was only a second. "Would you like some company?"

The soft smile came from his heart. "I think I'd like that."

Kathryn wasn't sure why she had made the offer other than she was afraid to leave him alone. Kelly was right. He was not handling this very well at all. Of course, she had suspected as much, but seeing the emotional turmoil up close was more disconcerting than she had thought it would be.

He got chicken, a small salad, and some Jell-o. She got a salad and some water. Truth was, she hadn't planned to eat, but she didn't think sitting and watching him eat would set him at ease, so she got something. They took their trays to a table along the side wall. The cafeteria area was busier than usual, which was fine with her. More action, less down time.

When he had emptied his tray onto the table, she reached for it and didn't let him protest her taking it. She took the trays over to the little stand and let herself take a breath before she headed back. "God, please take this situation and use me to give Ben Your love. Please help him to find peace." It was the only way she got her feet to turn back to their table.

By some strange twist of fate, she'd somehow been suspended between really liking him and really knowing she shouldn't, not like that anyway. As she walked back to the table, she fought not to catalog his good points, and there were many. But this was professional. He certainly didn't need her drooling all over him right now.

She sat down and let out an exhale. Slowly she spun her plate. "So."

He looked up at her. "So." A moment and he picked up his fork and touched the Jell-o. "Is this stuff edible?"

"I think it's safe."

He nodded as silence descended on the table.

A moment and then another as he cut into the slab of chicken. "What do you want to talk about?" he asked before he took a bite and looked over at her.

"Well, we could talk about what's going on, or something else if you want."

Slowly he nodded. "I think something else." He reached for his water.

She followed his nod as panic rose inside her. "Okay." *Think, Kathryn. Think of something else. Not about him or his dad or the bills...* Picking up a forkful of lettuce, she held it there just above her plate. "So what do you like to do? Are you into music, sports, cars, what?"

"Music. Yes. Sometimes. Sports. Yes. Not a have to be there for every game kind of thing, but I like to kick back on a Sunday and watch football with the guys. Cars. Like them but don't know a thing about how they work, and as long as mine runs, that's all I care about." He took a bite of the chicken. "You?"

Kathryn let out an exhale and shook her head before smoothing her hair over her ear. "I mostly work and go to church. I'm not that big into sports. Misty took me to a hockey game back in February. Never want to do that again." She kept her head down as she ate her next bite.

"Oh, really? Why not?" He was cutting his chicken again, and was now looking at her as if he really wanted to know.

This is a diversion for him, Kathryn. Don't get sucked into believing it's real. "Too violent. They like slam everybody into the walls, and then this really big fight broke out. They were punching each other, and it took like five minutes to break it up. Not my idea of a fun night out."

"So what do you do... when you go out, I mean?"

Boy, she had gotten into this trap quick. How did that happen? Her heart revved up, wondering when this got to be about her. But then she remembered, he didn't want to talk about himself, so she needed to keep the conversation here to let him have a moment of peace. "I don't really go out much. I mean, I work and I go to church. Sometimes I go visit my family, but not that often anymore."

"Oh, really? Why not?"

Why not? Why not? Good question. Because they treat me like an alien from another planet? Because all I hear is how depressed I must be because I don't have a ring on my finger? "A lot of reasons I guess."

"Name one."

She looked at him in annoyance and then shrugged as her gaze fell to her salad. "If you must know, I'm the spinster of the family. Mom thinks it's a recessive gene or something."

Ben reached for his water bottle and took a drink. "So you're not married then?"

"Huh. No." Kathryn laid her fork down and scratched the base of her neck. "Pretty much no."

He nodded as he set the bottle down. "Any prospects?"

Her patience slid over the cliff as she slumped forward and looked at him. "Do we have to talk about this?"

"Oh!" His whole body snapped upward. "Too personal. Sorry."

The slump grew. "No. It's not that. It's just..." She picked up her fork again and pushed the lettuce leaves around and around the little plastic bowl. "I get tired of trying to figure it all out, you know? The whole dating scene and guys in general. It's all such a big mystery, and I feel like I haven't been given the key to unlock it that everyone else has."

"Guys are not that big a mystery. Feed us and give us some love, and we're happy campers."

Kathryn laughed softly. "Yeah, right. I think it's a little more complicated than that."

Ben smiled. "Maybe some but not much." He picked up his fork, cut a piece of the Jell-o, and put it in his mouth. "Mmm. Now that's good."

She couldn't help but laugh at him. "Well, we've got the feed you part down."

He took a drink and joined in the laugh. "Looks that way."

The meal had been more than pleasant. Not once had Kathryn pushed about the situation or about his father or his life. True, she didn't seem over-eager to open up about herself, but he couldn't fault her for that. She was, after all, just doing her job. When they were finished, Ben knew he couldn't put off going back any longer although he wanted to. Had it been up to him, he would've chosen to just stay right there with her forever. That would not have been a problem at all.

However, hiding out in the cafeteria with the counselor wasn't going to win him any points in the good son column, so when she was obviously finished, he suggested it was time to go back. She agreed.

Somehow he had expected her to turn at the front doors, but she walked with him into the hospice. When he held the door for her to enter, a waft of her soft perfume danced around his nostrils, and he wondered if she always smelled so good after a long day.

"Well," she said when they got to the empty nurse's station, "I guess this is it."

Ben put his hands on his hips to keep from reaching out to her. "I guess so." Then he just couldn't help himself. He reached over to her and pulled her to him. Closing his eyes, he breathed in her smell and her softness. Maybe it was the day or the situation or his desperate need for a hug from someone, he didn't know, but this one felt better than anyone ever had. "Thank you."

Her hand rubbed up and down across the length of his back as he held her there. "You take care of yourself."

With a nod, he stepped back although he kept his hands on her arms. His gaze dug through hers. "Will I see you tomorrow?"

She nodded but never broke the connection.

After a moment his heart smiled for him. "Good."

Kathryn gathered her things from her office slowly. What she really wanted to do was to go down to their room once more. But that was crossing a line, and she knew it. No, his brother and his best friend would have to take care of him now. However, her heart hurt as she got to the front doors and her gaze betrayed her by slipping across the room to that door. It was closed. Somehow that seemed appropriate although it killed her to think that. A moment and she dropped her head and shook it.

It would have been a nice dream if he had been anybody else, but he wasn't. As much as she wanted him to be, he wasn't. And with that thought, she pushed through the door and left.

Ten

"No, I think you should come home with me," Kelly said for the sixth time. "Jason can stay tonight. You need to rest."

"I can rest here." Ben fought not to let his voice get too loud. The last thing he needed was a yelling match. Not now. Not after those few moments of peace. Moreover, he felt like he needed to be here. The time was drawing short, and even if that meant he still had a week, it was only a week. He didn't want to leave.

"You won't get any rest here," Kelly countered. "There are people coming in all night."

"Look, Kelly. I appreciate the offer really I do…"

"I think you should stay," Jason suddenly said, and both of them looked at him. "I do. Who knows how much longer… it could be."

Ben hated that last part, but he was infinitely grateful for the first. He nodded and looked at Kelly in challenge.

Finally Kelly shook his head and lifted his hands. "Okay. Okay. Do what you want." He checked his watch. "I really do need to be getting on home though."

Jason was first to offer his hand. "Thanks for everything, Kelly."

"You're welcome, man." Then Kelly turned to Ben. The handshake became a hug. "You take care of yourself, okay?"

When Ben let go of his friend, he nodded and smiled. "Okay." Kathryn was right. They were worried about him. He still didn't want to admit he needed the worry, but maybe it wasn't so bad to think that they cared. "Thanks for everything."

Kelly's smile was both warm and sad. "You got it."

The drive home seemed longer than normal, mostly because of the dream-like state Kathryn had somehow fallen into. It was like a super-reality. One that existed somewhere outside of the world that went on as if nothing was different. She saw that world, but it didn't feel like it ever had.

As she drove, her gaze slipped out the side window to the mass of people moving there. They each had their stories. They each had their loves and their losses. It was like being an apparition rather than a part of it. She wondered if anyone could see her, if she was even real, or just some imagined piece of an illusion. The feeling itself was odd, and she had no way to account for it. But some part of her suddenly saw the illusion of the world and could almost apprehend the realm of the physical and the realm of the spirit fusing as one and then separating once again.

She shook her head to get the thoughts to leave, but they didn't. Not really. For a moment she wondered if anyone else had ever felt like this—like they could see the reality of the illusion.

At that moment her cell phone bleeped to life, and she shook out of the meditative state to rejoin reality. "Hello?"

"Oh, good. I caught you."

"Hi, Misty."

"I tried you at home, but I kept getting your answering machine."

Kathryn arched her gaze out the window to the now ever-so-slowly darkening sky and glanced down at the clock. It was nearly eight. "Yeah. I haven't quite made it home yet."

"Oh, I forgot Wednesday night. Are you headed to church?"

Church. Bible study. She hadn't even thought about that. "Uh, no. I think I'm just going to go home. Not really feeling up to church."

"You're not sick, are you?"

"No. I'm not sick." Reality was starting to regain control. "I'm just tired and ready to take a shower and hit the hay." Answering for her every move was getting annoying. "Did you want something?"

"Oh, yeah. Um."

The pause told her she was not going to like this. "Mist. What's up?"

"Well, I kind of gave your number to Nathan…"

"You *what?*" The words were more of a shriek. "I told you I

121

didn't want you giving out my number. I don't want strange guys calling me."

"Nathan is not some strange guy. And we happened to run into each other at the grocery store, and he asked for your number."

"That's a lot of coincidences there, don't you think?"

"I'm just telling you what happened. He said he might call you later, and I wanted to give you a head's up because I know how you are about answering your phone when you don't know the number."

Do you blame me? "I'm not interested in going on a blind date."

"It's not a blind date. He's going to call you. You can talk to him. There's nothing blind about it."

There was too, but Kathryn was too out of sorts to argue the point. At a stop light, she reached back and pulled the clip out of her hair. It was pinching her head every time she tried to put her head back onto the headrest. For good measure she pulled the ponytail out and shook her hair out. She put her head back just as the light turned green.

"Just don't hang up on him, okay? He really is a nice guy. Promise me you won't hang up on him."

"I won't hang up on him."

"And you will talk to him like a civilized person."

"Misty."

"Sorry. I just want this to work… for you."

Kathryn sighed. They were never going to give it a rest. "I'll take the call, but I'm not promising anything."

"That's all I ask."

"So, how was dinner?" Jason asked from his position in the chair.

Ben was sprawled on the couch, sitting but barely. He let his head roll to the side to look at his brother. "It was nice. Cafeteria food, but not bad."

Taking that in, Jason nodded. "Kathryn seems really nice."

"Yeah, she is."

The pause settled between them, but it wasn't particularly arduous.

"Kelly's great," Jason said after a long moment.

"Yeah."

"So have you guys been friends long?"

"Since high school. We played soccer together. I was the forward. He was my wingman. We made All-State together our senior year." Ben took in a breath. "Man, that seems like a long time ago." He let his head roll back and forth on the back of the couch. "Eons. I introduced him and Tamitha in college. She's really nice. You'd like her." Rolling his head again, he focused on the ceiling. It was so strange how his whole life was right there in his memory banks if he just looked, but how it all seemed like some kind of weird dream. "Her mom died a couple years back. Car accident. It was really tough on her."

"I can imagine."

Ben tried to recall any specific thing he had done at that time for them. He found nothing. He hadn't honestly thought more than a minute about what it must have been like for her or for Kelly. Now he wondered how they had weathered those awful days in the aftermath. With two kids, they hadn't been able to just drop out of life. Somehow they had gone on. Only now did he wonder how.

Jason cleared his throat. "Have you given any thought to the... services afterward?"

And they were back to topics Ben would rather not even have to think about. True, his spirit was somewhat calmer now, but he still did not feel adequate to this task. "No, not really. I've just been kind of trying to get through this minute, you know?"

With a small nod, Jason pulled forward in the chair. "I think we need to start thinking about it, don't you?"

Where was that answer? It was nowhere to be found in Ben's head.

"Have you called Dad's pastor? I guess that would be the logical place to start."

Logical. What was logical about this situation? "I guess."

"We should do that in the morning."

We. Ben wondered if that meant he would have to participate. "Okay."

"Hi—hi. Um, this is Nathan Saffron. Is—is Kate Walker there?"

Kathryn curled into a ball on her couch, pulling her knees and feet up under her as she held the cell phone at her ear. She shouldn't have changed into her pajamas so early. It felt strange to talk to this stranger sitting here in her pajamas. She reached over and pulled the afghan over her as a sudden chill attacked. "Hi, Nathan. This is Kath... Kate. Misty said you might call."

"Yeah. Well, she mentioned that you might be interested in... going out sometime. She said I should call and maybe we could set something up."

It sounded like making an appointment with the dentist. "Um, well, sure. Okay. If you want to..."

"I thought... Oh, okay. That sounds great." He hesitated, and she wondered again why all of this dating stuff had to be so hard. "Um, well. What are you doing on Friday? Maybe we could go to a movie or something."

"Um. Okay. A movie sounds good." She hated the way her voice sounded so uncertain. Wouldn't it be better if she was jumping to accept his invitation? Didn't this sound like she really didn't want to go but she was just being nice. Then again, she kind of was just being nice. Did she really want to go on this date? No. Not really. But she beat those thoughts back. He was a guy, a supposedly nice guy, and he was asking her out on a real date-date. And what was she doing? Analyzing. That's probably why no one asked her out. Too much analyzing.

"Okay. Great. Um, I guess if you want to give me your address..."

This was like Chinese water torture. Death by a thousand tiny drops of awkward humiliation. "Okay."

Jason was asleep in the chair. Ben lay on the couch breathing and almost wishing he had taken Kelly up on his offer. He put his arm on his forehead and looked up into the darkness punctuated only by a single shaft of light from the window. Although he didn't want to think about it, his mind went to those days that were barely faded memories right after Tamitha's mother had passed away.

He searched and searched his memory, trying to recall just why he hadn't gone to that funeral. He hadn't. He knew that. But why? What had been so urgent? A sales call? An out-of-town meeting? As he thought about it now, he couldn't imagine what had been that important.

It brought tears to his eyes to realize the depths of his self-absorption. He hadn't even really cared. That's what hurt the most to realize. Their world was falling apart just like his was now, and he had blithely gone on with his life as if theirs didn't matter a whit to him. In the darkness, he shook his head, rolled to the side, and squeezed his eyes closed. If he could just make the thoughts go away, just for a minute.

The sun was already up when Kathryn pulled into the hospice parking lot the next morning. She scanned the vehicles, wishing she knew which one belonged to him even as she told herself that was not the reason she was looking. It was for a close parking spot so she could get out at noon to head to Mrs. Baker's funeral. She didn't go to many of them, but this one she didn't feel like she could miss.

It was always so odd how quickly things went after a patient passed on. There were the preparations, which she did not have a hand in, and then the funeral, and then the family went on with their lives. Sometimes she would pull up a chart and realize it had been a year or two, or five. Her heart filled with the thoughts as she wondered if when Ben was gone if she would remember forever how long it had been since he was here.

She batted those thoughts away. It really was pitiful how quickly they could snatch her sanity. Grabbing up her things, she headed inside. The weatherman had said to expect rain today, but he had obviously been wrong. There were only puffy white clouds in the beautiful blue sky.

"Good morning," she said to Misty who looked up, and it took little to nothing to know that they had lost another. Her heart slammed forward as she glanced toward the door at the far end of the lobby. "How are you?"

Misty's smile was sad and regret-filled. "Mr. Gunthrey passed away this morning at six."

"Ah." Kathryn let her things rest on the counter as she absorbed the news, stupidly thankful the name was Gunthrey not Warren.

"They all went home last night even Mrs. Gunthrey. Her kids thought it would be best for her to get some rest. They took a night off, and that's when he left."

Kathryn's heart fell with the news although it did not surprise her. There were too many times that the person passing on waited for just such a moment. While they were waiting, it was rarely clear just what they were waiting for. After, many times, it was abundantly clear. This was one of those times.

"Have they come to get their things?" Kathryn asked.

"They'll be here in about thirty minutes. Her daughter just called."

"Okay." Kathryn picked up her things once more. "Oh, I'm going to Mrs. Baker's funeral at one."

Misty nodded. As Kathryn walked down the hallway to her office, she thought how hard it was on all of them. It would have seemed like they would get used to it, and some of them did, but something told her that Misty never would. Kathryn was glad for that. It gave her the sense that she would never be left to face this job alone.

She left her things off in her office and went down to Mr. Gunthrey's room. At least she could make sure there was no trash to sift through when the family showed up.

It had been a long night. Ben had awoken with every sound, tossed, turned, and thought far too much. When he opened his eyes to the morning light, he found Jason sitting in the chair, looking far too much like he was sure he, himself looked. Haggard and worn out.

"Morning," Jason said.

"Ugh." Ben pulled himself up. "Morning." He rubbed his eyes. There wasn't even an adjustment to the room. It felt like he'd been in this room for his whole life.

"I was thinking about running down to get some coffee," Jason said. "You want to come?"

"Oh, uh. No. You go on. I'll just hang out for awhile."

Jason stood and stretched. "K. I'll be back." Instead of walking to the door, he stopped first at the bed, and the knife of self-recrimination ran through Ben once again.

He put his head down as he laced his fingers and tried to stop the ever-present thoughts. After a moment, Jason moved on and departed. Ben flopped back onto the couch. Another day in this depressive hell. Lovely.

"Oh, Kathryn." Jason stopped her in the lobby as she got to the door to Mr. Gunthrey's room.

She turned and smiled. "Hi, there." Without pause she left the door and came over to him. "How's everything this morning?"

He shifted feet, gazing more at the carpet than her. "We're okay I think. Um, I was wondering if you knew how we could get in touch with Dad's church. I don't think anyone has called them yet, and I thought they should know."

"Oh, gosh. Yes. Of course. Let's go to my office. We can call them from there. The information should be on some of the paperwork somewhere."

He followed her down the hall, glancing back, his hands shoved in his pockets. "I probably should've told Ben before I said something. I mean we talked about it last night... kind of, but I don't really know him all that well, you know? I sure don't want to step on his toes or anything."

Now that they were at her office door, she didn't really either. She turned. "Do you think we should go back and say something?"

Jason looked like he'd been caught coming in after curfew. He slid his hand through his hair at the side of his head. "I don't know." He glanced back down the hallway. "I just don't want to make anything any worse, you know?"

Kathryn nodded, considered, and then opened her door. "Why don't we talk it through a little? We don't have to decide right away."

"Okay." He followed her into the room and sat on the opposite side of the desk as she took her seat.

She thought about looking for the paperwork but decided to wait.

With a sigh and not more than that, he started. "I've always dreamed about what it would be like to see Ben again. I mean it was so long ago when we left, and there were just these vague—I don't know what you'd call them—memories, dreams, hallucinations of what he was like, you know? I would make up stories in my head about what he was like, what they were like."

"They?"

"Him and Dad. What were they doing, what they were like, what they would think of me if I ever saw them again." For a moment, Jason paused in thought. "And then Dad came for the wedding, so that piece was kind of filled in, but Ben was still this big mystery."

His gaze came up to meet hers. "I just don't want to mess up with him. I've waited so long to have a brother, and now that I have one, I just feel like if I make the slightest move out of square, he's going to pitch me back into the pond."

"This must be really tough to want to be a part of the family but not really have a place."

"It's not his fault. I mean he's been here. I haven't. I get that. It's just…"

"You're not sure where you fit."

"Something like that."

Pieces floated around in no discernible order. Should she ask? Finally she decided she needed to if for no other reason than to have something of a grasp of the situation. "So you were with your mom then?"

"When I was about five, Mom and Dad split. The court said I had to go with Mom, but Ben was thirteen so he got to choose."

"And he stayed with your dad."

Jason nodded. "Dad had to pay child support for me, so we never really lost touch. I mean I always knew his address and stuff. But Ben… I don't think Dad really told him much about where we were or anything. I'm kind of surprised he thought to call me at all if you want to know the real truth."

Kathryn was nodding just to keep him talking. He seemed to need to get the story out, and she wasn't going to stop him.

"When Dad came for our wedding, he said that Ben was real busy, but Ben said Dad never said anything to him about it. At least that's what I got out of it. I don't know. This is all just really confusing. I want to be the brother and the son, but I don't know how to do that."

"Well, I don't think it's something you can just step into and know how to do. Being a family takes more than just blood. It's sharing a history and knowing each other too. I mean there are families that come through here that are in a battle with each other. They are far more enemies than families. But every family is different. Every family has to find their own rhythm. Maybe that's what you're doing now, finding your own rhythm."

"Maybe." Jason sat, thinking without really moving.

Kathryn thought about everything he had told her and his earlier idea of calling the church. "I don't want this to sound too personal, but I'm curious, do you have God in your life? Is He important to you?"

Slowly Jason nodded. "My best friend back home was the youth minister's son. I know all the stories about youth minister's sons, but Ty was nothing like that. He got me through some really tough times. A lot like Kelly and Ben I'd guess. They brought me to the Lord when I was twelve, and God's been in my life ever since."

Without even looking, Kathryn saw the sticking point. "But Ben doesn't agree."

"We haven't really talked about it." Jason shook his head. "I thought about bringing it up, but I feel like I'm walking on eggshells with him. I don't know what is safe to talk about and what's not."

Kathryn knew the feeling.

"It's not that he's a bad guy," Jason continued. "He's just…"

"Closed," Kathryn finished, and Jason nodded.

"Yeah. I mean I know he's scared. I am too. I know he's dealing with a lot and I don't want to make it any worse."

"But you don't know how to have input without doing that."

"Kind of."

"Tell you what." Kathryn turned and rummaged through the file folders lined in the slots on the side file cabinet. "Why don't we…" She found the one she was looking for and rolled back. "… just look here and see where your dad went to church. Ah, here it is. St. Jude's. Father Patrick. Oh, good. You'll like Father Patrick."

However, when she looked up, there was a definite tinge of fear in Jason's eyes.

"Is something wrong?"

"Dad… Dad was… Catholic?"

She looked down to verify. "Looks like it." Her gaze came back up to his. "Is that a problem?"

His face said it clearly was though he was now fighting to disguise his surprise. "Uh, no. Well, kind of. I mean I'm an evangelical Christian. I don't know much about the Catholics."

Kathryn fought not to laugh out loud. He looked downright terrified. "Well, if it makes you feel any better, I'm Catholic."

That surprised him even more. "You are?"

She bent her head. "And, this is a Catholic hospital."

"Oh." He seemed to shrink.

"We're not so bad once you get to know us. I know we get kind of a bad rap sometimes, but…"

"I… I didn't mean."

She smiled to settle his concern. "I know what you meant, and it's okay. Trust me on this, you're going to love Father Patrick. He is one of the best."

Swallowing his trepidation, Jason nodded. "Do you think we should run this by Ben first?"

"I'm ready if you are."

Kelly had called to check on him. In a way that was nice, in another, it just reminded Ben how atrocious his own behavior had been when Tamitha's mom had died. Certainly he had fumbled the ball big time on that one. As he sat there, berating himself for all of his shortcomings, the door snapped and Jason followed by Kathryn came into the room.

Quickly Ben sat up, feeling like there were 900 pounds of guilt and shame piled on top of him. "Good morning." At least the greeting sounded almost human.

"Morning," Kathryn said. She stepped past Jason, and Ben got the impression they were about to double team him.

"To what do I owe this honor?" He was being sarcastic, and it showed.

Gracefully she sat down on the chair, and he knew by the look in her eyes something was up. His gaze bounced up to Jason who wouldn't even look at him. Yes, something was definitely up.

Before he could ask, she took a small breath.

"I know this has not been easy on you, and Jason and I want to honor what you want, but we feel like it's time to call in your dad's minister."

The words pushed Ben backward. "I… have no problem with that. I said that, right?" He looked up to Jason for confirmation.

"Yeah." But Jason still wasn't really looking at him.

"Okay," Kathryn said with no edge to the word. "We just wanted to make sure before we made the call."

"Y-yeah." Ben looked back and forth between them. "Yeah.

Make the call. What? Did you think I would say no?"

"No." How she stayed so calm on the outside when her insides were about to explode, Kathryn would never know. It had to be the Holy Spirit. "No, but we just wanted to check."

"Yeah, yeah. That's fine. Will they like, come over or something?" He tried to hide it, but the agitation screamed through his every shifting and fidgety movement.

"Yes. I'm sure Father Patrick will want to come and give your dad Last Rites."

Ben looked up to Jason who was getting that terrified look again. The prayer to the Holy Spirit was a breath as Kathryn realized this was going to take more guidance than she had initially thought.

"Last Rites or Anointing of the Sick is something the Catholic Church does when a person is either sick or dying. Father Patrick will bring the Holy Oil and say some prayers for your father. It is really a very peaceful prayerful time. Then I'm sure you can talk with him about anything you like—the services or what comes next or whatever. He really is a wonderful priest." Although she did her best to sound convincing, neither of them looked even a tiny bit more at ease. "Don't worry. I'll explain everything to him when I call."

Ben was the first to nod, followed by Jason. They both looked shell-shocked.

The last thing she wanted to do was to walk in and start imposing her will upon them. "Um. Would you like for me to let you two talk it over some more before I call?"

Older brother looked to younger brother for guidance, and she felt the conversation pass between them.

"No," Ben finally said, "make the call." He sounded infinitely more certain than he looked.

Kathryn left to make the phone call, and Ben watched as Jason sat down in a heap in the chair. For someone who had brought this whole thing up, he seemed rather reticent.

"I guess this means you're not big on this God stuff either, huh?" Ben asked, sensing a connection he hadn't realized was there.

"What? Oh, no. I mean, God and me, we're cool. I just didn't realize that Dad…"

Ben waited, but there was no end to that sentence. "That Dad… what?"

Jason laced his fingers and glanced over to the bed. "That Dad was Catholic."

Not sure why that should make any difference at all, Ben frowned. "And that's a problem?" After all, he'd grown up Catholic, not that it made a dent in his thought processes today. He was just surprised that Jason was so surprised.

"Well, no. I guess not." Jason's brow furrowed. Then his gaze jumped up to his brother's. "I'm sorry."

That surprised Ben even more, and worry dropped over him. "For what?"

"For… you know, questioning it."

The farther they went, the more confused Ben was getting. "Questioning what?"

"Him being Catholic. I mean I…" The sentence trailed off into oblivion as Jason watched his fingers lacing and unlacing.

This was getting them nowhere.

"I thought you believed in God," Ben said, but it was closer to a question than a statement.

"I do. It's just…" He looked like Ben might punch him if he kept going.

"Just what? Jase, whatever it is, say it."

It took more than fifteen seconds for him to even start, and the hesitation did not settle Ben's nerves at all. "I don't know. I just… I only know some about the Catholics, and I've always thought they were kind of… weird."

Ben was trying to follow, but it wasn't working all that well. Religion was really not his forte. "How so?"

"Like it was more of a cult thing. That's just the way they taught it where I went. I never really thought I even knew a Catholic. Now I find out Dad was Catholic."

"So you don't remember going to Mass when you were younger?"

Jason shook his head. "I don't really remember much about anything when I was younger. It's all just blurs and feelings, not really much of anything concrete. Then sometimes I catch something I think might be concrete, but I don't know if it really is or if that's just how I wanted it to be."

In a strange way Ben had never really thought of what it was like for his brother. Of course he didn't remember much. He was so young when he left. Love or something very much like it touched his heart. "What do you remember? About back then?"

The look in Jason's eyes was at once panicked and terrified. "Oh, uh. I don't know. Not much really."

Sensing his brother's struggle though he didn't really understand it, Ben leaned forward. "It's okay, you know. I'm not giving you a test."

His brother never picked up his gaze. "It feels like you are."

Anger and confusion reached for him, but Ben ducked them at the last minute. "I'm sorry about that. It's just things have been coming at me like rifle blasts. Half the time I don't know if I should duck right or left, or just be a man and take it in the chest."

"I know the feeling." Then Jason looked up, and there was a glimmer of hope and connection there.

Ben considered all the avenues he could go. Finally he took a slow breath. "I want you to feel a part of this. I do. I just... I'm having a really hard time here. I've never faced anything like this, and I guess I'm realizing that was kind of on purpose."

Confusion traced across the worry on Jason's face. "How do you mean?"

A moment's thought and Ben leaned back on the couch. "I don't know. I... I'm not real good at serious, important life stuff. I do much better if the whole thing stays up here." He glided his hand horizontally through the air. "On an even keel. Nothing big. Nothing major. Just living."

"Go to work. Earn a living. Go home. Maybe have a little fun," Jason said.

Ben nodded, surprised his brother knew anything about living like that. "Last night I got to thinking about Kelly and Tamitha and her mom. I remember giving Kelly a hard time about feeling left out when he missed the poker game like three weeks in a row. He said he wasn't trying to duck out, but Tamitha was really having a hard time with everything."

That conversation came back to him with a snap. It felt like a punch to the gut. "I told him we were going to forget about him if he didn't get his butt over there." His heart ached with the callousness with which he had treated his friend. Why they were even still friends, he had no idea. He let the couch back catch him. "I was such a jerk."

Jason said nothing to contradict him, and silence engulfed them as Ben thought through everything.

It would've been easy to traipse off down the self-pity path, but then he realized he would be doing life the way he had always done it, and enough was enough. He needed to find a different way, and here was as good a place to start as any. Yanking himself forward, he focused on his brother. "So tell me about this Catholic thing. Does it really bother you that much?"

There was a breath followed by a long silence. "I don't know. I really don't. I mean it did at first, and it still does, kind of. I just... I don't know what to think. Not that I'm going to take off or anything. I'm just not sure what to expect. I mean what's that whole thing about anyway? Is it for real, like something normal people are part of?"

"I think you're asking the wrong guy that one." Ben's gaze went over to the bed. "I do know that Dad believed in it very strongly. He always wanted me to take it as seriously as he did, but I was too busy... being me I guess." Then he had another thought. "What about Mom?"

"What about her?"

"Didn't she go to Mass?"

That stopped Jason. His eyes went wide. "Uh, no. Not that I remember anyway. We didn't go to church at all."

Ben thought that through and then nodded. "Maybe going was more his idea than hers."

"No, Mom thought church and God was a big waste of time. That's what she always told me when I went."

"Went?"

"My friend Ty talked me into going where his dad was the youth pastor. We went every Sunday and Wednesday. They really were a rock for me when I could very easily have gone floating off down a different twist in the river."

When Ben leaned back this time, it was to get more comfortable as he wanted to hear this whole story. "So you had a tough time then?"

"Oh, yeah. Not that I got into trouble or anything. I was just a really lost. I didn't fit much of anywhere. I didn't play sports or band. I wasn't all that smart or that talented. I just kind of floated through school. Then when I was a freshmen in high school, Ty moved in, and he invited me to church. I guess I finally found the place I fit."

"So you like church?"

"I love it. I feel safe there, like I belong."

A pang twanged in Ben's heart at the thought of his little brother feeling so alone for so long. "I wish I could've been there."

The smallest of smiles came to Jason's face. "Me too."

"Mrs. Gunthrey," Kathryn said as she crossed into the room. On one side the woman's daughter stood, a small box in hand to collect their mementos and belongings.

"Oh, dear Kathryn." Mrs. Gunthrey turned to her, and Kathryn gathered the old woman in. "Thank you so much for everything."

Tears slipped into Kathryn's eyes. "I'm so sorry for your loss."

"It was time, dear. It was time."

Kathryn stepped back and leveled her full attention on the woman. "So, do you have everything? Do you need anything else?"

Sadness clouded the woman's faded blue eyes. "Prayers."

With a nod, Kathryn fought to keep the tears from falling. "You've got it."

"Misty, please let me know when Father Patrick gets here," Kathryn said five minutes later as the door closed behind the Gunthrey's final exit. "I've got to get some paperwork done."

"K." Misty bent her head back to her work. "Oh, did Nathan call you last night?"

"He did." Kathryn was already headed down the hallway. "And that's all I'm telling you."

"Oh, come on!"

Making sure she sashayed just a bit more, Kathryn kept walking. Of course that would drive Misty crazy, but the truth was Kathryn really didn't want to talk about it. Nathan and Friday night was freaking her out. Trying to sound excited for her friend's benefit was too much to ask. In her office she sat down and slipped the paperwork for Mr. Warren back into its folder. "Dear

Lord, please hold the next couple of hours in Your hands. I know Jason is freaked, not to even mention Ben. Please, please be with them and with Father Patrick, and with me too."

She smiled at that request. He was probably tired of hearing that request by now, but there was no way around the fact that she needed as much help here as she could get. She glanced at her watch. It was already almost 11:15. She hoped Father Patrick would hurry. And with that thought, she got back to work.

Eleven

"Knock. Knock." Kathryn pushed into the room with her head down and then picked her gaze up and peeked in.

Ben saw her first and came up off the couch. Jason followed from the chair. The center of Ben's chest vice-gripped into a knot when he realized it was her. She really was beautiful. Where that thought came from, he had no idea, and he readjusted the waistline of his jeans at the thought that she might be able to read his mind.

"Hi, guys." She came all the way in then, followed by a little, balding man of about 55.

He had only a ring of dark hair around the low perimeter of his head, and he was dressed all in black with the little white collar thing at his neck. Ben knew the outfit well from his days of serving for Mass. That seemed a different lifetime now, and in a way it was odd that there were still priests on the planet. It had been so very long since he'd seen one. He'd almost forgotten they existed.

"Ben, Jason, this is Father Patrick," Kathryn said, indicating each in turn.

Ben's gaze snagged on her hand, which moved with such grace and confidence. He really liked that hand. Then he yanked his attention back to the reality of the moment. He held out his own hand to shake the older man's hand. "Father."

"It's nice to meet you, Ben. Your father spoke about you often."

"Oh. Well." Ben stepped back, his gaze bouncing to each person in the room. "That's... nice."

Jason shook Father Patrick's hand as well but got only the

word, "Father" out.

Looking over, Ben's heart went out to his little brother, and lest it become too awkward for him, Ben took over.

"Well, Father, Kathryn says you want to do some ceremony thing?" He looked to Kathryn for confirmation of that, but she was looking only at Father Patrick.

"Yes, I brought the oils to give your father the Anointing of the Sick," Father Patrick said. His manner was quiet and completely respectful. "Are you familiar with the Sacrament?"

Ben hadn't realized there would be a test. "Uh, well, no, not really." He looked to Kathryn for help. "I'm not really all that religious…"

He had expected a rebuke and harsh words. Instead Father Patrick only smiled softly.

"I understand. If you would like, I can explain a little about it?"

It was more an offer than a question, Ben was touched by it. "Yeah. I'd…" He looked over to Jason and for the first time felt they were both in the same boat. "We'd like that."

Father Patrick nodded. "We can sit if you want."

"O… kay." Ben turned back for the couch and headed that direction.

"I'll just leave you…" Kathryn started.

Instantly Ben spun. "I… Um, could you stay?"

True indecision went through her eyes, and his heart pleaded with her not to leave him with this one.

Finally she sighed and smiled as if forced. "Okay."

As they all took their seats, Kathryn resisted looking at her watch. *God, I'm going to have to be on Your time here. You know I need to eat lunch before I go to the funeral. How am I going to get all of this done?* But she couldn't leave Ben and Jason. They needed her. She just wished she could split herself into three people.

"The Sacrament of the Sick or Anointing of the Sick used to be called Last Rites," Father Patrick began, and Kathryn sincerely hoped he didn't launch into an all-out Catechism lesson.

Patience, Kathryn. Find your patience. She focused on breathing and pulling patience to her.

"It used to be given only when a person was on death's

doorstep, but we have come to the understanding that physical healing in the context of the spirit is needed many times throughout life, not just at the end. So now we give an Anointing of the Sick regardless of if the illness has progressed to the point of death or even if it might very well be healed outright."

Across the small space, Ben nodded, and Kathryn was grateful for that. He needed to find some peace, and maybe this finally had a shot at allowing him that.

"As for today, we can do either the simple anointing or we can do a reading from the Bible and maybe a prayer or two if you would like, but basically we are simply asking God to be merciful to your dad and to come into this moment to give you all peace and wisdom."

Ben sat for a moment and then shifted slightly, wondering why the priest hadn't talked about burning candles and strings of garlic. "And that's it?"

He knew he sounded skeptical, but truly he couldn't help it. He'd seen the movies with the priests doing exorcisms, and though he had also been part of the church and never seen one in person, he'd just assumed they did them when no one was looking or something.

"That's it. And it's totally up to you how much we do. Would you like to choose a Bible reading or just do the anointing?"

Boy, that question was way out of his league. He looked first to Kathryn and then to Jason, unsure of how they wanted that question answered. For himself, he had no clue.

"Uh, could we do 2 Corinthians Chapter 4:16-17?" Jason asked, and they all looked at him.

Father Patrick pulled his Bible out and found the reference. His smile affirmed the selection. "That is an excellent choice. Shall we?"

They all stood, and Ben followed but slowly.

The room suddenly seemed quieter and smaller as Ben watched them all go toward the bed. Standing, he adjusted his waistline and cleared his throat. It took actual force to get his feet moving, and his progress to the bed was slow and hesitant. The closer he got, the more his head swum for lack of oxygen. With the three of them buffering him from the sight of the bed, he heaved a breath, closed his eyes, and bowed his head.

It was a minor miracle that he didn't pass out right there. The swaying of his body told him that was a possibility, and he willed himself to be strong, to not think about what was going on, and to just get through it. That was much easier said than done.

"Father God, we come before You today to ask for Your mercy and Your love for our brother Ronald. In this life we are called to walk with You in faith. Ronald has done that, Lord. Now we ask for Your gentle arms to encircle him and to guide him on this his final journey home."

If he could just keep all the words outside of himself, Ben could get through this. He shifted on his feet carefully and willed a wall up between himself and what was happening just in front of him.

"A reading from 2 Corinthians," Father Patrick said. "Therefore, we are not discouraged; rather, although our outer self is wasting away, our inner self is being renewed day by day. For this momentary light affliction is producing for us an eternal weight of glory beyond comparison, as we look not to what is seen, but to what is unseen; for what is seen is transitory, but what is unseen is eternal."

A moment and he closed the Bible with the smallest of claps. In any normal room, the sound wouldn't even have been noticeable. Here, it was bone-jarring.

"Kathryn," Father Patrick said, taking something from his pocket. "Will you please hold the Holy Oils?"

She turned from her position next to the priest and accepted the small bottle. It took another moment before Father Patrick continued.

"Lord God, You have said to us through Your apostle James: Are there people sick among you? Let them send for the priest of the Church, and let the priests pray over them anointing them with oil in the name of the Lord. The prayer of the faith will save the sick persons, and the Lord will raise them up. If they have committed any sins, their sins will be forgiven them. Lord, we have gathered here in Your name and we ask You to be among us, to watch over our brother Ronald. We ask this with confidence, for You live and reign forever and ever."

"Amen," Kathryn said.

Father Patrick stepped just past Kathryn to the head of the

bed and put his hands gently on the white head of the man laying there. Ben watched him do this and then put his head down and let his eyes fall closed. To just keep standing there was taking everything he had. Watching would be more than he could do.

After a brief moment, Father Patrick turned to Kathryn and took the bottle. He tipped it, got some oil and put it just below the white shock of hair. "Through this holy anointing may the Lord in His love and mercy help you with the grace of the Holy Spirit."

"Amen," Kathryn said softly, solemnly, and Ben's gaze went to her. Of course, she had surely done this a million times, and yet she looked as if this time were truly special.

"May the Lord who frees you from sin save you and raise you up," Father Patrick said.

"Amen." This time it came from both Kathryn and Jason.

With a slight scowl, Ben glanced at both of them. What did they need him for? Certainly not this. He blinked those thoughts back, annoyed both with the situation and himself.

"Now, if we could say the Lord's Prayer together." Father Patrick reached to either side of him for their hands. "Our Father, Who art in Heaven…"

Ben didn't know the words, so he closed his eyes and prayed they would forget he was even in the room.

"Hallowed be Thy Name. Thy Kingdom come. Thy will be done on earth as it is in Heaven."

A moment and as the words continued, he sensed movement. When he opened his eyes, Jason was turned to him, gazing at him as he continued to pray.

"Give us this day our daily bread, and forgive us our trespasses."

With his free hand, his brother reached back for him. Ben flinched at the offer. Finally he lifted his hand and placed it in his brother's.

Jason immediately turned back. "As we forgive those who trespass against us."

A shakiness invaded Ben's soul. They all knew how to do this. He had no clue.

"And lead us not into temptation but deliver us from evil. Amen."

In the middle of the group, Father Patrick released the hands he held, and the others followed suit. Glad to be let go, Ben stepped back once again and crossed his arms over his chest, hoping this wouldn't last much longer. His stomach was beginning to clench so tightly he thought he might be sick.

"Father in Heaven, through this holy anointing grant Ronald comfort in his suffering. When he is afraid, give him courage, when afflicted, give him patience, when dejected, afford him hope, and when alone, assure him of the support of Your holy people. We ask this through Christ our Lord."

"Amen," Jason and Kathryn responded.

"Amen," Ben breathed.

Once again Father Patrick stepped to the head of the bed. "May the blessing of God, the Father, and the Son, and the Holy Spirit, come upon you and remain with you forever."

"Amen." Ben almost managed to get his in at the same time as the other two.

For a moment after the blessing, no one moved, and Ben wondered what came next. That sounded like the end. In fact, Father Patrick had closed the book, but still no one had moved. Father Patrick reached down and touched the pale hand that remained motionless on the bed. He bent his head and seemed lost in prayer or thought or something for a very long moment. The quiet of the room screamed through Ben's shredded soul, whipping through the tatters and sending a shiver through him. He reached up to scratch his ear and wondered at that just as he heard the thunder clap outside.

All four gazes went to the window which had the shades drawn and thus gave no view of the outside world.

"The storm was coming in as I was driving over," Father Patrick said to Kathryn.

"I was really hoping it would hold off," she replied.

He smiled. "Can't keep the storms at bay forever." Then he turned and addressed Jason who stood right next to him and Ben who stood slightly behind all of them. "We can talk here about the services if you would like, or there is a small conference room down the hallway if you would prefer."

"Uh." Ben hesitated, his arms now firmly crossed over his chest. He looked to Jason and then to Kathryn. "I guess the conference room if that's okay."

Kathryn nodded as she looked at them all. "It should be open."

Father Patrick nodded. "That will be fine."

Kathryn didn't want to have to leave, but it was nearly noon. The rain slithered down the large window in the lobby, giving testament to the fact that the storm had indeed arrived. Outside the room, she turned to the group, not wanting to go but knowing she had to. "I'm going to go on if that's okay."

From just behind the group, Ben's heart jumped in protest. She was going to leave him now? What was she thinking? Then he stopped himself and questioned his own motives. What was he thinking? She wasn't his guardian or even his friend. She was doing her job, and she'd already gone above and beyond the call of duty in that respect.

"That's fine," Father Patrick said. "I believe we can handle it from here."

"Please let Misty or one of the others know if there's anything you need."

"All right." Father Patrick held out his arms. "Thank you, Kathryn."

"You're welcome." She accepted the hug and then glanced at the other two. "I will be back after awhile if you need anything."

Somehow Ben got himself to nod. He had no clue what Jason's reaction was because he couldn't focus on anything other than his own distress. His arms were still crossed, but his head was bobbing because he knew nothing else to do.

"Okay, we'll see you later, Kathryn," Jason said, putting an arm out to her. "Thanks."

She gave him a quick hug because he was standing right next to her, and then she smiled in Ben's general direction. "Take care."

"We will. You too," Father Patrick said.

With that, she turned and walked away down the lobby. Ben's heart went with her. What did she have to do that was so important? More important than them? Of course that wasn't fair, but he really didn't want to do this alone. Maybe it would've been easier if she had stayed. Probably not, but there was always that thought.

"Gentlemen, the conference room is this way," Father Patrick said, opening his hand in front of them.

Even as his gaze fell, Ben nodded and forced his feet to follow.

With the rain, she was really going to have to hurry. Kathryn let Misty know she was leaving, ran through the cafeteria and grabbed the first small sandwich she came to. She would have to eat in the car. The funeral was only 45 minutes away in St. John's Lutheran Church. She'd been there several times so it wasn't like she needed a map. However, with traffic at a near standstill because of the downpour, her progress was slow and painstaking.

The rain came down in sheets, and she wondered as she drove where the beautiful blue skies from earlier had gone. Were it not for the weather forecaster's warning of this, she would never have seen it coming. Knowing that getting in a hurry would be dangerous, she defaulted to the only way she'd ever found to keep herself calm in tense situations.

"Dear Lord, be with us today." Her mind went back to the room and to the brothers so tentative and unsure of even the beautiful anointing Father Patrick had offered. "Dear Lord, please be with Jason and Ben. Open their hearts to Your love and to giving us Catholics a chance." She laughed at that softly. "I think Jason thinks we've got two heads or something. Please show him that we're not so bad, and that we really do love You. Show him that we are all Christians no matter what the sign out in front of the building says."

Then her thoughts slid back to his brother, standing behind them all. Yes, she had noticed, and it bothered her to no end. It was truly amazing how he could be in a group and be so separated at the same time. She wondered about that and then because she could think to do nothing else, she prayed about it. "God, Ben is having such a difficult time with this. I know how much You love him, and I know how very much he needs Your peace. Can You show him, Lord?"

A rumbling clap of thunder that tunneled down through the enormous buildings was her only answer.

"Lord, he needs You. Please be with him—with both of them."

"Your father has been in to discuss his final arrangements," Father Patrick said as he pulled some papers from his black notebook. "I think it would be helpful if we went over them, so that you both can see what he wanted."

On the other side of the table, Jason reached for the papers and began scanning them.

"As you can see, he wanted a simple Mass, not much fanfare. He was quite specific about the Gospel. The other things were mostly suggestions, so if you have other things you would like instead, I'm sure he would be okay with it."

Ben was less curious about the papers than the topic. "You said he came to discuss final arrangements."

Father Patrick's attention swung over to him. "Yes."

"How long ago?"

There was a small pause.

"Last month actually. It was right after the 9 a.m. service, and he wanted to put some things in writing because as he said he didn't want anyone to have to worry about it."

The smile that brushed Ben's heart was a sad one. That was his dad, always taking care of everyone else. He wondered then how clearly his father had known something like this was coming. The bills, the arrangements. He had to have known. It couldn't be that big of a coincidence.

Then Father Patrick's gaze fell, and Ben knew there was something else.

"He also gave me these," Father Patrick finally said slowly as he pulled two white envelopes from the notebook. "There is one for each of you. He told me to give them to you after his death as they were simply what he wanted to say that he was never able to. I can hold them until after if you would like. Otherwise, I see no point in not giving them to you now. Would you like to have them now or later?"

Jason's gaze snapped across the table. "There's one for me too?"

"There is."

Breathing had become a real issue again as Ben sat there, his mind screeching that somehow this was for real, that they were discussing his father's funeral and that his father was indeed dying. How was that possible again? How had he gotten here? It all seemed so very surreal.

"Well, I don't know about Ben," Jason said, glancing over, "but I'd like to have mine now."

Father Patrick nodded and slipped one of the envelopes across the table. He fingered the other as he waited for Ben's decision.

Ben looked at it, lying there on the table like it was a snake in the grass poised to strike. *No! I don't want that thing. I don't want it! I want my dad. No letter could ever take his place. I want him. Why can't anyone understand that?*

"I can hold yours until later," Father Patrick said as gently as words had ever been said. "It's your decision."

My decision? What part of any of this has been my decision? None of it. I hate this. I hate all of it. I don't want to make this decision or any other. What I want is for all of this to be over, gone, some stupid, horrible bad dream.

A clap of thunder shook the building, and Ben's gaze jerked to the ceiling. Even his arms uncoiled for a second. When his gaze came back, Father Patrick had not moved.

"I... Hm." Ben cleared his throat and pulled himself forward on the chair. It felt like he hadn't talked in months. "Um, I guess I'll take mine now too."

Father Patrick slid the envelope over to him, and Ben picked it up carefully. He turned it over and then over again.

"Do I have to read it now?" he asked, feeling the tears welling up inside him and really not wanting an audience when he opened that thing—if he ever did.

"When you're ready."

"We gather today," the pastor said, "to honor the memory of Emma Baker. I remember Mrs. Baker from the first time she showed up on my doorstep. I had just arrived as pastor, and Mrs. Baker came with a basket of cookies and breads like I'd never seen before. And every Monday morning she brought me something from her kitchen. She always said she wanted to make sure I was eating right because I didn't have a wife to look after me. Funny, I think her making me eat right put on at least a few of these pounds."

He patted his rounded belly, and the fifty people in attendance laughed. "Emma Baker was a quiet soul. She didn't command the fanfare of the world. She lived quietly and simply." His gaze fell to the seats in front just beyond where the casket stood. "When Emma's granddaughter Bonnie was killed in a car accident, Emma took in her two great-granddaughters, even though she was nearly 80, and she loved them with a fierce love and determination that were an inspiration to witness."

He smiled at them both. "She would have moved the moon for you girls. I want you to know how often her prayers were for you. She loved you both very, very much."

Kathryn sniffed her own tears back as she saw the heads of the two young women come together up front. Rachel was holding her younger sister, and Kathryn was glad that going forward they would at least have each other.

"In closing, I want you to take the lessons Emma taught through her life to heart. Make the right things important, step up when you are needed, and even if your life is not lived for the whole world to hear, your life can be a beautiful legacy to those closest to you. Emma, we love you and we miss you. May God and His angels take you home."

"I think I'm going to take a walk," Jason said when they got back to the room, and Ben noticed the envelope still in his hand. Ben's was in his pocket, mostly because he didn't want the reminder.

"Okay. I'll be here."

When Jason stepped out, Ben collapsed on the couch. He tipped back and pushed the shade back off the window. Sure enough the rain was coming down here too. It seemed to be everywhere, not the least of which in his soul.

A nurse stepped in and pulled up short. "I'm sorry."

"No. No. That's fine." Ben waved her onto her job as he pulled the envelope from his back pocket. Over and over he turned it in his fingers. What could his father possibly have to say to him like this? Not wanting to think about it, he flipped the envelope over onto the little table, spun so he could put his feet up on the couch, and leaned his head back onto the armrest. It wasn't even close to comfortable, but he was so tired, it hardly made any difference at all.

"Rachel," Kathryn said only the name as she stepped up to the first young woman in the receiving line at the graveyard.

"Kathryn." With that, Rachel grabbed her and tears flowed from them both. It was like this with some. There was just an automatic connection. Kathryn could never tell which it would be. At first she had felt guilty for that, but she had come to accept that that was just how it was.

"She loved you," Kathryn said, running her hand down over the long brunette tresses. Rachel was so very young to be the matriarch of the family, but sometimes those roles passed quickly and early.

"Thank you so much for coming." Rachel stepped back.

Kathryn followed suit. "Let me know if you need anything."

Rachel nodded, and Kathryn stepped on to her younger sister. In no time she was walking back through the rain to her car parked in the driveway of the cemetery. There was no good day for a funeral, but rain seemed a particularly bad choice. At her car, she looked back at the little knot of family left and said a quick prayer. They would get through this. God would see to that.

Her role in this passing was complete, so she got into her car and drove away.

"I got all the bills squared," Kelly said as he entered. Jason was on Kelly's heels, the two of them obviously in deep discussion. "I called the lawyer again, and I'm going to go pick up the will after work. All he needs is for one of you guys to call in so he knows I'm legit. He knows you guys don't want to be out running around right now."

Ben pulled himself up on the couch, trying to remember where reality was. Somehow he'd dozed off. In fact, the nurse was no longer in the room. He yawned and let his eyes go closed as he put his head onto the back of the couch. There was no telling how long he'd been out. By the feel of it, forever sounded about right.

"Kelly needs us to call the lawyer," Jason said clearly not sure that was his task.

"Oh, okay." Ben looked at his watch and nodded, really truly having a tough time snapping back on to life. "Why don't you go ahead and call him? We might as well get that done."

Jason agreed and stepped back out into the hallway. Kelly stood only a moment more and then sat down in the chair.

He reached over and hit Ben on the knee. "How are you holding up?"

Instead of answering, Ben let out a long sigh and glanced at the drawn shades. "I feel like I've fallen off the planet. Is there still life outside?"

"In fact, there is. It's raining today, don't you know?"

"Still?" Ben folded the shade back to find the same scene as before.

"It's not supposed to let up until like Saturday is what they said."

Saturday. That was such a strange thought. Saturday could be a month from now for all Ben knew. "What is today anyway?"

"It's Thursday."

Ben nodded as the thoughts from the night before came back to him. He reached up and scratched his head, figuring out how to get the words in his heart to come out onto the air. "Kell, I need to tell you… um. I'm so sorry about Tamitha's mom."

"Oh, that's…"

"No. Kell. Hear me out, okay?" Ben searched for the right words and then realized there probably weren't any. "I was a real jerk the way I treated you, and I'm sorry. I had no idea what something like this was like. I've been thinking about it since last night, and I was about as inconsiderate and obnoxious as anyone has ever been."

"Ben. Please…"

"No. I was. I see that now, and I want you to know I'm sorry about that."

Kelly's smile was tight. "Sometimes it's tough to see if you've never been there." He leaned back slightly. "Look at me. I've been there, and it took me four days to get my butt in gear and get over here. It's just… it's tough."

It was good to have at least apologized, and now, for the moment it was time to move on. "We talked about the funeral today, and we'd like you to be a pallbearer."

"Oh, dude." Kelly sat forward. "Are you sure about that?"

Ben nodded. "Dad had it in his notes. He loved you like a son."

"Well, I'm honored."

The windshield wipers slapped back and forth across the window doing no good at all. Buckets, sheets, cats and dogs—Kathryn had never seen a downpour like this.

"Remnants of the upper level disturbance will be with us for the next couple of days," the weatherman said on the radio. "Get out the galoshes. We're in for a deluge."

"Lovely." Kathryn reached over and turned the station. The last thing she needed was more depressing news. As a soft instrumental came through the speakers, her thoughts went again to Ben and Jason in that room. Ben looked so very sad and also so very lost. He hung back.

She snagged on that thought and slowly traced back through the times of being in the room with him. On the couch. In the chair. On the far side of the room. Worry came as understanding drifted through her. Had she ever once seen him get close to that bed? Had he ever once touched his dying father?

No, she decided with a snap in her spirit. He hadn't. He was there, yes. Omnipresent almost. But he stayed on the fringes.

That wasn't uncommon. Many people had great fear of seeing a person in their last days up close. Just as many couldn't go up to a casket of someone they loved. What was odd was how lovingly Ben spoke about his dad. His dad was his hero, and yet now, it was like he didn't want to see his hero this way.

She turned carefully into the parking lot and laughed when the thought went through her head that she hoped he wouldn't decide to come out and sit on the curb again. She really didn't want to get soaked. However, as she put the car in park, she knew she would brave even a torrential downpour to make sure he wasn't left to deal with this alone. Grabbing up her purse and her belongings, she got out and ran for the door.

"Holly just called," Jason said when he came back in the room. "She's decided to come with her mom."

Ben sat forward, worried for the sister-in-law he'd never met. "Do you think that's a good idea?"

Jason laughed. "You don't know Holly. It hardly matters much what I think." He let that settle. "They're flying in at nine, so I think I'm going to get a hotel. We can stay there tonight and come in tomorrow morning."

"A hotel?" Kelly asked. "Why don't you guys just stay with us? We've got plenty of room, and we're really not too far from here."

"Oh, I'd hate to put you guys out."

"It's no trouble. Tamitha would shoot me if I made you stay somewhere else."

Funny, Ben thought, how often Kelly said things like that. Tamitha would shoot him, Tamitha would have his hide, Tamitha would have him sleeping on the couch for a month… Ben wasn't quite sure what to make of that, but it went through his mind just the same.

Jason checked his watch and glanced over at the bed. "It's already almost four. I think I'm going to head on out so I can grab something to eat and figure out where we're going. Is that okay, Kell?"

Kelly jumped up, and Ben's gaze went up with him. "Yeah, sure. No problem." Then he looked down at his friend. "You going to be okay?"

No! screamed through Ben, but he forced a smile and a shrug. "Of course. I will. You guys go on." The words stuck in his throat as his heart asked if he really wanted to be here alone. No, he didn't, but he also didn't have much choice. Somehow he stood, but he had no idea how that had happened.

Then as if he had stepped off reality, he knew they were discussing something, but he couldn't even hear them. His gaze and focus had gone to the floor, willing his feet to stay standing there. Swallowing, he forced his gaze up and his mind to rejoin reality.

"Okay," Kelly said. "Then I'll meet you there." He looked toward Ben who straightened as his hands went up to the opposite arms and rubbed there. "Call us if you need anything."

The smile hurt. "I will."

"And let us know if anything changes," Jason added.

"I will."

As she stood giving Misty the quick version of the funeral, the door at the end of the lobby opened. Kathryn's attention snapped there as Kelly and Jason emerged, bending toward each other, deep in conversation. She tried to get her words and thoughts back on track, but she'd forgotten what she was even talking about.

"Kathryn," Kelly said, looking up and spying her.

"Hi, guys. Is everything all right?"

"We're taking off for the evening," Jason said. "My wife's coming into town. We'll be back in the morning."

They had stopped and were angled so that she had her back to the desk, and they were circled to the right and left in front of her.

"If you don't mind watching over Ben while we're gone," Kelly said, glancing back to the door.

"Say no more." Kathryn put her hands up. "I'll make sure he doesn't make a break for it."

They shared a laugh that was almost happy.

"Thanks again for everything," Jason said and leaned in to hug her. Kelly followed suit, and it panged through her heart that someday these two would have no reason to come by, no reason to want to see her. But she pushed that away.

"You're welcome. Take care, and drive careful."

"We will."

With that and a wave, they walked out.

"Too bad the young one is married," Misty said. "He's cute."

In annoyance, Kathryn turned. "You are hopeless."

Why did Kelly and Jason have to wake him up? Frustration crammed into Ben's chest, dispelling air and rational thought. He'd finally gotten to sleep. Finally. For one minute the thoughts had left him alone, and then they had to spoil it. Terrific. Now sleep was nowhere to be found. He looked at his watch. It was winding around to five o'clock. Actually it was nearly 30 minutes earlier than that, but his heart had already calculated that if Kathryn didn't come back before five, she wasn't coming back at all. And five felt like it was coming at the speed of light.

She'd mentioned having something else to do, and he wondered what that something was. Trying to think of something else, he pulled the shade back to look out. Same dreary, depressing gray was drawn in slithering streaks down the window. He let the shade go and heaved a sigh. Maybe he should go home too. What good was he doing here anyway?

He'd been here for days waiting for something that looked no closer to happening now than it had when he got here. If he could just think of something to do to keep his mind off the thoughts that streamed through his head like an incessant rain. Some were memories, some were accusations. The bills were a testament that something was wrong long before now, and yet he hadn't seen it.

Would he have seen it if he had been paying attention? He didn't know. One side was adamant that he would have, the other wasn't so sure. And they battled back and forth until he just wanted to scream, "Shut up already!"

Then there was the matter of his father going to talk with Father Patrick. Did that mean his dad knew something was wrong? Would he have told Ben if he'd have asked? How bad was it? Was he misplacing things, forgetting things? What? And if so, how long had that been going on?

The worst of all was that there would never be any answers to those questions. He would live the rest of his life and never know. Slowly he let out a ragged, hurt-filled breath. The beginnings of a headache gnawed on his skull. It was the missed sleep and the not eating. He sure could go for some of that cold cafeteria chicken right now. A tranquil, tired smile came at that thought, but it was quickly drown in the melancholy.

Sitting back, he considered going out to see if he could find her, but he discarded that idea. She didn't need to be babysitting him. She had other patients, other responsibilities. Besides, she would be gone in fifteen minutes anyway. He looked at his watch. Thirteen minutes.

He dropped his wrist back to his chest because it weighed a ton, and he put his head back on the couch. He was going crazy. That's all there was to it. He was just going to go stark raving mad, and then none of this would matter. He wouldn't even be sane enough to care. The middle of his mind contemplated how he might make that come faster.

"Don't think," he told himself. "Just stop thinking."

But it was all he had left to do.

Twelve

"You leaving early?" Misty asked, noting the coat and briefcase.

"Yeah. I'm just going to look in on Ben, and then I think I'm going to go home to a nice hot cup of tea and a long relaxing bath."

Misty shook her head. "Trade ya. You can go home for me and make mac and cheese for two whiny kids and a husband who says, 'We're having this again?'"

Kathryn laughed. "Thanks for reminding me why it's great to be single."

"That's what I'm here for." Misty took a handful of charts. "If I don't see ya leave, have a good night."

"You too. Don't have too much fun."

"I won't. I promise."

The ceiling was the kind with the little silver metal strips that held up white tile things in the middle. Ben hadn't noticed that before, but as he sprawled there, his head resting on the back of the couch, the rest of him stretched out like a waterfall over the couch, he counted the tiles. There were five vertical and five horizontal.

"Five times five. That means there are 25 tiles on this ceiling, plus those two over by the door." He didn't even try to stop the counting. It was much more merciful than the thoughts. "Let's just see if that's right. One, two, three, four…"

The snap of the door didn't even really jolt him. Propriety said he should sit up, but he really couldn't even find the energy to care.

"Eight, nine, ten, eleven."

And then, somehow Kathryn was sitting in the chair looking at him. "Whatcha doing?" Her gaze went up to where his was fixed.

He never moved. "Counting ceiling tiles. When I get finished with that, I plan to start counting the little black dots on each one. I have a theory."

"Oh? What's that?"

"I'm betting that each tile has the same number of little tiny black dots on it. I'm betting they make them all at some plant in Sheboygan, and they stamp all those dots in there with some big machine called the Little-Black-Dot-Maker."

Slowly Kathryn put her things down on the floor next to her, slid down in the chair, and angled her gaze up to the ceiling with his. "You think? It bet it's called a Dot-o-meter."

Intrigued, he nodded. "A Dot-o-meter. I like that. What else you got?"

She didn't remove her gaze from the ceiling. "I wonder how they get it to stay up there. I mean it's not glued to the ceiling, right? If it was, you wouldn't need the little steel strip-thing-a-ma-doogiys."

"Thing-a-ma-doogiys?"

"Yeah. Thing-a-ma-doogiys. Why? What would you call them?"

"Don't know I was too busy counting little black dots to think about what I would call those little steel strip thing-a-ma-doogiys." Ben was amazed at how peaceful he suddenly felt. Just drifting on a simpled-out cloud. He liked this even though he knew it couldn't last.

"Have you eaten?" she asked after minutes had slid into timelessness.

"I had a donut at ten, does that count?"

Nothing about her was quick as she sat up, leaned her elbows on her knees, and looked at him. "Well, I had half a squishy sandwich at noon, and I'm starving."

Something of his old bravado with women overtook him, and he looked over at her and smiled mischievously. "And you expect me to do something about that?"

"Well." Her gaze slipped back up to the ceiling. "I mean I know how busy you are solving the mysteries of the ceiling tile and everything, but if you could tear yourself from utter inanity for a few minutes..."

As if he was frustrated and annoyed though he was neither, Ben pulled himself forward on the couch. "Well, I guess, since you put it that way."

They got their table next to the wall again only this time Ben took her tray to return it to the tray holder. Kathryn had left her belongings back in the room, so she was glad she would have an excuse to go back after they were done. Counting dots on the ceiling. She shook her head and laughed at the absurdity of it. Not that it was bad, just a little weird in a surreal kind of way.

"I guess this means you don't have a hot date tonight," Ben said as he slid into the chair opposite her.

Emptying a packet of Sweet'N Low into her tea, she shrugged coquettishly. "I do tomorrow night, does that count?"

That stopped him, and he backed up slightly. "Really? So who's the lucky sucker?"

Petulant annoyance dropped on her, and she considered not answering. However, propriety got the better of her. "Well, if you must know, his name is Nathan, and he's Misty's cousin."

"Misty from the front desk Misty?"

"That's the one."

Ben nodded, and she couldn't tell if he was interested or merely counting more dots. "And this is a new thing, an old thing, a we're almost married thing?"

She about choked on her tea. "Um, no. Definitely not on the almost married thing. Actually I've never even met him before."

"Ah, a blind date." Ben rubbed his hands together and dug into his spaghetti. "Those are the worst."

"Tell me about it. I wouldn't even go, you know, if it weren't for Misty and my mom and sister thinking I'm going to die a spinster if I don't go out with someone."

His eyebrows reached for the ceiling. "Someone?"

"Anyone. As long as he's breathing and he has a pulse."

"And a pulse? Oh, now that's going to be tough to find someone with both things." He opened his bottle of water and took a generous drink.

This time she laughed. "Yeah, tell me about it."

"So you don't go out much?" he asked as he set the bottle down and started eating. He looked famished.

"Not a lot."

He wrapped spaghetti all the way down the tines of the fork. "So you work, you go to church, you don't go out. Sounds fascinating."

Defensiveness crawled up onto her. "It's just you know the kind of guys out there these days... They aren't exactly hero material anymore."

"Oh, so you're like Tina Turner then, looking for a hero."

Kathryn felt the heat creep into her cheeks as she reached for her tea. "I didn't mean it like that. I just mean, they've got this thing about you'd better impress them in five minutes or you're not worth their time."

"And you're not impressive?" The question sounded almost surprised.

"Hardly. Home, work, and church are not on the top of most guys' lists of a fun time out." She took a bite of her small piece of chicken. It was dry and had no flavor at all.

"Okay, well, minus the blind date guy, you got any others on the list?"

For someone just counting tiles, he sure was sounding interested.

"A couple." She shrugged. "Maybe."

"A couple maybes. Hmm..." He took another bite, and they both chewed in silence. "Well, that's a start."

A question snagged in her brain, and for a long minute, she beat it back, and then she decided what was the harm? It was something to talk about. "What about you? I see you've got no ring on that finger."

"Uh, yep." He held it up. "And proud of it thank you very much." His gaze fell, and twirling spaghetti, he looked only at his plate. "No, I'm one of those non-hero types. Trust me on that one."

She couldn't help it. Her gaze jerked up to him so quickly she felt the jolt.

"Marriage is definitely not for me." He only glanced up once as he picked up the spaghetti on his fork. Then he smiled at her like the Cheshire Cat. "I'm having way too much fun being single." Stuffing the forkful into his mouth, he chewed, and something about the way he did so made her want to smack him. "I've got a nice apartment, a nice car. I can go out when I want, come in when I want. I don't have to answer to anybody. Why would I want a wife?"

Suddenly Kathryn felt more alone than she had in a long time. "I don't know." The plate in front of her grabbed her gaze and held it. "So someone could hold you on rainy nights when it's cold or you've had a rough day. So you could have someone to talk to who understands and really cares." Her gaze came up to his but then fell again. "But maybe that's all just a nice fantasy." She sighed and cut into the last two bites of her chicken. It was something to do. "I see the other couples, you know, the ones who have been in love and who are screaming at each other and hurting each other now, and it just tears me up that they don't see how lucky they are."

The soft almost pleading of her words touched some long-forgotten space inside Ben. He felt it, and it took him completely by surprise. Quickly he disregarded it, pushing it away from his heart and his consciousness. "Yeah, well, people are people. The best thing to do is to remember that going in so you don't get your hopes up." He hadn't meant it to sound bitter, but it did even to him. He reached over and took a long drink of his water because he wasn't going to apologize for saying the truth although he felt like he should.

Her gaze still down, Kathryn nodded. "I guess with your parents and all that it had to have been pretty rough."

Shock smashed into him, and his face fell into a scowl.

"You told me some. Jason filled in a little more." She looked up at him, and there was only a deep, deep sadness in her eyes. "Some of it anyway. He said he went with your mom, and you decided to stay with your dad."

Hard hate for the details of his miserable life being aired for everyone to see slapped into his spirit. "Yeah? Well, Jason should learn to keep his mouth shut."

Her gaze fell to her plate, and after a moment, she pitched her fork there making it clang against the plate. Sad and contrite, Kathryn looked up at him. "I'm sorry. That was way out of line. I shouldn't have said anything."

Closing his eyes for a moment to squelch the pain, Ben took a breath. "No." When he looked at her again, he could see how deeply the error had mortified her, and knowing her, that didn't surprise him at all. "It's not you. I shouldn't be so crazy about all of this. I'm sorry." The lion of anger inside him stood down. "I know you were just doing your job."

"Yeah, not very well."

Compassion for the difficult lines she walked daily brushed past him. It was time to change the subject although only slightly. "It must be tough listening to sob stories all day."

Her smile brought up only one side of her mouth. "I don't mind. People need to be able to get stuff out. If they don't, wounds don't heal, and if they don't heal now, they might never get the chance."

"Still it's gotta be tough. I don't know how you do it." He lifted his eyebrows as he played with the spaghetti left on his plate. "I couldn't do it. That's for sure."

After a moment, she shrugged with only one shoulder and ran her finger over her glass. "Sometimes I wonder if I can." She let out a long sigh, and her eyes fell closed. Shadows of deep pain slipped across her face like gray clouds filled with wind and rain.

At first he thought she would say more. Instead she shook her head and looked out across the cafeteria.

Worry for what she wasn't saying crossed over his heart. "But you're so good at it." He knew the words wouldn't help, but he had to say them just the same. She had to know what she meant to them, and if she didn't, he wanted her to know.

"I wouldn't know about that. Half the time I have no clue what I'm doing and the other half I'm just hoping nobody figures out I have no clue."

That surprised him. He sat back, letting his fork rest next to his plate as he studied her. "I don't understand. You always know what to say, what to do."

She laughed softly as her gaze shot back across the room. "Hardly. I've just gotten real good at walking on faith rather than sight."

At one time he wouldn't even have asked. Now it felt like he had to. "That's one of those God-things, huh?"

"Yeah." She let her eyes go wide as she took in a long breath and then released it in a rush. "I guess it is."

Ben watched her for a long moment, seeing things he hadn't bothered to see before now. "You look tired."

Her gaze came to him then as her shoulders slumped. "Do I?"

"Yeah." He considered the question as she looked back down, and he wondered if it was his place. Still she had done so much for him, he wanted to pay her back even if it didn't fix everything. "Want to talk about it?"

Kathryn's heart panged forward. She knew what the answer to that question should be. More than that, she'd never really talked about her job with anyone not connected to it in some way. What could she say, and what was off-limits? She considered changing the subject, but nowhere in her brain could she find any other topic. Finally she sighed. "Sometimes I just feel so inadequate."

Her mind traced backward through the rain and the day, and there were plenty of examples. "Like today, these two beautiful young ladies buried their great-grandmother. She was the one who had taken them in when tragedy struck, and now she's gone too. I mean, what do you say to them? What good does, 'I'm sorry' do? Did anything I did even make a difference?"

Overwhelm was coming to the surface, and every onslaught hurt. "And I know that the next couple of weeks will be so hard for them." The center of her heart ached with the futility of everything. "I always think I'm going to remember and pray for them, but somehow I forget. I forget their names and their faces. I forget how long it's been since they were here. I've finally started just saying general prayers for all of them because I've forgotten so many that I thought I never would. And I feel bad about that. I mean I want to love them all, and I do. And I know… I know that God isn't mad at me for not being able to love them like He does, but I still feel bad about it."

When she finally stopped talking, the gaping chasm left in the conversation screamed that she had said too much. What was he supposed to say to that anyway? She wouldn't know what to say to that, how did she expect him to know? He just sat there, staring at his plate, and even through her own tears, Kathryn berated herself for dumping her life on him. That wasn't fair. Not now. Not ever.

"I'm sorry," she finally said, sensing she'd made him really uncomfortable. "This isn't your problem. I shouldn't have said anything."

"No. That's not it." For one second, he glanced up, and his eyes were filled with words she couldn't decipher, but then his gaze fell back to his plate. "It's just..." A moment and then another and his gaze came up to hers. As hard as she tried, she still couldn't read the words written there. "You have to know I never would've made it through this without you."

She brushed off the compliment. "You would have."

But he shook his head. "No. I don't think so. Everything is so... crazy. Half the time I feel like I'm going to outright lose my mind. The rest of the time I can tell I'm spinning that direction, and I have no idea how to make it stop. The thoughts are just... overwhelming."

Kathryn nodded. "Boy do I know how that is. Why do you think I spend so much time in the chapel?" It was supposed to be a joke, but he didn't laugh.

When he looked at her, it was with sincere hope. "So does that really work?"

"Better than anything I've ever found. It doesn't take away all the pain. That's still there. It's just that God is the only place I know to go with it. He probably gets tired of hearing from me." She laughed at that and then fell into seriousness. "No. I know He doesn't. Thank goodness because I can be really obnoxious sometimes."

"Obnoxious? I wouldn't say that." He looked at her with eyes that melted her insides. Although she could hardly hold his gaze, she couldn't break the spell he had her under either. Then he leaned back casually without ever breaking the connection. "I think beautiful would be a better word."

Utter disbelief dropped over her. She ducked and pushed a stray piece of hair over her ear. "Oh, yeah. Right. Now I think you're delirious."

But he did not laugh. A long moment and he leaned toward her. Serious was the only emotion on his face. He put his elbows on the table and laced his fingers together in front of him as he continued to survey her. Everything in her suddenly felt shaky and uncertain. Why was he looking at her like that?

"Honest," he said softly. "It's called being honest."

Not sure if it was because of where they were or the context of the situation or just that she wasn't at all sure what to make of any of it, Kathryn exhaled hard and looked at her watch. "Wow. We'd probably better go. I didn't realize it was getting so late."

"Oh, yeah." He moved to stand but slowly, and he hadn't quit looking at her either. "I'm sure you're ready to get on home."

She tried not to think about the loneliness of home. "Yeah."

They walked slowly side-by-side back to the room. Ben had his hand in his pocket lest it betray him and reach out to her. Yes, some of it was the kindness she had displayed to him and his family over the past couple of days, but it was more than that. At least one part of him said it was more. Then again, things were so very off-kilter, he couldn't be sure of anything at the moment.

"I can't believe it's still raining," Kathryn said as they walked down the long hallway, and he felt her voice in his heart. "I was hoping they were kidding about this lasting."

She still seemed so quiet and sad. Ben wanted to do something to change that, but when he opened the hospice door, he realized how few options he had in that regard. In minutes she would be gone. Nothing in him wanted to let her go.

"So Jason's wife is coming."

He didn't like how she could sound so very proper like that. It reminded him in colors far too vivid that she was just doing her job. Worse, she seemed to have gremlins telling her all of his secrets. That scared him far more than he wanted to admit. He realized that the two issues were on opposite sides of the spectrum, and he couldn't logically fault her for both, but he couldn't quite figure out how to stop his spirit from analyzing and re-analyzing everything she said either.

"Yeah, I guess so." He knew he didn't sound overly happy about that. The truth was he was almost to the point of not being able to feel anything that made any sense.

"You've never met her then?" Each word was slower and more drawn out so that they hardly seemed connected.

"No." At the door, he opened it and pushed it for her to enter. When she passed in front of him, he knew he needed to break this attraction. It was getting harder to ignore.

In the room he focused only on her moving before him as he put both hands in his pockets. Beautiful. She was so very beautiful. And now, she was by the chair, picking up her things. Leaving. She was leaving. His breath lodged in the top of his chest and refused to move from that spot. It scrambled the thoughts in his head, making them completely unintelligible.

"Um, you know." He scratched his head, hoping he didn't sound as desperate as he suddenly felt. "Father Patrick left us this little booklet thing about the... service." Lands, what was he doing? He should let her go. That was best for both of them. Still his spirit was flying forward with a crazy recklessness he couldn't quite take hold of.

When she turned to face him, logic scattered in all directions. The little light behind her made the strands of her soft blonde hair look like they were glowing.

"Um, I don't really know much about these things. I'm just... I mean I know you need to get home and everything." Like a pinball spiraling around, he reached up and slid his hand over his hair as his feet shifted. Then with great effort, he corralled his ricocheting spirit. "I'm sorry. I shouldn't..."

"No." She was looking at him with pity in her eyes, but now he was just absurdly grateful she was looking at him at all. "Don't apologize. I know how difficult these things can be."

"I... I would ask Jason, but he's kind of..."

"Not sure about the Catholic thing?"

His nerves began to relax. "So you noticed that too, huh?"

"Would've been hard not to." Kathryn laid her things to the side of the chair, and for the moment he could breathe again.

However, concern that someone close to him had made her feel uncomfortable surged on him. "Did he... Did he say something?"

She straightened, and her hand pulled down her blouse to straighten it as well. "Nothing I haven't heard before. It's all right. Really. I'm used to it. You would be surprised how many people think Catholics aren't Christian or are some kind of a cult, and all kinds of weird stuff I won't even go into."

"Like what?" Now that she wasn't leaving, Ben stepped to the couch, perfectly happy to discuss anything—even if it had nothing to do with his excuse for asking her to stay. When he turned and sat, he watched as she took her seat in the chair. She seemed hesitant, but he was so thankful she had agreed to stay that he chose not to dwell on that.

"Well, I've had people tell me to my face that I'm going to hell for being Catholic."

That pushed him back. Who would do something like that? "You're kidding."

"Oh, no I'm not. But it's okay. They don't get a vote anyway."

He didn't understand. "A vote?"

Her smile lit a warmth deep in him that he didn't quite comprehend except he could feel it in her eyes. "I learned a long time ago that only two people get a vote on if I'm okay or not. Me and God, and even my vote doesn't count."

The deep joy with which she said it drew him even closer to her. He wanted to understand even if he could never have that for himself. "Yours doesn't count?"

Resolutely but with a smile, she shook her head. "My grandma used to tell me that God loves me, and He's the only one that gets a vote—not even my vote counts, so I should stop being so darn hard on myself."

"So that's where the 'be gentle with yourself' thing came from?"

Sadness poured into her eyes and over her face. "Pretty much. It's good to remember when people try to run you down."

He couldn't stop the awe. "You're amazing, you know that?"

She laughed outright. "Where did that come from?"

But he was not to be deterred. "Why? You don't think so?"

Her gaze fell to her hands. "Hardly." She looked up and scratched her nose. "But thank you for saying it." Then her gaze slipped around the room. "Hm. You were saying something about the service readings?"

"Oh, yeah." Honestly, he wanted to continue the current conversation, but he didn't know how. So instead, he reached over to the little table and picked up the booklet that Jason had laid there. He swept it forward, dragging the envelope underneath it right off the table. It floated to the ground just in front of her feet, and Ben froze at the sight.

"Oh!" Kathryn bent to retrieve the vile thing from the floor.

His heart jerked hard with the vision of her picking it up. The last thing he wanted was for her to know about that thing. "I'm sorry. I forgot that was there." Nervousness jolted through him as he reached for it. When it was back in his hands, he just wanted to get rid of it, but his mind wasn't working nearly as efficiently as the rest of him. Where to put it? On the table? In his pocket? In the trash? "Um."

Swallowing, he finally replaced it on the table, shifted on the couch, exhaling slowly and knowing no way to explain it, he paged through the little book. His gaze stayed down though he didn't even focus on the little pages. He wouldn't look up, he couldn't. He didn't need to see what was in her eyes to feel her thoughts. "I think Jason said he had the readings, and Father knows the Gospel. It's one Dad picked out. I'm supposed to figure out the Proverb or something like that."

"Psalm. I bet it's the Psalm." Without questioning, she put her hand out for the book, and when he glanced up to transfer it, he came face-to-face with the softest kindness he'd ever seen.

Fighting not to fumble the transfer, he handed her the little book. And then, although he knew he should find something else to focus on, he couldn't take his gaze from her. She was fascinating, amazing, quiet, calm. All the things he wasn't. His spirit jangled at that thought.

"My favorite has always been Psalm 23." She paged through the book, sat back, and shook her hair out. "The Lord is my shepherd; there is nothing I shall want." She continued reading, but he no longer heard the words only felt the impression that they created in his soul. It was like floating on a feather buoyed on a gentle breeze. He leaned back, crossed his fingers in front of him, and just let the words and her voice brush over him. A moment and he closed his eyes. Sleep was a real possibility, not because he was tired but because everything in him suddenly relaxed.

"Only goodness and kindness follow me all the days of my life; And I will dwell in the house of the Lord all the days of my life."

The words stopped, and Ben nodded. "I like that."

"It's the one they read at my grandma's funeral, and I've never forgotten it."

He opened his eyes, and he couldn't help but feel that something had changed between them. Had she been anyone else, had they been anywhere else, he would easily have leaned over to her, kissed her, and taken her into his arms. However, the barriers between them were too obvious, so he stayed where he was and let only his mind play out the fantasy.

"What?" she finally asked, her face falling with concern.

Nothing in him could tear his gaze from her. "How do you do

that?"

Reaching up with the hand not cradling the little book, she slipped her finger under her hair and tugged on it. He loved everything about every motion she made. Although he blinked to get the feelings and thoughts back to reality, they didn't leave. Slowly he pulled forward, and when he got to the point that his elbows were on his knees, it was like trying to stop a thousand horses as he held himself back from her. The way she was looking at him, the dim light, the connection he felt with her but couldn't even come close to explaining.

Her gaze snapped from his and fell. "I... I should go." She stood even as she laid the little book on the table.

His heart leading the way, Ben followed her up as he reached out to stop her. "Please don't." His hand connected with hers between them, and the electricity of that touch was like lightning flashing through his soul. Every nerve stood on end as he found himself only a foot from her. She was shorter than he remembered, smaller. Somehow he got himself to let her hand go, but his heart would not let him let her go as easily as he looked down at her. "Please."

It sounded so selfish, so pathetic, but he didn't care. He didn't want her to leave, not now, not ever. "I don't..." Closing his eyes, he fought to breathe. "I don't want to be here... alone."

Kathryn fought the tears that welled up in her heart. She didn't want to leave him like this, but how could she stay when what she was feeling was so very improper? How could she stay professional when every look he gave her whispered words to her soul that she'd never heard before? How could she get herself to remember he was a client when he felt like so very much more?

God, please help me. I don't know what to do.

"I know I have no right to ask this," Ben said, his voice husky and strained, "you've already done so much, but I just... I don't want to be here by myself. Please stay."

If she could just get all right with leaving him... Kathryn wanted to growl her frustration at him, but that wasn't fair. He was vulnerable and frightened. It was her job to make this passage as smooth as she could. *Okay, God. I'll stay, but You're going to have to do this one because I really can't.*

Amazingly she didn't fall apart when she looked up at him. "Okay. I'll stay, but only for awhile."

He should have felt relief, but the panic in his soul that she might leave at all gripped him. Still, he nodded, glad for the momentary reprieve. "Thanks."

Backing away from him, Kathryn smoothed her skirt under her as she sat. Her gaze slipped over to the little table, and his followed. Terror seized his heart. *No! Please. Please don't ask. Please.*

She reached over and picked the envelope up. "Is this from Father Patrick?"

Ben collapsed back on the couch, wishing he had just let her leave. "No." The word was soft and ragged. "It's from my dad."

Her fingers ran back and forth softly across the lettering on the front. *Ben Warren* in his father's script. Ben read it even from his vantage point, and he turned his head to not see it. She didn't say anything for a long moment. One part of him thought she might just leave well enough alone. Then her gaze came over to him.

"Are you going to read it?"

He shrugged as if it hardly mattered. "I don't know. I think Jason read his, but…" His gaze drifted back to the letter now resting on her knees.

The moment hung in the room until the soft patter of the rain outside invaded the stillness.

"I don't know what there would be to say," Ben finally continued as defensiveness surging through his spirit. "I mean we know where the will is."

She was looking at him now, not arguing, just listening.

"What could he have to say to me that I don't already know?" Then as weird as it felt, he looked to her for confirmation. When she said nothing, anger smacked into him. "You think I should open it."

"I think you should when you're ready."

Frustration ground out of him, and he stood. "When I'm ready? What does that mean anyway?" He stepped toward the wall as he ran his fingers through his hair. "What is that, some kind of riddle? What if I'm never *ready*?"

He heard her stand, felt her coming closer, but she stopped a couple feet from him and came no closer.

"Letting someone go is the hardest thing you will ever do," she said softly. "It's not for anyone else to judge or to tell you when or how to do it."

"What if I don't want to?" The words knifed him on their way out, and he slammed his eyes closed at the sheering pain they ripped up. "What if I can't?" His breath gasped from him, raking up tears, and he couldn't stop any of them.

"Ben." Her gentle touch on his shoulder tore the last of sanity from him. Whether it was fair to her or not escaped from his consciousness. When he turned to her, there was no hesitation at all. Her arms came around him, and he grabbed onto her, gripping her, praying she would never again let him go.

"I hate this." The words clawed their way out of his heart. "I can't do it. I can't let him go." Tears blurred the rest of the world from his understanding. They pulled up fistfuls of pain from the center of him, and he had no power to stop them. "I don't want him to die. I know he's so sick, but I just can't let him go. I can't do it. I don't know how."

Every piece of everything he'd shoved down inside him started bubbling to the surface. "What am I going to do without him?"

Kathryn held him as the grief tore free and whipped through his battered, exhausted soul. She had been there. She understood what that grief could do to a soul that had loved so much and still did. Death was the cruelest of separations, especially if you didn't believe in a reunion in eternity. "Your dad knows, Ben. He knows you haven't let him go. That's why he's still here."

There were times she said things that there was no logical explanation as to how she knew them, but she did just the same because the Spirit said it through her. This was one of those times. She felt it. "He loves you, and he knows how hard this is for you. He doesn't want to go until he knows you're okay with it."

Next to her shoulder, Ben shook his head. "I don't know how to do that. I don't know how to ever be okay with it." He sounded so very tired, so very sad.

Although she didn't let him go, she backed up an inch. "Have you seen him?"

"Seen him?" Ben relaxed his grip and swiped at his eyes, feeling like an idiot for losing it so completely in front of her. "Of course I've seen him. He's right over there." But everything in him was backing up, away from the figure in that bed and what she might be asking. He didn't want to go over there. He didn't want to see. He was already far too close. Going over there would somehow make it real. There was no conceivable way he could do that.

Kathryn's hand was still on his back, rubbing there, and he could feel that she knew. "You don't have to if you don't want," she said, her voice softening even more. "I know how scary it can be, but he wants to say good-bye. He wants you to know how much he loves you even now."

With tears and short, hard breaths, Ben looked at her. "Why does this have to be so hard?"

"Because you love him so much." She sniffed, but her face was lit in a soft illumination that looked every bit angelic. "That's not a bad thing, Ben. It just means you love him a lot."

"It hurts."

"I know." Her face crumpled momentarily. "I know."

He let out a hard, angry breath. "Why does this have to be so hard? I just want it to not be so hard."

"There's nothing you can do to make it not be hard. It just is. It will be. But you can do it anyway. You can love him enough to do it even if it's hard." Her face furrowed farther, and tears slid down her cheeks. She didn't brush them back nor even seem to notice them, but he did. Those were not fake tears. They were not manufactured. They were as real as his own.

Gently Ben reached over and cupped her face with his hand. His fingers twisted into her hair. Very slowly his thumb moved up to her cheek and brushed a tear away. She laid her head into his strength. It felt good to feel her trust. When her gaze came up to his, she smiled.

"It really will be okay," she assured him. "This is just a step in God's plan. It's a step. It's not the end."

Never would Ben have thought he could even think about doing this, but suddenly the fear slipped away from him, swept aside by the gentle brush of an angel wing. A moment to gather the strength in her eyes and he nodded. "I think it's time."

Kathryn nodded with a sad, compassionate smile. "Okay."

Carefully, gently, she turned and reaching between them, she laced her fingers through his. It wasn't fair what that did to him. His heart dropped through his shoes, and his breaths swirled in his brain. And then she was moving and somehow he was following. A step at a time, she led him toward the bed, looking back every other step to see how he was doing. Had she pushed, he would no doubt have resisted with everything in him. Yet her gaze was far more an invitation than a coercion. There was no pressure at all, and as such, he would surely have followed her anywhere.

When they got to the bed after what seemed a million steps, Ben let his eyes fall closed as the jangling of his spirit began to settle somewhere deep inside him. The moment was more peaceful than he thought one could be. Only the soft sounds of the rain tapping on the window and the halo of light in the room that glowed around them as they stood together by the bed accompanied her in his consciousness. He felt her look at him though he couldn't quite tell how as his eyes were still closed, and then she carefully wound her arms through his and locked them around his waist.

After a moment, he felt her head arch to look up at him.

"It's okay," she said softly. Her hand drifted gently across his back. "Really."

The smallest of breaths and his eyes slipped open. Until that moment, he hadn't realized just how close they were to the bed. When that understanding broke through him, his heart jolted backward with the shock. For one second panic clutched him, and he stiffened in horror.

"It's okay," she said, holding him to keep him from running, but her determination was compassion not force.

Then forcing himself to breathe, he surrendered to this place, and the fight left him. A strange and all-encompassing peace drifted through him—body and soul. His gaze fell to the figure lying there, and grateful recognition filled him. He had forgotten how handsome his father was, how much of a gentleman. He'd always been so proud of the man lying there. The skin was paler now, but the face hadn't changed. It still looked so solid, wise, and intelligent. He loved that face so much.

Next to him, Kathryn relaxed, and then they were simply standing there holding each other, gazing down at the man in the bed.

"He had such a great sense of humor," Ben said, remembering as he laid his head on her hair. It was softer than he had imagined just as being in her arms was so much more peaceful than he had thought. In the circle of them, he let the memories have full rein. "He was always doing something crazy. At one point I went through a wicked punk rock stage."

Her gaze came up to him in questioning surprise, and he grinned and then laughed.

"Trust me, it wasn't pretty." Without question, he pulled her back to him, and she came without protest. Ben shook his head at how good the memories were. He hadn't expected that. "I don't know how he did it, but somehow he got a hold of the songs I was really into, and he learned every word."

"Ugh."

"Yeah. That's what I said. Snapped me out of that phase real quick."

"I'll bet."

Ben laughed and shook his head. "But he was always doing things like that. And he never complained about how nuts I got. Not once." Laughter drifted into seriousness. "I think he felt guilty."

"For?"

"For not being there early on." He let out a long breath, seeing life in a way he never had before. "I was pretty tough on him after the divorce. Not that I blamed him. I knew the score. But it killed me to see Jase leave, and I know Dad felt horribly about that.

"A lot of things changed after that. Not so much because Mom was gone, but more because Dad made it a point to be there like he hadn't before. I used to think that was because he didn't trust me, but now I think it was because he felt guilty about how things had turned out."

Kathryn's hold on him tightened but only slightly. "Blame is a weird thing. It ties us up in ways we can't really break free from until we forgive the other person or ourselves."

"I think he blamed himself even though it was really her fault." Ben swallowed that memory. It still hurt more than he wanted to admit. He waited for her to ask, but for some reason she didn't. Part of him tried to work on why, but it really didn't matter. He needed to go down this road even if he didn't want to. "I was there. I knew what she was doing."

Kathryn moved only a half inch on his chest, and Ben wondered how stupid he had to be to tell her this.

"She would take us, me and Jase, when she would go to the other guy's house. I was like twelve at the time, so she'd leave me in the car with Jase to babysit I guess."

There was now no movement at all in his arms, but she was listening. It was so quiet he could feel her heartbeat. He thought about that thing she had talked about keeping your arms opened, and he wondered how hard that was for her at this moment. It was truly incredible how many different directions his mind was going. Past, future, this moment, that moment, her, him, his father. Somehow he was thinking about it all at the same time.

"I hated her for it. I hated what she was making me do and that I was supposed to be okay with it and just go along with the program."

"How old was Jason?"

"About four." He shook his head at how deeply those feelings of hate, hurt—and love ran. "I loved that kid. I would've killed for him."

"And your dad didn't know?"

"Not for a long time. He'd come in some nights late from the hospital, and he'd come in my room and say, 'How ya doing, Slugger?' That's what he called me, and I'd just keep my head down doing my homework or whatever and say, 'Fine.' I hated lying to him, but I knew what she was doing would kill him, and I didn't want to do that to him."

"But he found out."

"Yeah. I don't even know how. We never really talked about it. It was just one day everything was like it always was. Then that night I heard them screaming at each other down the hallway. I figured he must've found out, and I remember going to lay with Jase that night so he wouldn't get scared. The next day Mom packed up and moved out.

"The house was so quiet after that." He exhaled hard. "It was like we were all trying not to talk about or even think about what was going on." Squinting, he tried to fit the next part into some timeline, but even now, he had a hard time doing that. "The next couple of weeks were just weird. I went to school and tried to act like everything was under control. I couldn't fall apart, not for Dad.

He was having too hard of a time the way it was. And then they had the court date."

It was strange how he could still smell the judge's office. Leather and books. That's what he remembered. "Jason was too young." Ben's heart contracted and refused to relax. He sniffed and blinked the tears back. With everything in him, he wanted to go back and do something to change those few moments. What he could have done, he still didn't know, but he should have done something. "He had to go with Mom."

"Oh, man." Her hug tightened around him, and he hugged her back as the tears slipped from his eyes.

"I didn't want him to. I wanted him to stay with us, with me and Dad. I... I still remember standing there in the judge's room because I'd just told him I wanted to stay with Dad. I was older, so it was my choice. I thought the judge would just see that Jase should stay with us. That seemed so logical to me.

"I remember walking out of that courtroom, and Mom getting in the cab with Jase. I was inconsolable, and I kept telling Dad to do something, begging, pleading with him, but there was nothing he could do." Ben's gaze fell to the face he had screamed at on more than one occasion. His heart ripped apart for one moment to say he was so, so sorry about all of it. "But he never gave up on me, no matter how tough I made it on him." He shook his head. "Never once." He sniffed the tears back though they were still slipping over the spillway of his lids. "I never had to wonder if he loved me. Nobody could take the abuse I gave him and just love anyway."

The tears came faster and harder now, and Ben's whole being crumpled into them. "He was my hero. I wanted to be just like him. And I wanted him to be proud of me. He deserved a better son than I was."

Kathryn shook her head next to his chest even as she held his grief. "He knew the burden you were carrying. He understood even if he didn't always know how to ease your pain."

Ben knew the truth of that. He still didn't know how to ease the pain from back then or from now. However, the slow methodical motion of her hands on his back was doing a good job of dissolving the hardest places inside him. After standing there longer than he'd ever stood in one place, Ben picked his head up a little and angled his gaze back to his father.

"I just wish I could tell him how sorry I am. You know? Just once. So he would know," he said, his gaze sliding back and forth over the immobile figure.

"Tell him now," she said softly. "He's still right here."

Her words hung, suspended in the air above them as Ben closed his eyes and absorbed them.

Had someone told him what he was about to do, he would've called them crazy, but this felt right, more right than life had felt in a long, long time. Kathryn let go of him but didn't so much as move. She looked at him and after a moment, she took his hand and lifted his father's hand from the bed. Gently, she formed the bridge upon which they met.

With the first touch, every broken place in Ben that he had duct taped, strapped, nailed, and glued together collapsed inside him. His heart plummeted, finding no landing place. "Dad..." Tears overtook him, and he shuddered at the avalanche of emotions. "Oh, God, I'm so sorry." The tears came out gasps. "I'm so, so sorry for everything."

His knees gave way, and he started for the floor. Somehow she came under his arm, and he grabbed onto her even as he now held his father's hand with only his own. That hand. It was so warm. Still so warm.

"If I would've known how not to be so dumb... If I would've known what to do so you wouldn't be hurt..." His other hand came over then and gripped the old, withered hand in his. It was the hand that had shaken his as he held first one diploma and then another, the hand that had driven the car to come get him when he'd drunk far too much at that party junior year. It was the one that had rubbed his back when Becca broke up with him just before prom and the one that had welcomed him back home every time he was smart enough to come back.

He held that hand now, gazing down at it, amazed that it was still warm after all this time. "You gave everything, Dad. You loved me even when I was unlovable. You cheered me on when I didn't think I could take another step. You believed in me even when I had no idea how to believe in myself. And I took all of it for granted. I thought you would always be here with me, so I forgot to say thanks. I forgot to tell you how much you meant to me, and now, I'm afraid it's too late."

For a moment he thought the tears would take him again, but

then the clouds cleared, and his gaze did too. His breathing slowed. "I wish I could go back and do it all over again, not to change anything but so I wouldn't miss so much. It all went so fast…" He closed his eyes then and tried to imprint the memory of his father's hand in his. "I love you, Dad, and that's never going to change."

As Ben's words slowed and then ceased, Kathryn let her gaze slide back and forth between them. There was a definite resemblance. Father and son. Son and father. The love of the son for the father was palpable, and so strangely enough was the father's love for the son. The father had given his all to right the son's world after chaos exploded around them, and it was easy to see that love had transcended the connection past the tragedies.

Ben sniffed softly and turned toward her just enough to acknowledge her continued presence in the room. "Do you think he can hear?"

"Yeah, I do. I think his spirit hears just as yours probably hears his message to you."

He nodded. "I wish I could hear his voice again." His gaze went back to the face, and he touched the man's shoulder tenderly. "He had such a great voice. He never raised it either, not to me. Even if he was furious, he would grit his teeth to keep from yelling." The memories lapsed into a long breath. "We used to sit in the mornings, and he would read things out of the paper to me. I don't know why. Maybe we didn't know what else to talk about. I learned a lot about what he believed—not so much religion but about politics and the world and people. He knew a lot about people."

"That doesn't surprise me. If you hang out in the medical field very long, you either deepen your soul connection or disconnect completely."

Ben nodded. "I think he almost did disconnect, right before Mom left, but her leaving changed him. I know it did. I watched it."

"It takes a very courageous soul to see mistakes and decide to change."

"I think he was a lot braver than I ever gave him credit for." Ben pulled in a slow ragged breath. "How much longer do you think we have with him?"

"It's hard to know. It depends on the unfinished business and when he feels it's finished." When Ben looked at her, Kathryn realized he thought she was nuts. She laughed softly. "I've been at this a long time. I've seen a lot of things. Some of it I can explain with anatomy charts and medical records. A lot of it can only be explained if you believe in the realm of God. We had a man the other night that had been here for 21 days. Someone from his family had stayed every single night, and then one night they all went home, and he passed on.

"I can't explain that any more than I can tell you why we're standing here right now, but I believe that the person who is transitioning has an awareness of the plan that we just don't. Trying to control that plan or to figure it out is next to impossible. It's much better to just let go and surrender to the process."

"Transitioning. Is that what you call it?"

"If I believed that this was the end, that this was all there was, I couldn't do this job. It would be too hard. But I don't believe that. I choose to believe that death is a transition into a different type of existence."

"Like a ghost?"

"Like into who we really are. Into the love we really are."

Strangely Ben didn't protest or even raise the question. Instead, he looked down at his father and smiled ever-so-gently. "He's going to be okay then."

"Yeah. He will."

Thirteen

As they stood at the bed together, Kathryn's gaze went up to Ben. He was a good guy with a gentle heart. Sure, he was confused on some points, but she couldn't fault him for something she was guilty of herself. He turned then and looked down at her, and her heart snagged on the ocean-colored eyes.

"Thank you," he said, and there were no tears, no fear, only sincerity all the way to the bottom of his gaze.

She smiled, sensing her mission had been accomplished. "You're welcome." For one more moment she held onto the feeling of being with him. Then her rational side took over, and she glanced back to the chair. "I guess I should be going. I don't want to keep you up all night."

In that instant panic enveloped Ben, not because he didn't want to be left alone but because he really didn't want her to leave. "Oh." His gaze slipped over to where hers was looking. "I... Yeah... I guess so." Then as she stepped to the chair, his gaze fell on the envelope on the end table. He stepped over and picked it up, knowing it was unfair to keep her, but something in him said when she walked out that door, he might never see her again.

"Um. I know you need to go home," he said as he turned the envelope over and over in his fingers. "But I... Um." His heart was hammering in his chest, and he had no way to know just why.

Lifting his gaze, he found her soft, compassionate gaze trained on him.

Without comment, she nodded and sat in the chair. He understood the message perfectly and let his knees lower him onto the couch. Once down, he knew what should come next but he couldn't get himself to make the next move.

"Um." His gaze stayed on the envelope. "I don't..." Emotions started colliding once again. He tried to breathe them down, but the breath came out in ragged jerks. "I'm not sure..."

Gently, she reached over and touched his hand, the gesture and contact jolted through him like an electric shock to his soul.

"It's okay," she said. "Really."

It was like a super-conductor had set off explosions in him, and he had no idea how to get them to stop. Looking up at her, he found only strength and peace in her eyes, and he nodded, understanding what she didn't say. Feeling the couch to be too difficult to continue sitting on, he slid all the way onto the floor and crossed his legs. Gracefully, she followed him, and he fought not to notice the soft curve of her leg and the gentle peace of her presence next to him. They snagged his breath and refused to let go.

He fought to remember how they had gotten here and where they were supposed to go. The clock was crawling back up toward midnight, and somewhere far outside his consciousness he heard the rain still pattering on the window. Still this moment seemed designed just for the two of them—no outside interference whatsoever.

Ben exhaled hard and looked at her. "I almost don't want to open it." His gaze fell to the envelope. "It's like this is it. The last thing he will ever say to me."

Then, though he had no explanation for it, she smiled with a mystery behind it that captivated him. "No, it's not."

Everything else slipped away from him. "What does that mean?"

She tipped her head and shrugged. "You might be surprised how he will find ways to talk to you. It won't be the same exactly, but you'll know he's still here."

He couldn't quite understand what she was saying, but he had no question that she meant it to the depths of her being. "So this isn't the end?"

Slowly she shook her head. "It's only the beginning."

There was no way to really ask what she meant, and in a strange way, he knew what she meant. He turned the envelope over once more. "It's time, huh?"

"Only if you're ready."

A half nod and then a full one coupled with a breath. "It's time." His hands came together, his elbows resting on his knees. It wasn't difficult to open, not nearly as difficult as he had thought it would be. In seconds the envelope fell away, and he took one more breath, opened the tri-fold, and put his hand, wrist up to his lips. It was a sure bet he would need the help keeping the emotions under control.

Kathryn sat, watching him without words. He laughed softly at something in the letter, and she wondered what it said. But this was his letter, his moment, and she knew not to intrude. Instead, she let her gaze fall to her hands on her skirt and a prayer went through her—a silent prayer for him. She wasn't even sure what words went with the prayer, only that she felt it all the way through her.

"Huh." Ben laughed softly, smiled, and shook his head. He looked over at her, and her heart flipped.

Suddenly her breath vanished, and she felt like she was falling far and fast with no way to stop.

"Want to read it?" he asked, and she had no idea how to answer that question.

"I don't…"

"No." The word was soft. He turned the paper over to her. "I think you should."

Not understanding, she took the paper he held out to her. "Okay."

She was intensely aware of him watching her even as she bent over the paper. Reading what was in his eyes was as impossible as reading what was on the paper in the dim light. Pushing his gaze from her consciousness, she adjusted herself so she could make out the handwriting. It was in a script that would take all of her deciphering ability to read.

Dear Ben,

Since you're reading this, I guess the end has definitely come. Please don't be worried about me. I've known this was coming for some time, and I'm okay with it. I know God's love has a plan for me even after I leave this earth. Much of me is excited to start the next chapter. It will surely be an adventure. The only thing that concerns me is you and how alone my departure will leave you. That's why I've made some extra special requests of God, and He has assured me that He has a plan for you as well. I wish I could be there to see what those plans are, but rest assured I will be checking in periodically, so enjoy what is coming into your life. It, too, will be a grand adventure.

If you will indulge your dad in giving one more little piece of advice, I'd like to tell you from one who has been where you are: Do not take the good things for granted. There is a plan, but if you get too caught up in your stuff and doing things your way, you will miss the blessings God is sending. Unfortunately, I did that with your mother, and I almost did it with you. I hope you can find it in your heart to forgive me for being so selfish and for aiming at the wrong goals for so long. I messed a lot of things up in your life, but I hope I got a few things right, too. Please let the good outweigh the bad in your heart, and know that I tried the best I knew how.

Regardless, do not let my mistakes hold you back from living the life God has worked out for you now. He loves you—of that much I am perfectly sure. We've had many, many conversations over you—me and your Heavenly Father. He loves you even more than I, which I still find difficult to believe, but I know it to be true. I know you don't buy into religion and all of that, but I hope that will change for you as it did for me. God brought me through, Ben, and He can do the same for you if you will let Him.

See, I told you this would be a lecture, and you've heard too many from me already. So I will close now, not because this is the end, but because it's time to step into the next chapter. Ben, I want you to know that you are and always were an awesome son. I have been so proud to call you my son, and I would never have traded even a moment we had together. I look forward to the ones we will share on the other side.

For now, last piece of advice, I promise: Make the right things important, don't settle for pleasure when true happiness is possible, and always love like there is no tomorrow. You will never be sorry for it.

Goodbye for now.

Love,

Dad

When Kathryn looked up, the tears streaming from her eyes were reflected on the ones he was wiping from his own.

"I think he knew," Ben said, his words so soft they hardly found the air.

"I think he loved you very much."

Ben nodded. "Yeah. He did."

Looking at her, Ben had the feeling that his father had known far more than just his love for his son. "A grand adventure." He let out a breath. "And here I thought we just lived."

"Maybe living means something more than just existing."

He nodded, sniffing although the tears had faded into numbed exhaustion. "Maybe so." A moment and he forced himself to look down at his watch. "Oh, man. You'd better get home. I've kept you..." He reached back to the couch to pull himself up. However, her hand stopped him, and on his knee, he stopped.

"It's probably not my place, but I have to say, your dad was a very smart man. I see too many people come through here who have made the wrong things important." She stopped and let her gaze fall. "I guess what I'm saying is... I want you to know... Being here, with you... tonight..." Her words faded out into silence, and it was clear she didn't know how to finish that thought.

Ben pushed all the way to standing and then put his hand down for her. It was the most natural thing in the world to feel her hand in his, and his heart began asking just how much his father had prayed. In seconds she was standing there, just inches from him. Kissing her was wrong though that's what he wanted to do. Instead, he stepped over to her and wrapped her in his arms.

"Thank you so much for being here," he said, and his whole body felt the mesh of his spirit with hers. It went through him, all the way to his toes, and he closed his eyes to savor the feeling. He had never felt so not alone.

Next to him, she sniffed, and he felt her tightened her grip around his waist once more. "Will you be okay?"

"Yeah." He nodded, knowing now it was the truth. Gently he rubbed his hands up and down her back, reluctant to let her go, but knowing she needed to get home. A moment more and he backed up, holding her arms in his hands, wishing she wasn't leaving. "Will you be back tomorrow?"

A glint shot through her eyes. "It is tomorrow."

He laughed. "Good point." With that, he let go of her, grabbed up her jacket and belongings, and helped her get ready. "How far is it home?"

"Thirty minutes. Not that bad."

His spirit tugged on him that sending her now might not be safe. "Will you be okay... driving?"

She resettled the jacket on her shoulders and retrieved her purse from him before picking up the rest of her things. "I'll be fine." When she caught his worried look, she smiled. "I promise."

It took him a long moment to get himself to be okay with that answer. "Do you want to call me when you get home?"

"I'll be fine."

"I know you will, but I want to make sure."

She smiled. "Okay."

Kathryn walked through the quiet hospice unit. No one was around, and she was glad for that. Her head was spinning so badly, she couldn't decide how bad it would be for anyone to see her. She decided it was better to not have to worry about the question. Outside the rain had settled into a soft drizzle, and she ran to her car, her keys out and ready. She slipped into the car, brushing the memories back. Could it have been real?

In one way it felt like a dream. In another, it was the most real she had ever felt. She started the car and pulled out into traffic. As she drove, her heart replayed the time with him over and over. One part of her tried to remind her that he was a client nothing more. But there were whole sections of her that wanted nothing more than to forget that detail.

Him, sitting in the dim light. Him, reading the letter. Him, holding her. That one gripped her breath. She could still feel his arms around her. Strong and safe—they felt like Heaven. In her purse on the other seat her cell phone beeped, and she looked at the digital numbers on the clock in surprise. 1:13.

Knowing slipped into her spirit as she dug for the phone with one hand. She pulled it out and beeped it on. "This is Kathryn."

"Well, what a coincidence. I just called Kathryn." Ben's voice sounded like tinkling bells. It was difficult to remember he was sitting in a hospice unit with death itself closing in.

"Well, that is a coincidence." She shook back her hair and fought the laugh. "What are you calling me for? I thought I was supposed to call you."

It was clear he, too, was fighting the laugh. "You were taking too long."

She laughed outright at that. "I didn't know I was being timed."

"Call it insurance. Thirty minutes was going to make me nuts."

"More than you already are? That would be bad."

"Hey." Even over the phone, she could imagine him relaxing back into the couch. No one said anything for a long moment.

"So how are you doing?" she asked more because she wanted to know than for some professional reason.

"I'm good."

"That's good."

"Good? I'm thinking a miracle would be closer."

"A miracle?" The bright lights from the last strip mall spiraled across the hood of her car as her heart jumped in her chest. "That good, huh?"

"Better."

It was nearly two in the morning when Kathryn had hung up with him. The conversation had no earth-shattering qualities to it. In fact, the next morning besides the quietly peaceful feeling she had when she thought about it, she couldn't really recall anything they had really talked about. Truth be told, there were several long stretches when no one said anything, but they were hardly awkward. When she thought about them, thought about just hearing him breathe, it danced across her heart.

She tried to keep herself from floating off the floor as she got ready, wondering what his favorite color was and if he preferred skirts or pants. For whole stretches she even let herself think about what a first date with him might be like—a restaurant or something simpler? She wasn't sure of anything other than it would just be wonderful to be with him.

"Slow down, Kathryn. Don't get ahead of yourself." Her mind traipsed to the calendar. Friday. Then it hit her like a steam roller. Friday. Oh, no! Today was Friday. Her heart plummeted like it had just taken a plunge off a ten-story building. Tonight was her date with Nathan! She hadn't even thought of it in 24 hours.

Her whole body went into rush-and-trip mode. Nerves overtook her. She looked at her watch and realized she was already late. Worse, she was tired and now outright panicky. With a sigh that helped nothing, she grabbed her briefcase and headed out the door.

"Ben... Ben, wake up."

"What?" Ben asked, coming back awake. He'd been having the most wonderful dream featuring him and a blonde-haired beauty walking on a sun-drenched beach. Fighting to figure out where reality was, he reached up and raked his fingers through his hair.

"Ben, wake up, man."

"Kelly?" Squinting into the memory of where he was and why he was there, Ben searched his friend's face and then looked just beyond him. With one glance he awoke, sitting up so quickly, his head spun. At the bed stood Jason, who had his arm wrapped around a small woman Ben didn't recognize, and she was crying. Next to Jason and on the other side of the bed stood three medical personnel. Ben couldn't remember hearing anything. When had everyone come in? He looked up at Kelly who had compassion etched on his face.

"Ben, he's gone."

"Please. Please. Please don't let this take too long." Kathryn nearly twisted her ankle as she scrambled from her car and slammed the door behind her. The gas station was busier than normal, which had already cost her another eight precious minutes. Clutching her credit card and hoping she could focus long enough to make the transaction, she went through the process of entering all of her information. Her whole body seemed set on slow motion even though she was trying to get it to move. When the nozzle was finally in the tank and the gas was flowing, she took a moment to look at her watch. She was already ten minutes late, and she was still fifteen minutes from work.

"Ugh." She needed to call in and let them know. As the numbers on the pump rolled up, she stomped back to the car and pulled on the door handle. It slipped from her grasp. Not understanding, she tried again with the same result. "Wh...?" Then a horrible feeling dove through her. The keys. The pump behind her snapped off, but she was too busy trying to see in the tinted windows. "No. No. No. Oh, please..."

But there they were, hanging from the ignition as if to put a stamp on how rotten the day was going to be.

"I... I don't understand," Ben said, scrambling up. "I... he was... I went to sleep about 2:30. He was still here."

"I checked an hour ago," the nurse beside the bed said. She was the same one with the bobbed black hair from that first day. Her gaze was filled with compassion. "You were asleep. He was still here."

The doctor nodded and stepped back as if to say *it is finished*.

The nurse looked at all of them. "I'm really sorry."

Stunned. It was the only thing Ben could register. His whole body went numb in one instant. He swallowed hard, not from grief but from utter shock. Not really wanting to but knowing he should since the doctor and nurse had moved away, Ben put his head down and stepped over to the bed.

The face was already losing the pink-white tint, and Ben had to force himself to breathe. The woman next to Jason let out a sob that did nothing to calm Ben's racing heart. Standing there, next to Jason, he reached down to touch the hand that he had held only a few short hours before. A soft gasp jolted through him as tears yanked to the surface. The hand was already cold. Ben's heart fell, knowing this really was, finally the end. All of the heartache, all of the wrenching decisions—they had all led to this one horrible moment.

He could hardly breathe, hardly think. How had they gotten here so very quickly? He blinked back the tears now blurring his vision. The feeling of being completely alone washed over him. How was he ever going to go on?

At that moment his brother turned to him, and through the tears shimmering on his lashes, he opened his arms. Ben had never been more grateful for someone to grab onto.

"I've already been out on six calls this morning," the locksmith said as he worked on Kathryn's car. "Must be something in the air. Maybe it's a full moon tonight."

Kathryn knew she should be saying something witty and cute, but she couldn't think of anything. She looked at her watch, wanting to ask how long this was going to take but figuring that would just slow him down.

The lock clicked, and he pulled the slim jim out and opened the door. "Good as new."

"Hallelujah."

"We have arranged for transport," the balding man in the well-worn suit who had arrived shortly after the doctor had left said.

The four of them had stepped away from the bed. There was no longer a reason to stand in that spot. The soul that had been there was gone.

"We just need to know the name of the funeral home."

Ben's mind slipped into the understanding that this man was arranging something that Kathryn should have. "Is..." He scratched the back of his neck. "Is Ms. Walker here?"

All four gazes went to him, and he felt completely exposed.

"No," the man said. "She was having some trouble with her car, so I stayed."

"Oh." Ben nodded as his heart panged. He tried to listen to the rest of the conversation, but it swirled away from him.

"Come on!" If Kathryn didn't know better, she would think the whole universe was against her this morning. The workers in the construction area had traffic down to one lane as they worked in the manhole. What could possibly be so important it had to be fixed this morning? "God, come on, here. Clyde is going to shoot me on the spot already."

Cars honked all around her as traffic snarled to a halt. Frustration began to twine around her, and she hit her horn for no reason other than it let out some of the steam.

"Hey! Lady! Can't you see..."

She didn't hear the rest, and part of her was glad for that.

Reining in the overwhelm, she put her head back. "God, please, I'm asking here. Please." Then as she breathed and forced herself to calm down, she forced herself to put the day in His hands. It wasn't easy. In fact, she wasn't even sure how successful she was, but at least she no longer felt like screaming at everyone around her.

After many long, agonizing minutes, traffic began moving again, though at a crawl, and she realized she needed to let work know she was going to be even further delayed. The only good thing was she didn't make a habit of being late, so they would surely forgive this one time.

Together, with the three of them, Ben exited the room for the last time. Transport would be here any minute, and there were now new issues to deal with—clothes, services, obituaries. The thoughts were overwhelming, but somehow Ben was holding himself in one piece. Kelly, Jason, and Holly headed for the doors, but Ben just couldn't leave without knowing, without asking.

He stepped over to the desk and waited for the nurse from before to get off the phone. Leaning on the counter, he prayed she wouldn't put more pieces together than were there.

"Can I help you?" she finally asked.

Ben purposely didn't notice the pity in her eyes. It would bring up all the other things he didn't really want to deal with at the moment. "Um, we're just about to leave, but I was wondering... Uh." Words failed as his heart twisted in his chest. "Is... Um... has Ms. Walker come in yet?"

"Oh." The nurse started. "That was just her on the phone. It sounds like traffic is a major mess this morning. She wasn't sure when she would get here. I'm sorry."

"Oh." His heart slipped into the abyss even as he forced himself to nod. "No. That's okay. Well, tell her..." Then he thought better of that. What he wanted to say he couldn't. What he could say, he didn't want to. He let his fist fall to the counter. "Just tell her I'll catch her down the road."

A moment and the nurse nodded. "I'll be sure to tell her."

At the rate she was going, Kathryn wouldn't have been at all surprised to break a heel and wipe out completely on the parking lot. That would be just her luck. Corralling her belongings, she swung the outside door open and hurried down the hallway. How many favors was she going to owe Clyde for this one? She hoped she didn't look as out-of-control as she felt. Then again, there wasn't much hope that she didn't.

She swung the interior door open and gathered herself as much as she could with a long breath. Striding purposely in, she squared her shoulders and put on her brightest smile. "Good morning."

The second Misty looked up, it was clear the world had fallen apart in her absence.

Kathryn stopped short. "What?"

Misty's face fell even further.

That drove fear and panic into Kathryn. "What? What happened?" Her mind instantly started down the list of horrible things that could have happened.

"Um." Never one to be unsure, Misty looked completely rattled. She stepped from behind the desk, glancing around—either for someone to be watching or for someone to take over, neither of which appeared. "Let's go down to your office."

Misty took hold of Kathryn's elbow and steered them both down the hallway.

"What?" Kathryn asked as sheer panic spread through her. "What happened? Misty, talk to me."

"I will. Just not here."

At her office door, Kathryn managed to find the key and open the door with hands that were now shaking away from her control. She forced air into her lungs. Whatever this was, it was bad, but she didn't have the space to fall apart. She had to keep it together.

The door finally, mercifully opened, and Kathryn went in followed closely by Misty. Kathryn dumped her belongings on the floor near her desk as Misty reached back and closed the door quietly. That set off alarms in Kathryn. Misty never closed the door unless it was really, really bad.

"So what's going on?"

Carefully Misty reached across the abyss of tiles between them and took Kathryn's elbow once more. She led her friend to the two chairs that faced the desk for guests. When Misty sat, Kathryn watched her and then followed her because she knew nothing else to do.

"Mist, seriously, what's going on?"

There could be no mistaking those eyes. They were too sad and concerned to warrant anything but the worst news. "Kate, Mr. Warren died this morning."

"What...?" In one snap the walls pressed in next to her. She searched her friend's eyes for something that said this was all a really bad joke. "But he was here... last night. We..." But she couldn't finish that sentence. "No. Misty. Are you sure? Where's Ben? Is he okay?"

Calm resolve came into Misty's eyes. "He's fine. He asked about you before he left, but..."

"He's..." All breath left her completely. "He's... gone?"

Slowly, sadly, Misty just nodded.

Fourteen

When Misty left after Kathryn had assured her sixteen times she would be all right, Kathryn somehow made it from the chair around her desk—but no farther. She sat, trying to sort through everything. One part of her wanted to call him, just as a friend to give her condolences, and she almost did, but doubt and fear stopped her. How could she know if they were friends like that or if it had only been because he was trapped in an awful situation and needed her help?

As she thought through the situation, heaped with her own grief, she finally decided that she simply could not be objective enough about any of it to risk making that call. The last thing she wanted was to make him think she was chasing after him. Then it occurred to her that it was going to be hard to chase him anywhere since he was gone. Her heart fell at the thought of someone else occupying that room. How could she have been so blithe in their time together last night? Why hadn't she made it a point to get up early, to be here for him—for them—this morning?

She hoped that Jason was at least there. The thought flitted through her mind that she could conceivably ask Misty how it all happened—who was here, who wasn't. But that would surely tip off Misty that there was more to Kathryn's interest in the situation than just that they were clients. Sitting at her desk, Kathryn picked up the phone for no real reason other than it was something to do.

At that moment there was a knock on the door and Clyde poked his bald head in. Instantly Kathryn put the phone up next to her shoulder.

"Oh, good," Clyde said. "You're here."

Kathryn fought to get the smile onto her face. "Where else would I be?"

"I think this one," Kelly said, coming out of the expanse of closet with a suit Ben wasn't sure he'd ever seen.

"That's really nice," Holly said when neither of the brothers offered an opinion. She looked to her husband who looked as shell-shocked as Ben felt. The introductions had been fast and only slightly awkward outside of the hospice unit. Holly was nice enough although Ben was still trying to get used to the idea of having a sister-in-law.

Jason shrugged. "It's fine with me."

They all looked to Ben who hadn't realized he would be consulted. He put his hand up on his head and rubbed there wondering where the reality-numbing headache had come from. "Oh, yeah. Yeah. It's… It's… fine." The absurdity of the word that finished that sentence knocked into his heart. *Fine? Appropriate? Great? Fantastic?* Fine was going to have to do.

"Okay." Kelly flipped the suit over his arm. "I guess we should go on to the funeral home then."

Eating wasn't exactly on Kathryn's most important things to do list at the moment. Her stomach was in one big constant knot. But when the clock said 1:15, she knew if she didn't go eat, she was going to get a monstrous headache. She didn't slow down as she walked past the front counter. "I'm going to lunch. I'll be back."

Misty's sympathetic gaze traveled with her. "Okay."

"This one is nice." Holly was trying to be helpful. Ben couldn't fault her that, but standing in a room with half a hundred open coffins was just not a place he thought he would ever be. They were in every color—blue, a purplish-pink, black, brown. Somehow he'd never considered the fact that there would be a selection.

"That particular one is 10,000," the funeral director said.

"Dollars?" Jason asked with a gulp.

"Yes, sir."

Wide-eyed, Jason looked to Ben for some decision, but Ben had no clue. What could they spend on a casket? What could they spend on anything? Yes, they had looked at some of the finances, but without the whole picture, guesses of what was and what might be were only shots in the dark at best.

"Um," Ben stumbled for words as he rubbed over his jaw, which he realized hadn't been shaved in more days than he had could remember at the moment. "Could we see some others in a little lower price-range?"

"Certainly, sir. We have a wide variety. We even have some with the logos of sports teams if that would be appropriate."

Tired pounced on Ben and he put his hands into his back pockets. Nothing seemed appropriate at this particular moment. "Um, no. I don't think we want any logos, just something nice that's not going to send anyone into major debt."

The man nodded, but it was a condescending nod. "I see. Then you would want to visit the room over here where we have our more modest line."

"Yes," Ben said, matching the man's condescension, "I think we'd like to see the modest line."

For some reason Kathryn's shoulders simply wouldn't lift higher than her heart. In the cafeteria, she sat hunched over her salad. She wasn't really eating it, more picking at it with her fork. Her heart hurt. Her stomach hurt more. It was like it was filled with a grief she couldn't fully comprehend. She'd lost patients before. In fact, that was kind of the point of her job, and yet... yet... this one felt so very, very different for reasons she wouldn't even admit to herself.

"Really? You're in sales?" The voice from two tables over carried to her with no obstacles, and she looked up in recognition.

However, her heart fell like a rock plummeting off the steep side of the Niagara when her gaze caught on the speaker. Dr. Martin. And he wasn't alone. Kathryn wanted to disappear through the floor, but the best she could do was to hunch further over her salad.

The young lady with Dr. Martin looked right out of high school. True that was probably Kathryn's jealousy talking, but still, the girl couldn't have been 25. She was now giggling at something he said. With a roll of her eyes, Kathryn decided she really didn't need the in-your-face reminder that her life was a completely deplorable wreck.

Swiping up her tray, which she hadn't bothered to empty, she skirted the other tables and dumped the whole thing into the trash. The meal had done nothing for her stomach or her mood. She stalked back to the unit, determined now more than ever to have a thoroughly rotten day.

"Parents," the funeral director said, glancing at Jason and Ben over his reading glasses.

"Uh." Ben shifted forward in the chair. "Our parents?"

"No, sir. Your father's parents' names. We will need it for the official records."

"Oh. Uh." Ben looked to Jason who was clearly not stepping up to help. "Um. Gertrude." He tested that name in his brain. Yes. That was right. "And Gregory Warren."

"Mother's maiden name."

Opening his eyes wide as if that would help him remember, Ben searched through the files in his brain. "Val..." He cleared his throat, still testing the name with his brain. "Valadine."

"Spelling?"

Everyone in the room was looking at him. He had no answers. It was all a not-very-well choreographed act. "V..."

"So, are you ready for your date tonight?" Misty asked when they were in the supply room. Misty was counting sponges and shampoo; Kathryn was counting brochures. At least that's what she was supposed to be doing. But she kept getting hung up somewhere between 23 and I-don't-want-to-do-this.

"I guess." Holding one stack that she had counted twice with no real clue how many were in her hand, she bent into the task of trying to figure out which brochure on the list these were.

"Wow. Don't sound so enthusiastic. You might bowl him over."

"Sorry. I'm just a little frazzled right now. I've got to get this done, and then we've got a new patient coming from oncology. I need to have the family packet prepared, and they'll be here in like ten minutes." She looked at her watch. "Eight minutes."

"Oh, you know, they don't ever get here when they say they're going to."

She put the brochures back on the metal shelf. "Yeah, but the way my luck's going today, they'll be early." With that she headed to the door. "Be good."

"Back at you."

"We really should stop somewhere and get something to eat," Kelly said as they drove out of the funeral home parking lot. "Then I can take you back to your car."

Jason and Holly had gone in the rental she had gotten at the airport, which was just as well. At least this way Ben didn't have to worry about how badly he was failing in the big brother column.

Kelly looked across at Ben with sympathy. "How you doing?"

Ben wanted to lie, but he didn't have the strength. Instead he just shook his head and let out a long sigh. "That was the worst thing I've ever had to do."

"It'll get better."

"When?"

"Well, not soon, but it will. Trust me."

It would've been nice to believe that, but Ben had been down this absurd rabbit hole for so long, he no longer believed in any other kind of existence.

The sinking feeling hit with both fists when Kathryn stepped into the room at the end of the hall. Her mind still remembered him being there—sitting on the couch, sitting on the floor. But now there was someone else in the bed. A lady with sparse white hair. A tall thin elderly gentleman turned from his vigil by the bed when Kathryn stepped in.

He tried to smile, but there were tears in his eyes as he did so.

"Mr. Davis. I'm Kathryn Walker with the hospice social services."

"Oh, hello, Ms. Walker." He extended a very thin, vein-laced hand. "It's nice to meet you."

"Nice to meet you." She shook his hand and then held up the

little brochures she had brought. "We didn't get a chance to get these put out before your wife's arrival. Feel free to look them over, take them home, whatever you want." She walked over to the nightstand and had a heart snag when she remembered the letter lying there the night before. Would she ever see Ben again?

Pushing that down, she turned. "We have many services available to you and your family."

"Go home," Kelly said as they sat in the hospice parking lot an hour later. He was worried about Ben, that much was clear from his tone and the look on his face. Ben was worried too. Nothing felt real anymore. In fact, nothing felt like it made any sense at all. He wasn't even sure that his dad had gotten the worse end of the deal. "Get some sleep. I'll give you a call tomorrow, and we can be at the funeral home when you go."

Slowly Ben nodded though he wasn't sure why. After a moment, Kelly put his hand over onto his friend's shoulder. "We're here for you, okay?"

Again Ben nodded, but his gaze stayed on his shoes. Tired grief mixed in his soul so that he wasn't sure if he would go to sleep or cry first. "Thanks."

So many things about so many things made absolutely no sense in life, and it was getting worse. Kathryn could feel everything closing in on her. She knew that feeling well, and only one place could come close to soothing her battered soul when she stared into the throes of depression. At the door of the chapel, she pushed in, and although she knew it was akin to running from the problems, it still felt good to go somewhere that had a chance of making something better.

Without a noise, she walked down the side aisle all the way to the front and slid into a bench. Sitting was too arduous, so she bent and pulled out the little kneeler. Carefully, slowly, she slipped down all the way onto it. Her eyes closed as anger, frustration, and despair wrapped around her.

"God," she whispered, but she choked on the word as tears slipped into her eyes. "I don't know how much longer I can do this. I don't. I just wanted to help. You know that, but I'm no good to anyone if I'm such a mess all the time. I feel so out of control. Please, help me, Lord. Please. I just want to quit, but I feel like I'm letting You down if I do that. I'm so confused, Lord. I'm just so confused."

Ben walked to his car and got in, watching as Kelly pulled out of the parking lot. The exhale took the last of his strength from him. It was a 20 minute drive to his apartment, but he felt like he didn't have the energy to move 2 inches. He reached down for the key, but his gaze snagged on the little building protruding from the monstrosity of the hospital beyond. That little building. In a strange way it had become home. He smiled a wistful, sad smile that he wouldn't have need of going in there anymore, and he shook his head.

A thought split through all the others, and he stopped completely. No. That was crazy. She wasn't there, and even if she was, she wouldn't want to see him. He wasn't her client anymore. Still, he didn't move. He couldn't. It was as if he was frozen there in time—somewhere between what used to be and what now was. His heart said to go see. His head said she was already busy with new patients.

Finally, forcing himself not to think about what he was doing, he turned the keys and yanked them from the ignition. It wouldn't hurt to just check.

There was no real way of knowing how long she had been on her knees—not long enough to find any peace that was for sure. Her soul was still caught in the effects of the wind and the rain that pelted her from every direction. Though they had finally cleared from the sky a day early, the storm in her hadn't subsided. If anything, it had intensified. What good was she to anyone in her life? Her mother thought her a failure. Her best friend had chastised her about the upcoming date that truth-be-told she had no desire to go on. Dr. Martin had no real interest in her beyond a day or two of flirting, and she'd probably misread even that. It felt as if her whole life was out of kilter, and she had no way of putting it back on course. She was too tired to fight anymore, too tired to even convince herself that it could get better. All she wanted to do was give up and quit for good. The only thing stopping her was the whisper that if she did, Satan would finally have won.

The door snapped open behind her, and she pulled herself upright and swiped at her eyes and her nose. The state of her being at that moment would have inspired confidence in exactly nobody, and she knew it. The last thing she needed was for some client to see her like this.

"Um, excuse me. Is this seat taken?"

Like a shot, the timbre of that voice burst through her, and she yanked her gaze up to the man standing there. Understanding hit her like a sucker punch, and she couldn't quite believe what her eyes were telling her. "Ben?"

His softly amused smile said it could be no one else.

Her heart led, and her body followed. She jumped to her feet and in the next heartbeat she was in his arms. Together they took a breath of remembering. It felt better than anything had a right to. He felt better than anyone had a right to. She closed her eyes to absorb the feeling. Then, as her brain caught up with the thoughts streaming through it, she pulled back, cleared her throat, and swiped at her eyes. "Um. I… What…?" She stepped back, hoping she wouldn't fall as her hands went into perpetual motion smoothing her hair and her outfit. She was a complete mess, and she knew it.

He smiled again, and the last shred of sanity scattered away from her. That face. That smile. How was she ever going to live without it? He looked down at the bench. "Mind if I join you?"

All motion stopped.

"W-what?" She looked down at the bench as if she hadn't realized it was there. Her heart was having a hard time catching onto the fact that this could really be happening. "Oh. Yeah. Yes. Of course." Corralling all the stupid, inappropriate things rattling through her heart, she slipped her hand under her skirt and sat primly on the edge of the pew, praying she could get through this without humiliating herself even more than she already had.

Close enough to touch but not reaching out, he sat too. It was then that she saw the streaks of grief marring his countenance, and she remembered. She ducked at her own presumptuousness, and her own grief furrowed across her brow.

Forcing her gaze up to him, she lowered her voice. "I'm really sorry… about your dad. I know that's really hard."

He nodded, and a shadow of a heartrending smile flitted across his face.

A moment and she blinked, realizing she should say something else. "I'm sorry I wasn't here this morning."

But his smile only tilted up a little more. "Don't worry about it."

"I am worried about it. I've been worried about you all day. I wanted to call, but…" Those words hadn't been planned, and she had no idea how to finish that thought without sounding hopelessly unprofessional.

He looked up at her in surprise. "But what?" His intent gaze searched hers.

Knowing he would be able to see the whole answer if she let him, Kathryn ducked. Slicing pain ripped across her heart. "I didn't know if I should."

Surprise and worry jumped to his face. "If you should? What does that mean?"

She glanced at him. Saying it was either stupid or embarrassing or both. "Well, I mean, you're just a patient here. I mean your father was a patient here. I don't… I didn't know if…"

Her stumbling and the obvious torment she was in touched Ben's heart in ways he never could have articulated. In that moment all he wanted to do was comfort her. He didn't know how she would react, but that was only a secondary concern. Carefully, he reached over to her, his hand coming first to her shoulder, then to her back, finally pulling her all the way to him. "Come here."

Kathryn's breath snagged on the gentleness of his tone and his touch. Although it should have been a given that she not put herself into that position, she couldn't resist the offer. His offer. Of solace. Of strength. Of someone to lean on. Slowly she slid across the bench into his arms which both came around her and clasped there. With her head resting on the strength of his shoulder, she closed her eyes—relaxing for the first time all day.

As her being rested in his, life settled around her.

"How's Jason?" she finally asked with real concern for all of them in her heart.

"He's okay. Holly made it. They're at Kelly's."

Kathryn nodded, wishing she could stay right here forever.

As he held her, Ben turned his head and bent his lips to her hair. It was soft, just like she was. However, halfway down, his gaze caught on the crucifix hanging there, seemingly in suspended animation on the wall. He had never been this close to one, had never had cause to really look into that face.

It was amazing how sad it was and how deeply he felt the look. Yes, it was only a statue, but it seemed so much more.

He settled back, holding her and gazing up. "Do you think He really understands?"

The other-worldliness of the moment drifted around him, and he chose not to fight it but to surrender to it.

She shifted on his chest. "Yeah, I think he does."

Something about that calmed all of the jangling pieces in Ben's soul. Either that, or holding her did, he wasn't sure which, but truthfully, he didn't care. Instead, he slipped back onto the pew a little further and relaxed into the peace around him. "They scheduled the wake service for tomorrow night at seven. Would you come?"

It was a weird question, one of those that you never foresee ever saying until you've already said it and then wonder if you should have.

Without really moving much at all, she nodded. "Yeah."

And then pure, unfiltered peace floated through him, encapsulating every last shred of dissonance left.

They stayed like that for several more minutes, just resting. Then, although Kathryn didn't want to, she knew she needed to get back. She felt much more stable now and once again prepared to handle the tasks at hand. However, she sighed heavily and pulled herself up from his embrace. Although she should have been embarrassed, she was surprised to find only gratefulness in her heart when she looked at him. "Thank you."

His fingers drifted gently across her shoulder blades, and his blue-green eyes held an amusement that yanked her breath from her. "Thank you." After a moment, he pulled his hand from her shoulders and put it on his knee as his gaze fell to it. "The truth is, I was having about as bad a day as you were."

When she moved to protest, his gaze stopped her.

"The nurse told me about you being late. I guess I should apologize for keeping you up all hours."

Kathryn couldn't stop the smile. "Yeah, maybe that's why I'm such a mess."

It was supposed to be a joke, but instead, he grew serious as he put his elbow back on the pew once more. His fingers brushed through her hair on her shoulder as his gaze burrowed into hers. "Then you're a very beautiful mess."

Her cheeks flushed, both from his touch and from the way he was looking at her. Not knowing what to do with any of it, she smiled and shook her head. "I think you need glasses. I'm hardly beauty queen material at this point."

"Well, I would beg to differ, but I'd hate to argue about it now."

He wasn't making this going on with life thing any easier.

Stuffing all the feelings he'd ignited in her down, she sighed. "I should get back to work." She looked up at him thinking she could end this professionally, but professional had long since been left in the dust.

"And I should let you," he said, but he didn't move. Instead, his eyes traveled across her face and back again. Once. And then again.

The moment held on pause as she looked at him, grateful for his presence in her life and never wanting it to end. Finally he half-smiled, nodded, and pushed up to standing. She bent and replaced the kneeler, and when she straightened, his hand was there to help her up. He stepped out but only enough to let her go first. All the way to the door, he shadowed her steps, and Kathryn was beginning to wonder how they would make it out without everyone and their dog seeing them.

At the door, she pushed through and turned to him, determined to put professional up between them again. She turned to him as if they were simply continuing an appointed meeting. "Did you say what funeral home?"

"Oh, uh, Clark's."

Kathryn nodded and folded her arms in front of her. It was a straight shot from Misty's desk to where they now stood, and

Kathryn knew it. "Okay. I'll be there. Tomorrow night. Seven, right?"

"Yeah," he said, putting his hands in his pockets as he glanced toward the desk and then back at her, clearly becoming as uncomfortable with the increased scrutiny as she was. "Seven."

"Okay. I'll be there." She nodded briskly, hoping this little act was covering all the butterflies flitting to and fro in her stomach. The truth was they were making even thinking straight impossible.

There was an awkward moment in which he leaned a half-of-a-fraction of an inch toward her, and her alert system blared on, pushing her backward. But then he simply smiled, and backing up, he picked his hand out of his pocket and ran his fingers through his hair. "Well, I'd better get going."

Still not really breathing, she couldn't stop nodding even though she felt ridiculous for it. "Thanks for stopping by." Her thoughts were running faster than her brain. "Uh, and tell Jason and Holly they have our sympathies."

"Will do."

Again, the moment paused only this time it contained massive amounts of awkwardness.

"I guess I'll see you later," he finally said, and with a push he started slowly down the hallway.

She wanted to follow him, to walk out with him, to go to his car and never look back. But those were not options. So she stopped at her office door. "Take care of yourself, okay?"

He turned and smiled, but it was a tight, sad gesture. "I'll try."

Leaving her there was like ripping his soul in half, but Ben could think of no reason good enough to warrant staying. As he walked by the front desk, the nurse from before said, "Take care, Mr. Warren."

"Thanks. You too," he mumbled, and then he pushed out of the unit, wondering if he might never see the place again.

"So…" Misty said two minutes later when she showed up in Kathryn's doorway.

"So… what?" Kathryn asked, not really caring as she went through the new patient's folder. She was 89, had had cancer three times. This one would be her last.

201

"I see Mr. Warren came for a visit."

"Hm." Kathryn continued to peruse the chart.

"Does this mean he'll be back?"

"He just came to tell me when the services are going to be." Kathryn shrugged although her heart was hammering in her chest. "It was no big deal."

"Uh-huh." Misty nodded up and down once as she folded her arms across her chest and leaned on the doorway. "It didn't look like no big deal to me."

Kathryn pushed a strand of hair over her ear. "What? Were you spying on us?"

"Observing. It's called observing."

"Well, I think it should be called minding your own business. Ben and I are just friends. That's all."

"Friends?" The word tilted upward. "I thought he was a client."

Frustration crawled up Kathryn's patience. "He was. Now we're friends. Is that a problem?"

Misty held up both hands. "No. No problems here. But if you ever want to be more than friends with him, you have my blessing."

A scowl punctuating her face, Kathryn looked up. "Am I, or am I not going on a date with *your* cousin tonight?"

Now Misty was backing out. "I'm not pushing. I'm just saying."

"Yeah? Well, saying isn't helping, okay?"

Misty's smile was small but knowing. "Got it. I won't say anymore."

"Thank you."

As Kathryn got ready for her date later that evening, she couldn't help but wish it would be with Ben. She even chose the outfit she thought he would like—though she knew how desperate that seemed, no one else would ever have to know. Every so often her thoughts let her wonder if this was what it was like to be in love. He was so great. Kind. Gentle. Strong. And handsome. He blew every guy she'd ever been out with out of the water.

Then again, maybe he was just being a friend, and she was reading far too much into it. It wouldn't be the first time that had happened. Besides that, he had all but said he wasn't interested in marriage. She thought about Dr. Martin and a sigh slipped through her though she knew that too was stupid. He'd seemed nice enough, but there was no real abiding connection there— apparently. Then she wondered about Nathan, who would be showing up in less than ten minutes, and her stomach flitted away from her. Maybe they would hit it off. Maybe he was the one.

But even as she tried to be excited about the prospects of Nathan, her thoughts trailed back into Ben land. She wondered what he was doing, how he was, if he was with Jason and Holly now. As stupid as that sounded, she wished she was there with them rather than here with herself. Then she berated herself for thinking so foolishly. They were a family. She had no place with them.

The doorbell sounded, jolting her out of her revere. She quickly applied the last of her mascara, fluffed her hair, which had already fallen flat, and headed for the door.

Ben was sitting on his couch as he had been since he'd gotten home. The images on the television flickered in no distinct pattern. He wasn't watching anyway. He thought back through the past couple of days and then into the next couple. Strangely his thoughts, no matter where they went, always found their way back to that little chapel in the front bench.

He'd always thought of religion as hokey and stupid, now he wasn't so sure. Never in his life had he felt that kind of peace even in the midst of the worst day of his life. He was sure most of it had to do with her, but there was a small part of him that attributed it also to the chapel. In fact, if it wasn't 20 minutes away, he would consider going there right now.

The phone rang, and he looked at it as if he'd forgotten it existed. Reluctantly, he pulled himself up off the couch and walked over to it. "Warren."

"Ben?" The high-pitched voice pierced through his ear drum.

"Yes. This is Ben." It sounded more like a question.

"Ben, oh, good. I thought something terrible had happened to you."

Something terrible had, but he had no way of knowing if he should say that or not as he had yet to voice print who this was.

"This is Charissa."

His heart fell at the recognition, but he fought not to let his disappointment sound in his voice. "Oh, hi, Charissa." He sat down on the little stool by the counter. "What's up?"

"Hey. I've been calling. I thought you forgot about me."

"No. No. I didn't forget." He put his elbow on the counter and held up his head with his hand. "What's going on?"

"Well, a bunch of us are going out partying tonight. I was wondering if you might want to come."

A party? Nothing in him even wanted to hear the word. "Oh, uh. I don't think so. I'm not really in the partying mood."

"Ah, come on. It'll be fun. We're going club hopping."

His spirit fell through the absurdity. "No, really, Charissa. Not tonight."

"Oh." Her voice fell flat. "Well, then..."

Awkward dropped over the conversation like an anvil.

"I'll... I'll call you sometime," he finally managed, not really meaning it but having no idea how to get her off the phone.

"Okay." A split-second and playful came back into her voice. "But don't keep me waiting too long."

"Oh, I won't." Wow did this seem ridiculously surreal. He wrapped up the conversation as quickly as possible, promising once again to call, though that call would be on the other side of bizarre-land, if it ever came at all.

When he hung up the phone, Ben sat looking at it for a moment that lasted an eternity and then another. He closed his eyes, trying to push life away from him. If he could just forget for awhile, for ten minutes, for an hour. Standing, he went to the liquor cabinet in the kitchen. Maybe alcohol would have a chance of dulling everything.

"Kate?" The guy standing in her doorway had a fistful of daisies.

Kathryn's eyes widened at the sight. She had always been wickedly allergic to daisies. However, she couldn't tell him that, so she looked up at him and fought to smile. "Nathan?"

"Saffron," he said, fumbling with the bouquet so he could get his hand out to hers.

She shook hands with him, wishing there was an easier way to do this. "It's nice to meet you..." Air sucked into her nose, and she sneezed hard. "Ugh. I'm sorry. It's nice to meet you, Nathan." Taking the air in her lungs in both hands so it wouldn't make her sneeze again, she stepped back. "Please, come on in."

He stepped in front of her into the apartment, and she sent up a prayer of desperation to God—for wisdom and for sanity.

"Nice place," Nathan said, looking around.

"Here. I'll just put these in some…" Kathryn reached for the daisies, feeling the sneeze but beating it back with all the strength in her. "Water." She took the offensive weeds that were thankfully bundled in white tissue.

"I hope you like them. Daisies are my mom's favorite flower."

"They're lovely." She worked to keep them as far away from her skin and nose as she got them into the kitchen, filled a vase with water, and stuck them in. "Ah-choo!" Sniffing as her eyes started watering, she picked up the bouquet and walked it out to the living room. "Ugh. Must be the dust in the vents. Sometimes when the air comes on, it just gets to me."

Nathan tilted his head, and his face furrowed questioningly. "I don't hear the air on."

"What?" Kathryn stood and straightened her blouse. "Oh, yeah. It… it was on earlier." Worried that she would have an all-out sneezing fit, she smiled. "Are we ready?"

"Sure."

As they walked out into the spring evening, Kathryn took a moment to really look at Nathan. He was far from bad though he wasn't drop-dead gorgeous. Blond hair with just a hint of red, nice features, slim build. She tried to imagine the picture they made together, and it was a thoroughly nice one. Maybe this wouldn't be so bad after all.

Ten minutes into the drinking session, the phone rang. At the little coffee table, Ben poured another vodka, deciding to let the answering machine get it. His plan was to sit right here, on this sofa all night. If he got really lucky, he might be on the floor before too long. He downed the stinging liquid, glad he was one shot closer to the eventual outcome.

"Beep!" The answering machine clicked on.

"Ben? Hey, bud, where are you?" Kelly's voice split through Ben's skull like an unwanted chain saw.

He groaned. There was no way Kelly wouldn't know he'd been drinking, and yet, he knew Kelly enough to know he'd be over here to check on him if he didn't answer. Fighting to get and keep his balance—more from the grief than the alcohol, Ben stood and stumbled over to the phone. "Warren." It didn't sound friendly.

"Ben! Oh, good. Listen, Tamitha decided to make up one of her lasagnas for Jason and Holly. You want to come over?"

"Oh, I don't know, Kell…"

"No, man. We want you to come. You're not going to sit there in the dark all by yourself. Not tonight. Come on. The lasagna's already in the oven."

Ben sighed as he looked back to the coffee table. Why couldn't they just leave him alone?

"You've got time," Kelly said. "Ya don't have to break your neck to get here. Just come."

What could he say? "Okay."

"So you work with Misty," Nathan said from his side of the black truck that somehow surprised Kathryn. She'd never been in a truck like this. It stood several feet off the ground, and Nathan had to help her so she could even get in. Once in, the high perspective made her woozy.

"Yeah." Playing with the strap of her purse, she fingered through the files in her brain trying to think of more to say. She was so hopelessly bad at this.

"I've always thought that would be such a hard job. I don't think I could do it, watching people die all the time."

With a rush, memories from the day swept back over her, and she put her head down to hide them. "It's not always so bad. I guess you kind of get used to it."

Nathan shook his head. "Not me. I couldn't do it."

For a long moment, Kathryn searched for something to say.

"Hey, do you like jazz?" Nathan asked, reaching for the stereo knobs.

"I… guess." She shrugged. Honestly she'd never had an occasion to listen to jazz, so she really didn't know.

With five clicks, the purr of a saxophone floated between

them. She slid down in the seat just a bit, relaxing. Maybe this wouldn't be so bad after all.

"Hey. You made it." Kelly met Ben at the door with an out reached hand that turned into a pat on the shoulder hug. Ben couldn't recall ever being hugged so much in his life. In fact, he had always been pretty much a hands-off person. But apparently that had changed sometime in the last week.

"I made it."

"Ben," Tamitha said, coming to the door and extending her arms as well. "I was so sorry to hear about your dad."

He hugged her—kind of. "Th-thanks." It was weird. What do you say to something like that? He'd never really thought about it. Following them through the little entry, he stepped into the living room, feeling hopelessly ragged. His hair was far longer than he'd ever let it get. Sometime back before time stopped, he was scheduled for a haircut. Now he wondered if he'd ever even canceled that appointment. He'd tried to shave earlier, but about all he'd accomplished was making his face bleed almost as much as his heart was.

"Hey, Ben." Jason stepped from the kitchen with Holly next to him. "We're glad you could come."

Ben picked his chin up as if he was going to say something, but movement at Holly's knee yanked his attention there. With one look, his heart plummeted to his shoes. Carefully Holly reached down and swung the little child up to her ample waist. The little golden curls danced around the little pixie face.

It was a challenge to hold to reality. "Well, who's this?" Ben asked through the lump. The truth was, it could be no one else.

"This is Ryley," Jason said, turning with pride in his eyes.

On rubbery legs, Ben stepped toward them. Seeing him approach, the child stuck her thumb in her mouth and bent her head to her mother's shoulder. Ben didn't want to scare her, so he stopped several feet away and just stood trying to figure out how that face could be so similar to the one that had haunted his dreams from the moment his mother and brother had left to this.

"Hi, Ryley," he said, his voice catching on the lump in his throat. The thought that his dad might never have met this beautiful little child brought tears to his eyes. The pain was all still so fresh, so raw inside him. It was as if life had suddenly become brighter, harsher, everything in perfect relief to that moment he had awakened to a new reality.

"And this is my mother-in-law," Jason said, stepping back to reveal a smallish woman who looked like she would backhand you if you crossed her. Ben decided right then he'd better be on his best behavior.

"It's nice to meet you, Ma'am." Ben bowed slightly, hoping the Ma'am would help. At this point, he wasn't sure anything would.

However, her gray eyes lost some of their harshness as she came toward him. She took his hand in both of hers. "I'm very sorry to hear about your father's passing. Please accept my sympathies." The sincerity in her tone touched a chord deep in him.

"Well, thank you." He had to swallow the lump.

Everyone stood there for a gaping eternity.

"Well," Tamitha finally said. "I'm sure the lasagna is ready. I'll go call the boys."

"That's fantastic." Kathryn sat on the opposite side of the table in the quiet restaurant. Nathan had certainly gone all out, and now she felt obligated to make this night not-a-disaster. She looked at him, thinking again he really wasn't bad. They would make a good couple. He was a good height for her, and their coloring was similar. "So you really graduated from MIT?"

"I did. Why? Is that so hard to believe?"

"Well, no." She reached for her wine. "You just don't look like a geek."

He laughed. "Well, thank you for that."

Then she realized how dumb that sounded. "No. I didn't…"

But he waved her off. "It's okay. Nothing I haven't heard before."

She wasn't sure if that was any better. "And you work in development?"

"I do." Nathan cut into his steak. "It's not as glamorous as it sounds, but it's a job."

"So what else do you like to do? Do you read?"

He laughed again. "Not much. I really love to rock climb. I'm planning a trip out west at the end of the summer with some friends. We're going to go repelling."

Her eyebrows reached for the sky. "Really? You jump off of rocks?"

Nathan shrugged. "I wanted to sky-dive, but my mom nixed that idea."

Something slipped into her consciousness. "You're close to your family then?"

"Oh, yeah. My younger brother and I go out nearly every weekend, and we're always getting together for something—birthdays, anniversaries—there's always something."

Nothing about that was bad, but it added pressure she wasn't sure she was ready for. "So how many brothers and sisters do you have?"

"Four brothers. Two sisters."

"Big family."

"Born and raised Catholic." He stopped and looked at her. "Didn't Misty say you were Catholic too?"

"What? Yeah." Kathryn didn't want him to notice how desperately she was working to make all of this information fit into her dream guy.

"Oh, good. Because you know I only date Catholics. Mom says it makes it easier that way."

Mom again. She was becoming a fixture. "Oh, yeah? How's that?"

"Well, you know how crazy some people are in the world today. I sure don't want to hook up with someone who doesn't have a good perspective on life."

How could something so logical sound so stifling?

"Not that there's anything wrong with other religions. It's just that, you know, getting some girls to agree to the Catholic thing can be a real nightmare."

She didn't know what to question first. "The Catholic thing? I don't follow."

"Well, you know, like having a big family. That's really important to me."

Kathryn nodded. "And how… big are you thinking?"

"Oh, I don't know six… seven."

The walls started closing on her. Six or seven children? Her eyebrows started for the ceiling, but she forced them to stay down.

"And your wife will work?"

Nathan laughed. "Of course not. She'll stay home and home school like my mom did. It's really the best way to raise a family." He reached for his glass and took a drink.

Nodding, because she didn't know what else to do, Kathryn ducked and wiped at her mouth with her napkin. If Misty knew all of this, she sure hadn't let Kathryn in on it.

"That's why when Misty said she had a good Catholic girl working there at the unit, I just had to meet you." Nathan smiled at her in a way that creeped her out.

Kathryn swallowed, praying that God would get her out of this before Nathan proposed.

"Terence! Sit down!" Tamitha said as her youngest knelt up on the chair next to Ben.

For his part, Ben was trying to eat without being noticed. The way he figured it, the faster he ate, the sooner he could go home.

"Have you talked to Kathryn?" Jason asked through the children and the clank of the plates, and Ben's whole awareness snapped to his brother.

"Um. Uh." Ben wiped his mouth with the little paper napkin. "Yeah for a few minutes today." He reached for his water as gazes from around the table landed on him. "But just for a few minutes." It was as if he couldn't stress that part enough.

Jason picked up his garlic toast. "Did you tell her about tomorrow night?"

Ben nearly choked on the water. Did they have to do this here? "Uh, yeah. I did. I don't know if she'll come though, you know. She's really busy."

"Kathryn?" Holly asked. "Is this the nurse at hospice?"

"Social worker," Jason corrected her.

"Oh, that's right." Holly trained her gaze on her brother-in-law who suddenly wished nothing more than the ability to disappear. "Jason says she's really nice."

Trying to figure out how not to make an idiot of himself, Ben nodded slightly. "She is." He picked up his fork and let his gaze drop to the plate. His heart turned over at the thought that she was probably out on her date right now. He wondered about the guy, and one major part of him wanted nothing more than to knock the guy's head of his shoulders. It must be the lost sleep and the stress. He'd never had such a desire before toward someone he had never even met.

"Well, I hope she comes," Holly said. "I'd love to meet her."

Ben bent forward farther and scratched his ear. The truth was he hoped she would come too.

"I figured we could catch the 9:30 show," Nathan said as they drove away from the restaurant.

With everything in her, Kathryn wanted to ask him to take her home. She wanted to put on her warm, fuzzy pajamas, get a cup of hot chocolate and curl up on the couch. But she knew the details of this date would get back to Misty. "Sounds good."

"No. Really," Ben said as he pulled on his jacket. "I'm beat. I haven't slept in my own bed in forever."

"Are you sure you're going to be all right getting home?" Tamitha asked as the four of them stood around him, looking like chaperones at a high school dance where he'd just been caught smoking.

"I'll be fine." He reached over and air kissed her. Then he shook Kelly's hand. "I swear."

Kelly didn't look pleased. Neither did Jason, but they clearly couldn't come up with a way or a reason to keep him there.

"Okay, but you drive carefully," Holly said as he barely brushed her arm in farewell.

"I'm fine." He looked over at Jason. "And stop looking at me like that. You guys get some sleep. I'll see you at the funeral home tomorrow evening." He pulled his jacket closer around him. The night wasn't all that cold, but his spirit was shivering. Quickly he exited and turned only once, barely, to bid them all good-bye. Then he hurried to his car and with only a bit of trouble crawled behind the wheel.

They were still looking, so he wasted no time. In seconds the car was started, seconds more and he was pulling away from the house and then the neighborhood. His whole body relaxed from the strain of trying to appear all right. Honestly, he couldn't be sure he was all right or not all right. Mostly he was just numb.

His gaze chanced on the little cell phone, and he thought about calling her. But he shook that thought away. He wouldn't disturb her now. That wouldn't be fair. She had her own life to live, and it didn't include him.

The laser guns cut across the dark black screen as the saviors of the universe fought evil personified. It wasn't as gory as some, but it was hardly in Kathryn's realm of enjoyable. Ten minutes after the lights went down, Nathan had stealthily reached over and taken her hand. She hadn't been prepared for that move, and now that her hand was stuck, she couldn't come up with a good way to extract it without him getting the wrong idea—or the right idea.

As the spaceship zoomed to a different galaxy, her brain went through her options. He was a nice guy. Yes. But his idea of marriage was so far separated from hers, she couldn't quite see how the two could ever mesh. She looked at their hands together and couldn't help but remember how Ben's had felt. That wasn't fair, of course. Nathan wasn't Ben.

And that was as much of a problem as anything else about him.

Although he hadn't gotten any real sleep in more than a week, Ben's mind just wouldn't shut off. Had she said she would come? He thought she had. He hoped she had. What if she did? Could he keep his feelings for her—such that he still couldn't figure out—from being broadcast to the entire world? He certainly didn't want to embarrass her. Especially since she was only coming because it was a part of her job.

That was the part that confused him the most. How much of her spending time with him was because of her job, and how much was something else? Was any of it something else? His heart panged forward in hopes that it was, but he couldn't tell how much of that was real and how much was just wishful thinking.

If he didn't get to sleep soon, he'd be counting non-existent dots in the dark. How depressing was that?

"I had a great time," Nathan said at her door. He was definitely making a move on her with his hand pressed against the wall next to her door.

"Yeah, me too." All she wanted was to get in that door without him following. "Thanks for dinner. The movie was great too. It's been a long time since I've been out like that." She was rambling because her mouth was stuck on talk.

Slowly he leaned over to her, put his hand on her shoulder, and bent his lips to hers. Air jammed into her lungs, and she slammed her eyes closed just as his lips met hers. Whatever she'd thought it would feel like, this was not it. His hands came around her waist and then her back, gripping her closer as she fought with herself not to push him away. It felt wrong, all wrong. And the only reason she didn't run was because she couldn't.

Finally the kiss broke, and she nearly lost her balance careening backward. "I... I'll see you later." And with that, she fled inside. When the door was closed and locked between them, she leaned on it, praying he wouldn't knock. For ten whole seconds she fully expected him to, but when he didn't, she finally breathed a sigh of relief. Her gaze slid up to the ceiling. "Oh, Lord, please tell me he wasn't the one You sent."

Ben had never prayed for anyone or anything in his lifetime. However, as the clock wound around to 1:15 in the cold, dark bedroom, he could think of nothing else to do. He wished he could call and talk to her. Just talk. That always calmed him down and made life seem to make a little more sense. But she was probably sleeping. Or she wasn't, which twisted his gut. He rolled over and put his wrist onto his forehead. "God, please, please be with Kathryn, wherever she is. Keep her safe for me, and give her peace."

The apartment was dark, but Kathryn never slowed down. She picked the bouquet up from the coffee table, went into the kitchen, dumped the whole thing in the sink and flipped on the garbage disposal. Four flowers down the drain, she started sneezing, but she didn't quit until they were all gone and Lysol had chased them down.

Fifteen

Although Kathryn had been to many funerals and wake services, this one felt very different. She dressed in her smoke-black dress suit and twisted her hair up into a loose knot. A little make-up and she was ready. Seven o'clock on a Saturday night. Without really even thinking the words, she thanked God that her schedule was so free that she hadn't even had to worry about changing plans. She checked her watch as she grabbed her purse and headed out to the car. There was plenty of time, but she didn't want him to think she had forgotten.

The dark suit. The white shirt. The black tie. They were all so formal, all so somber. Ben checked his reflection once more in the full length mirror on his closet. He looked about as good as he was going to. The air escaped from his lungs in a long, protracted whoosh. If he could just keep his nerves from overtaking him, he'd be all right. Grabbing his wallet and keys, he headed out to the car, trying not to remember how much he was hoping she would actually show up.

He knew that wasn't what he was supposed to be thinking about at this juncture, but it was better than the alternatives. In fact, it would be much better if she actually did come. If she didn't, he wasn't sure there would be enough glue in the world to hold him together.

Thirty minutes later, Ben was standing with Jason and Holly as the funeral director gave them the 411 on the itinerary of the service. "We'll have the service in the main chapel. There's more room in there."

The front door of the funeral home opened, and the movement at the far end of the hall grabbed Ben's attention. The sight snagged his heart and jerked the rest of him around. He blinked twice at the vision that could be no other person on the earth.

"Kathryn," Jason said also looking up and seeing her. He held out his hand for her to join them, which she did like she was walking on a cloud.

She looked eternally graceful and more beautiful than Ben had even allowed himself to remember. "Jason." Walking right to his brother, she wrapped an arm around his waist. "I'm so sorry about your dad."

Jason accepted the hug and then turned her to his wife and daughter. "Kathryn, I'd like you to meet Holly and Ryley."

"Holly." Kathryn smiled and offered her hand. The two women shook hands, and then Kathryn laid hers on the little blonde curls streaming down the head ducking into Holly's shoulder. "Ryley. It's nice to meet you." She returned her attention to Holly. "I'm so sorry to hear about your father-in-law. I had the privilege of meeting the family at the hospice unit. They've become very special to me."

"I've heard good things about you," Holly replied with a smile as her gaze jumped over to Ben who felt like he'd been jolted with a 1,000 watts of pure electricity. He couldn't even trust his own mind to tell him logical things to do—with his hands, with his voice, with his heart. Holly replaced her gaze on Kathryn. "Thank you for coming. We're very glad to have you."

"Thank you," Kathryn said, glancing around at them. When her gaze got to Ben's, awkwardness dropped between them just before she let her gaze plummet to the carpet. She lifted it with effort, causing his heart to jump into his throat. Her smile was so soft, it was barely there. "Ben."

He nodded. "Kathryn." Why couldn't he get any more than that out? Words jammed into feelings making any more impossible.

A moment and she smiled softly. "I guess I'll just go get a

seat."

People were now streaming in the front doors. Somehow Ben hadn't noticed that. His whole attention had been fixed on her as the oxygen had suddenly dissipated from the room around him. He should say something, do something to keep her from walking any and taking his heart with her. *Pound. Pound. Pound.* His heart thudded in his chest and ears making it impossible to think straight.

"I'll talk to you later," she said, and then somehow, horror of absolute horror, she was walking away. All the gazes in their little knot, especially his, went with her. He felt every step she took.

When she got to the door, however, Kelly and Tamitha came in and stopped her just before she turned toward the chapel. Ben couldn't tear his gaze from them even though the funeral director resumed his checklist. Kelly and Kathryn talked for a short minute, and then Kelly looked over at Ben who stood somewhere in the vicinity of shell-shocked and non-functioning. With a knowing smile, Kelly lifted his chin and then lowered his head to hear what the women next to him were saying. Then, taking charge, he put his hand on Kathryn's back and the three of them turned for the chapel.

The funeral director prattled on about protocol and practicalities. Ben heard none of it. He only wanted to be the one walking with her. Why hadn't he said something like that to her? Why hadn't he invited her to sit with them? Okay, that would be over-the-top obvious, but his heart really didn't care. All it cared about was that she wasn't right there with him, in his arms, at his side. Everything else seemed ridiculous to even think about.

Kelly and his wife accompanied Kathryn right into the pew. She was thankful for their presence. After seeing Ben, she needed something normal and real to hold onto lest her heart talk her into doing something immensely stupid. The chapel was filling up around them. There were many she recognized from the medical community, and she was glad she hadn't taken the bait of wanting to sit with Ben. Others might well get the wrong idea.

She shifted in her seat as the family walked in from the front. Her gaze dropped to her hands when he entered, but it couldn't stay there. It flitted back up to his face, and she shifted again feeling what just looking at him did to her. Rolling her eyes to get herself to calm down and think rationally, she willed sensible over her. She was, after all, at a wake service. This was hardly the time to think about making a move on the deceased man's son.

Ben had never been good at religious services. He fought not to squirm. The problem was there was nowhere to put his gaze that didn't include a casket, flowers, or a body. Worse, there was nowhere to put his mind that didn't include either death or her. That seemed the height of disrespect to be thinking about how good she looked and what she did to his heart while he was at his father's wake service. Horrible. Yes, he was a horrible, rotten, awful human being.

He shifted before he realized he was moving. He was getting a headache. It started at the back of his neck and was now radiating up and over his brain in spasms so excruciating, he felt like he might throw up. As the woman who had read the short reading crossed in front of them, he smiled at her though he didn't even really see her. What he wanted to do was reach up and rub the back of his neck, but he couldn't do that. Instead, he squeezed his eyes closed and begged for this to be over quickly.

It occurred to him then that he was either begging someone who was real or the air. He closed his eyes, not in a squeeze but a sigh. He really didn't want to have a philosophical debate with himself about the existence of God at the moment. Why couldn't he just get through this without thinking? That would be a blessing.

Blessing. Ugh. He almost moaned out loud. Quickly he put his elbow on the edge of the pew and rubbed his hand over his chin. Letting out a slow but shallow breath, he pulled his shoulders up. The whole service was going right over his head, streaming by without him even catching hold of any of it. Then again, due to the headache, that was probably better anyway. A rip of pain slashed upward through him, and a hard breath escaped. Jason looked over at him, but Ben just mashed his lips together, determined to get through this in one piece.

Then, like a creeping fog, the understanding of how alone he was in this place slipped over him. There were over a hundred people in the room, but he sat pressed up against the edge of the pew with a full-body of space between him and any other human being. That's about how he felt in his spirit too. Totally alone. Like no one understood or wanted to be close to him. Maybe that's why Kathryn hadn't said more. Maybe she didn't want to be close to him either. He couldn't blame her really. He was hardly get close-to material.

"Amen," the crowd said, and Ben snapped back from his thoughts into reality.

"If you would like to view the body or speak to the family," the funeral director said from the little pulpit, "please feel free to come forward at this time."

Dread and exhaustion hit him like bricks. Why couldn't they just go home? This was torture.

An elderly lady stepped up to speak with Jason and Holly. All Ben wanted to do was run. He definitely did not want to sit there, receiving people he didn't even know and would never see again.

"You must be Ben," the lady said, stepping over to him.

Somehow he got rational snapped back over everything else as he held out his hand. "Yes. Thanks for coming."

"Oh, you are as handsome as your father always said you were."

A flush of embarrassment heated over him.

"I'm Mrs. O'Rorke. Your father tried to set you up with my granddaughter a couple years ago."

Ben blinked at the statement, trying to remember. "Oh, yes," he finally said because he had to say something.

"But you had some trip already scheduled when she was coming into town."

"Yes. Yes." He nodded as if he really remembered. "How is your granddaughter doing?"

"She's married now."

"Oh, really." He smiled as if he was pleased and surprised by that.

"A lawyer out of North Carolina. I guess you missed your chance."

He laughed although he wasn't at all sure why. "I guess so."

There was a line forming behind Mrs. O'Rorke.

"Thanks for coming," he said. She said something he really didn't hear and then she moved on. Glancing up at the line, his heart sank. He didn't want to do this. He didn't even know these people. One-by-one, they came by to give their condolences. Some stopped to tell him a longer memory of his father. Every one felt like an arrow to his heart, and he wasn't at all sure how many more arrows he could withstand.

Waiting for the next person to finish talking with Jason, Ben put his hand on the back of his neck and let out a long, slow breath. The headache was getting worse.

"Ben." The soft voice behind him whirled him toward it. Like an angel alighting on earth, Kathryn stood there, leaning on her hands across the bench. "I'm sorry. Father Patrick is here. He stopped by on his way to the hospital. He needs to make sure he has everything you want for the funeral."

"What? Oh, y-yeah. Of course." Ben was having trouble following anything. Life seemed to be circling around him. He looked back to the line which had diminished, and he reasoned that he didn't know anyone left anyway, so he exited the bench and followed Kathryn to the side door where he found Father Patrick waiting just as she had said. That almost surprised him as one part of him had thought maybe she was just making an excuse to get him out of there. But then again, she wouldn't do that because what would be the point? It wasn't like they could escape together to some remote island and sip mix-drinks together...

He shook those thoughts away truly wondering where they had come from. It was like he had no control of any part of himself any more. "Father." He put out his hand, thankful that he at least sounded semi-normal.

"Ben. I'm so sorry about your dad. Please accept my condolences."

"Thank you." He still wasn't sure if that was right, but he hadn't come up with anything better. "Uh, Kathryn said you needed to speak with me." He had to clear his throat after saying her name because he glanced over at her as he did, and her beauty and compassion was on full display. Forcing his gaze away from her, he reanchored it on the good father.

"Yes. I'm sorry to bother you, but I wanted to make sure I had everything for the funeral." Father Patrick opened his little black book and proceeded down the checklist.

Ben wasn't following much of anything. Looking at the list, he put his hand to the back of his head, wishing he had paid more attention in church. "Yeah, okay, that sounds good." It was about all he could think to answer.

As she stood there, just off to the side, Kathryn watched him, and her alert system went on full-blaring blast. He was about two inches from the edge. Everything about him screamed, "I can't take this anymore!" And she wasn't at all sure that Father Patrick was helping. *Father God, please, bathe this moment in Your peace. Ben needs You, Lord. He needs You. Please be with him.*

"I think that's everything I need," Father Patrick finally said. "And again, I'm sorry for the interruption, but I have another anointing to get to at the hospital."

"Don't worry about it." Ben half-smiled as he offered his hand. "Thanks for everything. We'll see you on Monday morning."

He almost sounded like he was setting up a meeting or making a dentist appointment.

In minutes Father Patrick skirted out of the darkened back hallway, leaving them alone together. Kathryn's gaze went to Ben who exhaled hard and long. He glanced at the doorway that would take him back to the front of the chapel. Then he looked over at her, his eyes sad and tired.

"I guess I should get back."

The smile broke her heart. "Yeah."

But he didn't move. Instead, he nodded and closed his eyes. The battle in his spirit was on full display.

Her heart screamed the question through her as logic screamed back not to say it. He needed to go. He didn't need to be hanging out in dark hallways with her. Still, her spirit wouldn't let her let him go. "How are you?"

His eyes said it all when he looked at her. Exhaustion. Overwhelm. Sorrow. "I'm fine."

Kathryn nodded, wishing she had some kind of magic wand that would make it all better. *Help, God. Please. Help me help him. He's hurting so much.* "You know, they have a smaller chapel down this way. I mean, I know you need to get back and everything, but later, if you need somewhere to decompress."

When he looked up, there was the barest hint of a smile in his eyes. "Decompress? That would be a switch."

"Tell me about it. These things can take the legs out from under the best of us."

He looked surprised. "I figured you'd be a pro at this."

Sadly she shook her head. "It never gets easier. I've just

learned to keep taking it to God, keep taking it to God, and when I think I can't move another step, I take it back to God."

Ben glanced at the door as thoughts streamed across his face. "I think they can handle it." He reached over and snagged her hand in his. "What do you say we go find that chapel?"

For one full second Kathryn looked stunned, and then her soft smile, which he had grown to so love drifted onto her lips. "You don't think they'll miss you?"

"Not any more than usual." He smiled because it seeped up from his heart. "Come on."

Together, they turned down the hallway and crossed all the way past the intersection that led to the main lobby. At the little door, Kathryn stepped in front of him and pushed open the door. He followed, feeling lighter than he had in hours. The chapel could hardly be called that. It was more a room with a cross at the front and a few chairs. As he followed her in, Ben wondered at this cross. It was more like the others he had seen, with no statue on it.

She slipped into one of the chairs to the right, and he followed, sitting right next to her. His hand never let go of hers, and that settled him in ways he couldn't really explain.

They sat like that for a few moments, not talking nor moving, and then Ben couldn't take even the small distance between them anymore. Although they were ostensibly in church, he reached over and put his arm around her. She slid closer to him, though the chairs made that less comfortable than the pew in the other chapel.

Her gaze drifted up to him. "So, how are you doing, really?"

He looked down at her, sure she could read every word on his face. The breath was hard and sharp. "I've been better. All the people tonight. I mean, I'm glad they came and all, but…"

"It's overwhelming," she finished for him when he didn't.

"Yeah. I'm not much of a big crowd kind of a guy, and I'm sure not much into hugging everybody in the place. I'm big on personal space." He sighed. "I don't know. I don't even know what to say to people, you know? I mean, they come up, 'Oh, Ben. I'm so sorry…' and I don't even know who they are. It's like I'm the host of a party I didn't throw."

"Well, for what it's worth, you're doing better than some I've seen."

He angled his gaze down to her. "You're kidding." He'd thought he was in about as bad of shape as was possible.

"Oh, no. I've seen people throw things at each other over who was going to carry what during the funeral. I've seen family members show up drunk and stoned. I've seen people argue over who was going to give the eulogy and which wife was going to sit where."

He laughed softly at that. "Well, at least we don't have *that* problem."

Her side of the conversation went silent for a moment. "Does that bother you? That your mom's not here?"

Ben shifted slightly under her, causing her to shift. "I don't know. Yeah? No? I don't even know how to answer that. I mean I haven't seen her in so long, and when I talked to her on the phone the other day, it was like I was some salesman from Borneo trying to sell her coconuts from a banana tree. But then, part of me thinks she really should be here, as much for Jason's sake as mine."

"Are you still mad at her?"

"For what she did?"

"Yeah." Her hand drifted up and down his as it lay on his knee.

He wasn't sure how to answer that any more than he had been about the last question. He'd never talked about it with anyone. "I don't know. I guess." He shrugged. "It's like she doesn't even care, you know? Like we're just little trophies on some shelf that she doesn't want to play with anymore."

"That must hurt. To think your mom doesn't even care."

It hurt more than he had even realized. He shook his head and sniffed. "I can't help but think if the tables had been turned, if she was the one to go, and Jason was out there dealing with that, Dad would have been on the first flight out." He felt the tears, but he beat them back. "Although I'm not totally sure that's even fair because I didn't know Dad was going out there to see Jason until two days ago."

Kathryn pulled herself from his embrace and looked at him with concern. "You didn't know your dad was going out there to visit Jason?"

Stuffing everything into a hard knot blocked by the scrunch of his face, Ben shook his head. "Nope. Why should I know? I mean, I'm just the big brother that had his heart smashed when his little brother left."

For one second, she absorbed that, and then gently, slowly, Kathryn picked her hand up to his face. It slipped onto his jawline as her gaze held his. "Ben, I'm so sorry. I can't imagine what that's been like for you."

He tried to be strong, to fight all of the emotions rising in him. Glancing away from her, he sniffed, desperately trying to corral the hurt. "Yeah, well, it happened, right? Big deal. Time to move on. I mean, what can they do now? Dad can't come back. Mom's gone. And it's not Jason's fault."

"But it still hurts."

Slamming his eyes closed, Ben put up every battle front in him. Never before had he felt the pain like this. It came in great waves, washing over him, dragging him under.

"Ben, I'm so sorry," she said as she reached over and gathered him into her arms.

Tears overran their banks and ache cascaded through him as he let himself be really held for the first time in a long, long time. The signals in him were firing from his emotions rather than his brain, and he reached up and anchored his arm over hers, holding on lest he fall right into the pain and never make it back out again.

"I'm so sorry," she whispered again and again, holding him to her. "They didn't know. They didn't know what this would do to you."

Anger split right through him. "Or they didn't care."

She didn't even move to contradict him.

"You know what really fries me?" he asked, yanking himself back and swiping at his eyes, furious with himself for being so weak. "That Dad knew where Jason was, and he didn't tell me. Not even a hint. I don't understand why he didn't tell me."

Kathryn's hand now rested on his arm, like a butterfly announcing spring. "Maybe he didn't want to see you hurt again. Maybe he was waiting for the right time. Ben, there could be a hundred-thousand reasons or there could be none. The truth is, we're all doing the best we can. Your dad loved you. That much I'm sure. He loved you, and whatever the reason he kept this from you, to him, he was doing it out of love. Now you can second-guess him, and you can even be angry, but the truth is, he did not do this to hurt you and you know it."

Everything in him wanted to lash out at her, to say she had no idea and what right did she have to make any judgments one way or the other, but the truth was, at that moment, he believed in her love for him more than he had ever believed in any other single thing. She wasn't saying this to hurt him. She was saying it out of love, just like she'd done every other thing since they had met.

Somehow that understanding drifted into him and settled everything else in his heart. As his gaze came back up to hers, he knew that life would never again be the same without her. He let out a breath, trying to talk himself out of saying it, but it wasn't leaving. "Listen, this is going to sound... I don't know... nuts or something, but..." He put his head down. He couldn't watch her reject him too. "Monday, at the funeral..." Reaching up, he scratched his head. "...will you..." The breath snagged on the words. "... will you sit by me?"

Shock overtook her in one split-second, but she beat that back when he looked right at her. Expectant and hopeful, his gaze grabbed hers, and although all training and professionalism said she should find a graceful way to say no, Kathryn couldn't do that to him. Not after everyone else had abandoned him. Not after she had sworn to see him through this horrible time. It went against every wall she'd ever put up to protect herself from getting hurt doing this job, and she was most assured that her heart would get completely smashed, but she would never be able to live with herself if she said no. So she let her smile escape from her heart as she nodded. "Sure."

Sixteen

The guy had sat in front of Kathryn at church again on Sunday, but she hardly noticed. She was too concerned with praying about the coming day. In fact, by Monday morning, she was sure God was tired of hearing from her.

"Mrs. Davis passed away over the weekend," Misty said, handing Kathryn a stack of files that Yvonne had left to be processed. "That was short and sweet."

"Sometimes…" But Kathryn couldn't finish that sentence. She looked over the files in her hands, counting the hours of work they represented. "I'm leaving about 9:15 for the Warren funeral."

"Oh." Misty deflated. "How are they doing?"

"Holding up."

Misty nodded and then straightened with a look of near excitement. "Oh, hey. I never got to ask, how was the date?"

The date. It felt like centuries had passed since then. Kathryn looked up and smiled on cue. "Oh, good."

"Good? Just good? Come on. I need details."

But Kathryn laid her hand on the files. "And I need to get to work." She turned and started down the hallway.

"You're no fun," Misty called, leaning over the counter.

Kathryn only put her hand in the air to wave at her friend. She had been sincerely hoping that Misty would have a short or better yet non-existent memory. What was there to say about that date that wasn't borderline awful? She escaped into her office just as her cell phone beeped. In one click she had it up to her ear. "Kathryn Walker, St. Anthony's Hospice." It was then that she realized she hadn't even forwarded the calls yet.

"Well, hello, there, Kathryn Walker from St. Anthony's."

She smiled at the voice. "Hello to you too. How are you? I've been wondering how you're doing."

"Tell me you're coming, and I'll be better."

Sitting down in her chair, she spun slowly away from the door. "What time do I need to be there?"

"Well, we're following from the funeral home in about thirty minutes or so, so I'm guessing we'll be at the church about 9:30."

She nodded the information in. "Then 9:30 it is."

Ben was having a fight with his stomach. It just wouldn't settle down. That's why he had called her, hoping that would help, and it had, just not totally. At the steps to the large, imposing church, he stepped out of the limousine and helped Holly and then Ryley out. Jason was last, and they shook hands.

Kelly came in the car behind with the other pallbearers who hustled up to the big black hearse in front of them all. Cars lined every highway, driveway, byway, and street. Completely unbelievably there were more people today than at the wake service. Ben breathed that in along with the trepidation. He'd never really thought forward in his life to this moment. To the strange question of how many people would show up for his funeral. Would Kelly come? Tamitha? Maybe Jason and Holly if they even kept in touch after this weekend. It was odd thinking about it, but that didn't stop the thought from going through his head.

The pallbearers extracted the solid oak coffin and began their slow, unsteady walk up the steps of the church. It hardly looked easy. Still, Ben thought his position was even harder. He surveyed the gathering crowd around the steps of St. Jude's Catholic Church, but he didn't see her. His heart fell. Maybe she hadn't been able to get away after all. Maybe she got stuck in traffic.

Head down, heart tightly clenched lest it completely fall apart, he followed the little procession up the steps. Somehow he had learned some responsibility somewhere along the way as he herded his family—Jason, Holly, and Ryley—through the doors, holding it for them. Then it was his turn to enter. His heart fell further as the overwhelming feeling of wanting to run overtook him. He swallowed it back, but it choked him. How was he ever going to do this alone? He ducked into the cool, darkness beyond the door, praying that somehow he would make it through this even though his strength and willpower had somehow slipped away from him. Reaching up, he raked his fingers through his hair, knowing that would do no good but hoping it would anyway.

It was only when his hand came back down to his side that movement from the side of the entrance snagged his attention. He turned to it, and his smile came right through the surging ache. Like it was the most natural thing in the world, she stepped up next to him and put her hands up to his face. His hands were on her waist before he realized they were moving. The greeting lasted only a second and there were no words that accompanied it, but he felt it all the way through him.

Then she turned at his side, and his hand joined hers.

Kathryn tried not to think about who was saying and thinking what as she walked down the aisle with Ben in full view of all those already gathered. But she felt all of the questioning looks. She lifted her chin. God would just have to take care of all of that. She was here for Ben just as she said she would be. At the front, he stepped back to let her enter the bench, and in the next second, she found herself between Jason and Ben. She reached over for Jason who looked surprised but recovered quickly. A small wave and smile at Holly were enough.

She'd been to many funerals. They were all different. But none had been anywhere near like this.

It was a very good thing for Kathryn. Ben thought that every time they sat and every time they stood. The first reading was something about a large army and some guy who saw angels that weren't there.

"O, Lord, open his eyes that he might see," the reader said.

Ben closed his, thinking how nice it would be to have angels he didn't know were there. When he opened them again, he almost laughed out loud when Kathryn looked over at him and smiled. Maybe angels weren't so far away after all.

The psalm started and though he hadn't known he knew anything about the Bible, he remembered her saying those verses in her sweet, calm, patient voice. It took next to nothing to remember sitting there with her in the hospice, and his heart said he would never forget. The second reading started.

"Rejoice in the Lord always. I shall say again: rejoice!"

The words took Ben off-guard. Somehow he hadn't expected to be enjoined to rejoice at his own father's funeral. He probably should've given a little more thought and opinion to what Jason had chosen.

"Your kindness shall be known to all. The Lord is near. Have no anxiety at all, but in everything, by prayer and petition, with thanksgiving make your requests known to God. Then the peace that surpasses all understanding will guard your hearts and minds in Jesus Christ."

Requests? At that moment, Ben only had one, and it had to do with the woman sitting right next to him, holding his hand. He would have glanced over at her, but he didn't have to.

"Finally, brothers, whatever is true, whatever is honorable, whatever is just, whatever is pure…"

With each whatever, Ben realized he had no standing to make the request he'd just made. Pure? Just? Honorable? He wasn't any of those. His spirit sank.

"Whatever is lovely, whatever is gracious, if there is any excellence, and if there is anything worthy of praise, think about these things. Keep on doing the things you have learned and received and heard and seen in me. Then the God of peace will be with you."

The reader finished and stepped away.

The truth stared at him, and he felt it laughing. How could he even think of Kathryn joining him in life? She was all those things. Gracious. Lovely. Loving. Hopeful. Prayerful. He was none of them. As they stood, he let her hand go and crossed his arms. Somehow it was hard enough to be standing here with his father's casket sitting right there in front of him, he didn't need the reminder of how surely his life was sliding into the pit.

He wondered how much was left of this torture session. As Father Patrick approached the lectern, Ben fought not to look at his watch. The headache was coming back.

Father Patrick announced the Gospel. All Ben wanted to do was figure out how to speed up time. Shifting feet, he reached up and scratched his head. If he'd paid attention as a kid, he might know how much longer. As it was, there was no telling if this might in fact last into the next eternity.

Kathryn noticed Ben let her hand go. That worried her, but what worried her more was how fidgety he suddenly seemed. She closed her eyes and knocked Satan away with a one-two punch of the Sword of the Spirit and then called all of God's angels into the situation. *Satan, let go of Ben by the Blood of Jesus. You can't have him. Not anymore. Let go. God, please, come in here, flood Ben with Your love. Please.*

"If you love Me, you will keep My commandments. And I will ask the Father, and He will give you another Advocate to be with you always, the Spirit of truth, which the world cannot accept, because it neither sees nor knows it. But you know it, because it remains in you, and will be in you. I will not leave you orphans; I will come to you. In a little while the world will no longer see Me, but you will see Me, because I live and you will live. The Gospel of the Lord."

"Praise to You, Lord Jesus Christ," Kathryn replied with most of the rest of the congregation. When she went to sit, she realized Ben hadn't followed. She reached up and touched his arm.

He looked down and realized his mistake. Quickly he sat next to her. Smoothing, shifting, moving. There wasn't a thing about him that was calm. His head twisted one way and then the other, and he closed his eyes clearly struggling.

It was impossible to know how he would take it, if she was over-stepping her bounds or doing something that would push him away forever, but she took the leap and reached across for his hand. His gaze snapped to hers, and she ducked her gaze in seriousness at him, asking without asking if he was all right.

At first his eyes were wild, like they were looking for an escape hatch, but then the wild fell away, revealing only a deep, heart-wrenching sadness. She understood. After all, he'd just lost his father.

Ben dropped her gaze with a shake of his head even as he left his hand in hers. She was an angel. He was scum. What other conclusion could any sane person possibly come to after hearing all of that?

Father Patrick stepped down the stairs to address the congregation, and Ben wondered again how long this might take, hating himself for wondering even as he did so. He was sure she wasn't thinking that. She probably had the readings memorized.

"We gather today not only in sadness over the death of our brother, Ronald Warren, but to rejoice in Ron's life. Our readings illuminate so beautifully the point of reference that Ron had learned over the course of his life. During one of our last meetings together, he told me about this point of reference—how he had been reading about survivors and the tricks they use to survive. One of those tricks that Ron was most enamored with was that of the point of reference. He told me that there was a time when his life had spun out of control, and he very nearly lost everything. But then he spoke of the point of reference he had found right here." Father Patrick picked up the Bible in his hands. "I remember Ron telling me how he had learned to go to his point of reference when life and death decisions had been placed in his hands and how that single decision had made such a dramatic impact upon his life.

"We spoke at length about the Gospel. How Jesus had sent an Advocate in the Holy Spirit to be with us, and how Ron had found in the Spirit an emotional point of reference, a single point that was there always and did not move. Having found that, it gave him the freedom to take risks like reaching out to his younger son and reestablishing contact with him." Father Patrick looked across at Jason and smiled. "That moment was so very precious to your dad. He spoke of how frightened he'd been to take that leap, but how very grateful he had been for the opportunity."

Ben's attention shifted from the self-loathing ones back to the present situation. His father. This was the last he would hear from him, about him. That thought drown all the others.

"In fact, I believe in choosing this particular reading, Ron was giving us all a clue about what he most wanted for each of us." Then Father Patrick looked right at Ben. "Finding that point of reference for your life is critical. When life has you coming all undone, it can mean the difference between surviving and succumbing." His gaze slipped away, but Ben still felt it there. "When we find God and make Him our point of reference, we find just what St. Paul talked about in our second reading. We begin to become people of honor, justice, purity, love, graciousness, peace, and excellence. Not through a force of our own will but by the gracious direction of God's love working in our lives. When those things begin to permeate our lives, our eyes are open, and we can begin to see what God is doing in our lives. Like Elisha from the first reading, we don't see empty hills and an enemy army surrounding us. Instead, we begin to see the angels coming to our aid. We begin to see God's power working in our lives just like Ron did in the later stages of his life. I have to say, I believe that was his greatest wish for all of us." He paused. "Let us stand and remember our brother Ron."

Dutifully Ben stood, but he didn't let go of her hand, or maybe she didn't let go of his. He couldn't clearly tell who was holding onto whom anymore. And he wasn't at all sure that was even a bad thing.

Although Ben asked, Kathryn chose to drive herself to the graveyard. It would have been too weird to ride in the limousine. As she drove slowly amidst the string of cars, she let her thoughts trail back to the church, standing there, holding his hand for all the world to see. She wondered again if that's what it felt like to be in love. True, she would do anything for him. That was a given, but today would not last forever. At some point it would end, and there would be a tomorrow, and tomorrow life would go on—for him and for her. Where that would leave them was anyone's guess. Still, she pushed that back, determined to be here for him today. Tomorrow would have to take care of itself.

After the short ceremony in the graveyard, the crowd broke up, and Ben stood under the little awning for one more moment looking at the casket as the others dissipated. The spray of flowers had been removed, and the casket now stood over the hole in the ground bare but stoic—ready for its fate. A hand clapped him on the back, and Ben turned to find Kelly, eyes sad and knowing, right behind him. Wordlessly, they embraced. Gratefulness for his friend tore through Ben. He didn't deserve such a good friend as this one.

When the embrace broke, they turned together, looking at the casket.

"So do you think this is it?" Ben asked, feeling the utter pointlessness of it all if it was.

"Nah, man. You'll see him again. He's probably up there right now getting everything all organized for the rest of us."

Ben laughed. "He certainly tried to get me organized."

Kelly joined the laugh. "Like that ever worked."

The laugh fell away as Ben shook his head. "It just went so fast."

A moment and Kelly sighed softly. "It all does, man. That's why we've got to make the right stuff important instead of taking for granted it's always going to be here."

Ben thought about that and then put his hand out. It took Kelly a minute to react.

"Thanks," Ben said.

"For what?"

"For... I don't know... for being here, for not blowing me off when you could have and probably should have."

Kelly laughed and waved. "Oh, that. Well, you know, what did I have better to do, right?" After they shook hands, his gaze slipped past Ben, who turned to follow it. Across the graveyard, Kathryn stood, holding Ryley and talking to Jason and Holly. She looked like she'd found a new little friend. The sight made Ben's heart jerk.

"You know," Kelly said, "it's none of my business, but..."

He wanted to hear, to think down the road Kelly was going, but Ben knew the story was all but over, her job was over, she had done exactly as she had told him she would do—she had seen him through. "We'd better get over there. Jason was talking about going to eat somewhere. Are you and Tamitha going to come, or do you have to get back to work?"

Side-by-side they started across the grassy hill dotted with gray and brown headstones.

"Yeah, we'll be going back probably tomorrow," Jason said. "I've got to get back for work."

Without really realizing she was doing it, Kathryn ran her hand up and down the little child's back who snuggled into her arms. Sometime in the last hour as her parents spoke with everyone, the little girl had attached herself to Kathryn, and Kathryn wasn't arguing. She laid her cheek on the soft, blonde curls, wishing this never had to end. They had all become like family to her. How would she ever let them go?

"So." Ben stepped up with Kelly, and his brash manner surprised Kathryn. He looked more on top of his game than he had since they'd met. It made her heart collapse to think he no longer needed her. "I was thinking Orlando's or maybe Vencini's. How does Italian sound to everyone?"

Just like that Kathryn felt her place with all of them evaporate. She was no longer needed—he no longer needed her; they no longer needed her. Her spirit stepped back and away from them. It hurt, but she breathed that down, praying God would get her through the next few minutes.

"Sounds good to me," Jason said. "I'm starving."

Tamitha came to stand by Kelly. "We could go for some Italian."

"Great!" Ben said, clapping his hands as if he couldn't wait. "Then what are we waiting for?"

The shattering of Kathryn's heart was taking all of her willpower to keep down. It hurt worse than she could ever have imagined. "Well." She shifted Ryley slightly and with one more rub across the child's back, she detached from the child, handing her back to Holly. "I'd better be getting back to work."

Like a whipsaw, Ben's heart hit his shoes. "Work?" His gaze jumped to her. "You're not...? You're not going to... join us?"

She smiled, softly, serenely, as he had seen her do a hundred thousand times. "No, I'd really better get back. But you all take care."

He heard what she was saying loud and clear, and suddenly he couldn't breathe. She really was leaving. Not for an hour, not for a day, but for forever. He stood there, helplessly, not knowing how to make it stop.

"You guys travel safely," she said, giving first Holly and then Jason a hug. She stepped to Kelly and Tamitha and offered her hand. "It was nice to meet you. Take care."

She had to be kidding! She had to be! She couldn't just leave. Not now. Not like this. And then she was standing right in front of him, looking like the professional, in control woman who had walked into Dr. Vitter's office an eternity before. Her soft smile tore his heart out. "Let us know if you need anything." She put her hand out, and Ben looked down at it not comprehending anything.

"I… Okay." He shook her hand and then couldn't take the distance between them one more second. With that he pulled her to him, latching on, praying she wouldn't just walk out of his life. "Thank you."

Her hand rubbed up and down his back, and although he wanted it to be special, he knew she was only comforting another bereaved client. He let go and looked at her, but she wouldn't look back. Instead, her gaze was melded to the ground between them.

She sniffed softly and nodded. "You're welcome." Then for one small moment her gaze came up to his. It held for only a heartbeat and then fell again. "Take care." Her hand stayed on his arm, squeezed once more, and then dropped. For one whole moment he thought she was going to say more because she didn't move. Then, head down, she turned from their group and walked off, taking his heart with her.

Keep walking, Kate. Keep walking and don't look back. Tears streamed down Kathryn's face with each step she took, and she hated them all. If anyone had seen her, they would've thought she had completely lost it. But this was her *job* for goodness sake. Her job. Professionals didn't lose it like this. What was wrong with her?

Again and again on the trek to her car, she pushed his face from her memory and her heart. She had to get away, to put distance between them. It was the only way she could hope to keep any pieces of her heart that were left together.

"What are you doing?" Kelly asked, heat permeating the statement he hissed at his friend. "Why are you just standing there? Go after her already."

Ben's gaze fell from the sight of her walking away. Seeing that was tearing him apart anyway. He turned back to the group with a little shrug. "She needs to get back to work."

Kelly let out an exasperated exhale. "You've got to be kidding me."

Facing how little he really meant to her was hard enough,

doing it with an audience was horrific. "So are we going to eat or what? I'm starving." He really wasn't. In fact, he might never eat again.

"Dr. Lightner just called from the heart wing," Misty said as Kathryn stood at the counter thirty minutes later.

She was proud of herself for the solid snap-mask she had been able to force over the emotions in the hospice parking lot. True, it had taken all the way to there to stop crying, but once she had, it almost seemed like life could go on like normal. "Okay. Did they send the paperwork down?"

"It's on your desk."

"Have they assigned a room yet?"

"Twelve."

Mrs. Davis's room. And before that Mr. Warren's. Her heart lurched at that thought, but she yanked it back.

"How was the funeral?" Misty asked with some hesitation.

Kathryn barely looked up from the phone messages Misty had given her. "Oh, fine. It was nice." She could feel Misty about to ask more questions, so she looked up and smiled her best *all is right with the world* smile. "I'd better get to work."

"Yeah."

The conversation floated around Ben. He laughed when everyone else did though he could hardly follow the conversation for the pain in his heart. He tried to look interested as Jason told everyone about his job and the little town where they lived. He tried, but it didn't work very well. In a strange way it was like being able to see that life was all some fancy, elaborate play. He was watching it rather than being in it. They were talking, about what? Did any of it matter? Was any of it even real?

In twelve hours they would all be back to their own lives, no longer connected by the tragedy that was now over.

"Is something wrong with your manicotti, sir?" the waiter asked, stepping up behind him.

"What?" Ben spun, taken off-guard. He looked down at his barely touched food. "Oh, no. I guess I wasn't as hungry as I thought."

He felt the concerned looks from the others at the table. Even Holly who had been preoccupied with keeping marinara off of Ryley's dress for most of the meal looked over at him. He smiled at all of them and shrugged. "I guess I'm not used to eating at two in the afternoon."

"Are you going to break for lunch?" Misty asked, standing at Kathryn's door.

"Oh, I ate something on the way over." She barely looked up from the paperwork, hoping her stomach wouldn't give the lie away.

"I could bring you something back."

"No. Really. I'm fine."

"So," Jason said, standing outside of the restaurant. He turned to Ben who could hardly take the relentlessness of the heartaches being thrown at him like debris in a hurricane.

"So." Ben turned, determined to not make his last minutes with his brother some kind of weep-fest. He put out his hand, and Jason shook it. "Don't be a stranger. You know where we live now."

"Yeah."

"And I'll be in touch with you once we get the whole estate thing pinned down."

Jason half-smiled and half-nodded. "Okay."

As long as he could swim in the details, Ben convinced himself he would be fine. "I don't think it should take more than a month or so to go through everything. If you want something in particular…"

"No. Just whatever."

Ben nodded. Then sensing he couldn't take a second more of that conversation, he turned to Holly. "You take care of yourself, you hear me. And this little one and this little one too." He reached over and slid his hand over Ryley's curls, the feel of which brought the vision of Kathryn holding her in that graveyard rushing back. He could hardly keep the onslaught of emotions from surfacing. "Have a safe trip back."

"We will."

Again Ben nodded, feeling like he was on display for the whole entire world to see. "Well, I'd better be getting home." He reached over and shook Kelly's hand, feeling like he was abandoning his own responsibilities to his friend. But what was new there?

"Take care of yourself," Kelly said, and it sounded like a warning.

"Oh, you know me."

"Yeah, I do." And that didn't sound like a good thing.

Ben stepped backward away from them, hoping he wouldn't fall. "See you guys later." He lifted his hand and then ran it over his head as he turned for his car. It felt like lasers going through him. He knew they were watching, but what did they want from him? He couldn't stay and babysit all night. Besides they were going to leave at some point. He was doing them all a favor, getting it over with sooner rather than later.

Down the block, he crawled into his car and revved the engine. Back to real life. Finally. He couldn't have been happier to be back.

Seventeen

Jason and Holly were gone. Ben had gotten that much from the call from Kelly on Thursday. Kelly called him, not the other way around. The truth was for all the show he put on for the rest of the world, Ben was hanging on by a thin thread. He went to work, even made some sales. He came home and dragged a beer out of the refrigerator. That was the only thing left.

One part of him tried to remember the last time he'd eaten, but that took too much energy so he abandoned the search. He considered going out, but the question of where he would even go kept him glued to the couch. Besides, he couldn't think of anyone who would agree to meet him "out" wherever anyway.

So he sat on his couch, staring at the TV that he didn't have the energy to turn on, sipping a beer he didn't taste. Life was wonderful.

"I am so ready to be out of here," Misty said, the next Friday. "I can't wait."

"So what time's your flight out?" Kathryn had learned that short bits of very focused conversation were the only things that kept her from thinking about the pathetic state of her life and heart. She had seen Dr. Martin in the cafeteria with yet another blonde who might or might not have a connection with the hospital. Nathan hadn't called. And even the guy two rows down had skipped church on Sunday.

The one guy she really wanted to think about, she made herself not. It just hurt too much. One small piece of her had hoped he would call, but he hadn't. That was more than enough evidence to demonstrate that he hadn't been anything other than another client. She needed to move on. However, knowing that and doing it were on opposite ends of the emotional spectrum, and she couldn't figure out how to get them to come together.

"Nine-fifteen. I'm leaving early."

"And you're coming back next... what?"

"Friday. A whole week away in paradise." Misty sighed. "No kids. No work. No house to clean."

"Just make sure you come back."

Misty sighed again. "Why?"

That was a good question.

The bad thing for Kathryn was that even the chapel wasn't safe anymore. Going in there reminded her of their time together and that just hurt all the more. She prayed for him as much as her heart could take, but it was becoming more and more fragile with each passing hour. She needed to go out, to get out, to go do something.

Picking up her cell phone after work, she punched in Casey's number. Maybe they could go get Chinese or go to the moon.

"Hello?" Her sister sounded like death warmed over.

"Case? What's wrong?"

"Ugh. Hi, Kate. What time is it?"

"Uh, five-fifteen. Where are you?"

"Bed. Stomach bug. Paige came down with it yesterday, so we've been trading off throwing up all day."

"Oh, Case. Why didn't you call me?"

"Trust me. You don't want this stuff. The doctor said it's like a 48-hour thing, and we're going to be lucky if Taylor doesn't get it."

"How's Ethan?"

"Fine. He's working. He's probably safer there anyway."

"He left you with both kids?"

"Duh. Work or staying home with two sick-to-their-shoes people and a screaming baby? What would you choose?"

"I should come over."

"No. Kate. Really. Ethan should be here in an hour anyway. And there's no reason for you to get sick too."

"Are you sure? I could bring some Sprite or..."

"Oh, Kate. I've got to go. Paige is looking green again."

"O…kay."

"I'll call you later." And with that she was gone.

Kathryn clicked off the phone, seriously considering going over to her sister's. But it was a two-hour drive, and what could she really do once she got there anyway? Her phone rang, and with a sigh, she answered it. "Hello."

"Katie. I'm glad I caught you."

"Hi, Mom."

"Have you talked with Casey?"

"I just did. Why?"

"Because I'm headed over there. She doesn't need to be there with those two babies like that."

There was no argument in Kathryn.

"I just wanted to let you know that I'll be over there at least through the weekend so you don't worry if you call and I'm not here."

"Oh, okay."

"Darling, are you okay? I hope you're not coming down with something. You sound like you could use some rest too."

That didn't sound like a bad suggestion. "I'm fine, Mom. Just take care of Casey and the kids."

Her mother sighed. "I just wish you had someone…"

Ugh. Not now. Please. "I'm hanging up now, Mom."

"I'm not being pushy. I'm just saying…"

"Seriously. I'm hanging up." She pulled the phone from her ear and then put it back. "I love you." And with that she clicked it off and flipped it into the other seat. Maybe she was getting sick. She sure didn't feel great. Friday night, alone again. What a surprise.

"Ben, it's been awhile. I haven't heard from you," Charissa said on the machine as Ben stood at the counter drinking a beer and listening. "I'd love to see you again. Call me."

She left her number just before the beep. The machine clicked off. Staring at it, he took another drink.

He was alone, and he was bored. It wasn't like it would be the crime of the century to call her. Maybe they could go out. He hadn't been out in so long, he couldn't remember the last time. Or maybe they could just stay in. That sounded even better. Maybe that's just what he needed to get his head back on straight.

Reaching over, he tried not to think about what he was doing as he called her number. "Charissa!" He sounded fake even to his own ears, but he pushed that back. "I just got your message. Yeah. Listen..." He leaned back on the counter, letting the old bravado slip over him. Finally, Ben Warren was back in the game.

Kathryn took the book off the shelf. She had read it before, mostly for understanding for the job. For a moment she thumbed through it, and then stopped for no apparent reason. She flipped her hair over to the other shoulder and laid her head on her couch. As she read, it was odd how she didn't remember reading this part. It was about loving someone without expectations and how if you simply loved no matter what the outcome, that was real love.

Six pages in, she let the book fall closed. They all made it sound so easy, but what about when you did that and you still got your heart smashed? Standing, she walked over to the window where the raindrops slithered down. With the tips of her fingers she reached out and touched the cold glass as her heart searched for him no matter how stupid her head said that was. Love so wasn't fair, not when you went all in and got burned anyway. It hurt to know he'd never had any intention of being with her. He had used her, and when her job was over, when her use to him was over, he went on with life as if nothing had ever happened.

She would cry, but it would change nothing. She was out of tears, out of hurt, out of hope. What was the point? No matter what she did, she still ended up here, in her apartment, alone. With a shake of her head, she stepped away from the window and the depressing thoughts. She needed sleep. Maybe she really was getting sick.

"So," Charissa said as she sat on his couch. Her skirt was so short Ben had no trouble visualizing anything even through the alcohol.

"So," he replied, knowing full well where that would lead. What was the point of wasting time? They both knew why she was here. He reached over and put his hand on her leg. It was soft. He pushed that thought away as he leaned over to her. He didn't want to think anymore. He didn't want to feel. All he wanted was to get lost in the ways that had always worked before and to find a way to stay there forever.

For the third time, Kathryn pulled herself out of the bed. This time, however, she treaded into the living room and to the couch where she plopped down. The rain had chilled everything, so she pulled a blanket over to her. Her glance at the clock on the DVD player confirmed that it was in fact after midnight. Because she simply couldn't fight it any more, she let her thoughts go to him, wondering where he was. Probably somewhere fabulous. At a bar or on a date with some gorgeous super-model. She could see them now. It wasn't even all that difficult. They were perfect for each other.

She laid her head back against the cushions and pulled the blanket up higher. No wonder he had no real interest in her. Her life was pathetic. She was pathetic. A tear slid down her cheek, and she brushed it back, annoyed that she even still cared. It would be so much easier not to.

Charissa was asleep in his bed, but Ben felt like a hammer couldn't put him to sleep. He had thought this would help. He was wrong. Desperately, hopelessly, horribly wrong. Padding out to the living room, he sat down on his couch, and in the silence, he heard the rain. Just like that, he was back in the hospice unit, on the floor, with her. He could pull her face up with no problem at all. It was so easy, and it hurt so much.

With a hard sigh, he reached over to the end table and picked up his cell phone. Would it be so horrible to just call her? Sure, she might tell him to get lost, but at least then he would know. However, what would happen then stomped over his heart. How could he go on without her? It was like he suddenly couldn't even find life because she was gone. His gaze went over to the doorframe where Charissa slept, and hate for how repulsive he was drilled into him.

He let the cell phone drop between his knees as he flopped back onto the couch. "God, I can't call her. I can't do that to her. She's so much better off without me. Please, please, help me to let her go for her sake."

Halfway back to the couch, Kathryn spied the cell phone on the counter. She picked it up as if she was simply going to check her messages. Once back on the couch with her hot chocolate, she took a small sip and set it aside. Curling up, she clicked the phone on and had to fight against the intensity of the backlight. Was it always that bright? She hadn't remembered that.

When her eyes adjusted, she scrolled through the options. No messages. No voicemail. No nothing. Not that there should have been. Misty was already on the plane or maybe they had already arrived. Kathryn said a short prayer for them. She surely wouldn't hear from her mother or Casey until tomorrow, if then. Still, holding the phone, she took another sip. Even the warmth of the drink didn't help her chilled spirit.

Picking the phone up once more, she scrolled through her meager friends folder. Of course, it was well after midnight, so she couldn't call any of them. Then suddenly, there in her fingers, she held his name. Ben Warren. She had shifted him into the friends folder sometime after he had called her on the way home from work. Settling back into the cushions, she relived that moment. What it was like for someone to care that she made it home, what it was like just to talk, what it was like to hear his voice.

For one implausible second she thought about just hitting the call button. What would that hurt? Just to see how he was doing… But thankfully, at the last second, logic overrode the absurd idea. Closing her eyes so she wouldn't have to see herself, she closed the phone and flipped it to the coffee table. She must seriously be going insane to even think about calling him. How desperate was that? Disgusted with herself, she stood and headed back to the bedroom. It was time to get some sleep.

Sometime after two, Ben gave up trying to force himself to go back to bed. He just couldn't. Instead, he curled up on the couch, still holding the phone. It was the only way he could sleep.

"I don't know." Ben put his hand to his head the next afternoon as he surveyed the stacks of things around his father's living room. There were candle sticks and picture frames and statuary that he didn't even remember ever seeing before. So much stuff. So many things, but bereft of the man who had loved them, they meant nothing. "I don't even know what to do any more. I mean I've boxed and stacked and tried to get things semi-somewhat-organized, but you just wouldn't believe the amount of stuff."

"I wish I could come help," Jason said, sounding really very concerned. "It's just with work and the baby coming…"

"No. No. I'm not saying you should come. I'm just… Ugh. I'm freaking out here. And I thought the finance stuff was a mess. I met with the lawyers again yesterday. Everything seems to be in order there, I guess. I'm supposed to meet with the trust bank on Tuesday to go over everything. Apparently he didn't want to cut Mom out completely, so there's some going to be set aside for her and of course for you and me…"

"I don't really care about the money."

"Well, that makes two of us." Ben sighed as he looked around. "I have half a mind to just box this stuff all up and call Goodwill. If I didn't have some idea that it's worth something, I'd probably do just that. But I don't even know where to start at this point. I mean we've got Grandma Rose's china. What am I supposed to do with all of that?"

"I could talk to Holly. Maybe she would want it."

"That's fine by me. The more stuff you guys take, the less I have to get rid of. I sure don't need any of it."

Ben sat down in a heap on the couch because he simply couldn't stand any longer and sighed.

"So how are things?" Jason asked. "I mean besides all the stuff and the lawyers and everything."

Strangely Ben couldn't really see anything other than that right now—mostly because he didn't want to. "Fine. I mean, except for this whole estate mess, everything's good."

"You went back to work?"

"Yeah. Yeah. Back to work. Back in the game. You know. I can't duck out forever."

There was a long pause.

"How about Kathryn? Have you talked to her lately?"

"Kathryn?" The name was like a bomb explosion, but Ben managed to sound like he didn't even know anyone by that name. "Ah, no. I haven't… We haven't talked. Why?"

"Oh." Jason sounded surprised. "Well, that's too bad. I just thought… you know, with how you guys were at the funeral and all…"

Ben didn't want to think about how they were at the funeral or any other time. "Nah. It was just... you know... whatever. She was just doing her job."

"Her job is showing up to hold hands with the deceased's son at the funeral?" Jason stopped. "I'm sorry. Ben, really I am. I just... you guys were so good together."

Together? Had they ever been together? Ben sighed and ran his hand down his face. "Yeah, well, I can't drag her through the muck of my life. That isn't fair. Didn't you hear the preacher about that noble and excellent stuff? That's what she deserves. Not some jerk off the streets who can't keep his life together no matter how hard he tries."

"Ben..."

"I know. I know. It's just all this stuff I'm supposed to know what to do with and everybody waiting for me to get on with it, and I just feel like I'm stuck in quicksand that won't let me go."

"Well, for what it's worth, I'm glad you're there dealing with things. I would be clueless where to even start."

For some reason that made him feel just a bit better. "Well, for the record, I wish you were the one here trying to figure out what to do with 100-year-old candlesticks and furniture that probably came over on the Mayflower."

Jason laughed. At least the doom and gloom part of the conversation was over, and Ben hoped that was for good and for forever.

Kathryn spent all of Saturday scrubbing her apartment. If her life couldn't be in order, at least her apartment could. She scrubbed the stove with a toothbrush and the shower door with a Brillo pad. How long had it been since she had cleaned anyway? She dusted the shelves and all of the knickknacks, swept the floors and shined them up right. Even the television got a good cleaning.

By seven o'clock, her entire apartment was shining, and she was not even a step closer to out-running his memory.

"Dude, seriously," Kelly said as Ben sat on his couch later that evening. "Why don't you just call her? You know you want to."

Did he have to keep having this conversation over and over

again? It was like being stuck on the spin cycle with no way to shut it off.

"Dude," Ben said back mockingly. "She's gone on with her life. She wants nothing to do with me. End of story."

"And you know that... how?"

"Well," Ben hedged. "It's been two weeks, and she has my number too."

"Oh, for the love of Mike. You are unbelievable. You really expect *her* to call?"

Charissa had. That thought went over and through him like an airplane buzzing the tower, rattling everything in him. Did he really want Kathryn to be like Charissa? The thought sickened him to the core.

"Ben, listen to me," Kelly said slowly. "Kathryn is classy. She's not like the other bimbos and whores you've gone out with. She's not a woman you rent. She's a woman you buy."

Ben jerked forward. "Buy? I'm not..."

"Look. Hear me out. Okay? Tamitha got this CD thing she's been listening to about marriage for that class she's taking at church. She was telling me about it the other night. She said the guy says that there are three kinds of people you're going to meet in the dating world. There are the freeloaders who come in and take everything you give with no expectation of ever having to give anything back to you. There are renters—people who give you something in exchange for something else. They aren't freeloaders, but they aren't permanent either. The second the deal isn't working for them, they're gone. And then there are buyers.

"Buyers are serious. They aren't flipping houses. They buy into the relationship to stay. They invest in the relationship. They have a stake in it. They see things as permanent or at least that they could turn into permanent. Buyers aren't in it for some temporary fix. They are about forever. Kathryn is a buyer."

"Yeah, but I'm a freeloader." The statement broke him to the core, but it was true, maybe the truest thing he'd ever said, and he hated himself for it.

That stopped the conversation.

"What? I am." Ben felt it to the bottom of his soul. "You said it, 'They take and take, and they don't think they have to give anything back.' That's me, Kell. It is."

Kelly's voice shifted and dropped. "You may think that's you, but I think you're lying to yourself on that one, my friend. I think you've told yourself that and you've tried to make yourself believe it, but I think that's because you're too scared to admit the truth—that you want to buy more than anything else in the world."

"Right, Dr. Phil. Thank you so much for that psychoanalysis."

But Kelly's voice didn't lose the seriousness. "Here's what I think. I think you saw what your mom did to your dad, and you decided you never wanted anything to do with that, that you would never let any woman close enough to you to do that."

Ben beat back the fear and tears that surged into his heart.

"So you decided you would use women and then cut them loose before they got too close. You thought you weren't going to get hurt that way. But look around you, Ben. Are you happy? Have you been happy? Is living like this making you happy?"

Kelly took a breath. "Is going for it with Kathryn going to be easy? No. It probably won't be. Heck, Tamitha and I have times we'd like to kill each other. But the bottom line is, we've bought in. We're committed to each other and to making the relationship work because we can't imagine living without each other."

That part Ben heard loud and clear. He still couldn't imagine living without her. In fact, he'd felt like he'd come completely undone ever since she had walked away, and nothing upon nothing had helped to change that.

"Call her."

"But…"

"Call. Her." Kelly waited two seconds. "Seriously. Dude. Call her."

Eighteen

Kathryn went to bed at ten o'clock. At quarter to eleven she was back up again. She didn't know what was up with the whole not being able to sleep thing, but it was going to kill her sooner rather than later. She was in the kitchen, over the sink, making another cup of hot chocolate when her cell phone on the counter beeped.

Curious and worried, she went over to it. Her mother had called earlier. Who else would it be? She squinted into the darkness, trying to read the caller ID. Giving up and hoping it wasn't a telemarketer, she flipped it on. "Hello?"

The line was dead silent, and the thought that it was indeed a telemarketer went through her. "Hello?"

Ben's whole system—mouth, heart, and brain stopped with that one simple word. "Uh, hi. Kathryn?" Suddenly he couldn't breathe, couldn't think. "Um, this is Ben. Ben Warren. Did I… did I wake you up?"

Actually hearing his name in his voice gave new meaning to the term "wake you up." She almost dropped the phone. "Ben? What? No. I mean… what?"

"I'm sorry for calling so late. Maybe I should let you go."

"NO!" The word surged through her heart and right out of her mouth. Barely getting control of her rushing feelings, she cleared her throat. "No. I mean. I was awake. I was up."

"Oh… good."

"Hm." She cleared her throat again, trying to get her heart to stop pounding the fact that Ben Warren was actually on the other side of the line. "Did you… need something?"

At 11:15? She was seriously asking him that question at 11:15? Ben almost laughed out loud. How about directions to downtown or to the metro or to LaGuardia? "Um, no. Not… not exactly." He shifted on the couch, berating himself for thinking this was a good idea. "I was just wondering how… hm… how you're doing."

How I'm doing? He calls me out of the blue at 11:20 to ask how I'm doing? "I'm fine. How about you?"

She sounded so cold, so detached.

"I'm cool. I was just, you know, going through some things, and I thought about you. How's work?" Man, he was a bad liar.

"Oh, it's work. We got a new patient in Friday."

"Oh?"

"Yeah. A young kid. It's kind of sad. He's had a real tough battle."

What was she doing? He didn't want to hear this. "I'm sorry. Did you need something?"

"What? Oh, no. I was just… you know… wondering how you are. Hm. How you're doing. I'm sorry. Maybe I shouldn't have called you at home… unless you're not at home. I never thought… I'm sorry."

Kathryn let out a small laugh. "No. I'm home. Of course I'm home. Where else would I be—out on a hot date?" She reached down and stirred her hot chocolate.

"Oh? No hot date, huh? What happened to what's his name?"

"What's his name? Which one? The one that showed up with flowers that made me sick or the one that didn't even know I was alive?"

"Well, that can't be good."

"Good and my love life in the same sentence? Yeah, there's a laugh. I've been stuck here in my apartment all day, trying not to become completely pathetic."

"Oh, wow. Well, what a coincidence, I've been at my father's house all day, trying to figure out what to do with all the stuff and feeling completely pathetic."

She laughed again, telling herself not to get sucked in but finding it irresistible just the same. Carefully, she took a drink of hot chocolate.

"So, what do you say we meet somewhere and try not to be pathetic together?" he asked, and she almost dropped the cup.

"What?" She looked down at herself as she fought to carefully set the cup on the counter despite her shaking hands. Gray sweats, hair up in a twist, cleaning hands still visible. "Now?"

"Sure. Why not? You can just come the way you are. Whatever. I don't really care. I just... I want to see you."

And then she understood. He needed someone to talk to. This was going to kill her outright. She knew it, and yet she couldn't get herself to say no. "Okay."

By the time he got to the little coffee shop, Ben was a nervous wreck. What was he thinking? He should have asked her out on a real date, to a nice restaurant. He should be in a coat and tie, not in sweats looking like he'd been on a six-day drunk, which actually wasn't terribly far from the truth. In the little booth near the big window scrawled with Ned's Diner in red and yellow, he sat, watching the traffic and people pass by beyond that window. It felt like so very long ago when he was part of them—if he ever had been.

"Can I get you something?" the cute waitress asked, stepping up.

"Hm, well..." He turned to her putting his arm over the booth back, but his smooth move ran smack into horror of what he was doing. What was he doing? Hitting on a waitress he didn't even know while he was waiting for Kathryn? He pulled his arm back down. "Just coffee. Thanks."

She nodded and headed for the counter meeting Kathryn coming the other direction. At least he thought it was Kathryn. She looked really different in a way that wasn't wholly unpleasant.

"I'm sorry. I kind of got lost." Sliding into the booth across from him, she rubbed her hands together. "It's freezing out there. What happened to May?"

Ben couldn't stop the smile or the admiration from coming to his face and his heart. She was truly worth considering buying. He shook out of that thought. "Thanks... thanks for coming. I know it wasn't right of me to ask. It's so miserable outside."

"No, it's okay." She shrugged and refocused on her purse, digging in it.

The waitress returned and set his coffee in front of him. "Could I help you?"

Kathryn looked up, seeming not to realize she was being questioned. "What? Oh. Yeah. Coffee. Just coffee. Please. Thank you." She dug for a moment more but came up empty-handed. Finally she put the purse down with a determined thwack and turned her attention to him as she laid her forearms on the table. "So what's up?"

He was caught in the awe of her for one more second. "Oh, you know..." Putting his arm back on the booth, he tried to look cool as if they'd just run into each other in the middle of the afternoon between meetings. "Just trying to keep on keeping on. You?"

"Yeah." She rubbed her hands together again and raked her fingers through the strands of hair that had fallen out of the ponytail. "Trying to stay warm. This rain is ridiculous."

The waitress set her coffee in front of her, and Kathryn smiled up at her with that smile that brushed his heart.

"Thank you."

When the waitress was gone, Ben refocused on his coffee because he truly did not know what to do next. "So, you've been working?"

"Oh, yeah. Not today though. Off today. And tomorrow. I'll be back on Monday though." She seemed stuck in talk mode. "How about you? Are you back to work yet?"

"Pushing pills," he said, remembering Jason's assessment of his job. "Pretty exciting stuff."

"And your dad's estate?" She took a sip. "That's going okay?"

He widened his eyes and let them fall back almost closed in overwhelm and surrender. "'Okay' might be stretching it." Shifting, he looked only at his coffee. "It's kind of crazy dismantling all of it.

I mean, I've got boxes of just stuff. Stuff he loved, stuff I remember from growing up, but I don't know what to do with it all. It's crazy." He took a drink.

The frantic fidgety thing dropped from her demeanor. Suddenly, she was keenly focused only on him. "You know, a lot of families go through that. Have you considered having an estate sale, or maybe going through an auction house? I have some contacts. I could give them to you if you want."

"Yeah." His gaze fell. "Yeah, that would be great." The center of his heart hurt. This was not how he'd pictured this. He didn't want to talk about estates and funerals. He wanted to find some way to tell her that he was in love with her. The thought pushed him back into the booth. Blinking it back, he fought to figure out why he had thought something so bizarre. Love? Could it really have gone that far? They hadn't even been on a real date.

As she watched him, still struggling so hard, Kathryn forced her nerves and feelings to stand down. He needed her—not freaking out and wondering if maybe he liked her, but Kathryn. His friend. "I guess this has all been pretty rough on you, huh? I know it can be really hard to get back into the swing of things after the death of someone close." Counselor slogans slipped into her mind. "Don't push yourself though. You've got to give it some time. You'll be surprised how soon normal feels normal again."

His gaze came up to hers, far more lost and sad than she had apprehended upon her arrival. "I'm not so sure about that."

"No, Ben. Really. I've seen this a thousand times. The first couple of weeks are the hardest, but it gets better. It really does."

"No. Kathryn. That's not what I mean."

That stopped her.

"Oh." She sat back in the booth, more worried than stable. "What... what do you mean?"

Ben let out the breath slowly. He closed his eyes, begging God to let him out of the feelings—for her sake. But they weren't going anywhere. Finally, he opened his eyes and picked his gaze up to hers. How could he tell her this and not sound like a complete idiot? He'd led her on and then dropped her like a rotten sack of potatoes when it was time for him to invest something of himself. Now here he was, wanting to lay his heart out but sure he was ruining her life by doing that.

"Ben." She finally sat forward and laid her hand across to his wrist softly. "Whatever it is, just tell me. I want to help."

If only it was that easy...

He let his gaze fall to the table for another moment, and then seeing God wasn't going to do as he had begged, he looked back at her. However, instead of saying what he wanted to, he carefully turned his wrist over until he caught her hand in his. Surprise jumped into her eyes followed by concern. But he was already moving, and he wasn't going to stop now. Gently, slowly, he lifted her hand to his lips. Kissing it drilled right through him all the way to the center of his being. He'd never felt anything like it. His eyes fell closed with the feeling. When he opened his eyes again, her gaze was on him, panicked and concerned.

"Ben?"

His other hand came across to feel her hand in his. It was completely unbelievable what that did to him. "I'm sorry, Kathryn." He looked right at her. "I haven't been honest with you. I've taken advantage of you without giving anything in return, and that wasn't fair to you."

Panicked. She looked completely and utterly panicked. "I don't... I don't understand."

"When you first showed up, I was so grateful for you, for what you did, for how you helped me. I'd never... No one had ever done anything like that for me before." His fingers continued to rub over hers, learning, memorizing every inch. "You were right there the whole way, and I thought that was, you know, because of your job and everything, but these last two weeks, being away from you..." He pulled his gaze to hers, vowing to be strong if she told him to get lost. "I know I have no right to say this or to ask you, and to tell you the truth, I'm probably going to tank the whole thing because I really don't even know how to do this..."

"Ben?"

He couldn't tell if she was scared for herself or for his sanity. He was scared enough about all of it for both of them. Finally, he looked right at her. "I just need to know. Was this all about doing your job, or is there something... more there?"

A stab of joy pierced right through her, but she yanked it back. He couldn't be serious. Her? Why would he choose her? "Ben, I don't... Are you serious?"

"I've never been more serious about anything in my life. I just didn't know how to say it, and then when you walked away that day. I thought I'd have time to maybe come up with something or to you know, talk myself out of it. But I can't do that. And the truth is, I don't want to."

Shell-shocked. It was a good word for how she felt. "You're serious? You want... to like... go out or something?"

He almost laughed. "You seem surprised."

"Shocked."

Amused, he leaned closer. "Why?"

Tears bunched up in her eyes, stinging. "Because look at you, and look at me. You're like wow, and I'm like blech."

His eyebrows arched. "Blech? I'd hardly call you blech."

She was still spinning. "But wait. I thought you didn't want anything to do with marriage. I thought, you know the whole single thing, 'I like being single.' That's what you said." It sounded like an accusation even to her, but she was almost sure of it because that was one of the few logical parts of her that had kept her from getting her hopes up.

The flippancy fell from his face, and suddenly she knew he was serious.

"I was talking to Kelly earlier, and I was trying to tell him I wasn't interested..."

"In Kelly?"

The laugh was back. "In you."

She sank back. "Oh." It was so hard following because her mind was mush.

"I was trying to tell him I wasn't cut out for the whole marriage thing and it wasn't fair to you to pretend I might be." He grew silent and thoughts flitted across his face. After a moment, his gaze came up to hers. "That's what I always thought, that I was so much happier single. I wasn't tied down. I could come and go as I pleased. Whatever. I didn't have to answer to anybody. But I see now what a lie that was. All those years, I went out and partied and everything, and then I'd come home, and I was so miserable."

She knew that feeling all too well, except for the going out part.

His gaze fell into a serene softness. "But I wasn't lonely and miserable when you were around. Even when you weren't right there. I would think about you, about what you were doing and stuff. I couldn't wait to see you again… even if it was all kind of weird."

Kathryn was holding her heart back. She'd read about this, how patients fell for their nurses because it was the first time they had been given attention. "Ben…"

"No, please, Kathryn. Let me finish."

How could she argue?

"I know this isn't how it's supposed to happen. I know what people will probably think. But I don't care about any of that. All I know is that somewhere along the way I fell in love with you, and all I need to know from you is if there's a chance for us. If you hate me and want me to get lost, I will." He rubbed his fingers over hers once more. "It will kill me, but I will."

Holding onto her heart, holding onto professional had seemed like such a good and noble idea. But the truth was, they were holding her back from the life with him she really, really wanted. "Okay, but I think we should probably take this slow," she said, measuring every word and hating the wisdom in each one. What she really wanted to do was say, 'Who cares' and go for it. But if this was the nurse syndrome thing, she would surely get hurt worse by doing that. "After all, who knows—you may decide next week that it was all some fantasy that wasn't even real."

He smiled. "Not going to happen. But that's okay about the going slow thing. If that's what you want."

"I just want to make sure this isn't all built on rose-colored glasses because I helped you or something."

Ben had no trouble agreeing because he'd already worked out that argument in his heart. "So you're not saying no?"

How her reluctant smile could play with his insides like that, he had no idea.

"I'm not saying no."

Ben raced around his apartment frantically trying to get ready. He had made the mistake of agreeing to go to church with her, and then she was going to come to his dad's with him. It wasn't a terrific first date, but evenings were out for sorting and boxing—it was just too far to drive every night, and he needed to get the house done. Sunday would be his best bet.

"Good grief. When in the world did this happen?" Ben stood at the mirror, adjusting his tie which looked all wrong. "What was I thinking? I don't know how to do this. God, I really hope You've got a plan here because I've got no clue."

Kathryn had tried to talk him into meeting her at church, but he wouldn't hear of it. At nine-thirty, her doorbell rang, and she sprinted for it. Only at the door did she stop and breathe. Wrenching the doorknob, she swung the door in. "Good morning."

"Wow." His gaze traveled down the length of her.

"Like it?" Like a little girl, she turned slowly in front of him.

"Love it." But his gaze said he was talking about more than the dress.

"Hang on, let me get my purse."

He stepped in, his hands in his pockets. "I would have brought flowers, but I didn't want to make you sick."

She came back to the door, laughing. "Great plan. We'd better get or we're going to be late."

"Wouldn't want that."

Somehow the thought of this being their first real date surged in him again as he was opening the door of his car for her. That thought coupled with where it was they were going bowled him over. On his way around the car, he raised his eyes to Heaven. "God, listen, man, You're going to have to do this because I'm way out of my league here." He got in beside her. "You good?"

She smiled a mega-watt smile back at him. "Great."

They held hands into church and all the way down the aisle. Only eight rows from the front did she stop. This church was nothing like the little chapel. For one thing, there were people. Lots of them. For another this place was huge. It was decorated in cream and white so the whole thing was bright, from the shiny floors all the way up to the cream-colored curtains flanking the wooden altar.

Although Kathryn knelt, Ben simply sat. He felt like everyone was looking right at him. Strangely, he had never felt the need for God more than at this moment. He wasn't sure if that was because he was in church or because he was just so far out of his comfort zone, he was willing to take any help he could get. After a few minutes, she sat down next to him. Who was supposed to reach out to whom? He didn't know. Where there rules about that here? He wished this was St. Jude's. At least there he would've known Father Patrick wasn't going to throw him out for a mistake.

Her hand rested on her leg. It was right there, and he wondered if that was a sign. Swallowing, he reached over, and in the next second her hand was once again in his. That was right. He knew it the moment the connection was made.

The service started. They stood, they sat, they stood again. It would have been dizzying had his hand not been in hers. Because it was, he knew she would guide him rightly and never let him fall. That was a nice thought. He thanked God for his angel, even if he didn't deserve her.

"Today's Gospel of the walk to Emmaus," the priest said. He was older than Father Patrick, taller, thinner, and frailer. However, he spoke with that same quiet confidence Ben had noticed in Father Patrick. "There are several symbols that we miss because we do not understand the geography of that time. Emmaus wasn't just another town. The disciples weren't going there to get groceries. In fact, although this passage is referred to as the *walk* to Emmaus, there is reason to believe the disciples were doing more than just walking.

"To put it bluntly, they were running. They were high-tailing it out of Jerusalem. You see, Jesus had just been crucified—dying a horrific, very public death. They had heard the stories of His resurrection, but to them, they were just amazing stories that couldn't be real. Now Emmaus led away from Jerusalem back to the Roman Empire. The symbolism is that they had turned their backs on Jerusalem. They had made the decision to turn away from what God had shown them, what Jesus had done for them and run back into the world."

Ben shifted in the seat. Did these little talks always hit so close to home? He didn't remember that from before.

"And then Jesus came and was walking in their midst, but they were prevented from seeing it was Him. Some scholars think this was God's doing, but I'm not so sure. I think maybe they were prevented from seeing Who Jesus really was because they were so focused on running away from Him. Many of us do the same thing. We are so focused on the world and its trials and tribulations, that we often don't realize Jesus is walking right there with us. And if you notice, Jesus does not stop until they ask Him to. He was going to go on, but then they asked Him to stay.

"That is hardly an irrelevant line. Jesus walks with all of us, but He will never stay where He is not invited and welcomed. Our Protestant brothers call this getting saved. Basically, it amounts to recognizing Jesus for Who He really is in our lives and asking Him to stay with us. And I don't care if you've known Him for years or if you just got baptized two weeks ago, take a few moments right now to close your eyes and ask Jesus to stay with you. He will stay if you just ask. And just like at Emmaus, He will then reveal Himself plainly to you."

The priest stepped away from the podium, and although Ben's rational mind said this was stupid, still he bent his head. He didn't even know the right words. *God, that's me. I've been running to the world. I don't know how to do this or even the right way to say it, so please hear what I mean even if I don't say it right. Please stay with me. Please. I'm tired of running. I'm tired of feeling so empty. Please show me how to get back to You. Please.*

On his hand, Kathryn squeezed, and when he looked at her, he knew God was answering his prayers. He turned back to the front as Mass continued, but his prayers continued as well. *Lord, You and I both know I don't deserve Kathryn. Show me how to love her, and please help me not to ever hurt her.*

When Mass was over, they walked hand-in-hand back out to his car. He opened her door again, and Kathryn marveled that he was what she had always asked God for—a gentleman who wasn't out for a one-night stand. How that had happened she wasn't at all sure because part of her knew that had been who he was, but somewhere down deep she suspected it had something to do with all of those prayers she had sent up on his behalf, even when she didn't know who he was.

They started out of the parking lot and were already on the way to their next stop when he looked over at her.

"Mind if I ask you something?"

She was so happy she really didn't even hear the question. "Shoot."

"You and God are pretty close, right?"

"Yeah, pretty close."

"Well, how do you do that? I mean how does it get from being all stinky incense and boring words to really believing like you do?"

She anchored her gaze outside. "Well, it's kind of like going with somebody I guess. I mean we've just gotten to know each other."

"Like reading the Bible and going to church?"

"Yes and no. You can do all of that stuff out of duty, but miss what He's really about."

"Which is?"

"Letting Him get to know you and you getting to know Him. He really is like my best friend. I know that sounds weird or whatever, but it's true. I tell Him things I wouldn't dare tell anybody else."

"Like what?"

It was always hard to see these traps before she was in one. She glanced over at him. How far could she trust him? "Well, like with guys and dating. We've had a lot of conversations about why He wasn't sending my knight in shining armor and what was taking Him so long."

"Knight in shining armor, huh? Wow. No pressure there."

She laughed. "It's a girl thing. We hear about the prince that's going to come and sweep us off our feet, and we want it to be like that. What I've had to learn is to let God be my prince… even though sometimes that worked better than others."

"You've waited a long time, huh?"

The sigh was sad and soft. "Yeah. I kept wondering what was so wrong with me, you know? And I'd ask God that. 'God, what's wrong with me? Why is this happening for everybody else but not for me?'" Her smile was tight. "That's pathetic."

"I don't know. Maybe it's just real."

"It's weird though even though Mr. Magic Wonderful didn't show up, I always knew he would." Her gaze was down on her lap, but then it slid over to him. "I always believed God would answer my prayers and send me someone I could love and maybe even someone who could love me."

Ben had never been given a more delicate, fragile responsibility in his life. Just the look in her eyes, that vulnerability and hope, made him see with his heart as much as with his eyes. He vowed to never let her down, but he knew without God, he was sure to do just that. Reaching across the seat, he took her hand, liking how soft and small it was in his. "Maybe God just had to get the prince's attention first."

She smiled. "Maybe so."

The whole day was wonderful, not because it was stress-free but because she was there every step of the way. Ben had never in his life felt this way with anyone else. He could count on her. She didn't push. She didn't demand or force or even manipulate. She was just there, with him, no matter what.

When he took her back to her apartment after the sun had gone and the stars were out, he still didn't want the day to end. It had all gone so fast, and suddenly he knew the danger of going slowly. Still, she had asked, and he wanted to respect her wishes. However, at her door slowly was one skip away from his grasp. Before she had the chance to get to her door, he arrested her movement and pulled her into his arms.

"Kathryn." His voice was husky because he felt the meld of her body on his. "I hope you don't mind, but there's something I've been wanting to do all day."

"Oh, yeah?" She looked up at him. "What's that?"

"This." Slowly because she had asked for it to be, he lowered his lips until they brushed hers. It was a good thing he was holding her because she relaxed with one breath. Far from relaxing, his whole body bolted to attention. He let his lips find hers again, and then he was spinning on the feel of her and how she breathed and how she moved.

"Ho... hold up," she finally breathed, backing up. "Um..."

"I know," he said, pulling her back into his embrace. "Slowly."

Not that that was going to be easy.

It was probably a good thing that Misty was gone. Kathryn had no idea what she would even tell her best friend. Life had spun around so very quickly it was hard to hang on. All day Monday she floated through life. She even managed a short trip to the chapel to say thanks. Not that they were a done deal, but it was nice to think they might be someday.

He called Monday night to see how she was doing, and they talked for nearly two hours—about the day, about themselves, about life. Kathryn still sensed that he was less than sure about how to be in a real relationship; however, she couldn't really blame him. She wasn't wholly sure how to do any of it either. But as long as she didn't think about that, it was easy. It was easy to be with him, to talk, to just be. She couldn't remember ever having the opportunity to just be with anyone before. It was freeing and exciting and exhilarating. All she wanted was to be with him in that safe, wonderful place.

By Tuesday evening, she was headed home, looking forward to his call. If things went well, maybe he would even ask her out for Friday. She thought about calling her mom or Casey to find out how they were as she turned near a strip mall with cafes and shops she had never actually been in. That was odd because she'd lived in her apartment for years and had never had occasion to stop there on the way home. Maybe they could stop in sometime. Maybe on their first date, or their second. They could hold hands and just explore all of life that she had missed until now.

The light in front of her changed to green, and she glanced at the car turning right next to her as she slipped into the intersection. In the next second she heard the brakes and braced though she didn't even really think about it. Life slid into slow motion as she saw the blur of the car to her left coming at her. It seemed to not even be moving, but somehow she knew it was. She slammed on the brakes, praying the impact wouldn't send her careening into the other car.

Like bomb explosions, sounds erupted around her. Metal, horns, brakes. She was slammed one way against the seatbelt and met the air bag coming the other way. It jolted all thought from her. When the motion stopped, she could tell she was still breathing. That was all.

Ben had put off calling her all day, not because he didn't want to but because he didn't want to be a pest. She had work to do and a life. So when he got home, he called Kelly instead. They needed to get together for another poker night. That was as good an excuse as any.

"Hey, dude, what's up?" Kelly asked.

"Well, I just wanted to let you to know I took your advice."

"There's a switch." Kelly paused a moment. "Oh, wait a minute. This wouldn't have to do with a certain lady friend and actually making a move you've wanted to make for weeks now, would it?"

Ben couldn't stop the smile. He relaxed back onto the couch. "It could."

"Y-es! I knew it. You called her, and…"

"And we went out to church on Sunday."

"To church? Wow. This is serious."

"She was going. I just tagged along." But Ben couldn't help but think he'd enjoyed it more than that. "And then we went to Dad's and sorted some more stuff."

"All right. All right. This is definite progress. So you're going out this weekend, right?"

"Thinking about it. Thinking about it. I just don't want to push her, you know. I'm not interested in renting with this one." The admission yanked up excitement he hadn't expected.

"Awesome."

"Don't move, honey. It's best if you don't move." The face swam somewhere above her.

"My… car?"

"Oh, darling. I think that's the least of your worries right now. Just lay still. The ambulance should be here any minute. Would you like me to call somebody for you?"

"My phone?" She turned and tried to find it in the darkness of the passenger seat that hovered and swam before her, but everything was a mass of haze and blurs.

"No, honey. Don't go doing that right now. Just lay still as you can. Here comes the ambulance. Just sit tight. They'll have you out of there in no time."

"Well, listen. I'd better go," Ben said to Kelly. "But if you don't mind, say a few prayers for us. Okay?"

"Prayers? Man, she got to you quick."

"Kell…"

"No, dude. I get it. It's cool. I'll say some prayers."

"Thanks, man."

"No problem."

"You got very lucky, Miss," the doctor was saying. The previous hour or so had been a maze of lights and sounds with no connection to anything solid. "Some stitches, a nice headache, and a badly sprained wrist after all of that is pretty minor."

The stitches were the least of the issue. She could hardly think straight, and everything was blurry—not because it was but because her head hurt so badly. Her whole right arm hurt besides, and she couldn't quite understand why.

"We could keep you overnight if you want, but nothing in any of the tests indicates you got much more than a slight concussion."

It was strange how she could follow what he was saying even though she could hardly decide if she was even still breathing. "My car? What happened to my car?"

"Yeah. I don't think that will be much help. They had it towed," the policeman who was still standing near the bed waiting to get her statement said. "It was basically totaled."

"Not that you should be driving anyway," the doctor added. "Not for a few days anyway. These meds I prescribed are serious stuff. No driving. No operating heavy machinery…"

She would have laughed if she could have.

"I can call you a cab after we're finished," the policeman offered, and Kathryn thought she should probably thank him, but that got lost in everything else.

"Or we could call someone to come pick you up," the nurse said as she finished with the stiff bandage on Kathryn's wrist.

"You're going to need to get this wrist looked at by a specialist," the doctor said, "just to confirm there isn't a break we missed."

Like a fun house full of mirrors and multi-colors, Kathryn thought through who she could even have them call. Misty was gone. Her mom was at least two hours away. The thought of calling Ben flitted across her mind, but she didn't want to bother him. He probably couldn't come anyway. Finally she looked around at all of them. "I guess I'll need a cab."

"Okay," the officer said. "But first I need to ask you a few questions if you're up to it."

"Okay."

It was the third call Ben had placed to her phone in twenty minutes, and she hadn't answered a single one. That wasn't like her. Worry hit him as he hit the off button and frowned. Where was she? He glanced at the clock and frowned deeper. She should be home by now. It was too bad he didn't know a number for her family. He was going to have to ask that question. They weren't into texting, but he tried that anyway. Still nothing. He waited another couple of minutes and tried calling again, but it went to the voicemail after four rings. None of this was making any sense. She always carried her phone with her. Always. Realizing he was probably being silly, he pitched the thing to the counter.

In the kitchen, he pulled out some take-out from the day before and smelled it. It didn't smell deadly, so he threw it in the microwave just as his phone buzzed. Leaving the food, he raced for it, and a smile came to his face when he saw the Caller ID. "Well, hello, there, sweetheart. How was your day?"

"Um, I don't know who this is, but I saw you had called. I thought you might be someone who knows the lady in the wreck."

He came up straight, his hand on his waist, his heart hammering to life. "Wreck? What wreck?"

"Yeah, it happened awhile ago. They took her in the ambulance…"

"Ambulance? Kathryn was in a wreck and they took her in an ambulance?" This was getting worse. Without another thought, he was racing through the apartment, grabbing his coat and keys on the way out the door. "Where did they take her?"

"Um, I don't know for sure. Probably St. Luke's. We're not too far from there."

"And you have her phone? How did you get her phone?"

"It was in the car. She kept trying to find it after the wreck. When they were cleaning everything up, one of the firemen came up with it. He said it was just ringing, so I hit redial."

At his car, Ben jumped in. "How was she? How was Kathryn?"

"Woozy. Kind of out of it. The crash fired off the airbags. She was in and out of consciousness when they took her."

He peeled out of the drive and into traffic. "And who is this?"

"Corretta Daniels. I saw the whole thing. That other car was coming mighty fast through the intersection. I don't think she ever even saw them."

Turning at the first light, Ben sped through the traffic, changing lanes and flooring it on the straightaways. "Where are you? How can we get Kathryn's phone back?"

Ms. Daniels gave him some information for the fire station where Kathryn's things would be, and he tried to think straight, remember, and drive.

"I really hope she's all right. She seemed like such a nice lady."

"Yeah, yeah, she is." Ben hit the gas again. Wherever she was, he had to get to her. Now.

"And you didn't see the other car approaching?" the policeman asked again.

Just staying upright on the little chair, Kathryn fought to remember through the haze that clouded her brain. "No. Not until I heard the brakes. But the light was green. I never thought to look..."

Commotion from down the hallway pulled her attention that direction. She turned her head before she realized how much that would hurt. She squeezed her eyes closed and fought to breathe through the nausea. When she managed to open her eyes again, like some vision she had dreamed, Ben was running toward her. In the next second he was on his knees in front of her.

"Kat? Kathryn?" His hand came up and brushed her face. "Oh, my God. What happened? Are you okay?" Fear crowded across his face just before he gathered her into his arms, and truth be told, it was the first time she had taken a good, solid breath since she'd heard the brakes. Relaxing felt good. She might just go to sleep right here. He backed up and put his hands on her again as if he thought she might disappear altogether. "What in the world happened? Why didn't you call me?"

"Ben? How did you…"

"They found your phone. They called the redial and got me. Why didn't you call me? I was completely freaking out."

"She was very lucky," the officer said. "Two more feet, and he would've been right in her door."

Ben crumpled forward into her with that news. "Oh, thank God. Thank God you're all right. I knew something was wrong when you didn't answer. I knew it." Even when he let her go to slip up into the chair next to her, he really didn't let go. His arm was securely around her as he turned to the officer. "Can I take her home now? How much longer does she have to stay?"

"I think we're about done here." The officer checked his notes. "I'm sure someone will be in touch with you in the next couple of days. If you'll just sign this statement."

With the world swimming in front of her, Kathryn reached over and got her name to come out of her brain. But it was a struggle. The headache was coming in waves now, yanking her down into pain she couldn't fight off.

"Good luck, Miss Walker." The officer stood from his chair. "You take care of her, you hear?"

"Oh, uh, yes, sir. I will."

When the officer was gone, Ben looked at her, his eyes wild with worry and fear.

"What happened?"

"I don't know." Tired attacked her with a vengeance. "I was driving home, and I went through this light, and…" The fear and terror began to surface. Tears punched into her eyes when she realized what could have happened. With no more than that, she was in his arms.

He held her there, stroking her hair, and breathing softly. "Shhh. It's okay. It's going to be okay."

"I was so scared."

He backed up only slightly. "Why didn't you call me? They would have called me."

She felt the absurdity of the statement. "I didn't want to

266

bother you."

"Bother me?" The words knifed through Ben like a single-edged sword with a dull tip. "You didn't want to bother me? Kathryn..."

"I knew you would just be getting home from work. I didn't want to be a burden."

"A burden?" This wasn't getting any better, but he also knew she wasn't in her right mind. Besides fighting wasn't going to help anything. "We can talk about this later. For now, we need to get you home. Did they discharge you?"

"Yeah, a little bit ago."

"Okay. Then let me get my car so you don't have to walk so far. I'll be right back." He stood and held out his hands as if she might in fact fall to the floor when he let her go. That looked like a real possibility. "Don't move." And he raced back out into the nightfall beyond.

Kathryn tried to maintain some semblance of sanity when he had gone. At least she wouldn't have to ride home in a taxi. That was something. Those things scared her when she was alive and alert. Other people in the waiting area looked her way, but she kept her head down. That wasn't hard because it was pounding. They had given her some pain killers and a prescription for more. She wondered at that moment how she would manage to get them. In fact, she wasn't sure how she would manage anything with the headache and no car to speak of.

"Okay. The car's waiting." He was back. How he was back so fast, she didn't know. In fact, she didn't remember how he had gotten there in the first place.

"Oh, okay." It was a struggle to stand, and when she did, the whole world shifted one way and then the other. Her hand shot out for something to keep her upright.

"Whoa. Take it easy there." He was right there then, holding her up. Slowly they made their way through the lobby and out the door.

It was dark. That was weird. It wasn't dark when she was in her car. How much time had passed anyway? At the curb, he helped her in and reached across her to click her seatbelt in place.

Ache hit her like a truck. Everything ached—every muscle, every bone. Her wrist was throbbing. She felt like she'd been through a meat grinder.

"Hang on. We'll be home in no time."

For some reason when he had said home, she had assumed he meant her home. So when she awoke to him saying they were home, it occurred to her that nothing upon nothing looked at all familiar. "Where are we?"

"My place."

"Your place?" She tried to digest that, but it got caught going down. "I thought you were taking me home."

"Your things are at the fire station. I'll go over there tomorrow and get them. For tonight, we're here." He got out and in seconds was at her door to help her.

The headache was unbelievable. Not a step, not a move could she make without making it ache all the more. Still she didn't have to take even a single step on her own, and it was a good thing. She felt like a marionette that had been cut loose from its strings.

"Did they give you something for the pain?" he asked, worry punching through the words as they made their way from the elevator down the hallway.

"Yeah, something at the ER and a prescription. It's here, in my pocket."

"Okay. We'll get you settled, and then I'll go get that prescription."

Kathryn was aware that they had entered his apartment though little of anything was making sense.

"Do you want to lie down?" he asked, guiding her forward in no definite direction.

"Uh, yeah."

"Okay."

He was right there every step. At the bed, he pulled the covers back and helped her in.

"Do you have that prescription?" he asked as sleep crowded over her.

"Uh, yeah. It's… right here." Somehow she dug it out and handed it to him, and that was the last thing she remembered.

Ben wasn't at all sure they should have let her go. She had him worried silly. Still, rather than get caught up in anger and fear, he forced himself to think logically. He couldn't just leave her like this. That wouldn't work. What if she woke up and freaked out or got sick and needed him? He checked his watch. It was after ten, but some things couldn't be helped.

Hurrying out to the kitchen, he dialed his phone.

"Y-ello." Kelly's voice was calming.

"Kell, it's Ben. Kathryn was in a wreck. I've got her here at my apartment, but I can't leave to get her meds."

"Ben. Whoa. Hold up, dude. Slow down. What happened?"

It felt good to take a breath and better that he wasn't in this alone. Kelly agreed with the general plan and in no time they were smoothing out the path in front of her.

The world shifted slowly back and forth as Kathryn woke up. She couldn't figure out where she was at first, but then the headache reminded her. Trying to sit up, she coughed which hurt like fire. "Ben? Hm. Ben?"

Like a shot Ben was off the couch. He hadn't slept more than five minutes in six hours. "I'm here. I'm right here." Racing to her, he got to her just before she made it up and out of the bed. For one solid second he had no idea what to do as he watched her moving. Then she reached her hand out for something to stabilize her, and what to do snapped into place. In the next instant he was right there to help. "Careful. Just take it slow."

She stood, holding onto him with every movement.

He looked around. "Where are you going?"

"Bathroom?"

He hadn't seen that one coming, but he swallowed the questions. "It's right down here. Do you want the light?"

"No." She sounded pitiful and looked worse. Her normally soft blonde hair hung in strings, and even in the darkness, he could see that her face had bruises on it from the trauma of the wreck.

"Okay. No light." He'd never done this kind of thing before—helping someone. Some of it was natural, like holding her and feeling her reliance on him. Some was not, like not knowing the proper way to help someone who was so weak she could hardly stand up. It was a slow, awkward shuffle down the hall. "Careful here at the corner." At the bathroom door, he hesitated. "Do you want me to…"

The little night light coupled with the ambient blue light illuminated the bathroom enough to see.

"It's okay. I can. I'll be back," she said, hanging onto the wall. "Just don't go anywhere."

"Don't worry."

Shaky. Everything about her was shaky and weak, but Kathryn managed the bathroom, wondering at one point what had happened to her shoes. However, that seemed irrelevant in a way she couldn't even put into words. When she was finished, she carefully made her way back to the door and opened it. "Ben?"

"I'm right here." His hand followed by his body came out to support her.

She liked the feel of that, of him. He was so solid. His T-shirt was soft, and he smelled so good.

"I think I need some aspirin or something." The headache had come back with a vengeance. It was going to be a long, hard crawl to morning.

"We got your meds. Do you want that?" he asked even as he walked right beside her, holding her up every step.

We? But she didn't ask. "Yes. Please."

Back in the bedroom and once again seated, she looked down at her clothing. She couldn't believe she had been sleeping in her best suit and silk shirt. The dry cleaners were going to love this.

"I'll be right back."

When he was gone, she carefully pulled at the suit coat and had it halfway off when she realized that to tug on the other side was going to send her wrist into screaming pain far worse than it already was. She felt like a walrus trapped on an ice flow—unable to move in any direction.

"Here. Let me help you with that," he said, suddenly reappearing and setting the glass on the nightstand next to her. Gently he worked the coat off from around her before tossing it into the darkness beyond the bed. "Here's your meds." Handing her the water first, he got the pills ready as well.

"Just one," she said, knowing her intolerance for strong drugs.

His concern was written all over his face. "You sure? One's not very strong."

"It's strong enough." She took the one he offered and downed it with some water. The headache was unbelievable. When she was finished, he took the glass and set it on the nightstand.

Anchoring his hands at his hips, worry scrawled across his face, he gazed down at her. "Better?"

"Yeah." Her gaze traveled down to her blouse and helplessness drained through her. She couldn't worry about that now. Sleep was already making a comeback.

"Are you all right? Do you need something else?"

She looked up, trying to get impish to her face. "My pajamas?"

"Pa...?" Then he looked down. "Oh, my gosh. Of course. Um." He stepped back and sent his fingers digging through his hair. "Here. How about these?" He went over to a chest of drawers shrouded in the darkness at the other side of the room. "I don't know if they'll fit. They'll probably drown you, but... it's the best I have." When he came back, he was holding a pair of pajamas. Only then did she realize he hadn't left to get them, and the thought ripped through her.

Not a piece of her moved to accept the gift he held out. Instead, she looked around the room and swallowed. "Wait. Is this... your... room?"

He seemed confused by the question as he looked around the room himself. "Uh, yeah?"

Horror crashed into her. How could she have been so presumptuous? "Oh, my gosh. I'm sorry. I've taken your bed and your room." She started upward but snagged on the earth shifting the other way out from under her. "Oh!"

"Ho..." Just like that, he caught her downward momentum, halted it, and righted her back onto the bed. "Slow down there. Okay, first of all, I'm fine on the couch. Second of all, no sudden moves like that again, or we're both going to end up on the floor. Got that?" His hand brushed the top of her shoulder making sure she wasn't going to make any more sudden moves.

She nodded, chastened as much from the stumble as from being humbled by his generosity and the feel of his warm hand on her with only the thin silk in between.

"Good. Now here are some pajamas." He laid them in her lap, and she missed his hand on her shoulder. "You just get into those. I'll be right out here if you need anything."

She nodded again. What could she say? *Don't be so nice to me. I don't deserve it.* That's what she wanted to say. Or better yet, *Don't be so nice to me, I might actually think you mean it.* Could he really mean it? Could this actually be happening to her? Or was it just some crazy dream that she was going to wake up from?

As she changed into the pajamas, the part of her brain that didn't hurt like crazy thought about that. She had always thought she wanted someone who would be there for her, but letting him be there for her was humbling in ways she hadn't expected. Worse, it was scarier than she had expected. What if she really started trusting him and he let her down? What if this nice fantasy turned out to be just that... a fantasy? Wouldn't reality then hurt worse than never seeing the dream?

Pushing away those thoughts, she buttoned the long, soft pajama top. It smelled like him. Where that thought came from, she wasn't sure. Not many of her thoughts were making much sense. Carefully she removed her skirt and hose and got into the pajama bottoms. They, too, were soft. They felt so very, very good. Sleep was not going to be hard like this. She had already climbed back into bed and under the covers when he knocked.

"Everything okay?"

"Yeah," she called back already drifting and assuming that he was going to go back to bed. It didn't matter. Sleep was already winning.

He opened the door but not more than that. "Do you need anything else?"

Ben listened at the door for the answer that didn't really come. He pushed it opened a bit more. "Kathryn?"

Through the darkness he could see her already on the bed. Her clothes were in a heap on the floor. He knew he should let her sleep, but wanting to make sure she was all right just one more time, he stepped in and over to her. Carefully he pulled the covers closer around her and then sat next to her on the down mattress. He reached over and picked the strand of hair off her face and moved it to the side.

With a long sigh, he closed his eyes. "Thank You, God for Kathryn. I don't know what I would've done if You'd taken her away from me tonight." His heart literally hurt at the thought. "Please, God, please be with her. Help her to recover quickly." He turned slightly and laid his hand on her shoulder, feeling her presence in his heart more than he ever had. "Thank You, God for letting her stay here with me." Emotion choked the words from his throat. He hadn't considered what it would be like to lose her until that moment, but suddenly he fully understood the gift God had given him in her by just giving them more time together. "Thank You, God. Thank You so much."

Nineteen

"Wow," Ben said, coming to attention when she walked in from the bedroom the next morning. He'd been up since six, making phone calls to her work and his, downing pots of coffee so if and when she woke up, he would be awake as well. He'd been listening for her the whole night, jumping at every sound, so the fact that she was suddenly standing there, in his pajamas, hair tousled, and face marred by bruises jolted him right off the couch. He went straight to her and put out his hands out to steady her and to help her. "How are you feeling?"

Her hand came up to her head, and she looked like she might pass out right there. "Ugh. Like I fought with a semi and lost?"

"I can see how that could be." At the couch, he helped her sit down. "I hope you don't mind, but I called your work and told them what happened."

She looked up in surprised mortification.

"About the wreck," he clarified quickly, "and how you won't be coming in today."

A groan came from the bottom of her. She sat there, breathing in hard exhales. "Wow. I'm sore."

"I can see that." He stepped back and put his hands on his hips. He was in the same jeans he'd had on the night before. They looked like they'd been through the rinse cycle and dried in a heap. But he didn't care. He was far less into impressing her than just making sure she was all right. "Can I get you something?"

Her gaze was hollow. "Meds? Water? Something to eat? I'm starving."

"Meds. Water. And something to eat. Coming right up."

Most of the day passed with him fetching things and trying to make her more comfortable. She slept again in the mid-afternoon, and by the time she woke up again, life was starting to come back into some brand of normal.

"Wow. I'm glad that wasn't a serious crash. I'd have been in trouble," she said as she sat on his couch that evening, sipping the hot chocolate he had gotten for her at some point during her nap. She didn't know how that had happened exactly because when she asked for some with breakfast, he didn't have any, but now he suddenly did. Things were kind of like that at the moment for her—random, disconnected, and confusing.

"It was serious enough." His voice had a touch of anger and a lot of gravity. He rearranged the pillows behind her on the couch. "That better?"

"It's great." Gingerly she settled back into the cascade of pillows. They felt really good.

"So." He backed up and looked at her with those worried eyes as he put his hands in his pockets. "Do you need anything else? More meds? Something to eat? Another pillow?"

She shook her head and almost managed a smile. "No. I think I'm good."

"You sure?" He glanced around as if looking for bubble wrap to wrap her in. "'Cause I could like make some popcorn or get out the rice cakes... if you like those. I have some of those. But I don't know if you like those."

Taking a sip, she tried not to laugh. "Not really."

"Yeah. I don't like them either. I bought them when I was on this stupid health-kick thing back in January. I was going to go to the gym every day and exist on rice cakes and pineapple juice. That lasted a whole two days and I was so sore and hungry, I couldn't move."

She smiled and almost laughed. Through the dull pain it began to dawn on her how nervous he was. In fact, he was standing in the middle of his own apartment with his hands in his pockets, looking like he was afraid of breaking someone's good china. "You know you could sit down."

"Sit?" He looked around, his gaze darting here, there, and everywhere. "Oh, yeah. I could, huh?" Carefully he lowered himself to the chair next to the couch but just to the edge of it. A moment and he scratched his head. "You know, I could get dinner.

I'm not real big on cooking. I mostly do take out." He rubbed his hands together. "But I could try it. I can open cans. Soup? I have some soup I think."

With a small sigh for how hard he was trying, she leaned forward taking the pain with her. Laying her hand on his wrist, she fought not to let the pain from the movement show on her face. "Thank you."

He looked completely surprised. "Thank me? For what?"

"For being here." All of the things he had done for her drove into the softest middle of her core. "I was a mess last night."

His smile came almost all the way to his face. "You're never a mess."

But she wasn't kidding, and she wasn't about to be dissuaded by the joke. "It's been a long time since someone cared about me that much."

Concern went across his face. "But you have friends…"

"It's not the same. They have their own lives. They can't just drop everything to take care of me."

What she was telling him went through his heart. She took care of so many others without a single complaint. But who was there to take care of her? With everything in him, he wanted to be that person for her. Turning, he put his hand on hers, and the nerves dissipated in the wave of love and admiration. "Kathryn…" There were more words, but they choked at the top of his throat.

Her gaze fell from his, and she breathed for a moment before she shook her head slowly. "Maybe this is crazy, but I so don't want this to be a dream. I mean I keep thinking I'm going to wake up, and you're not going to be here, that it was all in my head." The pain was scrawled on her face when she looked up at him, but it wasn't physical.

And he saw it then—her fear of being left alone once again.

"It's not," he whispered as he slid from the chair to his knees in front of her. "It's not a dream. I'm right here, and I'm not going anywhere." His hands came up to gently touch her face. The bruises there tore his heart out. He never wanted to see her hurt like this again… never, ever again. "I was so scared last night." His gaze dug through hers. "I was so scared. When they told me you were hurt… I couldn't even think straight. I was freaking out."

"I couldn't believe it when you came. I didn't... I never expected... that."

Hurt and concern spiraled through him just as it had the night before. "Why not? Why didn't you think I would come? Where else would I be?"

Her gaze fell from his. "I don't know."

He exhaled, needing for her to understand what was in his heart more than he could even find the words to express. "Don't you get it, Kathryn? I can't imagine what I would do if something ever happened to you. I don't even want to think about it." Needing to reassure himself that she was really there, he pulled up to the couch next to her and gathered her into his arms, trying to remember not to tighten his grip too much. It was difficult not to. All he wanted was to hold her like that forever and forget all of the rest of everything. "Kathryn, you have to know what a difference you've made in my life. I would never have gotten through this last month without you."

The words stopped, but his thoughts didn't. "Look, I know I don't deserve you, but if you'll let me, I want to be here for you, just like this. I'm not perfect, and I'll probably screw the whole thing up more than once, but I couldn't live with myself if you were having to deal with things on your own without anyone there for you. I don't want you to ever be alone again." He kissed the top of her hair. "I love you so much."

All of her movement stopped. Slowly she twisted up to look at him with concern and confusion on her face.

"What?" he asked, looking at her. "I do. I love you. I think I was just too bone-headed and stuck in shallow to realize it. Okay, it took me hitting rock bottom with no way to get up on my own to realize that I needed someone, someone with passion and hope. Someone I could count on. But if that's what it took to get me to wake up, then I'm glad it happened because I never want to go back to being how I was." He pulled her head to his shoulder and kissed it again. "I thank God I hit bottom so you could find me."

Kathryn let his hand pull her in even as her mind struggled to contemplate all that he was telling her. Her? Passionate? Hopeful? Someone to be loved and counted on? She didn't feel like any of those things—especially now. He was so worldly. He had confidence that she couldn't manufacture if she tried. What could she have that would even come close to getting his attention or holding it? "Ben…"

"No, Kathryn. Don't even go there. Look, I know that other guys have overlooked you." He tilted his head, his eyes sparkling. "Personally, I think God put blinders on them so He could save you for me until I realized how stupid I was being about everything, and that took some doing. Not that you get a great deal out of the bargain, but…"

"I don't know why you keep saying that. Look around you. You've got a great apartment, a life most guys would kill for. You said it yourself you didn't want to be married, you liked being single."

"Yes, but that was then. Look, I can't really explain this, but something in me has changed, and I really feel like it's for the better. Before, it was all about me—what I wanted, what was best for me. I didn't care about anyone else, and I liked it that way. But then you came along and the whole thing with Dad, and I just started to see things so differently than I ever had before. I started seeing how selfish I was and how many people I had let down and looked over because it was too much trouble to care about them. Like Kelly. Did you know his wife's mother died a year or so ago?"

"No," she said softly.

"She did, and I didn't even go to the funeral, not even the wake service. In two days I was giving him hell for not coming to the poker game. That's how I was. And maybe it's how I still am, but it's not how I want to be. I want to learn to have what you have, to figure out how to be there for people and really see them, but I don't even know how to do that. I mean I see you do it, and it looks so natural, like it's just who you are. But then you said that you had to go to the chapel and stuff, and I've seen you do that, so I know it's not as easy as you make it look. And I don't know, maybe I can't even have that. Maybe it's not even in me. But I want it to be."

Kathryn heard the whole thing as much with her spirit as with her ears. She did not want to ask the question because she knew it could destroy even this tenuous connection that they had now established. Yet she had to know. "So where are you on the whole God thing? I know you have really been struggling with that."

"I still am, but I've been talking to Him again. You know. Like last night after you were here. I said some prayers, well, not the kind I got taught in Sunday School, more like just talking to Him kind of prayers. And it's weird, I really felt like there was somebody on the other side of that line this time."

"There is." She knew that now, more clearly than maybe she ever had. The answer to all of her prayers was sitting right next to her, and only now did she understand why God had made her wait.

"It's weird, you know," he said, the awe sounding in his voice. "I went to church growing up. Did all the stuff, got my sacraments, was an altar boy, the whole nine yards, but then when Mom and Dad broke up, I decided it was all just a big show for people who went. They all seemed so stuck up and holier-than-thou anyway. I had one kid in my Sunday School class that spread all kinds of rumors about my dad and why they had broken up, said he'd heard his parents talking about it. I think I decided if that's what church was, then I didn't want any part of it. When Dad started going again, I told him I wasn't going, and that was the end of that. Until now."

She let that settle for a moment. "And now?"

"I don't know. It's really hard to put into words because I'm seeing that yeah, there may have been a lot of stuck up people at my church, but that doesn't mean that everyone is like that. I mean Father Patrick was great. He didn't push all the religion stuff on us. He just helped us through. And you and all the staff at hospice. I know that sounds weird, but I could just tell you really meant what you did to care about us. It wasn't just a job or whatever. But you weren't superwoman either.

"That day I found you in the chapel crying… I can't explain it, but I was like, 'Whoa. Why would she do something like that?' I mean I couldn't get why you would go sit in front of that Jesus on the cross thing."

"The crucifix."

"Yeah, that thing. I never liked those things, even growing up. I remember having to carry it for Mass, and I was like, 'Ew.' It creeped me out. But then I started to see it the way you do—that Jesus up there understands what we are going through. I mean, he was beaten and spit on and hung on a cross. He knows. He understands pain. I think He even knew how much I was hurting when I turned my back on Him."

"He did."

"I know. That's what I mean. It just... amazes me that through all of that, even though I'd totally rejected Him, He still sent you to find me. I mean He could just as easily have left me out in my misery and said, 'See ya,' but He didn't. That He would love me that much to send you to get me. It's just..." He shook his head. "I can't even put it into words sometimes."

"I know," she said softly. "I was a little girl when He did that for me too."

Ben grew sincerely silent at that as he looked down at her, and she felt the shift from his story to hers. She'd never told anyone this story, not even Misty or those she worked with. And at weird times she wasn't even sure it had happened at all. But as the words came to her heart for the first time, she chose not to censor them out.

"My grandma was really like my best friend when I was little. I went to her house all the time, and we'd bake cookies and she'd read me stories. And then she got really sick, and the doctors didn't know why. When I went to the hospital to see her with my mom and dad, that was back before hospice was even invented. Grandma was really sick, and they wouldn't let me back to see her. I was too young. So Mom and Dad would go in and leave me out in the lobby by myself. There was this one nurse that saw me crying out there one day. She came over and asked what was wrong, and I told her the whole thing, not realizing who she was or why she was even there. She asked if I knew Jesus, and I told her I did, and she asked if I wanted to go see Him, to talk to Him about everything. I said that I did, so we went down to this little chapel that was there. It was a lot like the one at hospice come to think of it. A few benches and the crucifix hanging up there.

"She told me I could always go and look into Jesus's eyes as He hung on the cross and tell Him what was wrong and how scared I was, and He would always hear me because He understood about being in pain. I still think about that little chapel and that nurse. I don't even know her name, but she stopped what she was doing that day, and she helped me find Jesus when I was really lost and hurting. That's all I try to do for other people now because I know what a difference it made for me."

Love for her flowed through Ben along with gratefulness for her, for her grandmother, and for that nurse whom he would never know. The forks in the road that led to this place were amazingly complex. Had God been planning this all the way back then? And then another question, much more frightening occurred to him. What if that nurse had been too busy to comfort that scared little girl that day? What if she had thought it was someone else's business, that it wasn't any of hers? What if she had talked herself out of helping? Ben shuddered at the thought. "What happened with your grandma?"

"She died. A couple days later. I only found out years later that it was cancer, the real sudden and invasive type. I never really got to say good-bye."

"That's why it's so important to you to help others say good-bye."

Slowly she nodded. "I don't want them to have any regrets."

Ben couldn't help it. He pulled her even closer to him. "For what it's worth, I think God set it up that way... not to hurt you but so you could help others."

"I just feel so inadequate sometimes, like nothing I do really even makes a difference."

From this new perspective, he saw the lie of that. "Oh, it does. Trust me on that. It makes all the difference in the world."

The next day they went together to the tow lot, and Kathryn couldn't believe how bad her car looked. It was indeed totaled. The whole front side was caved in. There would be no fixing that thing. She would have to get a new one. Ben took her back to her apartment, helped her call the insurance companies and then took her to get the rental they set up for her. She was glad he followed her back to her apartment because she was still quite shaky behind the wheel. Never before had she looked both ways when the light turned green. Now it seemed she couldn't help doing so.

Her nerves were frayed strands by the time she got back to her apartment, and tired was once again overwhelming her senses.

"You look like you've been beat with a stick," Ben said as he stood behind her, waiting for her to open her door.

"Gee, I wouldn't know why." She pushed the door open and walked in, almost hoping he would decide to go so she could sleep even though it was only four in the afternoon.

However, he never slowed down upon entering. Instead he went right into the kitchen. "Do you want your meds now so you can take a nap?"

The question took her aback. He'd been on taking-care-of-her duty since the wreck. She had assumed that once she was close to back on her feet he would stop. "Sure."

In seconds he was back. "Here you go. I cut it in half like you did this morning."

She took the pill from him and the water, and her alert system saw him standing there in her apartment, hands on hips watching her take the medication. When it was down, he took the glass from her and headed back into the kitchen.

"I thought about ordering Chinese tonight," he said. "How does that sound?"

"Um, fine. It sounds fine." The whole thing was just so weird. Here was this guy, this gorgeous guy, in her kitchen, getting her medicine, ordering take-out for them. How exactly was that possible? Somehow she had to have slipped into some parallel dimension.

He strode back in and stopped when he saw her. "Oh. I thought you'd already be headed to bed."

She wanted to, but wasn't that weird to leave him here in her apartment... without her being awake and conversational? "Oh, I..."

"Seriously. You need your rest. We've got to get you better." He came over to her, took her arm, and turned her toward the bedroom. "Now get."

"I could..."

"No arguing. Go get some rest. I'll hold the fort down out here."

Once she was gone, Ben went into the kitchen and finished up the dishes that were sitting there. Her apartment was spotless otherwise, so he made a few calls in to work and to Kelly to update him. Then he thought about Jason. Life had pivoted so quickly since he'd last talked with his brother. He hit the numbers and waited for the connection to be made.

"Hello?"

"Jase, hey. How's it going? This is Ben."

"Ben. What's up? Have you made any more decisions on Dad's stuff?"

Wow. That had all gotten totally drown out of his consciousness. "Uh, no. Not yet. Kathryn kind of had a wreck, and we've been dealing with that…"

"Kathryn? Kathryn-Kathryn?" And Ben could hear the excitement, suspicion, and surprise in his brother's voice.

"Yes, Kathryn-Kathryn. I finally had to admit I was just being stupid and stubborn and call her."

"And…?"

"And we're going out. Well, kind of. We've been to church and then to Dad's and then the wreck happened."

"Wait. You went to church?"

"I did."

"So when's the wedding?"

What was most weird when Kathryn woke up was how un-weird everything was. Ben had indeed ordered Chinese, which was wonderful, and the two of them discussed work and what came next. She was going back in the morning, and so was he. As strange as that seemed, life was going to seem very strange without him right here with her. Just when that had happened, she wasn't at all sure.

When they went back into the living room after dinner, she didn't reach for the remote. Instead, they sat together on the couch. He put one arm around her, pulled her to him, and held her other hand with his. She wanted to stay like that forever. He made her feel so safe, so seen, so loved.

"I've been thinking," he said slowly as his fingers traced hers. "I know the church has all kinds of rules and stuff about getting married, and I know what you said about going slow, but I'm not going to lie to you. I don't want to waste any more time with God or with you. So, I'm thinking I'm going to go talk to Father Patrick and see what it would take to get back into the church."

That stunned her to the core. "The church? Ben, are you sure?"

"I've never been more sure about anything. I don't have all the answers, but I'm learning that God doesn't expect me to. And

I'm certainly not perfect, but God doesn't expect that either. What I do know is that I'm totally going to need His help to do this thing right with you, and so I want to get right with Him as soon as possible, so I can love you the best way He knows how instead of how I would try and mess it up."

"So what you're saying is…"

"What I'm saying is, when God says He will show you how to do it nobler and all of that stuff, that's what I want, but I know I can't do it on my own." He squeezed her shoulder gently. "I'm going to need God and my angel to show me how."

She fought the smile but not very hard. "Well, I know God will do that in a heartbeat."

He looked down at her. "And the angel?"

Kathryn's gaze came up to his, and what she saw there was hope and a glimmer of peace. "She's in too… all the way to heaven and beyond."

Epilogue

Coming undone had been the best thing that had ever happened to Ben. As Father Patrick gave him the vows to say, he repeated them with no trouble at all. "I, Ben, take you Kathryn for my lawfully wedded wife. I will love you, honor you, and cherish you in sickness and in health, for richer or poorer, in good times and in bad, no matter what life brings until death do us part."

Accepting the ring she put on his finger was even easier because he saw in her eyes her pledge to see him all the way through to heaven and beyond. It was all he'd ever hoped for, and more than he'd ever imagined. As they turned to the small congregation and Father Patrick announced them as man and wife for the first time, Ben had never felt more proud or more at peace. The only piece missing was the empty seat where his father should have been. A soft, dull ache brushed his heart at that thought.

Even so, he could see in the divine plan the reason, and he really couldn't be mad. His father had surrendered his life so that Ben could find real life—with her and with God. It was a gift he would always be grateful for.

"Ben, you may kiss your bride."

He turned to her, and in her soft, brown eyes was a trust and a hope he had never seen before. He knew the responsibility of it, the fragileness of it. The kiss would come, but before he did, he had to tell her what was flooding through his heart. "I love you so much."

Kathryn smiled back at him. "I love you too, Ben Warren."

He laughed, hearing her name come from his heart. "Kathryn Warren."

She laughed at that just as he leaned forward, closing his eyes, and his lips found hers. It was almost like coming undone all over again. And he wasn't complaining about that at all.

Chapter 1

"I do not believe I'm doing this." Jonathon Danforth strode past the knots of college students who were draped and drawn over every available step and statue. Had it been cold, they all surely would've taken refuge elsewhere, but New York was experiencing one of those fascinating if completely frustrating warm snaps in the middle of January.

It couldn't last. They never did. That's why Jonathon wore his black wool coat even today when it was 60 degrees out. He was ready for the moment the cold front, that one not even predicted yet, blew in. Climbing the steps, he asked himself again, "Ugh. What am I doing here? This is completely insane."

Still he reached for the large door and entered Bennett Hall. Inside was considerably more crowded and considerably colder as well. It was nice to see the good people of New York Central College didn't waste money on little issues like heat and light. His gaze slid to the ceiling where the lighting, such that it wasn't, glowed dimly. With a snort of derision and disgust, he made his way through the old lobby, dotted with students.

They were all young. Nineteen, twenty. No more than 22. Some looked at him. Most were content to ignore him. In the middle of the lobby, he stopped and dug out his schedule. *English Literature. Room 103.*

As he stuffed the schedule back in his pocket, he had to ask himself yet again why he was doing this. It wasn't like he needed an education. He had one. Two if you counted life experience which he definitely did. And yet, here he was, standing at the doors of an old lecture hall that held little if any fascination for him. *Why?* drifted through him again, but he beat that back. Did it matter why? Did it really?

He was here. He had made this decision, and now he was going to go through with it whether he liked it or not.

It was a thing of beauty. Lecture Hall 103. Elizabeth Forester had been here, in the lecture hall, since eleven a.m. It was not required that teachers, uh, professors get there two hours before the class was to start, but Elizabeth simply couldn't help herself. The old English wood, the desks placed just so. They didn't make them like this lecture hall anymore. It was a throwback to a time long before when students came and sat up straight, ready and eager to learn.

Of course in the past three years since she'd become an actual professor, she had seen very few of such students. Many today were not interested in doing more than minimal work and collecting a good grade (somehow that the two didn't go readily hand-in-hand never really made a dent in their social calendars until right before finals). She wanted to be angry about that, to make them understand what literature could do for a person, but she had no real way of conveying that except to her own heart, so she contented herself in presenting the material and letting what happened, happen.

But 103. That was a different matter altogether. First, it was storied—for her anyway. It was where she had first come into the hallowed halls of higher education as a wide-eyed freshman more years ago than she wanted to admit. And there was always the aura of Professor Avery, her first mentor, that hung about the place.

As she sat at the old desk which really served no real purpose anymore, save that they couldn't get it out of the room, she thought about Professor Avery. "Elizabeth, you are a fine student with a great passion for fine literature. Have you ever considered teaching?"

And thus had the trajectory of her life forever changed. It was odd, she thought, running her hand slowly across the smooth old wood, how one minute your life could be so one way and the very next, it would never be the same again...

See more about *"If You Believed in Love"* at:

http://ebookromancestories.com

About the Author

A stay-at-home mom with a husband, three kids and a writing addiction on the side, Staci Stallings has numerous titles for readers to choose from. Not content to stay in one genre and write it to death, Staci's stories run the gamut from young adult to adult, from motivational and inspirational to full-out Christian and back again. Every title is a new adventure! That's what keeps Staci writing and you reading. Although she lives in Amarillo, Texas and her main career is her family, Staci touches the lives of people across the globe with her various Internet endeavors including:

Romance Novels:
http://ebookromancestories.com

Books in Print, Kindle, & on Spirit Light Works:
http://stacistallings.wordpress.com/

Spirit Light Books Blog
http://spiritlightbooks.wordpress.com/

And…

Staci's website
http://www.stacistallings.com

Come on over for a visit…

You'll feel better for the experience!

Also Available from Staci Stallings

In Print

The Long Way Home

Eternity

Cowboy

Lucky

Deep in the Heart

To Protect & Serve

Dreams by Starlight

Reunion

Reflections on Life I

Reflections on Life II

Ebook Editions

Cowboy

Lucky

Coming Undone

Deep in the Heart

A Work in Progress

A Little Piece of Heaven

A Light in the Darkness

Princess

Dreams by Starlight

Reunion

To Protect & Serve

CPSIA information can be obtained at www.ICGtesting.com
Printed in the USA
LVOW07s2038200114

370194LV00002B/735/P